BONES OF OUR STARS, BLOOD OF OUR WORLD

BONES OF OUR STARS, BLOOD OF OUR WORLD

CULLEN BUNN

GALLERY BOOKS
NEW YORK AMSTERDAM/ANTWERP LONDON
TORONTO SYDNEY/MELBOURNE NEW DELHI

G

Gallery Books
An Imprint of Simon & Schuster, LLC
1230 Avenue of the Americas
New York, NY 10020

For more than 100 years, Simon & Schuster has championed authors and the stories they create. By respecting the copyright of an author's intellectual property, you enable Simon & Schuster and the author to continue publishing exceptional books for years to come. We thank you for supporting the author's copyright by purchasing an authorized edition of this book.

No amount of this book may be reproduced or stored in any format, nor may it be uploaded to any website, database, language-learning model, or other repository, retrieval, or artificial intelligence system without express permission. All rights reserved. Inquiries may be directed to Simon & Schuster, 1230 Avenue of the Americas, New York, NY 10020 or permissions@simonandschuster.com.

This book is a work of fiction. Any references to historical events, real people, or real places are used fictitiously. Other names, characters, places, and events are products of the author's imagination, and any resemblance to actual events or places or persons, living or dead, is entirely coincidental.

Copyright © 2025 by Cullen Bunn

All rights reserved, including the right to reproduce this book or portions thereof in any form whatsoever. For information, address Gallery Books Subsidiary Rights Department, 1230 Avenue of the Americas, New York, NY 10020.

First Gallery Books trade paperback edition November 2025

GALLERY BOOKS and colophon are registered trademarks of Simon & Schuster, LLC

Simon & Schuster strongly believes in freedom of expression and stands against censorship in all its forms. For more information, visit BooksBelong.com.

For information about special discounts for bulk purchases, please contact Simon & Schuster Special Sales at 1-866-506-1949 or business@simonandschuster.com.

The Simon & Schuster Speakers Bureau can bring authors to your live event. For more information or to book an event, contact the Simon & Schuster Speakers Bureau at 1-866-248-3049 or visit our website at www.simonspeakers.com.

Interior design by Hope Herr-Cardillo

Manufactured in the United States of America

10 9 8 7 6 5 4 3 2 1

Library of Congress Cataloging-in-Publication Data has been applied for.

ISBN 978-1-6680-6527-3 (pbk)
ISBN 978-1-6680-6528-0 (ebook)

*This one—and really everything I write—
is dedicated to Cindy and Roman.*

*Without the two of you,
without your support of all my wild ideas and notions,
it wouldn't be worth it, would it?*

BONES OF OUR STARS, BLOOD OF OUR WORLD

***T*HE MEMORY OF WITCH'S FIRE** *is burned into his skull.*
That's what some locals call it, muttering to its existence with high tide in their throats, gazing out across the ocean on black nights, when even the stars are smothered by a blanket of darkness.

For old sailors and fishermen—and, Lord, there were plenty of them on this island—witch's fire was a shimmering blue or purple glow in the mist, around the mast of a ship or even all along the sides of Cape Jordan Lighthouse. It was also called St. Elmo's fire (not so much around these parts), named after the patron saint of sailors, and it was said to warn of thunderstorms and lightning strikes.

But this is something different.

Something new.

Something old.

Witch's fire, like a slice in the night sky, dragging itself across the blackness like a blade through skin.

A cut.

Instead of blood, though, light spills out. Not lightning.

Not exactly.

And even once it's gone, once the wound has scabbed over, once the scar has faded, it leaves an echo.

His mind has imprinted upon the bright, searing light like a baby bird to its—

Mother.

It's a blister on his brain. He sees it even when he closes his eyes.

Which is odd.

Because he never saw it in the first place.

MONDAY

**FOR SO MANY,
THIS IS THE LAST WEEK ON EARTH.**

CHAPTER ONE

*O*NE BEER, BARRY THINKS AS he hobbles to the kitchen and yanks open the refrigerator door, would be the perfect way to flush this massive, stinking shit of a day right down the toilet.

Of course, he doesn't have any beer.

At least, not a *real* one.

Allie won't let him keep the stuff in the house, especially not after his last physical. Doc Maro had ordered blood work, and the blood had spilled Barry's dirty little secrets, revealing high blood pressure and bad cholesterol and a liver that simply didn't work half as well as it should.

"Too many years of hard living," the doctor had said, pausing to cluck out a *tut-tut-tut* that stung like a series of slaps, "and hard drinking to boot.".

Kind of ironic, really, considering how much Dr. Glen Maro used to drink back in high school. After a day of tormenting freshmen, he'd peel out of his pre-patched letterman's jacket and blow off a little steam with a few Budweisers, or the hard stuff if his father forgot to lock the liquor cabinet. Under the bleachers next to the football field, way out on the winding dirt roads nobody was watching, in the unused horse barn on Old Man Haney's overgrown farm on a Friday or Saturday night—the party was never too difficult to find. Going on damn near fifty years later, Glen, who would be called "Doc" when all was said and done, had once held the unofficial title of "Drunkest, Meanest Sonovabitch" on Wilson Island, North Carolina.

Now, though, he was a pillar of the community. Town physician. Deacon at the White Sands Christian Fellowship. Member of the board of aldermen. The local legend, the hellraiser who'd set the bar for all the shit-heels and delinquents to come, was a "fine, upstanding citizen." Getting pickled in the public eye wasn't in the cards anymore. Neither was bullying others.

Or was it?

Maybe some of Glen's bluster, swagger, and cruelty remained, manifesting as prescriptions and meal plans and dietary restrictions.

And judgment, Barry thinks. *Let's not forget that.*

Tut.

Tut.

Tut.

Barry can't help but wonder if Doc gets a perverse thrill out of the humiliation his patients experience every time he orders them to turn their head and cough. Now, thanks to the prick of a needle and some numbers generated in a lab somewhere, Doc wasn't just checking for a hernia.

He was grabbing hold and squeezing tight.

Betrayed by my own blood, Barry muses, *and some asshole who used to give younger kids wedgies and swirlies but now dishes out heart medication and condescending glares with equal abandon.*

And so, no beer.

None of that cheap bourbon that Barry likes so much.

No alcohol of any kind.

Not in the house and not in his gut. If Barry stops at the ABC store, steals off to the Tugboat, or so much as sneaks a peek at the beer aisle at the grocery store, his loving wife will know.

She'll smell it on me.

And then there would be hell to pay.

And he can't even get drunk to dull his senses during the dressing-down.

Instead, Allie keeps root beer on hand. *Root* beer. As if that somehow makes this easier, comforts the cravings, relieves the frustration, soothes the insult brought on by age and a failing liver and a rat-bastard doctor. Sometimes on really tough days, when Barry's thoughts go grim, he thinks maybe his loving spouse of forty-two years is taunting him.

Barry is an old man.

Wearing slouchy pajama bottoms and a baggy T-shirt.

Staring down the barrel of a 9 p.m. bedtime.

Not an ounce of fight—of fire—left in him.

Searching the fridge for a beer that doesn't exist.

Something reeks within the refrigerator, though. Leftovers that have gone forgotten for a little too long, maybe. Not his concern. He'll let Allie deal with it tomorrow. Pushed all the way to the back, behind cups of probiotic yogurt and Tupperware containers of tuna casserole, stand six tall bottles of brown glass.

At least they look like beer, Barry thinks. *If anyone peeks through the window, they'll see me taking a swig and think to themselves, "There's old Barry, still throwing them back like he used to! There's a guy who knows how to take life by the horns and live it up!"*

One bottle clinks against the others as Barry drags it out.

"You love root beer," he mutters to himself, casting his voice high and shrill, mocking his wife.

But not loud enough that she could possibly hear.

The glass is cold in his hand.

"It's caffeine-free," he whines in his godawful approximation of Allie's voice, "so it won't keep you up all night."

He shoves the refrigerator door closed.

"Don't forget to put the bottle in the recycling bin!" he singsongs through curled lips.

He turns the bottle over in his hand.

Diet root beer. Oh my God.

She's definitely fucking with me.

Barry twists the cap from the bottle, tosses it onto the counter. It's bedtime, and the alarm clock will be shaking him awake before he knows it. He's three steps out of the kitchen before he realizes he forgot to turn off the lights. Grumbling, he shuffles back through the door and snaps the switch.

The house is dark.

Midway down the hall between the kitchen and the bedroom, a nightlight is plugged into an outlet. It casts a feeble orange glow along the walls.

Dark.

And quiet.

He takes a swig of the root beer—correction, the *diet* root beer—as he shuffles toward the bedroom. He holds the cold, fizzy, artificially sweetened liquid in his mouth, savoring it. He has to admit, it tastes pretty good. Not good enough that he'd ever say as much to his beloved, of course. And definitely not good enough to make up for the day he's just had.

Not hardly.

His boss, Mr. Winslow at Surefire Pest Solutions, is just a kid. But he likes to throw his weight around. Enjoys yelling. During the best of times, yeah, but even more so when the sailing is anything but smooth. At the moment, with the crew unable to keep up with an ever-increasing glut of assignments, the water is choppy. And Mr. Winslow has made it obvious that he doesn't care for Barry. Why? Who knew? Sometimes one person just didn't like another, rhyme or reason be damned. One thing is certain: Mr. Winslow has no respect for Barry's thirty-five years of killing termites and cockroaches and carpet beetles.

Mr. Winslow has barely been alive that long.

When Surefire Pest Solutions isn't living up to its online customer reviews, it's Barry who weathers the full force of the boss's wrath. And today had been one of those days. It didn't matter that the company was painfully understaffed to handle the number of jobs they were receiving. It didn't matter that Barry shouldered half those jobs, late though they might be, all by his lonesome. It didn't matter that Mr. Winslow could stop riding a desk chair and kill a few bugs himself to help the company get caught up on service calls. It only mattered that Surefire's reputation—one built, at least in part, on Barry's back—was suffering. Bad Yelp reviews piling up. And that likely meant young Mr. Winslow was getting an ass-chewing of his own from the retired founder of the business, the *real* Mr. Winslow, a man "Li'l Winslow" called "Daddy."

That notion makes Barry smile and offer a cheers to the man upstairs.

Approaching his partially open bedroom door, he sees that the room beyond is filled with shadow. He sighs. Allie's already turned out her bedside lamp, which means she's sound asleep. He'll need to move carefully in the room to avoid stubbing a toe or waking his wife.

And he'll have to fumble with his CPAP machine, another form of torture imposed upon him by the Allie/Doc Maro tag team, to make sure the damned thing is filled with water and ready to—

The smell stops him cold.

A foul stench.

For a split second, Barry wonders if he left the fridge open, if the rank scent of leftovers is following him.

This is worse, though.

Much worse.

A sickly sweet aroma, not unlike spoiled milk.

But also not unlike the stink of an overwarm butcher shop.

Meat.

Blood.

As Barry pushes the door open and steps into the dark room, his toes brush against something crinkly on the floor. The curtains are drawn, but there's enough moonlight filtering in from behind the fabric, enough of the nightlight-glow coming in from the hallway, that Barry can get a feel for his surroundings, Looking down, he sees a white trash bag, dark and slimy fingerprints leaving smeared trails across the plastic. He nudges the bag with his foot. The contents are murky and dark, soft and wet.

Barry wonders if Allie has been fussing about, collecting trash to be taken out for tomorrow's garbage pickup. Leaving the spoils of her work on the bedroom floor like this, though, is not her style.

And what the hell has she been cleaning anyway? What's in the bag?

He looks to the bed where she sleeps. Still. Unmoving. He's about to risk waking her, about to ask her what's going on.

The words catch in his throat.

Allie sleeps on top of the covers. And she's not wearing a stitch of clothing. Her skin is pale in the gloom. Except where it's not.

From her throat to her groin, her skin is dark, almost black, deeper than the shadows of the room.

Not dark.

Hollow.

Someone stands in the corner. Not far from the bed. Lurking in the gloom. A man. Tall. Thin. He is dressed in light-colored clothing, almost blending into the eggshell-white bedroom walls. But an apron of black leather—also glistening—covers his chest and stomach. A belt around his waist is studded with implements of glittering metal. His arms are covered, up to his elbows, in black leather gloves. In one hand he holds something meaty, about the size of a softball. His face is impossible to discern, not because of the darkness, but because—

Is he wearing my CPAP mask?

The man most certainly wears a face covering of some sort, and a long, whipping hose hangs from it, trailing all the way to the . . .

. . . bloody . . .

. . . floor.

The stranger drops the hunk of wet meat.

It plops to the floor, spattering blood, and rolls a couple of inches, falling to a stop in a wedge of pale moonlight.

Is that Allie's heart?

And the masked figure is now racing across the bedroom, quickly, silently. The hose from the mask whips back and forth, clicking strangely. His gloved hand darts down to his belt—*a utility belt, just like Batman,* Barry thinks—comes back up grasping something metallic and sharp.

Where the hell are his eyes?

Barry should be able to see them, even in the darkness, this up close and personal, right?

Root beer arcs through the air in an undulating spray as Barry, now holding the bottle by its neck, swings with all his might. The brown glass shatters against the stranger's head in an explosion of foam and shards. The assailant grunts, stumbles back, bumps into the bed's footboard, rocking the mattress, shaking Allie's lifeless flesh, because it *is* lifeless, she's *dead* Allie's dead Allie's *definitely* dead—

As the broken bottle thumps to the floor, Barry lunges at the stranger with a roar of horror and rage. His hands—arthritic though they may be—clench into fists. He punches the man in his apron-covered stomach. He brings a fist down against the mask that covers the man's face.

Barry feels his fingers break against the unexpected hardness of the eyeless mask.

The intruder comes up, shouldering Barry in the gut, staggering him back, but Barry hasn't had enough, and he moves in, punching at the man who has just butchered his wife, feeling the agony of cracked bones, his ruined fingers shifting and crunching against one another. He drives a knee into his attacker. He claws at the strange, eyeless face with his good hand. He flails. He can't get to a phone, but he can yell his ass off, and maybe one of the neighbors will hear the disturbance.

At first his screams are inhuman and incomprehensible, raw, terrified bellows and shrieks, but the words eventually form in his head, coalesce on his lips.

"*Somebody—!*"

Something cold slashes across Barry's throat.

Something warm washes down his baggy T-shirt.

He feels a sliver of iciness—of metal—still jutting from his neck. Panting, the masked intruder grips it tightly by the handle, twisting, sawing through bone and digging up meat. Barry's arms fall limply at his sides. His legs begin to buckle.

One last thought races through Barry's mind.

One damn beer.

That's all I wanted.

Then it's lights out, promptly at 9 p.m.

CHAPTER TWO

MOONLIGHT DANCES ACROSS THE WATER, turning every ripple and crest into a jagged silver blade, flickering across the endless dark. Somewhere out in the distance, a buoy bell clangs rhythmically, reminding anyone who's listening that there's still something—*anything*—beyond the shore. Waves rush in, sizzling across the sand, seaweed and bits of shells and driftwood tumbling in their wake.

Willa Hanson stands on the beach, just barely within reach of the oncoming waves. By the time the water arrives, it has turned into bubbles and froth. Her sandals discarded a few yards behind her, she digs her toes into the wet sand, flexing them, as she watches the ocean. So vast and empty that it might swallow her up just because she dares to stare into its depths.

What's the old saying? If you gaze long enough into the abyss, the abyss will gaze back into you.

Willa chuckles.

Trust me, you wouldn't like what you'd see, abyss.

In her hand, pinched between her index and middle finger, is her last cigarette. Her final smoke for some time to come. The Marlboro Light is lit, the cherry aglow, ashes trickling into the sand in which she's buried her toes. A curl of smoke rises into the cool night air. She doesn't remember lighting it. Habit, she guesses. She wants to bring the cigarette to her lips, to take a long, deep drag. But despite what everyone has always said about her, what they will almost definitely say about her in the very near future, she's not completely irresponsible.

She flicks the cigarette out across the surface of the water, watches the pinpoint of red flare through the darkness.

Like a streak of witch's fire.

The blazing cherry spins and vanishes into the rolling waves.

Snuffed out.

Like her future.

Maybe.

It all depends on what she wants to do, on what she and Kenny decide. Even though she's pretty much already made up her mind. She's self-destructive that way.

Waves roll in, ceaseless, foamy and white, and her sodden, unsmoked Marlboro tumbles in the surf, along with smooth pebbles, broken shells, and shattered sand dollars shining in the moonlight. A couple of fiddler crabs, leaving crisscrossing tracks on the wet beach, investigate the cigarette. One of the crabs picks the butt up and dashes away with its prize. The second crab zigzags away in a *wait for me, wait for me* kind of pursuit.

Willa's hand falls to her stomach, lingers there.

It doesn't feel any different. *She* doesn't, anyway. But everything *is* different now.

All because I peed on a stick.

She knows better, of course. The at-home pregnancy test hasn't condemned her to a certain fate. Willa did this to herself, her and Kenny. Behind her, she sees her Honda CR-V parked several yards back, nestled in the dunes of the Point. This was the scene of the crime—just two months ago, she and Kenny rolled around in a tangle of sleeping bags in the back of his F-150 with the roar and sigh of the surf as their mood music.

It was all very romantic.

Shooting stars and everything.

Now the wind off the water is cold and bitter. The beach is quiet. You'd never know that the summer season is upon them. Tourists. Fishing charters. Bonfire parties. Part-time jobs.

For some of us.

Keggers at Mitch Bently's summer house.

For some of us.

Camps. College tours.

For some of us.

Somewhere out there, across the water, stand the ruins of the

Cape Jordan Lighthouse. The old structure hasn't been in operation for decades, but Willa wishes it would flare to life just one more time and guide her through the predicament she's in.

Willa pulls the folds of Kenny's letterman jacket tighter around her frame. Her father is going to shit a brick. Or maybe suffer a heart attack. Or, more likely, shit out his still-beating heart while it goes into cardiac arrest. And, as his heart sprouts spider legs and scurries around the floor, he'll try to stomp it to a pulp to end his impossible pain and disappointment and misery.

And then he'll commence stomping on Kenny.

Or he'll have Scraps or Bear do it for him.

Where is Kenny anyhow?

He should have been here by now, standing on the beach with her, his tangled hair blowing in the sea breeze, that charmingly goofy grin on his lips, probably slipping and falling into a disbelieving frown as she tells him how the pee-stick has eternally cursed them.

Maybe he's already figured it out.

Could he have read Willa's uneasy silence and distance—the unspoken worry written all over her face—over the past few days? If he had, was he standing her up? Avoiding her? Retreating like the waves, rushing out into the nothingness?

No.

That isn't his style, not by a long shot.

No matter what, Kenny wouldn't cast aside his responsibilities. He wouldn't turn his back on Willa, even if it meant kissing all those athletic scholarships good-bye. And he wouldn't even bat an eye over it, wouldn't hesitate. He's a solid guy, stands up for the people he cares about, would do anything for anyone if it's the right thing. It's one of the reasons Willa loves him.

Gag.

Turning to look toward the sand-swept road that cuts through the dunes and the patches of tall sea oats, Willa sees no sign of his F-150's headlights in the night.

Her stomach flip-flops.

Fishing her cell phone out of the letterman jacket pocket, she thumbs the screen, scrolling through a list of her favorite contacts—Sarah, Mom,

Dad, finally Kenny. She presses the tiny picture of his handsome face and waits for the line to connect.

"*Hey, babe,*" Kenny says, answering on the second ring, and she can hear the silly, disarming smile on his face.

"Where are you?" she asks. "I thought we were meeting up."

"*I know, I know. Sorry. I lost track of time at Charlie's, but I'm on my way now.*"

"How far out?"

"*Couple of miles. You want me to stop at Rudy's? Pick us up some snacks? If the Warlock's hanging around, maybe I can grab some smokes or a six-pack.*"

Willa laughs self-consciously.

"*What's so funny?*" Kenny asks.

"Nothing," she says, and she's glad he's still a couple of miles out, because it might give the wind a chance to dry the tears from her cheeks. "I uh, don't need anything. Just get here, all right?"

"*Miss me that bad?*"

"Something like that."

"*On my way. I should . . .*" His voice trails off for a second. Then: "*What the hell is that? Oh, shit!*"

His sudden full-of-shock voice competes with the warbling, whining sound of tires swerving on pavement screaming over the line. An explosive crashing sound fills her ear.

"Kenny?!" Willa cries. "*Kenny?!*"

The call is still connected, but there's no answer, no sound from the other end.

Willa grabs her sandals and races toward her car, the beach trying to pull her down. She tightly grips her phone, keeping the line open, hoping Kenny's voice will crackle back at her and tell her everything's going to be all right. Not just tonight, not just right now, but forever.

But he doesn't.

He's far too responsible to start lying to her now.

CHAPTER THREE

ALL THINGS CONSIDERED, KENNY SMYTHE is very lucky.
Primarily because he didn't have the chance to stop by Rudy's Mart and visit the Warlock.

Along Killdeer Avenue, sleeping houses spring to life. Interior lights brighten living rooms. Porch lights flare. Curtains are pulled aside so residents can see just what the hell made all the racket—which is Kenny's pickup, jumped up onto the curb, crunched over the twisted remains of a stop sign, and crumpled around a creosote-coated telephone pole.

Almost certainly calls are being made right now. Sheriff Buck or Deputy Fines will be on their way to survey the incident.

If Kenny had stopped by the Warlock, they might find beer or a bag of cheap weed or even a few of those red-and-blue pills in the truck. And that would be, as Kenny's dad likes to say, all she wrote. No trifecta of high school basketball, football, and baseball fame would spare him, especially not with the sheriff, an alumnus of Vickersville High just fifteen minutes up the highway, conducting the investigation. Buck was an all-star himself back in the day, and still indulges those old rivalries. Wilson Island High students like Kenny get more speeding tickets, have their parties rousted more often, are busted with booze or pot more frequently, and get assigned more community service than students from Buck's alma mater. That's just a local fact.

And if Kenny was arrested for possession or driving under the influence thanks to already kicking a few back at Charlie's house, then his athletic scholarships might be in jeopardy. Without them, college would be out of the question. Kenny would *never* get off the godforsaken island.

All. She. Wrote.

What would he do then, stuck living out his days on Wilson Island like so many others? Follow in Dad's footsteps and run charter fishing expeditions? Join the Warlock in peddling beer, weed, and pills to underage kids behind Rudy's Mart? Pull shady odd jobs for Willa's old man doing God-knows-what? Become a sheriff's deputy himself and, years from now, take out his bitterness and frustration on every athlete from every rival school in the county?

Kenny's head spins. He might not be too drunk or high, but he's shaken. By the adrenaline. By the collision with the telephone pole.

By . . .

. . . the *thing* . . .

. . . he saw.

Still, the thoughts of his future collapsing around him cement as fixed points in the turmoil of his thoughts.

"*Kenny?! Kenny?!*"

He is dimly aware of Willa's voice, distant, calling out to him.

"*Are you okay?*"

He shoves the driver's-side door open and hops out on shaky legs. A flood of dizziness washes over him. He places a hand on the truck's frame to steady himself.

"*Answer me!*"

He notices his phone now, glowing on the passenger-side floorboard. A photo of Willa is on-screen. She's smiling, wearing a white dress and cowboy boots, sitting in the shadows of a rickety barn. Maybe she should be holding an acoustic guitar and sporting a cowboy hat, but instead she embraces an electric Fender, and a jean jacket covered in rock 'n' roll band patches is thrown over her amp. It's a picture she might have used as an album cover. If she still played music.

Leaning into the truck, through the shadows, stretching, Kenny feels another dizzy spell. Maybe the collision was a little harder than he originally thought. His fingertips touch the phone, find purchase, and slide it closer. Rising back to his wobbly legs, he brings the phone to his ear.

"I'm h-here," he says, quietly at first, then more loudly. "I'm here."

"*Oh my God!*" Willa says.

"I'm here," Kenny repeats.

"*What happened?*" Willa asks. "*It sounded—*"

"I had an accident."

"*Are you all right?!*"

"Ran right off the road. Not sure if my truck is just sorta fucked or totally fucked."

"*You're okay, though?*"

"I think so. Dizzy, maybe. B-but I don't think I'm hurt."

"*Where are you now?*"

"On Killdeer."

"*Just hang tight, okay? I'm on my way. Did you call the sheriff?*"

Kenny looks around the neighborhood. More lights glow from stoops and living room windows. On some porches, men and women and children in house robes and pajamas are shuffling out to see what's going on. A few of them have phones in hand.

"I'm sure someone did," Kenny says.

"*Okay,*" Willa says, and again, "*I'm on my way.*"

Willa disconnects and Kenny slides the phone into his jeans pocket. He pulls himself away from the truck's door and moves toward the front to survey the damage. It doesn't look as bad as he expected, but he winces anyhow. The hood is crumpled. Underneath, something leaks onto the street, spreading out in rivulets across the pavement. Steam spews from under the metal. But Kenny imagines that if someone would just step on the edge of the bent, fallen stop sign, he might be able to back the truck off the curb and even drive it home without a problem.

He glances around—at the street, at the illuminated houses, at the rubberneckers.

He sees no sign of the . . .

. . . *thing* . . .

. . . that caused the accident.

Not a *thing*, he tells himself, but a *man*.

Kenny didn't get a good look at him. The guy—he had to be a guy, based on his height and build—had dashed out into the street right in front of the truck. He was wearing a white shirt, a black overgarment of some sort, a belt covered in dangling and glittering metal adornments, long gloves, and . . .

. . . a mask?

It had all happened so fast—

Kenny crying out. Dropping his phone. Swerving. Bouncing onto the curb, rattling across the stop sign, crunching into the telephone pole.

—that he can't be sure what he saw.

Kenny almost hit the guy. That much he knows. For a moment, as the sign wrenched out of shape and thumped against the underbelly of the truck, he thought he *had* run him over. In that instant, Kenny had felt an avalanche of horror roll over him. But, no, he hadn't hit the man. There he went, scurrying off into the shadows—without even looking back—just after the collision.

But there's a smear of blood on the street.

Black under the streetlights.

But blood just the same.

Maybe I clipped him, Kenny thinks.

Or perhaps he was hurt before he threw himself right in Kenny's path. Maybe he was confused, suffering, not thinking straight.

Even though his head is still tilting and whirling, Kenny turns in place, scanning the houses on both sides of the street and the faces of their residents, some of whom are drawing closer, asking if he's all right, if he needs medical attention, and he sees no further sign of the strange man he almost flattened, and there are no bloody footprints leading away from the scene, just the slash of crimson wetness, trailing toward—

—a plastic bag.

A trash bag, stuffed maybe half full, tied in a knot at the top. It rests on the street, up against the curb. Droplets of black blood sprinkle the plastic. More blood decorates the ragged edges of a tear in the side of the bag. Thick fluid oozes from within.

The feeling of horror and dread swells within Kenny again, almost strong enough to shove his vertigo aside. *Almost.* Instead, it all does a spinning dance—he thinks he might puke, but he forces his nausea down as he approaches the bag.

"Should we call an ambulance?" somebody asks.

"Sheriff'll be here soon," says someone else.

"What happened?" another voice asks from the gathering crowd.

Kenny nudges the trash bag with the toe of his sneaker.

A heart spills across the pavement.

A human heart.

The rip in the bag grows, widening, more blood oozing out.

A piece of meat, dark and curved like a giant bean, tumbles to the street. A length of intestine slithers out of the expanding, seeping tear. A fatty chunk of flesh.

A second heart.

Kenny violently reacts, vomiting, falling to his knees and losing his dinner and whatever remains of lunch. He pukes up his feelings of luckiness along with all the beer he drank at Charlie's and lets it boil in the spreading blood. Everything comes out—he throws up until he's sweating and trembling but strangely no longer dizzy.

He's still in a state when the red-and-blue lights finally pulse across the tiny houses of Killdeer Avenue.

CHAPTER FOUR

CARELESS, CARELESS, CARELESS!

From his hiding spot across the street, crouching behind a rusting, rattling, leaking air conditioner unit, the man watches and curses his own stupidity.

Ran right out into the street! Right in front of a pickup! Like a fucking toddler!

It's not all his fault, he tells himself. The mask makes it difficult to see. Like looking through a fog-veiled and rain-slicked window. Only it's not water washing down the glass in sheets. It's more like Vaseline. Like his plans, oozing and semisolid, clinging to some sort of vague shape but somehow still formless and shifting.

Mutating.

In a way, Barry and Allison Hadley were part of a mutation to what he'd done up until this point. Out of character, maybe. And a mistake. Necessary. Required. But a mistake anyhow. He hadn't been ready. Hadn't been prepared the way he should have been.

Sloppy.

Mrs. Hadley had been easy enough. Quiet. She hadn't made a sound, hadn't even opened her eyes until he made the first slice. By the time the blade slid sluggishly through skin and tissue, it was too late. Done and done. The old woman, wide-eyed and gasping, was finished before she realized what was happening.

If she realized what was happening.

He hopes she didn't. He liked Mrs. Hadley. She'd always been kind to him.

On the other hand, Mr. Hadley—Barry—had caught him off guard. The old guy fought back, and was stronger than expected. The back of the man's head still pounds where the bottle cracked across his skull. His cheek throbs where Mr. Hadley whaled on him, crushing the hardness of the mask into his face. He hopes the attack hasn't left a bruise. That would draw undue attention when he finally takes the mask off. Mr. Hadley had fought tooth and nail, giving everything he had, punching, kicking, and—at the end—scratching.

Mr. Hadley had screamed.

It was the sound, cut short with a series of stabs into the ragged meat of the old guy's throat, that had been startling. Mentally, the man had been preparing for the Harvest, but somehow had never anticipated the screaming. It was louder than expected, filled with agony and anger and fright that took him by surprise.

Someone must have heard that.

The thought had taken root in his brain and he couldn't shake it, not as his victim had crumpled to the floor, not as he started cutting, and certainly not now as he hid in the narrow alleyway between houses.

The houses are so close around here.

Normally, with the animals that had come before, he would have taken the time to dispose of the bodies, keeping only the meat that was necessary. These hadn't been animals, of course—livestock, actually. He had expected it to be more difficult, but—

Someone heard, someone heard!

And he hadn't so much sliced the vital organs as ripped and dredged them out. He had to work fast. Before a neighbor, roused by the sounds of struggle, came snooping and caught him in the middle of his sacred task. He'd thrown the meat into the bag, didn't even bother cinching it up properly. He'd left the bodies where they lay, on the bed and on the floor, hadn't got rid of them carefully, and fled the house, across the yard, and into the street.

All because—

Mr. Hadley had screamed. And someone heard.

They *must* have. They must *still* be hearing the screams. Because they're most certainly still echoing in *his* skull right now.

His heart slams. Sweat coats his skin, soaks into his clothes. He can't catch his breath, not under the mask.

People gather in their yards. Clad in pajamas and robes, they shuffle out to gawk, to see the pickup truck that had smashed into the telephone pole and now sits right out in front of their houses, hissing and steaming, to see why the driver—Kenny Smythe, of all people—is vomiting his guts onto the pavement.

Doesn't matter if they actually heard or not, because they damn sure know what I'm up to now.

The precious contents of his bag have spilled out for all the world to see. His hard work, the Harvest, has been ruined. He'll be empty-handed when he returns home. And that, he knows, will not suffice.

I'm not cut out for this.

Cut.

Not hacked *out for this. Not* slashed *out. Not* ripped *out.*

A nervous giggle rises in his throat as he stops himself. Now is not the time for childish jokes, especially not at his own expense. If he screws this up—

Something moves in the shadows behind him.

Shuffling. Rustling. Sniffing.

A dog, a little black-and-white beagle mix, trundles his way. It moves in a carefree pattern, nose to the ground, searching for something—anything—interesting. A tag jangles from the collar around its neck. A rambling, roaming dog-about-town making his nightly rounds. When the dog smells the blood on the man, it tenses. And when it spots him, squatting in what must be one of its favorite pissing spots behind the AC, it jumps back. The hair along its spine sticks up like a Mohawk. It growls, not quite barking but letting out six low, warning chuffs.

Not too loud. Yet.

Instinct guides the man's hand to his belt, his gloved fingers finding the handle of one of the ritual blades.

He reconsiders, pulls his fingers away from the weapon, clenches his hand into a tight fist. The glove's leather creaks.

The killer extends his empty hand, slowly, cautiously, gently. "It's okay," he says.

Speaking under the mask is strange. Uncomfortable. It's the first time he's tried to do so. Drool spills down his chin, down his neck. The words are muffled and slurred, but hopefully his soothing tone comes across.

Wagging his tail, the dog approaches, sniffs the gloved hand, and licks the fingers.

The killer runs a blood-and-saliva-slicked glove over the dog's head, roughs him up playfully.

He grabs at the tag on the dog's collar, leans in closer for a better look.

Through the haze of his mask, he sees that the tag reads BUSTER.

He exhales, his breath under the mask pluming over his face in a rank, humid cloud. He is thankful. Glad he doesn't need to kill Buster. It would be easier, yes. Everything has been up until this point. But he doesn't want to kill this dog any more than he wants to kill his friends and neighbors.

Want, though, has nothing to do with it. He only does what he must. What's required.

He can't stop now, even though his actions are no longer as secretive as he would like.

Will he need to be more careful? Yes. More efficient? Yes. More ruthless? Yes.

Can he dream of ever being able to stop?

No. Not ever.

He squints at the red-and-blue lights of the approaching vehicle. The colors, the brightness, even muted through the mask, hurt his eyes.

Maybe they sting more *because* of the mask.

Now that the sheriff is here, now that one of his bags—his bags of treats—has been found, it won't be long before they find the murder scene. The blood soaked into the bedsheets, into the carpet, spattered on the walls and even the ceiling. Mrs. Hadley's body, what's left of it, on the bed. Her husband's, ripped apart, bones cracked and spread out from its flesh, sprawled on the floor.

Buster shakes his head. His tags jangle. Still wagging his tail, the dog suddenly darts off.

Oh, shit.

Too late, he realizes Buster's owners might notice blood smeared on the little dog.

What's it matter?

They wouldn't find fingerprints.

Buster isn't going to be able to tell them about the masked figure he met in an alley between houses.

The killer follows the dog's lead, creeping farther into the shadows, knowing he's failed and there will be hell to pay.

The screams no longer echo in his head. Instead, one nagging thought rolls over repeatedly in his gray matter: *The job's gonna be a real bitch from here on out.*

CHAPTER FIVE

THE HOUSES ALONG KILLDEER AVENUE are almost all the same. Small, white, dark-gray shingles on the roof, a carport off to the side, a single door in the center of the structure, a one-frame window to the right of the door, a two-frame window to the left.

The yards are different enough, the homeowners showing off their personal decorative tastes. Here is a flower bed bursting with hydrangeas. There is a cluster of cement frogs and donkeys and roosters, all stripped of paint by years of exposure to salty air. Another has a pair of Adirondack chairs positioned alongside a sea buckthorn tree. Even in the dark, it's obvious the chairs are painted in "island escapism" colors. But they are peeling too, and it is likely they've never been graced by an ass to sit upon them. A mailbox is mounted to a stand that looks like a statue of a giant, goggle-eyed seahorse. Patches of rust coat the metal box, trails of brownish-red dripping along the seahorse's concrete scales, and the hinged door has fallen off. The small stack of junk mail that was dropped off earlier today is on display for all to see.

The houses, though, built by an out-of-town developer some fifty years gone by, are just about as cookie-cutter as they come.

On the outside.

Inside? Hell, that's anybody's guess.

Pulsing lights paint the houses in flashes of color, giving them, if only for a couple of seconds, different looks. Shadow and light, warm and cold, peaks and valleys. The shifting, changing glow cascades across the doors, the windows, the cement frogs, the seahorse mailboxes. Across the faces in the crowd.

"Ain't nothing good on the TV tonight?" the sheriff mutters quietly through a tight smile. He raises two fingers over the top of the steering wheel. No one else hears what he says, and that's for the best. "Y'all just had to throw on your slippers and come out to gawk at the spectacle of it all, huh?"

Sheriff Bartholomew Buckner ("Don't call me Bart, but you can call me Buck") knows damn near every person standing at the edge of damn near every yard. Sure, he does. He's called this stretch of North Carolina coast his home all his life, except for a stint in the Marine Corps after graduation. Most of that time, he's served as a member of the sheriff's department, the last ten years wearing the big, bright, shiny, head-honcho badge. He's gotten to know folks as a friend, as a neighbor, and now as the shepherd for the flock.

He laughs at that last idea. *Should have been my goddamned campaign slogan.* Not that he needed one. He'd run for sheriff of Fredericks County unopposed, and damn straight on that one.

Standing at the edge of their yard are Delmont Ferris and his wife, Paula. Sixteen years ago, Buck, then just a deputy, had busted Delmont's dumb ass for running an illegal cockfighting ring. He, along with fifteen others, had pulled a stretch in jail. Since that time, though, Delmont has turned things around, become an upstanding citizen. He works at the body shop, attends church a couple of times a week, and even coaches Little League. Hell, Buck and Delmont even played poker three or four times in the last year, and just ended up laughing about the bad old days.

Lincoln Wells, a confirmed lifelong bachelor, nods toward Buck as his SUV cruises past. Lincoln and Buck attended high school together. Both signed up for the corps—*Oorah!*—on the very same day. But Lincoln had come home just a year later, missing the lower half of his right leg thanks to an IED. Buck lasted a sight longer, leaving the military of his own accord and thankfully on his own two feet. The two don't talk much these days—Buck always gets the feeling that Lincoln is a little bent out of shape about getting maimed while Buck didn't.

"Fuck you very much," Buck says under his breath as he nods back, "you and your prosthetic leg both."

From a yard on the other side of the street, Bill and Nancy Wallace keep watch. Bill holds a protective arm around Nancy's shoulders. Those two have been together since the tenth grade. Buck smirks at that. As clear as day, he remembers nailing then–Nancy Patrick, head cheerleader for Wilson Island High, in the back of his Impala not two hours after he'd dislocated Bill's shoulder and near about broke his ankle during a football game between the Vickersville Raiders and the Wilson Island Devil Dogs.

Good times.

And Nancy still looks pretty damn fine.

Buck recognizes the F-150 that hugs the telephone pole too. The pickup belongs to Kenny Smythe, all-star quarterback, point guard, pitcher for Wilson Island High. *Speaking of Devil Dogs.*

Kenny himself paces back and forth near his truck. He looks pale, shaken, and uneasy.

Probably shitting himself thinking of telling his old man about the accident.

Buck and Kenny have had a handful of run-ins over the years. Nothing serious. Just a kid being a kid. Buck knows what the students of Wilson Island High say about him. That he treats them unfairly, always gives them the short and thorny end of the stick, old varsity rivalries never die. That, though, just ain't the way of things. Buck has always made it his mission to treat everyone fairly under the umbrella of the law, whether he likes them or not. Of course, teenagers, just like everybody else, have a way of interpreting reality through a lens of their own bullshit.

Eh, who cares. Let the kids think what they're going to think.

If pressed, though, Buck would admit that he'd like to be thirty-odd years younger and facing Kenny Smythe, Devil Dog Number 37, on the scrimmage line. *Oh, that would be one for the record books.*

Kenny is using the back of his hand to wipe puke from his chin. Buck's about to shove the door open and haul himself out of the SUV when the radio squawks.

"*Sheriff?*" It's Tessa speaking over the static-filled airwaves. "*We've got an opportunity.*"

An opportunity, she always says. Never a problem. Never a hassle or a headache. Always an opportunity.

"Go ahead, Tess." Peering out the window at Kenny, Buck depresses the button of the mic hanging from his shoulder epaulette. His tac vest is in the seat next to him. He doesn't wear the vest if he can help it. "What's going on?"

"*Mr. Renner called again,*" Tessa says.

It's all Buck can do to keep from openly groaning. "Is it those fucking kids again?"

"*Language, Sheriff.*"

"I know," Buck says. "Of course it is. Language is how we communicate, Tess. Language is how I ask you if those *fucking* kids are out there sneaking onto Mr. Renner's property again."

He tries to keep a cool head, but Tessa should know that Buck won't ever listen to her about the profanity.

"*He says it's the Cooper brothers. They're shooting at his chickens with airsoft rifles. Says they even killed one of them. He's asking for you to come out there and handle it.*"

Standing in front of the SUV, awash in the flashing lights, Kenny steps closer, then stops himself. He wipes the palms of his hands on his jeans, smearing leftover puke. He looks pale, haunted.

What did this kid get himself into, anyway?

"Nah," the sheriff says into his microphone. "I'm in the middle of something here. Send Reed or Keene."

"*Mr. Renner isn't going to like that. He asked for you specifically.*"

"I'm not sure I give a shit what Aldo Renner likes or dislikes. We're the sheriff's department, not a band playing down at the Tugboat. We don't take requests. Send Reed or Keene. Pretty please, Tess."

"*You got it, Sheriff.*"

Before hopping out to deal with the accident, Buck delivers one more message. "And do me a big favor, Tess. I'm tired of dealing with those idiot Cooper boys. Whoever you send, tell them to scare the piss and vinegar out of them. I don't want them to even think about getting into trouble without their guts going watery. Get me?"

For a moment, Tessa doesn't respond. Then: "*Understood. I'll send Keene.*"

"Thank you. I do appreciate it. I'll radio back soon."

Buck steps out onto the street. He hitches his belt under his bulging belly, letting his keys jangle authoritatively. Kenny looks toward him, worry crawling across his chalk-white, sweaty face.

"So. What the hell happened here then?" Buck asks. He half steps away from the SUV, his hand still on the frame of the open door. Kenny doesn't speak, but he looks to the street.

To the spattered puke. To the oozing blood. To the rumpled plastic trash bag. To the contents that have spilled out of it.

"Je"—Buck takes a step back—"sus!"

The blood runs in tiny, sluggish, reaching tendrils across the pavement.

Buck fumbles for his mic. "Tess," he barks. "*Tess!* Forget about Renner! Forget the Cooper brothers! You get Keene and Reed over to Killdeer Avenue, right now! Get Fines too!"

"*Sh-sheriff?*" Tess replies tentatively over the crackling signal.

Buck feels his own stomach kick and twist, like he might lose the Salisbury steak and mashed potatoes he wolfed down for supper.

Those look like human organs. Human body parts.

He wonders how well he knows—*knew*, come to think of it—the person they belonged to.

CHAPTER SIX

HISSING STEAM RISES FROM THE crumpled hood of Kenny's truck. It writhes and roils in the air, a pale-gray specter, trying to take some sort of shape, succeeding only in quarter measures. A quarter-measure rubber duck. A quarter-measure airplane. A quarter-measure grasping hand. Drifting mist works to turn itself into something *other* than itself, then just comes undone and—

Collapses.

Willa knows the steam isn't really trying to do anything. It's her own mind painting pictures in the vapor. There are no intentional patterns or shapes in the formless chaos. And she knows . . .

. . . deep down in her bones . . .

. . . something's not right . . .

. . . or it won't be . . .

. . . not after she tells Kenny what she needs to tell him. . . .

Yeah. Of course. No shit.

She tries to convince herself it's going to be all right, that he's a good guy, that he'll know the exact right thing to do, to say.

But now is not the fucking time!

It's more than that, though, more than the worry over her boyfriend's reaction to . . .

. . . fatherhood.

It's the feeling that *everything* is about to change, not for the better or worse, but *irrevocably*. Has life been grand and beautiful and paradisal? Not always, not by a long shot. It's not all bad, though, and at least Willa understands the status quo, warts and all.

What comes next?

What she can't foresee.

That part scares the hell out of her.

Parked a couple of houses down, she steps, stiff-legged, away from her car.

The feeling of impending doom—

—*not doom, not necessarily*—

—intensifies.

She's walking into a shifting future, as intangible and mercurial and unstable as the radiator mist drifting from her boyfriend's wrecked truck, and she can't will it to take on a clear and cohesive shape in her mind.

Kenny moves in slow, shuffling circles, looking down at his feet, down at the street. Willa's not even sure if he's noticed her. If he has, he's not acknowledging her.

She takes another couple of steps.

The sheriff's SUV, black and gold, is pulled up along the curb, the flare of the lights oscillating red and blue. Sheriff Buck himself crouches over a small, dark shape. He has his cell phone in hand, using its flashlight to illuminate his surroundings. Every few seconds, he snaps a photo.

Oh God, Willa thinks. *Kenny's run over somebody's dog.*

Her next move is more hesitant. She has no interest in seeing a dead dog. Especially not one her boyfriend and the father of her unborn child has pulped on the pavement.

People stand at the edges of their yards or gather in clusters on the sidewalk, watching wide-eyed, as if expecting a late-night parade to pass this way. A dog getting strewn across a couple of lanes wouldn't have brought them out in such numbers.

Or maybe it's not a dog.

Maybe a kid?

Another step.

Oh God. Maybe somebody's child.

Kenny spots her now. He doesn't look happy. No goofy smile tonight. But he appears somewhat relieved, like he's been holding his breath and finally, now that Willa's here, can let it out. Almost as quickly as he relaxes, even a little, his features tense again. Nervousness, bordering on panic, overtakes his face.

Willa takes another step as Kenny hurries to meet her.

"You're okay," Willa says, not a question but a declaration in need of validation.

"Yeah." Kenny draws her into a tight hug. "I'm all right."

He doesn't sound convincing.

And he reeks of vomit.

The stink triggers Willa into a reflexive act, a glance to see if there's any of her own vomit on her shirt. She is, after all, no stranger to sickness of late. The quick examination of her clothing is involuntary.

Like the puking.

"What happened?" Willa pulls back, looks into Kenny's eyes, then looks over his shoulder. "What is the sheriff—"

"Don't."

Kenny's hands are on her shoulders, squeezing firmly, and he moves to stand between her and Sheriff Buck. He positions himself so she can't see past him, even leaning in, pushing her back.

"Hey!" Willa says, startled. "What are you doing?"

"You shouldn't be here," Kenny replies.

"Let *go*." Willa brushes Kenny's hands away, breaking free of his grasp. Her voice is low but full of surprised indignation. "I really don't appreciate being manhandled."

"Don't come any closer, all right?" The look on Kenny's pallid, sweaty face is stern but pleading, an expression that makes him somehow pathetic, a scared boy pretending to be a brave man. "You don't want to see. Please. Really. Don't look."

The warning only ensures that Willa does exactly that.

She moves to the left, slips past him.

The blood—black in the shadow, but she knows it's red, red, *red*—crawling and creeping around islands of glistening organs, tries to spell out messages on the blacktop. The gray-pink length of intestine trailing from the ruptured trash bag loops and coils in the gore-streaked street as if trying to draw images.

More messages in quarter measures.

Willa's brain scrabbles to grab on to reality and mold it, shape it into something that's not so completely, so suddenly, out of control.

There's something there.

She almost deciphers the message. She chokes.

There are no revelations to be found on the street.

No answers to the questions spinning in her brain.

She's not a lucky girl. She's a pregnant girl . . . and ready-made answers don't come easily.

Looking up from his examination of the organs in the street, Sheriff Buck spots Willa. He rises to his full height and raises a hand in a halting gesture. Stepping over the blood trails as if he's playing a game of "step on a crack, break your mama's back," he stomps toward her.

"No, ma'am," he says. "No. No. You can't be in the street."

Willa stares at the blood and organs, still trying to puzzle out their secret pictographs.

"Hello? Are you listening?" There's a cold, dispassionate quality to the law officer's voice. Trained. Something he works at. Something being eaten away—ever so slowly—by whatever lies beneath. "Do you hear me? You need to step back with the others. Better yet, just go on home."

The sluggish blood paints a picture. Almost coming together.

It has something to say.

Something it wants to tell Willa. Half measures becoming whole. She's almost got it.

A large hand wraps around her arm. "Come on," Sheriff Buck says. He pulls her toward the sidewalk, where the others wait.

Another hand—Kenny's—falls to her shoulder, gently squeezing. "Hey—it's cool. This is my girlfriend," Kenny says. "She's giving me a ride home."

"I know who she is." The coldness in his voice begins to burn away. "Not that I remember asking."

Kenny and Sheriff Buck face each other, each with a hand on Willa, and they're not pulling her, not yet, but a vicious tug-of-war might break out at any second.

On the street, the blood's message has atrophied, incomplete.

"Let's go," the sheriff says, his grip tightening.

Willa snaps out of it. Twisting her arm, she yanks away from the sheriff. She also shrugs out of Kenny's grasp.

"How about I'll stay," she says.

Both Kenny and the sheriff blink in disbelief.

"Young lady—" Sheriff Buck starts.

"You damn well know my name," Willa says, and her words display an iciness too, different from the sheriff's, untrained, uncontrolled, and most certainly not dispassionate, a tone that says *Touch me again, and frostbite's gonna freeze your fucking fingers right off.*

"Willa." The sheriff speaks her name as slowly as possible, as if using a bit of extra time to mentally count to ten, to work at keeping his blood pressure and temper in check. Her name, though, is short, so he probably only makes it to a one or two count. "Come on. This is a crime scene. The area's secure. I need to ask Kenny a few questions. When I'm done—"

"I'll stay."

"I wasn't asking."

"Neither was I."

The sheriff's eyes narrow. *He might be looking at me*, Willa thinks, *but right now he's seeing Dad.*

Buck draws in a labored sigh. "Fine. Suit your damn self," he finally says.

Willa barely realizes he's given up the fight.

Her gaze falls back to the bloody street. To the secret messages she wishes she could decipher.

CHAPTER SEVEN

THE WARLOCK HOLDS HIS BREATH. Listens.

The sirens—distant, wailing—fade. His eyes narrow, dart back and forth.

The sirens fall silent. But he knows what he heard. The telltale clenching of his asshole does not lie.

Wilson Island is a peaceful place, not a breeding ground for trouble. Sure, some folks get a little too drunk from time to time. Locals and tourists scuffle every now and then. There's the occasional boating accident. But those events rarely stir the screaming calls of emergency vehicles in the dark.

"Foul spirits are at work tonight," the Warlock intones, casting his voice high and creaky—an approximation of the Emperor from *Return of the Jedi*. He pulls the hood of his ratty sweatshirt low over his eyes and takes a hit, a cloud of smoke from the joint filling the air around his head. Suddenly he's not so worried about the sirens.

The Warlock's real name is Denny Finn Danvers, but several years ago, some kids at the rec center started calling him by his much-cooler nickname. Back in those days, he was running Dungeons & Dragons every Thursday night and Sunday afternoon. He was, as some might say, a killer Dungeon Master. "Killer" because he was a skilled craftsman, telling tales of magic and adventure, of sorcery and diablerie, with gusto, challenging his players with clever traps, devious catacombs, and foul monsters. But also "killer" because he would maul, mutilate, and murder those same fighters, thieves, and magic-users with great zeal and delight. And his players loved him for it.

He savors the memories.

Ancient history now, all of four years gone by.

"It is the doom of men that they forget," he says, doing his best Nicol Williamson—Merlin from his favorite old movie, *Excalibur*.

Of course, the running game had ended when the rec center permanently closed due to budget cuts. Try as he might—and despite his cool nom de guerre and stellar reputation as a Dungeon Master—he was simply unable to keep the game going. He couldn't move the festivities to his house. His uncle had no interest in hosting D&D sessions in the dining room two days a week. And who the fuck would want to hang around anywhere near Uncle Terry anyhow? The Book Grotto, the used bookstore the Warlock frequented in search of works of fantasy, horror, and science fiction, was a brief possibility, but they were overstocked and had no space in their back room or attic. The town library was a no-go too, because despite evidence to the contrary, the librarian, Mrs. Slater, thought gamers might be a little too disruptive.

One would think the good people of Wilson Island would be more interested in keeping kids out of trouble and occupied with wholesome activities.

The Warlock even tried to convince Rudy, the owner of Rudy's Mart, to let him use his storeroom to play. It would have been a great quid pro quo for Rudy, since he'd sell the group soda and snacks hand over fist, but he wasn't biting. *You loiter around here too much as it is*, Rudy had said.

That's okay, the Warlock thinks as he leans against the dumpster behind the little convenience store, taking another hit. *Rudy still provides*.

After all, many of the kids the Warlock used to play D&D with are now some of his best repeat customers.

Not at the moment, though, and probably not for the rest of the night. Sirens tend to frighten the clientele back to their bedrooms and basements. No teenagers around to pay a few bucks extra for the Warlock to buy them six-packs. No one's out now purchasing his cheap weed or painkillers or speed.

His hand slides over the left pocket of his hoodie, where the bulge of his supply can be felt. He keeps his wares, neatly organized in old prescription medicine containers and little plastic baggies, safe and sound within the same Crown Royal bag where he once stored his beloved gaming dice.

No one to play D&D. No customers. All alone, as usual—

Something snaps in the darkness.

The Warlock jumps away from his usual lounging spot behind the dumpster.

"Hey! Who's there?"

Someone moves in the garbage-strewn copse of pine trees crowding up against Rudy's back lot. A dark shape in motion among many dark shapes. Footsteps rustle in the dead straw and underbrush, kicking and crunching twigs.

Switching his joint to his other hand, the Warlock reaches into his right sweatshirt pocket. His fingers wrap around a cold metal cylinder—pepper spray for just such an occasion.

"Go back to the shadow," the Warlock mutters, quietly mimicking Gandalf's bellow against the demonic Balrog.

Without heeding the warning, the shape draws closer. The Warlock pulls the pepper spray from his pocket. "You don't stay right where you are," he says, "and I'll fuck you up."

His voice breaks, no longer amused, no longer imitating his favorite wizardly types.

The figure shuffles closer.

A shiver skitters along the Warlock's spine, spreads out into his arms, his fingertips, his legs, lips.

"I said—"

"I know what you said." The figure speaks in a gruff, familiar voice. "And I can't say as I give a good, fiber-enhanced shit."

Madhouse Quinn emerges from the trees. Dirty, smelly, bearded. Filthy stocking cap pulled low over his long, shaggy, salt-and-pepper hair. Dressed in a tattered olive-green field jacket; fingerless wool gloves that reveal too-long fingernails; jeans so grime-caked they could probably stand up on their own; and mismatched boots. He drags a canvas duffel bag—full of crushed cans and whatever other treasures the homeless man has scrounged and hoarded in his travels—behind him.

The Warlock breathes a little easier. Through his mouth, not his nose.

"Damn, Quinn. You scared the hell out of me."

"That's what weed and pills do to you," Quinn says. "They make you all jumpy."

"More like make me aware." The Warlock taps his temple with one finger. "You want some?"

"If you're offering."

The Warlock passes the smoldering joint.

"You hear those sirens?" the homeless man asks.

"I did."

"Unclench, boy." Madhouse Quinn takes a hit off the joint, holds it like a pro, then exhales. "They ain't worried about pill-pushing pill-poppers like you."

Quinn regards the joint he holds between his fingers as if he's trying to decide whether to take another drag. Then he crushes it out with the thumb and forefinger of his other hand. A tiny wisp of aromatic smoke curls from the blackened tip. He opens his field jacket and slips the joint into an interior pocket. "Might need that later," he says. "No sense in using it all up."

The Warlock almost protests, then stops himself. He knows from experience that arguing with Quinn, with anyone called "Madhouse," for that matter, is wasted energy. Instead, he sighs and asks, "You know what all the fuss is about?"

How could he? the Warlock wonders almost as soon as he asks the question. *Guy's an outcast, an outsider, even more so than me.*

"Fuck, yeah," Quinn replies. "I sure do."

"Okay, I'll bite."

Quinn smiles, showing teeth that are almost brown. "Why are you wasting your breath?" he asks.

"I'm not. The way you were talking, I thought maybe you knew something, more than you should."

"I do."

"Enlighten me, then."

Quinn's smile stretches, becoming too wide. Thus speaks the doomsayer: "We have jobs to do, you, me, each and every one of us."

"A job," says the Warlock.

"No application necessary," notes Madhouse Quinn through his brown-toothed expression, pleased with himself, pleased with the spilling of secrets, "no interview required."

"What are you talking about?"

"You, me, them others who were out on the beach that night."

"I've never been to the beach with you."

"We were chosen." Madhouse thumps the Warlock on his forehead. "Don't matter if you remember it or not."

"Chosen?" The Warlock steps back. He cracks a smile, but the expression is nothing more than a bandage slapped over his growing discomfort. "You mean, like for dodgeball in gym class?"

"If you were half as stupid as you pretend to be, you'd be in a sorry state."

"All right." The Warlock waves his companion away. "I've heard just about enough. I'm going home. Enjoy the rest of the weed, man."

"Chosen," Madhouse Quinn says again. "Recruited. Conscripted. Enlisted."

"For what?" the Warlock asks, angry at himself for voicing the question.

"We're meat puppets."

"Like the band?" the Warlock scoffs.

"What?"

"The band? You know what? Never mind."

"Meat puppets," Madhouse Quinn says, "for the bone."

"You're so full of shit."

"One of us to sustain. One of us to speak. One of us to carry on. One who no longer matters. And one of us . . ."

Madhouse Quinn fixes his gaze on the Warlock, and his lips twitch with a kind of malicious delight.

He's talking about me right now, the Warlock thinks. "Yeah?"

"I'm not ready to tell that story," Madhouse says. "Not just yet."

CHAPTER EIGHT

"**T**ELL ME WHAT HE LOOKED like," Sheriff Buck says.

"I already told you," Kenny says, irritation creeping into his voice.

"I know, I know. Humor me. Tell me again."

He's trying to trip Kenny up, Willa thinks, *see if his story's going to change.*

"What did he look like?" the sheriff asks.

Willa tries to read Kenny's face as he answers Sheriff Buck's questions for the third time. He's not as difficult to decipher as the cooling blood on the street. He's pale. He's shivering. He's avoiding the sheriff's eyes, keeping his own gaze focused on his shoes. The muscles in his jaw clench and pop. Every now and then, even though he fights to keep it under control, a tremor ripples through his body.

He's rattled. On edge. Ready to be home. Far from Killdeer Avenue. Far from Wilson Island, more than ever.

"He was wearing coveralls." The slightest hint of anger twitches across his face, bubbling up to the surface of his unease, then sinking back down. "Or something like coveralls."

The rage, the frustration, turns his voice shrill.

Willa looks at the blood on the street, and can't help but think she's deciphered the message, can't help but think: *He's not ready.* And the idea has nothing to do with the accident.

Well, not this *accident.*

"More like fishing bibs," Kenny says, shrugging.

"Fishing bibs," Sheriff Buck says. "You sure about that?"

"I guess."

"A guess ain't being sure."

"Close enough, how about that."

Kenny would know fishing bibs when he saw them. After all, it's what his father wears whenever he goes out on the water, whenever he wants a bit of extra protection from sea spray and rough weather and blood and guts.

There are human organs in the street, Willa thinks.

"Definitely waterproof," Kenny adds. "PVC and canvas. They were wet."

The sheriff eyes the blood-slicked pavement, clears his throat, and continues his interrogation.

He doesn't even have a notebook.

"Definitely a man?" Buck asks.

"Pretty sure."

Shouldn't he be writing this down?

"But you couldn't see his face."

"He was wearing some sort of gas mask."

The sheriff sucks at his teeth. "And you weren't drinking?" he asks.

That's a new line of questioning.

"No," Kenny says.

But his voice quivers just a little. *He's lying*, Willa thinks. She *knows* when he's lying. *What does it matter if he had a drink?*

"You gonna agree to a field sobriety test?" Buck asks.

"If I have to," Kenny says.

There are human organs in the fucking street!

Three black-and-gold patrol cars are now parked near Buck's SUV. They came in with wailing sirens, but now they are silent. The lights flash red and blue, red and blue, casting strange shadows across the faces of the townsfolk who still watch from both sides of the street. Deputies Reed, Keene, and Fines—nearly the complete contingency of the Fredericks County Sheriff's Department, at least until the interim officers are brought on for the summer—work the scene. They wear matching khakis with short-sleeved black button-ups and tactical vests laden with guns, ammunition, Tasers, handcuffs, and an assortment of other military-grade ordnance needed to defend a besieged country or dole out traffic tickets in small-town USA.

A flash of bright, clean light erupts amid the flush of reds and blues.

Deputy Eric Reed crouches next to the open trash bag, using his cell phone like a camera, gathering photographic evidence. His face is weird and eerie in the glow. He's the youngest member of the department, not much older than Kenny, but he looks worn out and worn thin, aging with every photo he snaps.

Deputy Martin Fines, the oldest member of the department, unfurls yellow tape from a spool. He wraps it first around the post of a mailbox, extending it to the trunk of a tree, stretching it to a lamppost across the street. He's already set up road barricades, sawhorse-like obstacles adorned with flickering orange reflectors. The street is cordoned off.

Making it official.

Now, if they didn't realize before, the residents of Killdeer Avenue know this is more than a simple accident, more than a kid on a joyride fucking around and finding out, more than a traffic ticket. This is the kind of event that gets talked about at work the next day, gets written about in the local paper, attracts the attention of statewide news agencies, maybe even goes national. Some of the townsfolk shuffle closer to the curb and edge onto the street, craning their necks, trying to get a good look at what the hell is going on. After all, if they're gonna tell *I was there when it happened* kinds of stories, they'll need more details.

"Folks! Folks!" Deputy Melissa Keene raises her arms, waves to get the attention of the crowd. She's the deputy everyone genuinely takes seriously, the officer you never want to piss off. Nobody wants to be on Keene's bad side, or have her be the one who pulls you over when you've been driving a few miles over the speed limit. "We're going to need you to step back, stay in your yards, please, and let us do our jobs."

"Somebody get hurt?" Bill Wallace asks.

"We'll tell you what we can," Keene says, "when we can."

"Hurt? More like somebody got killed!" another voice calls out.

Nervous chatter passes from person to person, questions and exclamations bouncing back and forth like a hot potato.

"Did that kid run somebody over?"

"He found something!"

"I know him!"

"He found a dead body!"

"Part of one, anyway!"

"You think it's murder?"

"Did you see that bag? That's somebody's insides, all over the street!"

"Who is it?"

Faces—awash with red, awash with blue—turn toward Kenny. They look strange in the ebb and flow of shadow and light, strange in their confusion and fear, strange in their cold accusation.

What the fuck are they looking at? Willa wonders.

"Don't worry about them," Buck says. He doesn't acknowledge the staring crowd, but he must feel their presence, burning at the back of his neck, and he doesn't care. "Worry about me. We're almost done here. So, he dashed out in front of you from over this way." Buck points to his right, toward a bank of houses, then to his left. "And he ran off over yonder."

"I think so," Kenny says. "I was a little more focused on the telephone pole."

"Fair enough." Buck snorts. "What about the bag, though?"

"He was carrying it."

"But he dropped it, letting it spill out onto the street."

Willa regards the mess that's been made all over the pavement. The mess that used to be a person. *Two* people from the looks of it.

Kenny nods, all somber.

Sucking at his teeth again, Sheriff Buck surveys his surroundings. He draws in a breath, holds it for a beat, then exhales. He hitches his fingers over his belt and eyes Kenny. "Your old man gonna be pissed about the truck?"

Kenny shuffles back a step. "What?"

"Your dad." And, just for a split second, Buck fixes his eyes on Willa. "Dads can be a handful, as I'm sure you both know."

He's puffing up, Willa thinks. *Challenging us. Challenging* me. *Trying to prove he's not afraid of Dad.*

"Well, yeah. He won't be happy," Kenny says, answering the sheriff's question at long last. "No."

"Repairs like that"—Buck eyes the truck—"gonna mean a lot of extra hours on the boat."

"Guess so."

Kenny's voice is distant. Like he's not on Killdeer Avenue at all. Like he's not . . . anywhere.

"Are we done here?" Willa says. "We should probably take Kenny to the emergency room, you know? Probably see if he has a concussion or some other injury."

"He seems all right to me." Sheriff Buck actually grins at this. "Tough kid. But—yeah—I'd say we're just about done. For now. I mean, I'm gonna need you to come to the station, make a formal statement, but that can wait until tomorrow."

"A formal statement?" Willa asks. "What was all this then?"

"An *informal* statement," Buck says.

"Whatever," Willa says.

"In the meantime, I'll arrange to have your truck towed to Smitty's. That suit you?"

"That's fine," Kenny says.

Where else would you tow it? Willa thinks. *There's only one auto shop on this whole stupid island.*

Taking Kenny's hand, Willa leads him away from the scene. Kenny opens the passenger-side door of her car and slumps into the seat. Willa, standing with her hand on the door handle, feels the sheriff's gaze following her. In another circumstance, she'd force herself not to look back. As she gets behind the wheel, though, she finds herself staring right at the big man.

Kenny mutters, "Fuck that guy."

"No, thanks," Willa says as she throws the car in reverse and backs away, "though I agree with the sentiment."

"And fuck this town. Fuck everybody in it. I can't wait to get clear of this place. And when I do—when *we* do—we're not looking back."

Willa's breath hitches in her throat.

"What is it?" Kenny asks.

Willa forces a smile, but she knows it must look sad or apologetic, the kind of smile you plaster across your face when you're about to deliver some really bad news.

CHAPTER NINE

"I'M PREGNANT."

Willa tries to sound chipper, upbeat, positive, like the world isn't falling apart. It seems like the right thing to do, no matter how she's feeling. But her efforts fail. Those two little words thunder like a proclamation of global doom.

Kenny doesn't really respond. He barely moves, barely blinks, barely breathes. Still slouching in the passenger seat of Willa's car, he stares straight ahead, like he's witnessing his dreams rolling away like tumbleweeds, farther and farther out of reach.

They're parked in front of Kenny's house. It's dark. Quiet. In the driveway is a pickup—older than Kenny's, beat-up, white paint flaking from rusting metal, the bed loaded with tools, fishing gear, old shrimp baskets, and a cooler. The only other thing in the driveway, partially covered in a blue plastic tarp, is a rotting, barnacle-encrusted bulk of wood that might have once been considered a boat.

The boat—the *Jilly-Bee*—hasn't seen water in years, not since Kenny was in middle school. His dad always said he was going to fix it up when he had the time and money, but those two commodities always elude him. Willa and Kenny used to slip out to the boat with a sleeping bag and some cheap wine to screw around under the tarp, away from prying eyes. It was a decent enough change of pace from Kenny's truck. That is, until the spiders moved in, and they must've been screwing around too, because their numbers rapidly grew, making the boat inhospitable to two drunk, horny teens. Now, save as the breeding ground for pests, the boat wallows in its utter uselessness.

"Did you hear what I said?" Willa asks.

In the passenger seat, Kenny shifts slightly, but he continues staring straight ahead, never looking at Willa, never taking his eyes off the road, off the future that he envisioned lay somewhere far from here.

"Kenny—"

"I heard you," he says, not even glancing in her direction.

"And?"

"I wonder"—his voice is monotone, robotic, void of emotion—"why you're telling me this now."

"*That's* what you're wondering?" Willa grips the steering wheel, squeezes. "Well, I don't know, Kenny. Why don't you tell me when it *would* have been a good time?"

She knows he's right, though. This obviously *isn't* a good time. Kenny *isn't* ready. The decision whether to tell him had been batted back and forth all night. At first she wanted to spill the beans when he got to the beach. Then, when she realized he'd been in an accident, when she'd seen the gore on the street, the same as him, she'd changed her mind. And she might have done so one way or the other a hundred times before she finally just thought *Fuck it* and threw the revelation his way in her fake glib tone.

There was something more to it, though, wasn't there?

Just before she dropped the bombshell, all she could think about was his hand on her, pulling at her, trying to control her.

And it royally pissed her off.

Some part of her wanted him to know he wasn't in control. Not of her. Not of anything. Selfish and petty, maybe, but her question still stood: When *would* have been a good time?

When he was making his final decision about what school to attend? While packing his bags to leave and never look back? As the baby was popping out?

So she'd blurted out the news as they pulled up to his house, no preamble, ripping the proverbial bandage off without warning.

"This," Kenny says, "fucks everything."

"Yeah, well, I know it's not what we expected."

"What are you going to do?" he asks.

Willa flinches. "What am *I* going to do?"

Kenny shrugs in response. And now Willa's looking out the window too, looking past her hands tight-clenching the steering wheel, looking down the road that, she knows, leads Kenny to a very different place than it leads her.

"This isn't how I expected you to react," she says.

Kenny shrugs again. Infuriating.

"I know it's a lot," Willa says.

"You realize what you're doing here."

"This conversation feels like you're putting a lot of this on me."

"You realize what you're asking."

"I'm not *asking* anything!" What feels like a balloon swells in her throat. She forces herself to look at him again. She wants him to look back at her, but he resists the mental urging. "I'm telling you the situation that we're in. Me *and* you. *We're* in this, both of us."

"So now I'm supposed to give up on everything." Kenny's lips curl, just a little, into the slightest of disgusted snarls. It's an expression Willa has never seen before on his face. "You're asking me to stay here. On the island, this shithole. End up like my dad. Spend twelve hours a day on the boat. To break my back, and come back to nothing every day."

Nothing.

"Wow . . ." Willa says.

"Fuck. I had *plans*."

"Are you being serious right now?"

"Seems like a good time for seriousness."

"Huh. Okay then. What do you want me to say?"

"I want you to tell me that this is all some sort of bad joke. Tell me you didn't mean it. That you were kidding. Tell me you're *not* pregnant. Otherwise"—now he finally looks at her, fixes her with his dead eyes—"I don't know that I have much use for anything you might tell me."

Willa coughs out a humorless laugh.

"What?" Kenny asks. But he doesn't really want an answer. His hand is already on the door handle.

"Yeah, you know—go ahead," Willa says. "Just go. Asshole."

Kenny opens his mouth, starts to say something, then thinks better of it. He offers no more arguments. He mutters no more hurtful words. He damn sure doesn't try to comfort Willa. He shoves the door open, climbs out of the car, slams the door, and stomps toward the house.

He doesn't look back.

Willa sits in her car, parked outside her boyfriend's house, wearing his jacket, thinking about her future, thinking about *his* future, and about the rotting boat sitting in the driveway that likely played a part in this entire mess, as hot tears stream down her face.

It's the first time she's cried since peeing on that fucking stick.

CHAPTER TEN

STRETCHED BETWEEN SIGNPOSTS, TREE TRUNKS, seahorse mailboxes, and telephone poles, yellow police tape flutters and rasps as a warm gust of wind races along Killdeer Avenue. Pacing the perimeter of the barricade he's created, Deputy Martin Fines rubs his thumbs against his forefingers. The tape, pulled from the trunk of his patrol car, had felt dusty from years of disuse. The memory of the dustiness lingers on his fingertips.

The residents have been sent packing from the edge of the street, but they still cluster on their front porches and on the other side of living room windows, like shadows, watching, craning their necks for a glimpse of the carnage. The pulsing red-and-blue glow of cruiser lights floods across their faces, giving them a morbid, ghoulish look.

"Come on—go on back inside. Nothing to see here, folks."

A blatant lie when there are human organs splattered across the street. Blatant, yes. Untrue, yes. But simple to understand.

"Get back, please get out of our way—let us work."

Some of the onlookers are on their phones, shooting video.

By morning, word of the accident—and, more importantly, of the discovery made in its aftermath—will be spreading all over the island and beyond. *And that*, Fines thinks, *is gonna put Buck in a piss-poor mood.*

...

With a quarter pinched between his fingers, Deputy Eric Reed raps his knuckles upon the wooden door of 2146 Killdeer Avenue. The coin, he finds, kicks the sense of urgency up a few notches, gets doors open a little more quickly, even as he tries not to damage property. In this case, he needs the sense of urgency felt by the people inside to match his own.

To match the pounding of his heart.

He exchanges a glance with Deputy Keene—Melissa, though he never calls her that—who stands poised on the porch beside him. She presses a hand down, signaling him to take a breath, tamp down his nerves, play it cool. Without her saying a word, he can hear her voice ringing in his ears.

You carry a badge, Deputy Reed. Carry it with respect. Stand tall. Walk the walk.

She has offered that advice almost every day Eric has been on the job. Sometimes when he isn't.

He might be at the marina with his buddies, all of them dressed in deck shoes and shorts and tank tops, loading the boat up to go out fishing, and if Deputy Keene drove by in her cruiser, in her uniform, she'd pull to a stop, stick her head out the window, and speak those same words. And whenever she pulled something like that, regardless of the laughter of his friends, Eric always felt himself instinctively straighten up.

He stood tall.

Keene scans the street, which has gone silent now, then looks at Eric and nods, giving him the go-ahead.

"Sheriff's department!" Eric calls out, tapping the quarter against the door a little more forcefully.

Keene leans to the side, looking toward the front window. Light slices between the gently swaying panels. Shadows dart past.

"They're home," she says.

"They don't want to get involved," Eric says, shrugging.

"Answering a couple of questions isn't 'getting involved.'" Keene steps up, tired of waiting her turn, and bangs on the door with her fist. She doesn't need the quarter trick to demand attention. "Hello? Anybody home?"

After a beat, the lock is thrown and the door creaks open. A short, balding man greets the deputies. Behind him, clutching his shoulders, is presumably his short, wide-eyed wife, holding her phone in one hand. The pair wear matching bathrobes—black with pink flowers.

"Good evening," Eric says. "Sheriff's department. There's been something of a disturbance out here tonight, as you probably know. We were hoping to ask you a couple of questions."

...

Across the street, Sheriff Buck inches down darkened alleys between houses. In one hand, he holds his Maglite close to his face, directing the pale beam along the surrounding walls. In his other, held in the low-ready position, is his Glock 22.

He's drawn his firearm in the performance of his duties a time or two. Like when Teddy Lewis decided the live music at the Harvest Festival taking place across the street from his house was just too damn loud. Teddy had stomped right through the field, right past the pumpkin decoration station and apple cider vendors, right past the face-painting booth and the Blue Hills Siding & Roofing display, rifle in hand and a growling curse on his lips. He'd climbed up onto the stage as the band—some near-local screaming rock group—played, and kicked over one of the speakers, brandishing his weapon and demanding some peace and quiet. Buck had drawn his gun then, ordering Teddy to throw his own weapon down, and was damn glad when Teddy did as he was told. Teddy might've been loaded, but the rifle wasn't. And Buck knew the old guy was pretty damn lucky someone in the crowd hadn't drawn their own concealed handgun and taken him down.

It's been a long time, though, since Buck's actually fired his own weapon anywhere other than the range.

He thinks things might change. And soon. Maybe even tonight.

Whoever the Smythe kid—Devil Dog Number 37—almost clipped with his truck, whoever dropped that plastic bag full of human organs, had dashed off between the houses on this side of the street.

A KILLER ON KILLDEER!

Buck can see the headlines now.

His grip tightens, on both the Maglite and the pistol, as he rounds a corner.

Chances are, the murderer—and Buck's already determined that the person *is* very much that, because who the hell else carries a plastic bag full of human organs around in the dead of night?—kept on running.

But they *might* still be lurking about.

He thinks of Kenny Smythe, star quarterback, golden boy of Wilson Island High School.

The suspect might be waiting in the darkness.

He thinks of Willa Hanson, snidely mentioning her father.

The suspect might still be looking for a fight.

I damn sure hope you are.

•••

"You didn't happen to see anyone suspicious pass by here tonight, did you?"

"Were there any unusual vehicles in the area today?"

"Did you see or hear anything out of the ordinary earlier this evening?"

Deputies Reed and Keene move from doorstep to doorstep, stoop to stoop, knocking on doors, rousing the neighborhood, asking their questions.

The same questions. The same answers. Over and over. With every house, Eric feels less like an officer of the law—

Stand tall.

—and a little more like a door-to-door salesman. Or maybe an evangelical. Cruising neighborhoods on a bicycle, dressed in a white short-sleeved shirt, Bible in one hand, pamphlets in the other, spreading the gospel.

Only, the gospel Reed and Keene are peddling hinges on:

"Suspicious."

"Unusual."

"Out of the ordinary."

Eric reminds himself that his job here, in addition to gathering information, is to reassure the residents, his calm demeanor soothing their anxious concerns and worries. To squelch the fears surrounding "blood in the streets." With that in mind, he speaks confidently and with authority.

Walk the walk.

He's not sure he's fooling anyone. Let alone fooling himself.

Keene, on the other hand, projects a coolness bordering on ice-cold. It's no wonder people in town—adults and kids alike—clench up whenever she appears, including Eric himself.

The routine continues. House after house. Knock after knock. Question after question. Response after response.

"Didn't hear anything until that kid plowed into the telephone pole."

"No one strange . . . at least no more strange than usual . . . in the neighborhood today."

"While you're out here, could you ask the asshole next door to stop playing his music so fucking loud after midnight?"

"Did I hear someone say something about . . . blood?"

As they move to the next house, Keene shuffles to a stop, something catching her attention. She knuckles Eric on the shoulder—knocking for attention—and motions her chin toward the shadows the next street over. At first Eric doesn't see what she's seeing. Another row of houses, all dark and still and quiet. Beckner Street. The people who live in those homes probably have no idea there was a collision on Killdeer.

Frustration on her furrowed brow, Keene motions her chin again. She could just tell him what she wants him to see, but it's almost as if she's holding her breath. Holding her words.

Eric looks again, narrowing his eyes, concentrating. Then, finally, he spots it.

Among the silent houses, all locked up tight for the night, a single back door stands open, yawning into blackness within.

He looks at Keene and she offers a curt headshake. *That's not right*.

...

"*Sheriff*," Keene's voice crackles over the radio, "*we've got blood over here*."

Tucking his flashlight under his arm, Buck presses the button on his shoulder mic. "Where are you?"

"*Beckner Street. We're around back at one of the houses. There's no activity. It's quiet. Dead calm. But the door's open. And there's definitely blood."*

"Stay put," Buck says. "I'm on my way."

He whirls, hustles down the alley between houses, navigating grumbling AC units and overfull trash cans pushed up against walls and hidden behind vanity partitions. Crossing the street, Buck holsters his pistol. If there are prying eyes watching from the surrounding houses, he'd rather they not see him carrying his gun at the ready. He spots Fines, manning his barricade.

"You need me, Sheriff?" the deputy asks.

Buck keeps moving.

Buck wishes like hell he could swap Fines for Reed. Fines is more seasoned, a pro, and might be better suited to a crisis. But maybe, if he's lucky, this won't be a crisis scenario.

Across the street, in the darkness behind the houses, Buck sees the beam of a flashlight, waving back and forth. He crosses an unkempt backyard full of weeds and plastic children's toys, a small swing set creaking in the slight breeze, the yard of new parents, harried and busy and overwhelmed. There's no fence separating this yard from the one a street over.

He meets Reed and Keene, standing at the back door of one of the homes along Beckner Street.

"Who lives here?" Buck asks without looking at his deputies.

He feels like he should know, but he can't quite put a finger on the homeowner's name.

His eyes are drawn to the concrete back steps, and the spatters of blood to be found there. Over the threshold. Down the steps. Disappearing in the sand and grass of the backyard. The blood trailing off.

But prints—partially obscured by those of the deputies, obliterated by his own careless footsteps—are leading away.

He looks from Reed to Keene, seeing a hint of fear on Reed's face, resolve and forced resilience on Keene's, and he chucks his chin toward the darkened doorway, giving them the go-ahead.

"Sheriff's department!" he calls out, his voice deep and rumbling. "Anybody inside?"

There is no answer.

And he doesn't call out again before shouldering past his deputies and stepping indoors.

Buck barely registers drawing his pistol again. He's not worried about anyone inside noticing.

...

A snake of ice uncoils in Eric Reed's stomach. Aside from the thumping of his own heartbeat in his ears, the silence holds its ground.

There's nothing alive in here.

He follows the sheriff down the hallway. Keene is at his side, close, their shoulders almost touching. Three flashlight beams—Buck's, Keene's, and his own—crisscross in the darkness. Each of them holds a firearm in hand. Eric's hand is sweaty and trembling on the grip. Black patches spatter the carpet. An iron scent hangs in the air, as stark as the shadows.

Blood, for certain.

Framed portraits adorn the walls, memories captured and frozen and still. Some of the images depict a family, a mother and father, a daughter, a son. Some portray the father, smiling and sunburned, standing on the deck of a fishing boat, the ocean his background as he proudly holds a massive cobia. Others display high school graduations for both children, while still others are of vacations or barbecues or homecoming dates. A scattering of memories—the son in a football uniform, the daughter a cheerleader, the mother gardening, the father in his exterminator's uniform.

Eric recognizes the people in the photographs. Barry and Allison Hadley. Friends of his parents. Eric had gone to school with their kids—Jordyn and Scotty. Jordyn was in his grade, Scotty a couple of years older. Neither had waited around after graduating; they'd moved on from Wilson Island like pretty much everyone else, gone to college out of town or out of state, got married, started families, got away from here.

Eric wonders what the kids are doing now.

Jordyn's a pharmacist, right? And Scotty runs a construction crew somewhere.

But what are they doing right now? Right this very moment?

He wonders what he's going to say to them when he inevitably calls to tell them about their mom and dad.

"Oh, hi, Jordyn. Hi, Scotty.

"It's good to talk to you again.

"Jeez. How long has it been?

"You gotta get back out to the island sometime.

"And . . . while I have you, I've got some bad news."

Because he knows, without question, what they're going to find in the depths of the house.

That certainty is the freezing-cold snake writhing in his stomach.

Without thinking, Eric reaches out and flips a nearby light switch. The *snap* breaks the silence like a gunshot. Light floods the hall, illuminating the faces in the photographs.

Along with the blood on the floor.

Sheriff Buck and Deputy Keene look toward him, scolding, annoyed. They say nothing, though. Putting his flashlight away, Buck looks toward the portraits. His face betrays recognition. He damn well knew Barry and Allison too.

And that's their blood on the floor—Eric just knows it—leading the trio toward a bedroom door. Half open. Or half closed, depending on pessimism levels.

Buck leads the way, his boots sinking softly into the plush carpet of the hallway. The once-pristine beige fibers are marred by a series of dark crimson stains, drawing them inexorably forward. Each bloody spatter is a gruesome marker on a path toward—

I don't want to see. I don't want to see this.

You carry a badge, Deputy Reed. The words resound in his head. *Carry it with respect. Stand tall. Walk the walk.*

He swallows his dread down.

The sheriff presses the flat of his hand against the bedroom door. It creaks as he pushes it open. He steps through, into shadow. Eric follows. Absently, almost instinctively, the deputy reaches over and flips the light switch.

The illuminated room spins wildly. Eric's eyes widen, taking everything in against his own will. The blood on the floor. The walls. The fucking ceiling. The body on the red-soaked carpet. The second body on the red-soaked bed. Eric knows their names, but he blocks them from his mind, refuses to acknowledge these . . . piles of shredded . . . *meat* . . . as anything that was once human.

Stand tall.
Stand tall.
Stand tall.

The words pound through his skull.

But this time, they're not spoken by Keene. They're *hissed* by the icy snake in his gut. The one that slithers up from below, up his throat, out his mouth.

He slaps a hand over his lips to block its escape, but it slithers through his fingers.

And now the snake is hot. And stinking. A serpent of vomit that spatters uncontrollably down onto the floor.

CHAPTER ELEVEN

KENNY DOESN'T INTEND TO SLAM the door when he comes in, but he does, hard enough to rattle picture frames hanging on the wall, beer bottles on the rickety coffee table. If his old man had been sleeping—in his recliner, always the recliner—it would have startled him awake for sure.

He's not sleeping, though.

"Goddamn!" Larry Smythe calls from his seat. "Who the fuck stepped on your dick?"

Funny, the accuracy of that question.

"Sorry," Kenny says.

His father sits in darkness, surrounded by his cathedral of ten or so Keystone beer bottles. Staring into shadow. In one hand he holds, *surprise*, a near-empty beer. In the other he cradles an old, dirty football—Kenny's, from when he was a kid.

Kenny looks to the mantel above the never-used fireplace, to the spot where the football usually rests, along with the trophies and ribbons and dust collected over the years, along with a few more framed photos.

There's Kenny in his football uniform. There's Kenny in his baseball gear, a bat on his shoulder. There's Kenny in his basketball jersey. And there's Kenny, his dad, and his mom—gone four years now—smiling against a backdrop of the sun setting across the water.

The older man drums his fingers against the football. "What the fuck's got you so riled?" he asks.

Kenny hesitates, then says, "Nothing."

His father chews at the inside of his mouth, looks at the bottle in his hand, swirls its contents around a little, as if trying to conjure more of the blessed liquid into existence.

"That a fact?" he asks.

"Yeah."

"The way you slammed that door says otherwise."

His father is dressed in his work clothes, a well-worn sweater thrown over a greasy T-shirt, rugged work pants. His boots have been kicked haphazardly across the floor. His feet are covered in dingy socks, his big toe sticking out of a hole in the left one like in the old hillbilly comic strips.

His fishing bibs, if he wore them today, are likely cast off in the carport, where he could hose them off.

His fishing bibs. Like the garment worn by the guy who dropped the bag of gore.

His dad finishes the drink, sets the bottle on the side table along with its brethren. "Another dead soldier," he announces. Leaving the football wedged between the armrest and the seat, he pushes himself out of the recliner, not bothering to lower the footrest, and crosses the room toward the small kitchen.

Kenny instinctively presses his back against the door and smells sweat, salt, and fish.

The older man moves into the tiny connected kitchen. The counters are covered in chip bags, half-empty boxes of saltines, sardine tins, and unwashed dishes. He tugs open the refrigerator door, letting the weak light within wash over his face as he bends down to examine the icebox's contents.

"Got a call a bit ago," his dad announces, still looking into the fridge. His words slur together, but not so much as to be misunderstood. "Randall Haeger. You remember him, right?"

Kenny's guts go runny. His dad has a temper, especially when he's been drinking. From the looks of it, he's been consuming more than his fair share.

"Dad—"

His father, never looking away from the illumination of the fridge, curtly shakes his head.

"He says you drove your truck right into a telephone pole. Just down from his house. Says you fucked it up something special."

"Someone ran out in front of me," Kenny blurts out. "I was gonna tell you in a few minutes. I was just waiting for the right time."

When would have been a good time? Willa had asked.

Kenny's dad makes his decision, leans into the fridge, and rises again. Using his hip, he nudges the door closed. He has two more bottles of Keystone, one in each hand. He moves toward Kenny, hands him one of the bottles.

The knot in Kenny's stomach uncoils.

"You hurt?"

Taking the bottle, Kenny says, "No, sir."

"Damage as bad as Randall says?"

"Uhh . . . I'm not sure yet."

His dad settles back down into his seat, twists the cap off the beer, and raises it in a somber toast to his son before taking a sip. Kenny hesitantly removes the cap of his own, stuffing it in his jeans pocket, then returns the gesture and takes a swig.

"You could have called me, you know," his dad says.

"I—" Kenny starts to protest, to argue, to debate, then stops himself. "Yeah. I know."

"That girl of yours give you a ride home?"

"She has a name, Dad. Willa."

"What did I say?"

"It . . ." Kenny takes another swig. "Eh. It doesn't matter. Me and her, I think we're done. We're through."

"Well, hell." Kenny's dad instantly downs his beer, slams it on the table with the others. "Then I reckon you'd best hustle back to the fridge for us. Grab us a couple more, why don't you. A couple more *each*."

...

Willa sits in the car for a good fifteen minutes before going inside. Her eyes burn and her cheeks feel stiff from dried tears. The three-car garage is quiet and still, neatly organized. Unlike the monstrous, raging shitstorm in her head.

When she first pulled into the driveway, she saw lights within the house, in the living room, in Dad's office. Her parents are still awake. Not the most unusual of situations. Dad is a night owl, working till the wee hours, and Mom simply doesn't like going to bed without him.

They aren't "waiting up" for her in the traditional sense, not really, but she'll have to talk to them.

And during the course of the conversation, she knows she'll blurt out the truth, the way she did with Kenny. Just to lighten the crushing burden.

When she finally climbs out of the CR-V, the distance to the interior garage door—past Mom's Lexus, past Dad's BMW—feels a hundred miles long. Walking slowly, she tries to puzzle out how she'll tell her parents that their only child, their darling little girl, has just ruined her life. With every step, she tries to predict their reactions. Disappointment? Sadness? Anger?

Will they tell her, as Kenny did, that they effectively don't have use for her anymore?

That's not what he said. Not exactly. But . . . might as well have been.

At the interior door, she wraps her hand around the knob, closes her eyes, takes a deep breath to steel her nerves, and steps inside.

The scents of pine and fresh linen hang heavy in the air. The house smells renewed, like a clean slate.

She finds Mom standing at the kitchen island, leaning over the countertop, scrolling through different windows on her iPad. She wears a matched set of pink pajamas. Mom's always looked younger than her fortysomething years, but this outfit makes her look almost like a kid. Her blond hair falls to her shoulders. Blue eyes big behind round-rimmed glasses. She looks up when Willa comes through the door.

"You're out late."

No anger, no disapproval. Just an almost casual statement of fact. Sue Hanson rarely raises her voice.

"Sorry," Willa says. "Kenny was in an accident."

"Oh no! Is everything okay?"

"Yeah, he's all right, it was nothing big, but I gave him a ride home."

"You should have called."

Willa feels the tears bubbling up in her throat. The tears burning in her eyes. "Mom, I—"

"I know. I know."

"No. You don't understand what I'm telling you."

Mom smiles, a comforting, reassuring expression, one that says *I'm here for you and we're in this together.*

And Willa understands. Somehow, her mother *does* know. About everything. The waterworks start anew. Willa breaks, crying, and her mother joins her. Mom holds her arms out, and Willa moves to her in long strides, almost throws herself into her embrace. Mom squeezes her tight and they sob together for a few minutes.

"How did you figure it out?" Willa eventually asks. But she doesn't dare break the hug.

"The cleaning crew came today," Mom says. "And you didn't do a great job of covering your tracks."

Willa blinks, letting what she just heard settle in for a second.

"The pregnancy test," Mom says. "Hello? The box. They found it?"

Willa doesn't even remember throwing it away. She can't grab hold of the memory. For all she knows, she just left it on the bathroom counter. "And they told you," she says.

"Well . . . they thought they were doing the right thing."

"So . . . Janet and her crew . . . *they* now all know." Willa pulls away. She's looking down, not quite ready to meet her mother's eyes. "And that means they'll blab it to everyone in town."

"Ehhh, I don't think so. They know better. I'd like to think they know it wouldn't be great for them." For just a second, Mom sounds cold and menacing and dangerous. *She sounds like Dad.* Then her voice brightens a little. "It's honestly not their story to tell."

It's one of her catchphrases, one of her little mom-isms that keep Willa sane, that remind her that it's all right to mind your own business from time to time.

Willa smiles. "Thanks, Mom."

"We have a lot to discuss, and soon . . . but maybe not tonight, okay?"

Willa looks sidelong at her mother, asking the question without asking.

"Your dad's in his office."

"Does he know too?"

"He'll be upset if you don't say good night to him."

With Mom watching, Willa approaches the double doors of Dad's home office. Large windows are set into the doors, but they're covered with blinds, which are almost always closed. Willa taps lightly on the glass and, not hearing otherwise, pushes the door open and steps inside.

Heavy bookshelves line the walls of Wade Hanson's sanctuary, each packed with leather-bound volumes, the classics, many first editions, most of which have never been read to avoid damaging them. Her father has acquired them painstakingly, lovingly, and he's damn proud of the collection. A large oak desk consumes and dominates most of the space in the office. There is currently none of the usual stuff present: no papers, no pens, no blotter, no laptop. The rare clean desk from Dad. A couple of leather chairs are placed in front of the desk. A bay window serves as a backdrop. On bright sunny days, it floods the room with natural light. On nights like tonight, the glow from the room within attracts moths to flutter and tap against the glass.

Once upon a happier time, Willa used to play in the office, pretending to be a powerful businessperson like her father, brokering deals (whatever *that* meant) and managing a crack team of employees (stuffed animals from her bedroom).

Now she rarely sets foot in here.

Dad stands between the desk and the bay window, pacing. He wears a light-blue button-up shirt with the sleeves neatly rolled to his elbows, black slacks, meticulously polished black shoes. His dark hair is receding a little, thinning, but not much. There are deep-set lines around his eyes. The frames of his glasses are tortoiseshell brown. He's slim, not too tall, the kind of man who, if you didn't know him . . .

. . . *if you didn't know better* . . .

. . . you would assume worked as an accountant or maybe a stockbroker.

Phone to his ear, he paces between the desk and the bay window. He glances at Willa as she steps inside. Behind his glasses, his eyes warm. The corner of his mouth rises. As always, he's glad to see her. He holds a hand up to tell her he'll just be a second.

Forget the sheriff.

This is the most feared man in Fredericks County.

Dad.

"I'll get him out," he says. "Tomorrow, maybe the next day. Wouldn't hurt him to just sit there and cool off a bit."

He's talking to Scraps, she realizes, or maybe Bear.

Jeez, Dad. Don't any of your friends have real grown-up names?

Those are the only two brave enough, with enough rope, to call him this late. Right now, whoever it is—Scraps or Bear—is giving him a rundown of the day's events, of the associates who have gotten arrested for one transgression or another, of the deals that went through, of the ones that went south.

"If we can move it, yes, but we're not buying it sight unseen."

This is her father at work.

Not once in her life has Willa asked what her father does for a living. Nor has he ever volunteered a detailed accounting of his day-to-day. He doesn't hide his business from her, but he doesn't elaborate either. And Willa's never felt the urge to ask.

That's a conversation they don't really need to have.

She's overheard the gossip whispered by kids in school and the average person on the street. Hell, sometimes they spouted the rumors right to her face. She's eavesdropped on dozens of her father's conversations, all of them a lot like this one he's having right now. She's speculated wildly with her friends, giggling at the possibilities.

Dad does a little of this, a little of that, some of it just barely legal in the strictest sense of the word, some of it blatantly illegal. He runs with a tough crowd, men and women in his employ or in his debt ranging from here to Charlotte, here to Myrtle Beach.

Willa's always accepted him for who he is and what he does. He takes care of his family, gives them a nice life. He looks out for the people who work for him. He cares about the townsfolk of Wilson Island. For the most part, they return the sentiment.

For a "bad" man, he's a pretty good guy.

"That's the cost of doing business."

With her hands behind her back, Willa waits to make her own report.

"Tell them to take their goods elsewhere, then, and I mean at least a couple of hundred miles from here."

She wonders who her father is talking about. Who's trying to negotiate a deal? Who's trying to angle for the upper hand?

At the end of the day, it doesn't matter.

"They don't want me to find out otherwise."

There's an edge to his words. Just a hint. He always keeps his cool. Never raises his voice, never yells. He doesn't need to in order to get his seriousness across.

"Look, have you got this or do I need to drive down that way?"

Willa shifts nervously from one foot to the other.

"No. Let me worry about that."

He hangs up, looks at the phone in his hand for a second or two, draws in a deep sigh, then looks lovingly at his daughter.

"Do I need to have Kenny Smythe killed?"

It's a question he's asked her from time to time since Willa and Kenny started dating, since the very first time she came home just fifteen minutes past curfew with her hair slightly mussed and carelessly straightened. Over the last couple of years, it has become something of a running joke between them.

Only this time, she's not sure he's joking.

She knows that some people around town—the sheriff, for instance—think of her dad as a bad man.

Does loving him make her bad too?

...

Because he doesn't want to frighten his mother, he takes the mask off before he goes inside through the back door. Always through the back door, where no one can see.

She saw the mask once, when it was worn by someone else, and it terrified her. *Mr. No-Face.* That's what she called it. The mask, and the man who wore it.

He's done this since he was a teenager, sneaking in and out of the house at all hours. Somewhere along the way it just stuck with him, even when he wasn't being sneaky and creeping out into the darkness to get high with his friends down at the Bottoms, or slipping out just to get some fresh air, when he wasn't . . .

. . . gutting old folks, let's be blunt about that part.

The front door is for guests, for polite company, not that they ever have any, not anymore, not since his mother took ill.

He coughs as the mask pulls away, a gag reflex he hasn't yet figured out how to control. His face is hot, his skin flushed and sweaty, his damp hair plastered to his forehead. He gulps mouthfuls of air, as if he's been underwater for far too long.

Stepping into the darkened kitchen, he places the mask on the counter, right next to a grease-spattered ceramic trivet decorated with the phrase BLESS THIS MESS. He removes his belt—carefully, carefully—trying not to rattle the metal implements against one another. He sets it aside. He pulls his apron off, folding it inside out, placing it next to the mask and the blades.

The ritual blades. They had done their job. But he had failed, and miserably at that.

"Fucking stupid," he whispers.

Floorboards creak underfoot as he crosses the room. He's famished, but doesn't stop at the fridge or raid the kitchen cabinets for snacks. Later. Once he's attended to his other responsibilities. They always come first.

And, even then, how do I eat after what I've done?

The living room is lit by the glow of the television. There is no show playing, no situation comedy or late-night news. The screen shows only hissing static. No cable or satellite in this residence, do you have any idea how much that costs? The roof antenna blew down two years ago during a wicked storm and was never replaced. Sometimes they pick up a garbled signal from the local network out of Greenville. Not tonight, though. And it doesn't matter anyway. He never has time to squat in front of the idiot box (as his father, God rest his soul, used to call it), and his mother likes the static to help her sleep.

She's wrapped in her house robe, snuggled under a quilted throw blanket on the couch. She is so pale. So still. For a moment, he thinks she might be dead, and he holds his breath, just as he's done every night for months. And just as he has done every night for months, he watches in silence until he detects her shallow breathing. He finally exhales and speaks quietly, just enough to be heard over the TV.

"Mom?"

She doesn't move.

"I'm home, Mom."

He crouches next to the couch, reaches out, nudges her shoulder. At his touch, her eyes snap open. She gasps in confusion and jumps, but doesn't sit up.

"Hey, it's just me," he says. "I'm home."

Her eyes dart around the room, trying to catch shadows, and then they settle on him. She focuses. The startled look drains away from her face, replaced by a simple smile. She reaches out, touches his cheek.

Her fingers will come away sticky, but she won't notice.

"Lucas?" she says, blinking. His father's name.

"No, Mom. No. It's me. Sorry, I didn't mean to startle you."

"I was having a dream."

"A good one or a bad one?"

"A little of both, I think. Is it late? It feels late."

"Yeah. Pretty late."

She extends her arm, and he helps her sit up.

On the end table next to the couch are a spoon and a little plastic container of applesauce. He left it for her, knowing she wouldn't touch it until he came home to feed her.

"You hungry?" he asks.

"Very."

He peels the plastic lid from the cup, sticks the spoon into the applesauce, and stirs it. She watches, her eyes flashing in the television's glow. He scoops out a quivering spoonful of applesauce and guides it to her trembling lips. She opens her mouth like a baby bird, slurps the spoon clean, all the while looking at him lovingly. Dependently.

He repeats the action four times, then discards the spoon into the empty cup. Cleanup will come later, for that and other things.

"There were snakes in the dream," his mother says, bits of applesauce still clinging to her lips, "thousands of them, and we were carrying them out to the beach in these buckets. It was you, me, and your dad. We were throwing them to the seagulls like breadcrumbs. They were snapping them up and carrying them out over the ocean. And they were dropping them down into the water, where something was there, waiting to eat them all up, even though the snakes were hissing and biting."

"Sounds like a crazy dream."

"I don't know how I can sleep at all."

"Why's that?"

"Can't you hear it? The scratching? Something in the walls? It never stops."

He cocks his ear to the side, hears nothing.

But he knows it's there.

"Let's get you to bed, huh?"

With her arm over his shoulder, he reaches under her legs to cradle her. Her bones, pressing against her tissue-thin, spot-marked skin, pop. They creak like the kitchen floorboards. She's so light.

And she reeks. Her breath. Her thinning hair. Her pale skin. Her grimy robe. The nightgown underneath. All of it, sour and unclean.

She . . . sickens him.

"Tomorrow we're going to give you a bath."

"I'm still hungry," she says.

"I'll make you some soup. You can eat it in bed. Hang on."

He carries her up the stairs. He doesn't bother turning on the lights. There's a small window above the landing, and moonlight streams in to give shape to the threadbare stairs, the loose, scratched handrail. Even without the moonlight, he would be fine. He knows the way. He could navigate the steps in pitch-black without incident. All those years sneaking out taught him something about spatial distance in a familiar environment.

He reaches her bedroom. No lights on. The smell—the pervasive sour, unclean, slow-rot stink—is heavier here. Thick on the bedsheets, in the very air. His mother's bed is unmade, and will stay that way. He lowers her to the mattress, pulls the comforter up around her.

"Where were you tonight?" she asks him.

"I was just . . . out. I had some errands to run."

"Were you spending time with Jimmy?"

"No, Mom. He doesn't live around here anymore. He moved away. Remember?"

"Yes. He moved to Raleigh," she says. "Sorry, forgot about that."

Already sleep claws at her, tries to drag her down into the depths.

"You still want that soup?" he asks.

Sleepily she bobs her head, then murmurs, "I think Mr. No-Face was here again tonight."

He turns to the door without responding.

"Were you out with Jimmy?" she asks. "How's he doing?"

He looks back over his shoulder, summoning yet another way to say, *Yes, Mom, I was spending time with my childhood best friend who got the hell off Wilson Island as soon as he had the chance*, but she's sleeping peacefully.

He steps out of the room, looking across the hall toward the door to his own bedroom.

God, he'd love to stagger in there and collapse into bed. There's too much to do, though. He has to clean everything up: his apron, his gloves, his tools. Maybe not the mask, but everything else for sure.

As he descends the stairs, he hears his mother calling to him: "I'm hungry!"

Louder than before.

"I'm hungry! I'm hungry! *I'm hungry!*"

Not from her room. But from down below.

CHAPTER TWELVE

THE WARLOCK STILL HEARS THE sirens ringing in his ears, though he's not sure if they're still wailing—like ghosts, banshees, like demon-wolves—or if it's all in his head.

And why should he care?

They aren't out there looking for him. Madhouse Quinn said as much in his oh-so-cryptic way. Let them bellow and screech and howl, as long as they—

Just leave me the hell alone.

Crossing through narrow brick alleys, behind the kitschy consignment store Shop-and-Awe, through silent backyards, the Warlock weaves through the oily darkness and fishy stink of Wilson Island. All the businesses are locked up tight. All the houses are dark and quiet. All his would-be customers have scurried back into hiding to blast their minds into oblivion.

Can't believe I let that old jackass take my joint.

His own shadow plays along the walls of the Plaza of Lies.

Whatever.

His black Chuck Taylors leave tracks in the sandy, trash-can-lined path behind the Ashen Court. *Not like I don't have more.*

Head down, he hurries past the hulking remains of the Behemoth and scoffs.

The Plaza of Lies. The Ashen Court. The Behemoth.

After all these years, the names still stick.

The Plaza of Lies is the epithet he's given to the collection of businesses on Beaumont Street. Island Properties. Island Outfitters. The Island Boutique. Island Ice Cream. The Almighty Deli. A half dozen other pop-up shops that peddle the illusion of island life and pick the pockets of tourists who don't know better. The Ashen Court is what he calls Felton Lane, the gray cinderblock duplexes where a handful of his best customers scrape by from day to day. The Behemoth, well, that's the crumbling remains of the old high school, no longer in use since it was discovered that the walls were basically solid asbestos.

In his youth, he gave almost every house, street, and neighborhood on the island a different, more epic name, just to ease everyday drudgery.

When I grow up, I will put away childish things. He slinks past the entrance to the Warren, the trailer park he calls home. *Eh, fuck that. Childish things keep me from going insane.*

What he really can't believe is how badly he let Quinn get under his skin with those strange, doomsayer-lite proclamations behind Rudy's Mart.

"We have jobs to do, you, me, each and every one of us."

He tries to shake off the unease clinging to him like a barnacle.

"We were chosen. Don't matter if you remember it or not."

He knows Quinn was teasing him. Taunting him. Fucking with him for the sake of doing so with anyone who'll listen. Acting like he knows something he doesn't. And yet . . .

"We're meat puppets."

Something about Madhouse Quinn's ranting bugs him, tickles in his reptile brain, like the old man was almost speaking fact instead of lunacy.

Almost.

When guys called "Madhouse" start making sense, I might be in trouble.

"I have no memory of this place," the Warlock intones, quoting Gandalf in the orc-haunted mines of Moria. "And neither does fucking Madhouse Quinn."

He should—and he knows this deep down in the molten core of his being—ignore the crusty old hobo.

Everyone else in town does.

•••

Ghosts dance across the television screen.

At least, Terry thinks the static looks a bit like spirits, restless and uneasy, the way all the best spirits behave when the eyes of the living stumble upon them and actually *perceive* what they were looking at.

Ghosts on the TV, Terry thinks. *Like in* Poltergeist.

"They'rrrrrre heeeeerrrrre," he whispers.

The glow of the screen paints the mobile home's tiny, cluttered living room in a flickering gray wash. From his recliner, Terry thrusts the remote at the TV and punches a button to change the channel.

More static.

Grumbling, he pushes the button again.

Static.

Same as every night for the last week.

Terry taps the button again and again in rapid succession.

Insanity is doing the same fucking thing over and over while expecting different results.

Upon the remote control, his finger goes to town.

In the static, though, Terry can almost see the ghosts playing out scenes from his favorite shows and movies. He changes the channel, and there are ghost Sam and ghost Diane and ghost Cliff and ghost Norm hanging around Cheers. He presses the button again, and the ghosts scramble to win the Golden Power of Veto to avoid eviction from the Big Brother House. He switches the channel again . . .

No. Can't be.

"Hawk-the-fucking-Slayer!"

Terry hasn't seen this low-budget sword-and-sorcery epic since he was a kid. He tosses the remote onto a coffee table covered in takeout boxes and unopened bills.

He settles back in his chair. And lets the ghosts entertain him.

...

The rusting, sagging steps groan beneath the Warlock's feet, and the screen door screeches as he yanks it open. Hand on the inner doorknob, he looks over his shoulder, thinking he hears the sirens anew. Or maybe their echoes are just figments of his imagination. The door to the trailer is stiff, swollen in the frame, but he shrugs through into the living room.

The pale glow of a static-filled television screen flickers through the room.

"Back so soon?" Uncle Terry doesn't move from the sweat-reeking cushions of his easy chair. His bloodshot eyes are sunken in his skull. Chapped lips curl from his teeth. His stubby fingers drum against an empty, semi-crumpled PBR can in his right hand. His other hand unconsciously chases after an itch that moves from place to place on his body. "Thought you'd be out playing make-believe with your loser friends."

"You're kidding, right?" The Warlock pulls the door closed behind him with a slam and plods toward the back hall. "I was working, okay?"

But what he wants to say is *You know, it was you who taught me to play these games of "make-believe," right?* And what he really means is *I don't have any friends, loser or otherwise.*

Uncle Terry stares after the Warlock, glowering, as he hurries back to the sanctuary of his cramped bedroom.

The Warlock's fingers tremble as they close around the doorknob, and the familiar scent of dusty paper and week-old incense washes over him. This is his domain, his kingdom, his refuge from the rest of the world, from the crushing weight of reality.

Reality, wrapped up in the totality of Wilson Island.

His room is a museum to all the things that have brought him joy and comfort over the years. Every inch of every wall is covered with posters. His favorite movies—*Conan the Barbarian*, *Excalibur* (his all-time fave), and *Dragonslayer*—share space with his favorite bands—Slayer and Sepultura and Savatage. Dog-eared, broken-spine fantasy novels. Zelazny, Moorcock, Greenwood, Salvatore stacked in teetering towers, cover to back cover. Sagging particleboard shelves stuffed with D&D guidebooks—the *Player's Handbook*, the *Dungeon Master's Guide*, the *Monster Manual*. If the Warlock were to pull one off the shelf and crack the cover, he would find his uncle's name—*Terry Danvers*—scrawled inside, scratched out and replaced by his own signature.

Denny Finn Danvers. And that was scratched out too. Replaced with: *THE WARLOCK.*

His true name. His name of power.

Dice and scattered Magic: The Gathering cards and wooden treasure chests litter every surface. Spice racks, taken from kitchen cupboards and repurposed, display dozens of hand-painted miniatures.

Rust monsters and umber hulks and beholders. Skeleton lords and their ghoulish minions. Thieves and paladins, clerics and . . .

Warlocks.

Nearby, a plastic craft caddy holds countless vials of paints, brushes aplenty, and a magnifying glass to aid with the decorating of the smallest details on the figures. His open laptop, almost lost beneath piles of papers and dirty clothes, displays an active screensaver of a dragon billowing flames at a brave knight. The flames cascade across the knight's shield, with his sword drawn back for a killing strike.

Here, nestled in the clutter of all he's ever held dear, he can almost forget the drudgery of his day-to-day.

The Warlock's gaze drifts up, above his twin bed with the disheveled covers, to the longsword mounted over the headboard. The blade, purchased several years back at a Ren Faire in Kinston, has never gleamed and is instead the deep gray of cold steel. Upon the metal, dozens of names have been painted in various shades of green and red and blue and purple. *Stormbringer. Mourneblade. Excalibur. Death Dealer. Mjölnir. Baron Ass-Kicker. Wraithbane.* Some of the names are chipped and faded. None of them are the sword's true name.

The Warlock hasn't found that. *Not yet.*

"Hey!" Uncle Terry's voice booms from the living room. "Keep it down in there!"

The Warlock almost shouts back, almost angrily tells his stupid uncle that he hadn't been speaking, not a word.

But he's not sure he hasn't.

In what seems like ages gone past, Uncle Terry had introduced the Warlock and a small group of his buddies to the world of Dungeons & Dragons. With Terry as their Dungeon Master, they'd played at least once a week for several years, adventuring into catacombs and crypts, battling troglodytes and dark elves and goblins. Building myths.

Until Terry fucked it all up.

With his drinking. With his rudeness. With his cruelty to the others sitting around the table. With his bursts of insane anger when things—in a *game*—didn't go the way he wanted.

The Warlock had tried to keep the game going, taking on the mantle of Dungeon Master himself, rolling dice whenever they could, wherever would take him and his group. His friends—Rodney Ottley and Norman Smith and Junior Simms and Nate Moore—had followed him, despite the absolute mess his uncle had made of things.

The Warlock had a gift. All his players told him so, even to the point of encouraging him to find a way to make money through gaming. He should be writing his own adventures and getting them published. He should be turning the world he was creating into a fantasy novel of his own.

That world of myth and legend he crafted as part of their sessions might be his way out of Wilson Island. A *real* way out, not just a mental escape.

For a while, he'd seriously considered it. He started writing the novel, and researched submitting original adventure material as intellectual property to gaming companies. He'd even looked into game-mastering adventures professionally, running adventures online for hungry gamers everywhere. If he could just get some traction, he believed, he could climb out of the pit that was Wilson Island and slip away, bloody fingers and all.

But he never did find the right goddamn fingerhold.

And his frustration bled into his game. And when they struggled to find a decent place to play, it killed the group once and for all.

The Warlock flips open one of the decorative treasure chests that sit among his modules and magazines—*Dungeon, Dragon, Descent into the Depths of the Earth, Castle Amber*. Inside the chest, a half dozen joints await. This is his personal supply. Nothing he would sell to anyone in town. He lights up and takes a hit to calm his nerves.

Uncle Terry might smell the smoke.

Worst-case scenario, he comes sniffing around, wanting to share.

The Warlock lets the smoke wreathe his head like a spirit and tries to forget, even for a little while, the nonsense Madhouse Quinn had spouted.

And the loathing in his uncle's eyes. And the cement-like hold the island has on him.

A gust of wind rattles the windowpane, and sand hisses against the glass. The Warlock pulls aside the beach towel he uses as a curtain and looks out into the trailer park.

A man stands in a pool of moonlight.

He is void of color, as if he's stepped out of an old black-and-white movie. He is shirtless, his skin weathered and tan. A thatch of gray hair grows in the center of his chest. His belly hangs over a pair of camouflage shorts, cut off at the knees. It's impossible to tell if the camo might be forest green or urban gray.

This is the visage of a half-memory.

A ghost.

The Warlock recognizes the man.

He's seen him somewhere . . . and relatively recently . . . but he can't pull the pieces of the memory together.

But his heart races at the sight of him.

The shirtless man holds his empty hands out toward the Warlock. He speaks. Somehow, despite the distance, despite the wall separating them, the Warlock hears him.

"Look what I found."

The Warlock cranes his neck. There's nothing in the shirtless man's hands.

"Look what I found. Look what we've found. All of us."

With a sense of dread, the Warlock glances toward his sword—Stormbringer or Excalibur or whatever he most recently decided to call it. He's not sure if the blade will do him any good against ghosts—against memories—but he considers taking it up, brandishing it in warning toward the shirtless man. When he looks back out the window, though, the phantom has vanished.

There is the slightest hint of his form, a phantom in the weed smoke that hangs around the Warlock's head.

He drops the joint down a half-empty soda can, where it sizzles out. A wisp of smoke rises from the popped top.

Get it together. You're letting Madhouse get to you. This is no way for a warlock to behave.

CHAPTER THIRTEEN

AS TOWN HISTORY GOES, CAPTAIN Bob's Tavern and the Tugboat Saloon have been in a bitter, spit-in-your-eye feud for nearly two decades. The inciting incident—if there *was* one other than the mere existence of two bars on an island that could really only support one—has been forgotten. Some say the cold war started when Robert Hanratty (the "Bob" of Captain Bob's fame) put popcorn chicken on the finger foods menu not two days after Stu Gibbons (owner of the Tugboat) started offering the same deep-fried nuggets to his own patrons. Others believed the animosity between the two establishments stemmed from acts of infidelity, a four-way competition to steal each other's spouses that left Bob and Stu both divorced and, if the humiliating rumors are to be believed, their wives now living happily together in Charlotte. Still others said the feud started, and persisted, because both Captain Bob's and the Tugboat proudly boasted "The Best Margaritas" on the East Coast.

Truth be told, Delores thinks, the margaritas at both places are little better than sugary piss water. And she would know. In the war between Captain Bob's and the Tugboat, she's a double agent.

She frequents both dives, knows the daily specials and happy hour prices, knows all the employees, is familiar with all the regulars. If you were to ask Delores to pick a favorite spot between the two, she wouldn't be able to do so because, frankly, she didn't much care for either one.

But what else is there to do?

Tonight she sits at the bar in Captain Bob's. It's Tuesday, which means two-dollar Miller Lite flows all night long. Usually she would spend a Tuesday evening at the Tugboat, where well vodka is only a couple of bucks. There's a shitty metal band playing at the Tugboat, though. She has nothing against the genre per se, but Tuesday night Tugboat metal is in its own class of ear-bleeding bad. So, Captain Bob's gets her hard-earned Family Dollar money this time around.

There are a handful of other people here. The bartender, Ray, makes a pitiful show of wiping down every table in the joint whether they need it or not. Up front, Ozzie looms over a threadbare pool table, grinding a cube of chalk mercilessly against the tip of his cue. A trio of out-of-towners huddle around a table in the back, sipping beers and shots of bourbon.

Come the weekend, Captain Bob's—and the Tugboat, for that matter—will be packed. There'll be sports fishermen, a smattering of surfers, some hikers, some dirt bike and jet ski enthusiasts, fried flounder aficionados, and a bunch of sunburned kids looking to just get fucked up. There will even be a handful of nature lovers, hoping to catch glimpses of the wild horses on the Dresmond Banks, a few history buffs looking for stories of local pirates and the phantoms they left behind, and maybe a couple of conservation activists dedicated to cleaning up the eroding banks around Cape Jordan Lighthouse. Summer months are good for business. Always have been.

"Ready for another one, kiddo?" Ray asks as he rounds the bar and grabs up her empty. He always calls her that, even though she's at least a few years older than him. "This one has just about had it."

Without realizing it, Delores has shredded the label from her beer bottle like a jackal ripping meat from a bone. Slivers of silver paper carpet the bar top.

"Sure," Delores says. "Another'd be great."

Ray pops the cap off another Miller Lite and slides the bottle to her. Before she even takes a sip, Delores starts picking at the label again.

To Ray's credit, he doesn't make a crack about how that activity represents sexual frustration. He's a good guy, one of the few decent people on the island as far as Delores is concerned. He's also easy to look at in a rugged, Marlboro Man way, and his eyes tell stories and guard secrets.

"Tell you what," Ray says with a wink. "That one's on me."

Delores shreds a bit of the beer's label in his honor.

•••

Kibble rattles into a cracked ceramic bowl and all over the equally cracked concrete of Mrs. Abernathy's back patio. "Kitty-kitty-kitty-kitty-kitty!" the old woman calls out, and shakes the Friskies box.

In days past, the sound of fish- and chicken- and beef-flavored pellets clinking into the bowl, the high-pitched kitty-call summoning, would have been answered by a chorus of meows and an army of scruffy cats emerging from the brush. Lately, though, over the past couple of weeks, the number of visiting kitties has been greatly reduced. Tonight the offer of a free meal only draws a trio—a skinny orange tabby and two striped grays—hesitantly from the shadows.

Mrs. Abernathy's knees creak and pop as she crouches down to pet the heads of the purring cats as they chow down.

"Where have all your friends gone?" she asks.

The cats ignore her and purr-chomp kibble as a response.

"You've all vanished," Mrs. Abernathy says. "Like ghosts."

•••

Melanie might ask herself how the fuck she's ended up lost and alone on Wilson Island. She *might*, if she didn't already know the answer to the question. It's craziness—most of it her own—that has stranded her here.

You know what pirates used to do in these parts?

She can hear Ronnie, her boyfriend—correction, *ex*-boyfriend—in her head, asking his bandmates pseudo-philosophical/historical questions while they camped out in an abandoned and overgrown field behind an equally abandoned old barn on the outskirts of town.

They would tie a lantern to the neck of an old horse, Ronnie said. *On those so-called dark and stormy nights, they'd prance the horse back and forth along the beach. Ships out at sea would see the lantern, think it was the light of a ship that had dropped anchor in safe waters, and head that way.*

Then—smash! Ronnie exclaimed, smacking his fist into his palm for emphasis, and Melanie flinches at the memory of that and of his bruised knuckles. *The ship would crash into the shoals, and the pirates would scurry out to murder the crew and loot the ship!*

Nah, man, Rusty said, shaking his head. *I heard that was all a myth.*

What do you fucking know? Ronnie growled. And there was anger on his face.

Anger, Melanie had known, he would never take out on his bandmates, but very well might take out on a girlfriend he saw as little more than a needy groupie for the Gunrunners.

And so, here she is.

Thank you very much.

It was crazy to leave home the way she had, all shouted curses and middle fingers to her mom and dad; crazy to hook up with Ronnie and his band; crazy to be a tagalong on their road trip across the USA, from town to town, shithole to shithole, gig to gig; crazy to let Ronnie beat the hell out of her when he was drinking cheap tequila or arguing with his friends or had a headache or was stressing over gas money.

Ditching him, vanishing into the night while the Gunrunners played a godawful cover of Motörhead's "Ace of Spades" to a small group of drunk rednecks at a place called the Tugboat? Well, *that* was not crazy. That's the sanest she's been in a good long while.

And now?

Now what do I do?

She sits on a bench in a town she doesn't know, trying not to sob. She has no money, no credit cards, no ID. She left her purse in Ronnie's van, along with all the earthly possessions of the Gunrunners. All she owns is a tie-dyed shirt, a pair of ratty shorts, and some cheap rubber flip-flops. Maybe that's all she'll ever own again, because she's most certainly not going back to get her bag. She'd rather have no identity at all than be known as the girl who crawled back into Ronnie's lap just so she could have a roof—van or otherwise—over her head. She knows she'd go back to him if she saw him again. She is just that . . .

Crazy.

Most of all, she has no idea what she's going to do next.

And sitting out here, waiting for a sign isn't getting me any—

"Hey. You all right over there?"

A man, maybe thirty years her senior, approaches Melanie. He's bald, his head and chin dusted with gray stubble. In his hands he holds a filthy baseball cap, which he's evidently removed in a gentlemanly gesture, his fingers fidgeting with the bill. With a grunt of exhaustion, he sits down next to her on the bench, takes a deep breath, and tilts his head back to look at the stars.

"You ain't alone out here, are you?" he asks.

Is he talking to me? Melanie wonders. *Or the stars?*

"I guess I am," Melanie says.

"Not anymore," the bald man says.

Melanie smiles. "I guess not."

"You do a lot of guessing."

"I guess I—"

She stops herself.

"I hadn't noticed," she says.

"Name's Abel," he says.

"M-Melanie."

"Don't got no place to go?" the man asks, turning now to look at her.

Melanie shrugs, still fighting back the tears.

"Well"—the bald man rises, motioning for her to follow—"come on, then."

"Just like that?" Melanie asks.

"That's right. There's a place I know. A place for people like us. For people who ain't got nowhere else to go."

He doesn't look back.

For a second or two, Melanie doesn't move. She just watches the strange man as he walks down the sidewalk, moving from one pool of streetlight glow to the next.

A place for people who have nowhere else to go.

Maybe this old man is the sign she's looking for.

Probably not.

But I've got nowhere else.

Melanie rises, and hurries after him.

She *is* crazy, after all.

CHAPTER FOURTEEN

THE KILLER DESPISES THE MASK. Hates putting it back on and the overpowering smell—his own bad breath from the last time he wore it, the stench of old things cast up from the sea—lingering on the underside. Like aftertaste left on the pulp of a bitten and browning apple.

The stink of his own failure. Hates his No-Face.

"I'm hungry! I'm hungry! I'm hungry!"

Mother's voice. Shrieking in his head and from below.

He knows. And he's ashamed.

The mask muffles his curse. His hand—gloved once more—traces across the blades dangling around his waist. The tools of his faith. He feels a burn through the fingertips of the gloves, as if the glinting, jagged implements might reject him.

I fucked up. I know it. But I'll set it right.

He's not sure he believes what he's thinking. Doubt upon the cross.

His fingers close around the handle of one of the blades, squeezing it, reassuring the tool—and himself—that he'll do what must be done. And this time—*this time*—he'll do it right.

This . . . time.

Time, though, is not his ally. He can't waste what's left with failure.

"I'm hungry!"

"I know, Mama. I know you are."

Creeping between a pair of houses, he emerges onto Ingram Street. Here the homes are dark, quiet. Small residences in good repair, with well-manicured lawns and carefully maintained rock gardens and shrubbery, nice vehicles parked under carports. Just a couple of blocks over, and the houses are so much nicer than his own. Just a couple of hundred steps separating the good side of town from the bad, no railroad tracks required.

He knows the people who live in this neighborhood.

The two-story place with the yellow vinyl siding is home to Mr. and Mrs. Hawthorne. They attended church with him and his mom, back in the day. They'd brought a casserole—or maybe it was a lasagna?—when his mother took ill. "We thought you might be hungry," they'd said.

Next door are Mr. and Mrs. Greene.

Two doors down, in the white house with black trim, live John and his wife, Rebecca, last name unknown. They've only been married a few years, and have two young children. He thinks their names are Emily and Jack, but can't be sure, even though he sees the mother and the kids about once a week at—

Work. His other job.

The next house down the line, painted a light blue-gray and decorated with sand dollars mounted in a scattering pattern on the walls, belongs to Mrs. Jenkins. She's a fourth-grade teacher, the one every kid in school fears. He always liked her, though, finding her fair and kind with those students who followed the rules.

And—

Mr. No-Face. That's my name. Because there's nothing where my face should be.

—had always been a good student. Always followed the rules.

Everyone on this street, each and every one of them, is a family friend or neighbor, and he doesn't want to hurt them—not unless he has no other choice.

But someone has to die tonight.

That is the promise—the commitment—he has made.

What happened earlier, though, was too dangerous. Way too close to home.

"I'm hungry."

"Yes, I'm working on it. You just need to be patient. Just a little longer."

Mr. No-Face had thought the elderly couple might be a good choice. They didn't have all that much time left anyhow, right? That, however, had proved to be a colossal mistake. Barry had fought back, startling him. *Really* caught him off guard. Even though he'd escaped with his prize, he lost it on his way home, and hadn't properly cleaned up the way he wanted, or even disposed of the body. Bodies, actually.

Now that would cost him, and dearly.

Because currently people know—understand without really understanding—that they are in mortal danger, that there is a hunter, a predator, a murderer among them. They'll be on guard, making sure their doors and windows are locked tight come tomorrow evening. They'll have loaded pistols and shotguns close at hand should anyone dare creep down their halls.

Something jingles in the darkness.

Mr. No-Face does a double take when he again sees the little black-and-white dog—Buster—hustling down the street, his tags trembling on his collar, his nails clicking on the pavement.

Hey—are you following me?

Buster lets out a quiet chuff of surprise and cocks his head to the side. The dog sits in the street, watching him curiously, his tail wagging, his tongue lolling out the side of his mouth.

Maybe it's the dog who's wondering, "Is this faceless guy following me?"

Mr. No-Face crouches, staring at Buster. The dog tilts its head one way, then the other, eyes bright with innocent interest. Once again, Mr. No-Face considers plying his trade on the dog. But the hunger he needs to satiate is far more profound than what this small creature could provide. The time of killing dogs in the night, walking past MISSING PET signs in the light of day, is done. It would be easy, though, quick and mostly painless.

A reminder of simpler times.

The hunger might not be satisfied, but his own frustration and building anger might be assuaged.

He reaches out a gloved hand, beckons for Buster to come closer.

The kill might clear his head. So he could think. Avoid stupid mistakes.

Buster watches him with big brown eyes.

No.

The dog serves a purpose. But it is not meat.

Nor are Mr. and Mrs. Hawthorne. Nor John and Rebecca. Nor Mrs. Jenkins.

The dog reminds him of where he started. And where he must go next.

"*Still hungry.*"

"Yes, Mama."

He knows. Tonight he will feed her hunger.

For that, though, he needs animals. *Cattle.*

His mind racing, he darts back through the shadows, leaving Ingram Street behind. His heart pounds. His breath blasts, hot and sour, beneath the mask. The blades at his belt rattle like the tags on Buster's collar, that of a dog serving its master.

"*Hungry.*"

"Yes, I *know*. Just a little longer," he mutters. And the night, almost ravenous in its final hours, swallows him up.

CHAPTER FIFTEEN

"**L**OST SOULS, ADRIFT IN THE sea, spilling up like flotsam onto the shore."
Madhouse Quinn takes a drag on what remains of his recently procured joint. His eyes half closed, his body hunched as he trudges along the street. He inhales, holds it, then exhales an undulating cloud of smoke. In the timeline of tucking the joint in his inner pocket and lighting it back up, he had waited, oh, about thirty seconds after leaving the Warlock behind. There was, he decided, about as much sense in waiting as there was in sharing.

He owns almost nothing beyond the clothes on his back. The tattered and mismatched sneakers on his feet. A couple of pieces of chalk and some crayons. An ink pen and some Sharpies. A folding Swiss Army knife in case of emergency.

And his trusty old lighter, heavy and smooth and cold to the touch, always with him. The weight of it is his constant companion. The familiar click of the cover, scrape of the wheel, hiss of the flame.

For just such an occasion as lighting a stolen joint.

Not stolen, though. Not really.

The kid had given it to him, offered it up. *A willing sacrifice*.

The smoke follows him along the trash-littered lanes of Golden Dunes.

The sign at the entrance of the subdivision—now faded and peeling and defaced with both seagull shit and graffiti—proclaimed the area to be YOUR PARADISE AMONG THE DUNES. Never mind that the location was a couple of miles from the nearest natural dunes, and sand had been brought in by the truckload to create the landscaped illusion of a beachfront. And, while you're at it, please ignore the fact that a paradise needs constant upkeep or it'll fall into squalor and decay.

Once upon a time, the big city–big money investors had a big plan for Golden Dunes. Sixty modern, upscale housing units on twenty-four acres, with another forty-eight ready for quick and profitable expansion. Looking for a fresh start or a peaceful retirement or a summer vacation home, out-of-towners would flock to the area. And they'd happily pay a premium to live up to the promise of the SALT LIFE decals slapped on the rear windows and bumpers of their SUVs.

The development had brought a lot of excitement to the community. For a while, anyway. New houses meant new residents meant new money meant new jobs meant local businesses flourishing and families getting fed.

It turns out, though, that those investors might have bitten off more than they could chew. As houses started going up, so did expenses. Somewhere along the line, one of the key developers backed out of the project. The domino effect devastated the dream of what could have been for Golden Dunes.

Construction had begun on only half of the houses when the bottom fell out. And that's where it stopped. Many of the lots now stand empty and overgrown with thick patches of switchgrass. In other lots, foundations had been poured and abandoned. In yet others, housing framework had been raised and stands now like the skeletons of forgotten things. The few houses with actual walls and roofs are hollow and vacant.

For a while, local teens took to the spot, using it for parties and hangouts and hookups. When the local homeless community moved in, though, the kids abandoned Golden Dunes almost as quickly as the investors—the partying resumed at the Point—and let the bums have the development.

It is a long way from the "paradise among the dunes" it was intended to be.

Madhouse Quinn shuffles along, eyes darting from side to side. Drawn to his presence, drawn to the scent of the smoke, shadowy figures peel themselves away from the framed doorways and half-finished walls. Curious gazes trail after him. And some of the figures follow.

"Lost souls, ain't we all."

The ragtag congregation trails behind Madhouse Quinn on lethargic feet, winding their way through the decaying remnants of Golden

Dunes. He never glances back. Doesn't need to. He knows they're with him. He hears their dragging footsteps against sand-dusted pavement. He feels their weary gazes at the back of his neck. Once more, he has ventured out into the world—the "world" being the township proper of Wilson Island—and they want to know what revelations he's brought back this time.

He keeps his mouth shut.

For now.

This is not the place to deliver his sermons.

Past the final half-structures, beyond most of the empty and bulldozed lots, Madhouse Quinn climbs the last of the man-made dunes, brushing his hands across the tall grass, which hisses, whispering. He stands atop the dune and gazes across a field of death. Sand stretches out before him.

The wide expanse is scattered with small mounds of earth, each marking the final resting place of some unfortunate animal. These are the graves of cats, dogs, birds, possums, and even a few fish. Not all of the creatures—

The beasts of the earth.

—are covered. Some lie exposed, as if the ground could not accommodate their presence. Their remains are on display, and anyone who looks can see that they've been ripped apart, torn open, and—in some instances—gruesomely turned inside out.

The members of his congregation gather around Madhouse, their tattered sneakers and heavy boots and bare feet sinking into the sand.

The moon shines down upon the graveyard, on rotting carcasses and bits of uncovered bone.

Castoffs.

"Rejects," Madhouse mutters under his breath.

Left behind by the faceless man.

"Haven't seen hide nor hair of him," says Maryellen, clutching a tattered shawl around her shoulders. Her face is deeply lined and dry and dirty. "Not for a few days at least."

A shift in the wind carries the pungent stink of rot and decay.

"He's not coming back," says Al. Scabs dot his cheeks, and he scratches aimlessly at the raw back of his hand. "Is he?"

"He's finished with the field," says Varnie-Boy. He is tall and lean, his body etched in muscle, his blond hair long and greasy. He wears only a pair of faded and sand-dappled swim trunks. "Finished with this place."

"Good," says Archie, his dark eyes almost invisible beneath the stocking cap pulled down low over his brow. From the bushy recesses of his mustache and beard, the stub of a cigarette glows, threatening to set his whiskers ablaze. "Always got a bad vibe from him."

"Everything's different now," Madhouse says without looking back at them. "Yes, he's finished with the field. But I'm not so certain he's finished with this place."

"It's not over, then?" June asks. She's older, withered, sickly, her gray hair a tangled mess over her face.

"What did I just tell you?" Madhouse asks.

A suppressed and uneasy gasp passes through the gathering.

The faces of the homeless stare back at him, eyes dark pinpoints in the shadows. These people are his friends. His family. He has lived here, on the outskirts of Wilson Island, for years. Since long before they claimed Golden Dunes as their church.

But he knows his time with them is growing short at long last. Because the death of one man means little. Not when compared to the deaths of oh-so-many.

"What is this place?" asks a voice he doesn't recognize.

A young girl, maybe twenty years old, moves through the crowd. She's blond, pretty, pudgy-faced, dressed in a yellow tie-dyed T-shirt and ripped jean shorts.

Someone new.

Madhouse didn't expect to see too many more additions to their order, but here she is, another soul who's lost their way, lost their family and/or livelihood, finding their way to Wilson Island in search of purpose.

One of Abel's strays, maybe.

"This," Madhouse replies, "is not our world."

CHAPTER SIXTEEN

ALL RIGHT, MELANIE THINKS. So, I've found my way into the company of lunatics. It's all right. I've seen worse. Certainly been through worse. Endured. Persisted. At least for the past day or so, but as far as a home goes—

Her footsteps echo in the silence, a hollow sound, almost thunderous in the deserted half-town of Golden Dunes.

—this ain't it, girlie.

She sees no one else around. They're all back there, looking over that . . .

Graveyard?

Necropolis?

Killing field?

. . . with that guy, the one they're calling "Madhouse."

Good for them. They've picked one of their own as their . . .

Shepherd?

Priest?

Doomsayer?

The residents—the squatters—in Golden Dunes gather around a field strewn with the lifeless bodies of animals. Cats with their fur matted and eyes glazed over. Dogs with gray tongues lolling out of their mouths. Birds with their wings splayed awkwardly, scattered like fallen leaves.

Who killed them all?

Was it these homeless? The vagabonds? The drifters?

Melanie doesn't love the idea, especially since she is now one of them.

Maybe Madhouse, their freak-o priest, had a hand in it?

Upon first arriving in the abandoned subdivision, when she'd gathered with the others around the empty lot, Melanie had heard whispers among the group, stories of someone else who had brought the dead animals to the place, someone who had once visited them but had since vanished.

Whatever.

She's not going to blame them for chasing after crazy. After all, she's been doing that for some time now. That's how she ended up in this godforsaken place, isn't it? Leaving home. Hooking up with Ronnie and the Gunrunners. Following a stranger in the dead of night.

And now?

She's hunkering down in a homeless community—the unhoused, literally and figuratively, considering the state of this area—and they're holding some sort of sermon or communion or mass seance while she tries to find a place to sleep.

Right back to crazy.

Someone killed all those poor animals. Probably someone who lived among the Golden Dunes homeless community.

Maybe Madhouse himself.

But, really, it might be anyone. A lot of messed-up people in the world.

She knows this firsthand.

I've got a real nasty knack for getting tangled up with them.

She tells herself it will be for just one night. She'll find something that passes for shelter. She'll sleep as best she can.

And tomorrow?

She'll hike back to town. It's not that far. She'll find a phone. She'll call home and hold her breath when her mom or dad answers and she'll pray they forgive her the way parents are supposed to do and she'll ask if they can just put all this behind them.

And she'll cry.

Because she doesn't really want to go home but she doesn't have a choice.

Because she's gotten herself into this humiliating mess.

Because she's stupid and impulsive and crazy.

But mostly because she's just so damn tired.

Melanie pauses before an uncompleted house. Naked beams crown the framework, an open-air ceiling beneath the night sky. Beams of stark moonlight spill through the half-finished structure. Semitransparent curtains of plastic shift and rustle in the night's breeze. She crosses the threshold through the empty doorway. Graffiti screams from the walls. Weirdly drawn eyes and dancing skeletons seem to writhe and twist on the wood, tricks of shadow and light, among phrases scrawled in spray paint and marker and chalk—

> WE ALL PLAY OUR PART
> MOTHER MOTHER MOTHER MOTHER MOTHER MOTHERFUCKER
> THE STARS WENT OUT

Raising her head, Melanie looks past the ribcage frame of the incomplete ceiling. Above her, the sky is a vast black blanket. No clouds to be seen. She should see stars, yet doesn't.

There's a lesson in this somewhere.

With her back against the wall, Melanie slides down to the sandy concrete floor. Weariness floods through her muscles, through her bones, and she's not sure if, now that she's sitting, she'll ever have the energy to stand again. She releases a sigh. The stillness, at least for a few minutes, comforts her. She breathes in, the way the family therapist used to advise her to do, then breathes out.

This place is as good as any to crash in. With no money, no friends, and no family, what better option is there at the moment? She might have slept on a bench along a town street or in a park, but didn't like the notion of the police or, heaven forbid, Ronnie spotting her. She could have found a gas station restroom, she supposes, but the idea of the potential smell and filth disgusts her. She might have crashed on the beach, slept under the open sky, but there are crabs there, and crabs are essentially the spiders of the sea, and she loathes spiders more than life itself.

When she ran into the old guy on the street, Abel, he'd suggested Golden Dunes. *Lots of space, out of the way, quiet,* he'd said, and she was already sold, even before he muttered, *As long as you can put up with Madhouse Quinn.*

And so, here she is, bunking down—

—hiding out—

—in a vacant building in a vacant subdivision in a town that might as well be vacant itself.

How did things get so out of control?

Not even a year ago, all the possibilities in the world were available for her. Parents who loved her (whether or not they also loved being a pain in her ass). A softball scholarship to a decent (if local) college. A job waiting tables with a flexible schedule and decent tips (even if she had to deal with a few handsy customers). *And I literally drank a big glass of water and pissed it all away.*

Tomorrow, first thing, head back into town, find a phone, and call Mom. Will she be glad to hear from her daughter? Or be angry instead, spitting venom across the line before hanging up?

From across the structure, the soft click and scrape of shoes on the sandy concrete catches her attention. She peers through the moon-dappled shadows. She thinks she sees somebody moving out there past the framework walls and sections of drywall. Only for a second. Then, as she leans forward into darkness, she loses track of them.

"Hello?"

There is no answer.

"Is someone there?"

Melanie places her palms against the floor and pushes herself up, sliding to a standing position along the wall.

Again, she tracks movement, a figure creeping through the structure.

Whoever it is, they vanish behind a panel of drywall without a word.

"Oh." Melanie speaks to herself as much as to the unseen figure. "I didn't know anyone was here or this space was, y'know, taken or whatever."

A shuffling footstep.

"Sorry about that," Melanie says. "I can move on, find somewhere else, if you want me to."

More silence, then another footstep across the sandy concrete.

Melanie's mind races. Who is she dealing with here? One of the nameless few who follow that guy Madhouse?

Maybe a townie, come to rattle the homeless community?

"Hello . . . ?"

Could it be Ronnie and his fellow Gunrunners? Have they tracked her down? Are they going to drag her kicking and screaming back into the band's van, back on the road? Will Ronnie perhaps now beat her within an inch of her life, punishment for taking off?

Not this time. Not without a fight.

"Hey!" Melanie channels fierceness into her voice. "I'm not in the mood, all right? I don't want to be fucked with at the moment! So just move on, get the hell out of here, leave me alone. Okay? Leave me the fuck *alone*!"

A man steps out of the surrounding darkness, shrugs free of the blanket of shadows. At least, Melanie thinks it's a man. He's tall and lean, but he looks powerful, strong. He is dressed in a black leather apron and black leather gloves. Around his waist is a belt laden with glittering blades—knives and cleavers and fish scalers and scalpels. A pale mask covers his face. No eyeholes are visible, but some sort of breathing tube hangs down from his face, whipping back and forth, clicking noisily as he takes a step closer.

Melanie's brain almost cracks, but she holds on to sanity, at least long enough to form a coherent thought—*Oh, shit!*—like a starting shot. No sooner has it entered her mind than the masked figure is charging toward her, his feet slamming against the concrete. Something silver glints in both of his gloved hands. Melanie whirls, almost tripping over her own feet, and she runs, legs pumping for all they're worth. It's been a while since she's had the need to and she's out of practice, but the incomplete walls of the house offer dozens of escape routes, and she ducks low, avoiding a two-by-four obstacle, leaping into the sandy yard.

A little black-and-white dog sits in the sand before her, watching her with a curious tilt of its head.

"Uh."

The weirdness of it sets Melanie's head to spinning, but only for a moment. She blinks. Looks away from the dog. Turns to look behind her.

The masked figure is gone.

Was he ever here at all?

Blinding pain enters the side of her throat in a silent, stinging answer to her question.

Melanie gasps, lurches to the side, turns, clutching at her neck as blood sluices through her fingers and soaks down into her sweaty shirt.

The masked figure, now standing before her, calmly regards Melanie. He turns a bloody knife over in his right hand. The hooked blade in his left is clean and gleaming.

"Uh."

Melanie takes another step back, but now her legs are heavy and clumsy. She blinks, but suddenly tears cloud her vision. Spit bubbles on her lips.

The masked man moves toward her.

Help! she screams in her mind. *Help me! Somebody, help me!* But it all comes out as a pitiful gasp.

The hooked blade punches into Melanie's stomach, twists, gathers what's inside her, then rips back.

Then his right hand slices across her face, spattering blood into the sand.

Then the left. Then the right.

All the while, through her fading vision, the little dog watches.

Melanie's legs give out under her, and she falls to her knees. Then on her side. Then onto her back.

"Please!" she tries to shriek, but it comes out as a wheezing whisper. "Please! I want to go home. I just want to go home!"

But the eyeless face offers no reprieve, mercy, or absolution. Just an angry grunt.

The knife punches downward, cracking through her breastbone.

Twisting. Digging.

Melanie feels nothing. She's way past pain at this point. Her body's grown accustomed and desensitized to the violence and agony.

Lying there on the sand, looking up at the sky, she sees stars winking to life in the darkness.

One.
Two.
A hundred.
A million.
No. Not stars. *Eyes.*
That's just crazy, Melanie thinks as blackness swallows her vision for good.

TUESDAY

THE DREAM TURNS BLEAK.

CHAPTER SEVENTEEN

THE DEATH REQUEST LINE IS ringing off the hook.

That's how Slim likes to think of it.

When he was a kid, just a stupid teen, he had dreamed of being a radio DJ, but those dreams dried up real fast. He never made it off this godforsaken island, save for a couple of weekend trips, and the only local radio station had closed up not long after Hurricane Matthew leveled the station and near about every other structure back in '16.

He had, of course, big plans to rebuild and resume broadcasting from the old station. He just needed his ship to come in, one of his scratch-off tickets to pay off in a massive way. Failing that, maybe he'd just start his own pirate station, like in that old movie he likes so much, *Pump Up the Volume*. Of course, that cost money too. So, maybe an internet station was the answer. That, though, required funding as well, at least to license and play the kind of music he wanted, and not rely on internet access conveniently stolen from his neighbor in Apartment 3C.

And money was something Slim never really had in abundant supply.

Answering another call, asking the caller to please hold so he can help one of the other customers waiting behind the flashing white light, Slim thinks that maybe he should ask Winslow for a raise.

Especially if I'm gonna be the only poor sumbitch who shows up for work on time.

Winslow himself—Li'l Winslow, as he hates to be called—is nowhere to be seen, and he likely won't drag his lazy ass through the door of the mobile-home-turned-extermination-HQ for another hour or more. *If there are good employees on the payroll*, he might say, *the boss don't need to punch the clock.* Maybe that's fair. Slim's never been a boss, never been in charge of a damn thing, and he more than likely never will be until that radio station vision comes together.

But you don't have any good employees on the payroll, none except me. And maybe Barry.

He answers another call—"Morning, Surefire Pest Solutions"—as he looks over at Barry's especially cluttered little corner of the desk he shares with two other employees. Among the work orders and receipts is the old man's coffee cup. Empty. Across the room, the coffeemaker is cold and unused. Most mornings, Barry gets there long before anyone else; has the cranky, clunky machine working; and enjoys a cup or two in solitude until the phones start ringing and the rest of the team shows up. He says his wife won't let him have caffeine at home, so the office is a place of solace for him.

Not today, though. The lights on the phone blink. Calls holding. *Holding to request death.*

"Can you hold, please?" Slim says.

He sends the caller to limbo without waiting for a response.

The old man's never late, never calls in sick.

Over the years, Barry and Slim have become friends. Slim listens to Barry's complaints—about his health, about getting old, about the job, about his wife, about the world in general. Barry acts as a sounding board for Slim's plans. They go on calls together when the service crew isn't stretched too thin. They look out for each other when Li'l Winslow has got a bug up his ass. They're work friends, sure, but buddies nonetheless.

Slim genuinely likes the guy. And Slim doesn't really like anyone who wasn't in an eighties hair band.

He hopes Barry hasn't fallen victim to the attitudes and general laziness of the other employees. More than that, he hopes nothing bad has happened. Barry's old. So there's a reason his wife doesn't want him drinking caffeine or booze.

Punching a button, he grabs one of the waiting calls. "Thanks for holding." Sometimes Slim tests out different DJ voices on calls. Not this morning, though. No time for experimentation. "What can I do for you?"

"*Yes, hi.*" The woman's voice on the other end of the line is shaky and timid and worried. *"This is Annette Crewes. I was wondering if you could send someone out here to help me. I've never had this problem before, but I'm now having trouble with, well, rats."*

"Yes, ma'am. We can help with that. I'll be up front with you. We're getting a lot of calls right now and we're a little shorthanded." Through narrowed eyes, he looks at the office, empty of all the other team members. "It might be a day or more before we can come see you."

"Oh my." The disappointment in her voice, the concern about fighting off an army of vermin for another twenty-four to forty-eight hours, is palpable. *"I suppose, if there's no way you can—"*

"I'm sorry. There's really not. We're up to our ears in job tickets. But we'll get to you as soon as we can."

On the other end of the line, Mrs. Crewes clears her throat. *"I wonder if Joseph Winslow is available?"*

Here we go.

"I'm sorry," he says, "but Li'l Winslow"—he catches himself just a moment too late—"*Mr.* Winslow isn't in just yet."

"May I leave a message for him? I'm a friend of his father's. I'd like to speak to him about this scheduling predicament of ours."

Not a "predicament." The schedule is the schedule!

But he takes down her name, address, and phone number, tells her someone will call her when they're on their way to her house, and promises to keep an eye on the schedule for any cancellations. Dropping the handset back into the cradle, he looks again at Barry's empty mug.

Something cold slithers in the pit of his stomach.

The phone rings again. He grabs the receiver and answers without thinking: "Death Request Line."

CHAPTER EIGHTEEN

"**BREAKFAST, SWEETHEART!" MOM CALLS FROM** downstairs. "I hope you're hungry!"

An echo bounces along the walls.

Hungry...

...hungry...

...hungry...

Willa winces herself awake. Through the curtains at her window, green light spills across her bedroom. It's a sickly illumination to match the flipping and flopping of her stomach, an evil glow, one that does just about nothing to improve her mood. With a frustrated sigh, she casts the sheets and blankets from her legs and lets them fall to the floor. She swings her feet around and sits on the edge of the bed, shoulders slumping, as she urges herself to move, to stand, to slog her way downstairs before her mother shrieks for her again—

"Breakfast!" Mom calls.

Stumbling to her feet, feeling her legs tremble beneath her, Willa crosses her bedroom. Rubbing her eyes to dispel the remnants of sleep, she descends the steps, nearly missing a couple along the way.

The green light follows her.

She places an arm across her belly. Has it grown overnight? Is it larger than when she finally went to sleep? Is this what she has to look forward to? Noticeable, sudden changes in her physiology for the next several—

"Breakfast!" Mom calls.

"Yes, yes, I know," Willa grumbles. The smells of cooking food—bacon? toast? eggs?—fill the air.

What time is it anyway?

Still rubbing a hand back and forth over her swollen stomach,

Willa enters the kitchen. At the counter, Mom stands with her back to her daughter. The floor feels sticky under Willa's feet. The air too, heavy with smoke from the cooking food, like it's adhering to her skin.

"Breakfast!" Mom says once again.

"I'm right here."

"Sit down, then." Mom doesn't turn. "Eat. Food's on the table."

"When do we *ever* eat at the table?"

"Please," Mom says without looking over her shoulder. "Just for today."

With a sigh, Willa slumps into a chair at the table. Before her, a covered plate awaits. Her face, washed by the greenish light, plays across the silver of the covering.

"Mom?"

"I wanted to do something nice." Mom turns away from the counter, smiles widely and proudly at Willa. "It's your special day."

"Oooooookay, weirdo."

Willa's fingers close around the handle of the dish cover, which feels heavier than expected. Or maybe it's only the weight of her own hesitation. The kitchen seems to close in around her, the walls creaking and groaning.

"Go on, dear."

Why does she sound so calm? She's never that way.

Willa lifts the covering, and blood pours out from under it. Gushes. It flows in sheets, spilling across the table, into her lap, onto the floor.

Willa jumps up, lurches back, knocking her chair over, tripping over her own legs, slipping in the blood dribbling from the table. Falling on her ass, she kicks back across the floor. She looks toward the waterfall of blood, toward her smiling mom, then back toward the carnage.

"W-what?" Willa stammers. "What? W-what?"

"Breakfast!" Mom chimes.

Carried on the tide of spilling blood, organs—a kidney, a length of intestine, a heart—now ooze from the plate and topple from the table, splattering at Willa's feet.

"What . . . ?" Willa asks again, her voice a cough. A metallic stink floods her senses.

Willa throws herself to her hands and knees, crawls through the gore spreading across the kitchen floor, slips, sprawls, gets back on her hands and knees and crawls again.

"It's a special day," Mom says, "one that calls for a birthday breakfast!"

"It's . . . not . . ." Willa chokes between words as she slip-crawls away. ". . . my . . . birthday."

"Of course not."

At last Willa clambers to her feet, grabbing at the doorframe for leverage. Adrenaline surges in her veins, and she sprints down the hall toward the front door. She moves slowly, though, like she's running through jelly, like some unseen force is trying to keep her from leaving. By the time she reaches the door, she's out of breath and gasping, her heart hammering in her chest. With one last look over her shoulder—

Mom stands in the kitchen door, smiling, cradling human organs in her arms the way a new mother might hold an infant.

—Willa shoulders the door open and spills out of the house. She stumbles across the porch, leaping over the front steps, still in her pajamas, shoeless.

The neighborhood is awash in a sickly glow. Overhead, the sun is a writhing green ball of light, ringed in seething blackness.

"Morning, Willa!" calls Mr. Thompson from his front yard. He wears a white T-shirt, boxers, black ankle socks, and slippers. He picks up a rolled newspaper from the driveway and waves cheerily. As he straightens, a jagged wound across his belly suctions open, spilling his entrails out before him. He keeps right on smiling.

Willa looks back at the man as she hurries down the street.

"Hey there, sweetheart," says Mrs. Sutton, her voice syrupy. She's in a light-blue tracksuit, and a thin veil of sweat covers her skin. With two fingers she takes her own pulse as she jogs in place. The zippered jacket is soaked dark red, a hole ripped in the chest, a gaping maw where her heart should be. "Don't forget about the bake sale this afternoon!"

"Did I hear right?" calls Mrs. Carmody. She kneels in her garden, pulling weeds with glee. "Today's a special day, isn't it? Oh, Willa, you're simply glowing!"

As Mrs. Carmody lowers her head toward the garden, her brain spills out of her skull like cereal that's sat for too long in blackish-red milk. The top of her head has been sawed away.

Up and down the street, neighbors call out to Willa. They all smile and wave despite the ragged tears and gaping holes in their flesh. The green light turns their skin eerily pale, their gushing blood black as oil.

"What?"

Willa's legs don't wait for one of the mutilated, mauled neighbors to answer. Her pace quickens, even as she looks from person to person, and soon she's running, a desperate sprint. She has no idea where she's going, only that she has to get away from the madness surrounding her.

The greenish light. Maybe it's causing this, driving everyone crazy. She stutter-steps to a stop to catch her breath. *Everyone but me.*

Panting, she places a hand on her stomach. And feels a kick.

A simple "oh" slips out with her breath. She moves her hand around, chasing after the feeling. A nudge, a wiggle, a tremor passes under her fingers.

Dizzy thoughts dance through her head.

It's too soon. The baby shouldn't be kicking. Not yet. Right?

Willa raises her head toward the sun. There's no warmth radiating from above the green, undulating light. Could that glow be affecting the baby? Could it be hurting her unborn child?

The rush of the surf answers her.

She stands upon the hard, wet sand of the beach. The air tastes of salt. The vastness of the ocean stretches out before her, rolling, racing up the shore and over her bare toes. Seaweed twists and wriggles in the oncoming foam.

How the hell did I get here?

Looking back the way she came, she sees nothing but endless, rolling dunes. The sky is overcast now, the green light muted, the clouds seeming to press down like a smothering blanket. Flashes of green lightning dance in the distance.

Witch's fire.

A deep, mournful cry cascades across the water, alien and achingly familiar at the same time, a booming trumpeting, almost musical, a ghostly wail.

Beyond the shoreline, the water swells, and something massive breaks the surface, sending angry whitecaps crashing against the shore. Foaming water and tangles of seaweed spill from the colossal shape. It might be the bloated corpse of a whale, or a rising section of bleached coral reef, or even the wreckage of a ship. The details are lost to shadow and sea spray.

The somber trumpeting grows louder.

It sounds like whale song. And the weeping of an infant.

Something—not the baby, but *something*—kicks in her stomach.

The sensation weakens Willa's knees, and she gasps.

It's a feeling not unlike hunger.

Waves smash against the massive shape rising from the depths. The cacophony of bellowing whale song and infantile shrieking intensifies. Willa thinks, vaguely, that she can hear words forming in the maddening howl. She steps closer, ankle deep in the water, soaking the hem of her pj's, seaweed scraping at her skin. She listens—really listens—trying to understand what the behemoth in the ocean is trying to tell her.

A truck's horn blares, startling Willa from her task. She spins. Her eyes widen.

"Kenny?"

The F-150 roars and bounces across the beach. The front of the truck is crumpled and billowing steam. The grille is smeared with blood. Kenny is in the driver's seat, looking straight ahead, fingers gripping the steering wheel tightly as he drives toward the water.

He has no eyes. Only gaping, empty, meaty sockets. Bloody tears fall down his cheeks.

The truck doesn't stop. It rockets into the surf, sending a spray of stinging salt water into the air. And it keeps going, driving on top of the ocean's surface, gliding, heading straight for the indistinct, wailing leviathan rising from the depths.

The truck slams into the shape, and explodes in a ball of green flame.

CHAPTER NINETEEN

WILLA WAKES WITH A JUMP, sitting up, gasping for breath, legs kicking the covers to the floor. For a second, the nightmare feels real, like it actually happened, and her heartbeat slams in her chest. Her hand falls to her stomach. Not swollen. Well, not much. She at least feels nothing squirming within. She glances, hesitantly, toward the window, and is immediately thankful that the light streaming in from behind the curtains is not green and sickly.

Around her is her bedroom. That's her cozy chair in the corner. That's her old teddy, Bigsby Bear, in the seat. Those are all her photographs—pictures of her and her family and her friends and Kenny—strung up in fairy lights. That's her acoustic guitar leaning next to her electric Fender and her amp, all equally forgotten and unused.

Allowing herself a half dozen deep breaths, she rises. She moves gingerly, steadily, because she worries that anything sudden might somehow awaken the nightmare and drag her back down.

A little plastic aquarium filled with hazy water and chemical mixtures and a forest of colorful "crystal" towers sits on her desk. The underwater garden of bumpy, colorful, rocky spires had thrilled her to no end.

For a couple of days at least. Her Magic Crystals.

"Put the crystal solution in water and watch them grow-grow-GROW into strange formations!"

Her mom had gotten her one for Old Christmas when she was six years old, and she loved it. Now she receives one on almost every major holiday. If, for some reason, she doesn't get one, she feels rather slighted.

Sometimes she finds herself staring at the twisted, bumpy crystal spires, lost in their irregular, stalagmite shapes, lost in their knots and bulges and nodules, lost in the bizarre little world they form.

She picks the aquarium up and shakes it for all she's worth.

Water sloshes back and forth. The crystals sway and bend and collapse in the face of the tumult she has inflicted upon them. The towers crumble to colorful pebbles.

It is as satisfying as it is sad.

As the memory of the dream fades, though, the cruel truth of reality sets in.

Fuck. I had plans.

I want you to tell me that this is all some sort of bad joke.

Tell me you didn't mean it.

Tell me you're not *pregnant. Otherwise, I don't know that I have much use for anything you might tell me.*

The argument with Kenny—*that* happened. The coldness in his eyes, the betrayal, the anger. Those things had been real.

Willa grabs her phone from the bedside table, uses her thumb to rouse it to life. No missed calls or text messages from him.

Just making sure ur OK.

Nothing.

We can figure this out.

Nope.

I'm sorry.

Fuck, no.

There is, however, a message from Sarah.

Hey, loser. We're going to the Red Eye. Twenty minutes.

The text is about five minutes old.

Willa doesn't bother to respond. Sarah is likely on her way over already. And she never takes a simple no for an answer. Refuse breakfast with Sarah Mitchell?

Now, that *would be a nightmare.*

She feels a little better after a quick shower. Not much, but a little. She towels off and checks her phone, realizing she doesn't have time to dry her hair or do her makeup. Sarah's probably already parked out front, drumming her black-nailed fingers on the dash, grumbling curses under her breath.

A wet head it is. And no makeup. But, really, who am I trying to impress?

Although a little concealer would likely do wonders for the dark circles under her eyes.

She dresses quickly—khaki shorts, a light-blue Amish-style blouse, sandals—grabs her purse, and hurries downstairs.

The aroma of fresh coffee meets her halfway. It's comforting. Real. She's smelled it every day of her life, because her mom doesn't start the day without a fresh pot of coffee. Sometimes she doesn't even take a sip. Sometimes no one in the house does. And the pot gets emptied into the sink around 10 a.m. But the act of making coffee, that's a morning ritual she never forgets.

"Mom, I'm off!" Willa calls out.

Her mother emerges from the kitchen—a dish towel in nervous hands. She looks tired, like she didn't get much sleep either. She has an aura of hesitant expectance and disappointment—and maybe even a hint of relief—on her face. "So early?"

"Yeah. Sarah wants to go to breakfast."

"Oh."

"Is that all right?"

A smile—the genuine kind that's easily mistaken for something false—slides across her mother's face. "Of course. Of course. Take care, sweetheart. Tell Sarah I said hello."

Willa turns to the door.

"And maybe you and I can talk when you get home?"

Willa sees the hesitance on her mother's face again. Hesitance and hopefulness.

"Yeah, Mom." Willa opens the door. "See you later."

Willa slips through the door. It closes behind her with a *click*. She jiggles the handle to make sure it's latched, an old habit she picked up as a kid and never broke.

It's brighter outside than she expected, and she winces against it. Not even eight-thirty and it's already hot. Gonna be a scorcher.

God is aiming a magnifying glass at the ants again.

When is He ever not?

Two short, sharp blasts of a car horn draw Willa's attention to the street. Parked at the end of the walkway is Sarah's ancient, wood-paneled Buick station wagon.

In a town full of boats, it's the Battleship.

Salt air has done a number on the paint job, leaving the light blue fading and peeling across the hood. Dents aplenty mar the vehicle, a physical history of a half dozen fender benders, most of them not Sarah's fault, that had been endured. The windows, from the rear to the sides and even part of the front, are covered in stickers. Sugar skulls and Sex Wax. Ron Jon Surf Shop and Vans "Off the Wall." Baby Yodas and middle fingers. Calvins peeing on Ford logos. Calvins peeing on Chevy logos. Band logos—Gunship and Journey and Weezer and dozens of others. Bumper stickers proclaiming SAVE THE TURTLES and PROTECT THE OCEAN and HONK IF YOU WANT TO STUDY NAKED. Nearly every inch of glass is covered in decals. It's a wonder Sarah can drive, let alone never get pulled over. There are nearly two hundred thousand miles on the odometer, but the station wagon has not once been in the shop for any significant repairs. This is a vehicle every bit as indomitable as its owner. The Battleship is big enough for eight passengers to squeeze in—more if they're willing to get cozy. Thankfully, Willa sees only Sarah within, waiting impatiently behind the wheel, the dull throb of music pulsing against the glass.

The horn honks again.

The sticker-encrusted passenger-side window rolls down. The ragged edges of the torn stickers surrounding the seal lost their stickiness to dust and time long ago. Sarah leans across the seat.

"Is there something wrong with your legs?" she calls. "Do you need me to drive across the yard to come get you?"

Willa gives a small smile, waves, and quickens her pace.

As Willa opens the passenger door, there are so many stickers on the windows that the interior of the car is cast into eternal shadow. A burst of synthwave music shreds the morning stillness. It's upbeat and dark at the same time, a lot like the girl who sits behind the wheel. She's a few inches shorter than Willa, her frame just this side of waifishness, but she demands attention in any room she deems worthy of her presence. Her dark, curly hair is cut into a short pixie-like fade. Her eyes are big and bright.

"Morning, sunshine!" Sarah says.

"Hey." Willa instinctively reaches for the volume control, turning the music down. Sarah's mouth is agape, as if she cannot believe the blasphemy Willa's committed.

"Sorry," Willa says. "I like to hear myself think."

Sarah gives her friend a good once-over, and now her smile is tight and curt, showing no teeth. "You look like shit," she finally declares.

"Hey, thanks."

...

As the Battleship glides along the peaceful streets of Wilson Island, Willa watches the road with simple curiosity. Moving between neighborhoods, the chemical makeup of the houses changes drastically from one block to the next. The homes on Willa's street are large and well maintained, the paint bright, the garages capable of housing three or four cars, the lawns professionally manicured. A couple of streets over, the residences are small and quaint, the cars parked under carports or awnings bought at Lowe's. Another street over, and now some of the houses teeter on the verge of condemnation, their decay spreading to the homes next door.

"So," Sarah asks, "what the hell happened last night?"

"You mean the wreck?"

"Yeah, the wreck." The dappled shadows of the passing trees play across her face. "I heard Kenny ran somebody over, spread their guts all over the street."

"That's not what happened."

"Thank God."

"There was . . . something, though."

"That sounds suitably ominous," Sarah says as a song by Rosegarden Funeral Party, her favorite band this week, strums from the speakers.

"There were . . . like . . . body parts in the street."

"So he *did* run over someone!" Sarah cackles with joy. "I knew it!"

"I'm being serious," Willa says.

"Serious, serious?"

"One hundred percent."

"What do you mean, 'body parts'? Arms and legs and heads? Something more disgusting?"

"I don't know. Hearts. Kidneys. Organs."

"Ugh! Where the hell did they come from?"

"Kenny said he almost hit a guy—"

Sarah raises an eyebrow.

"Almost," Willa says.

Sarah shrugs a shoulder.

"But the guy he almost hit," Willa says, "was carrying a bag. He dropped the bag and—splat!—the street was covered with innards."

"'Innards' is an old-fashioned word. Too, too old-fashioned. Please never say that word again."

"Sarah."

"Sorry, sorry," Sarah says. "You weren't with him, though, right? You didn't see it happen."

"I saw enough."

"And Kenny?"

"He's all right. I guess."

"You . . . don't know for sure?" Now Sarah gives Willa the side-eye.

"We . . ." Willa starts, but is unsure she wants to finish, conjure those words into reality. "We broke up, I think."

Silence hangs in the air as they pass one house, two.

"You told him, then," Sarah says at last.

"I figured he should know."

"And he didn't take it well."

"Oh-ho, *that* is an understatement."

The station wagon glides past another couple of houses.

"You know, I never liked him," Sarah says. "That fuck."

"Sure you did—at first."

"Yeah, before the two of you got together—certainly not after."

"Yes," says Willa. "You made that abundantly clear."

"I'm just glad you're all right," Sarah says.

"Am I?"

"You gotta be."

"And what am I supposed to do now?" Willa asks. "How am I going to survive this?"

Sarah smirks at her. "Gravity, friction, and faith."

CHAPTER TWENTY

IN THE MAIN OFFICE, WHERE all the deputies write their reports and file their paperwork and kill time scrolling through fucking TikTok, Sheriff Buck perches on the edge of Deputy Keene's desk. He grips the desktop, his fingers drumming out a steady rhythm. He checks his watch. He has an appointment with Doc Maro to keep. Releasing a frustrated breath, he stares out the station's window.

A battered white pickup truck rumbles into view and jerks to a stop right outside. In the bed of the truck, fishing poles sway and shrimping baskets bounce. Larry Smythe sits behind the wheel, cigarette in mouth, greasy frayed cap pulled low over his eyes. He doesn't so much as glance at his son in the passenger seat. Kenny climbs out, his shoulders hunched, mutters something, and walks toward the station's front steps.

As Kenny appears at the glass front door, Sheriff Buck straightens his posture, sucks in his gut just a bit, and hooks his thumbs on his belt. A power move, show the kid who's boss here.

The door opens as Kenny steps inside, then whooshes closed behind him. Kenny has dark circles under his eyes and he looks worn-out, the kind of exhaustion one gets from partying too hard or worrying too much.

"Come on in," Sheriff Buck says.

He steps up to the partitioned counter, nicked and scratched from years of use but polished by Tess's own hand nearly every night, raises the gate. Buck watches Kenny move past, then closes the gate behind him.

"You ever been here before?" Buck asks.

"Not really," Kenny says. "Once on a field trip in third grade."

"My office is right this way."

Buck ushers Kenny into the small office. He spends as little time in here as possible. He'd rather be in the main bullpen, or out in his SUV, or just about anywhere else.

"Have a seat," Buck says.

"Am I in some sort of trouble?" Kenny sinks into the wooden seat across the desk from Buck's own antique chair.

"We're just having a friendly chat."

"My dad says I shouldn't really talk to the cops, not about anything."

"Your old man would say that." Buck laughs. "But, no, you ain't in trouble. So there's no point in playing coy, is there?"

"Guess not."

"I'm a little surprised, though, Kenny." Buck sneers a little, a smile through a foul taste in his mouth. "I expected that hotshot girlfriend of yours to be with you. Seems like she was dead set on representing your interests."

Maybe Buck should have let it drop. At the end of the day, it wasn't important. But he can't help himself, can't get past the girl barging into the area, shoving her way onto his crime scene, and throwing her daddy's reputation around like it was supposed to unnerve him.

Somebody needs to teach that girl—and her daddy, for that matter—some manners.

"She won't be coming. Can we just get on with this?"

"You in a hurry?"

"I'm supposed to meet my dad. He's got a charter."

"Okay. Let's get started then."

Buck leans back in his chair, smiling, enjoying making Devil Dog Number 37 squirm and sweat. Just a little bit. He slides a pad of paper closer. He grabs a pen and hits the clicker, then, with quiet delight, spits out a question he's already asked a few times.

"Why don't you tell me again what he looked like?"

CHAPTER TWENTY-ONE

THE RED EYE DINER'S GIANT coffee cup sign had once, fifty years ago, maybe more, depicted a soft-serve ice cream cone. When the ice cream shop went belly-up, the sign had been repurposed. A handle had been added to the side of the cone. Dark coffee had been painted within. The crown of the soft-serve ice cream had been converted into a haze of steam rising from the cup. In the ensuing decades, the paint had oxidized and faded, the ghost of the ice cream cone surfacing beneath the diner's logo.

It's part of the Red Eye's charm.

Sarah pulls to a stop across the street from the diner. The casual observer might think there was no way anyone could fit the overlong station wagon into such a tight spot, especially with all those stickers obscuring the back window. Sarah, though, maneuvers the bulky vehicle with calm confidence, never letting doubt enter her mind.

Willa wishes she possessed even a fraction of Sarah's drive, determination, self-reliance, and ballsiness.

Downtown Wilson Island is already bustling. The island doesn't draw anywhere near the crowd of, say, Atlantic Beach, but it snags its fair share. Families buying sunscreen and beach towels from the Islander Mercantile. A few college kids loading charcoal and coolers full of ice, light beer, and seltzers into the back of a pickup. A couple maybe older than the Red Eye's coffee cup sign tool down the street on a growling black motorcycle.

Fishing, though, is where the island really comes to life. Trucks and cars, almost every one of them from out of town, pull boats on trailers through the streets. Locals hustle down the sidewalks with rods and reels in one hand, buckets in the other.

Entering the diner, Willa and Sarah are met with a clamor of chatter and clinking coffee mugs, the hiss of the coffee machine, and forks and butter knives being scratched across dishware. The walls of the brightly lit restaurant are plastered with the menus of countless other eateries—other diners from all over the country. The air smells of roasting coffee beans and sizzling bacon and—by God—heavenly grease. The girls find a booth by the front window and slide into red-checkered seats. Mounted under the tabletop's veneer is an array of advertisements for local business.

In a world of drive-thrus and paint-by-number chain restaurants and fast food and DoorDash, the Red Eye stands gloriously alone.

"Morning, ladies." A tired-looking waitress, KAYLA in gold on her name tag, approaches the table with a coffeepot in one hand. "Coffee for you?"

"Yes!" Sarah quickly flips her mug over in its dish. She reaches across, a habit, and flips Willa's mug as well. "Two, please!"

Willa places her hand flat over the mug before the waitress can pour. "I'll just have water, I think."

"Oh." Sarah deflates just a little, then recovers with a grin and a shrug. "I forgot."

Without needing to peruse the menu, they each order bacon and scrambled eggs, pancakes, hash browns, grits, and whole wheat toast. It's more food than either of them can eat. At the Red Eye, though, it's a go-big-or-go-home scenario. Kayla scribbles down their orders as she hurries back to the counter.

"Sooooooo," Sarah says, "I've got news."

"Cheer camp?" Willa asks.

"Yes! Got the call last night! They want me as a counselor. I'll be heading to ECU for three weeks!"

Willa feels joy spread across her face. "That's really awesome."

"One last rah-rah-rah before senior year. Those clumsy skanks from all those other schools aren't going to know what hit them."

"When do you leave?"

"End of next month."

"Wow. This summer's going to go fast."

"Crazy fast."

"Sounds amazing," Willa replies, her words sincere even if her smile doesn't quite reach her eyes. For a fleeting second, she was swept up in Sarah's enthusiasm. How could she not be? But reality comes crashing back in.

"Not amazing," Sarah says. "Epic."

Willa's fingers trace the edge of the menu, her mind drifting to all the plans she and Sarah have made over the years, all the dreams they had every intention of manifesting together. Sarah is, after all, a big believer in visualization, in focusing on the things you want, in shaping the world around you through sheer force of will.

"Hey." Sarah reaches across the table, her hand covering Willa's with a gentle squeeze. "We can still do the girls' trip. There'll be plenty of time."

They've been planning to get away—somewhere, anywhere that isn't a beach—for a week or so before the summer's gone. Those plans built up steam, growing bigger and more exciting, but now they seem to be moving so quickly down the tracks that they threaten to crush Willa before she can leap clear. It feels like the threads holding the future together are shredding, unraveling in her grasp.

The waitress brings their food to the table in no time. Sarah excitedly rubs her hands together. Willa places her napkin in her lap and pours syrup. She looks at the mess on the plate and feels her stomach flip and flop as she remembers the dream and the scene of the accident last night.

"So," Sarah asks as she nibbles on a strip of bacon, "have you thought about what you're going to do?"

"Do?" Willa tentatively cuts her pancakes into triangles, moves the pieces around on her plate.

"Hello, you know." Sarah lowers her head a little, speaks in a whisper. "About the baby?"

Even as a whisper, the words carry black hole gravity. "No."

"Have you considered what we talked about?"

"Considered?" Willa feels pressure seize her chest. She nearly struggles to take a breath. "Um, Sarah—only every day. Every. Single. Day."

Maybe, she thinks, she should have just taken Sarah's suggestion to heart. She pokes at her eggs with her fork. *Before* she told Kenny. *Maybe I shouldn't have mentioned it to him at all.*

"I just want you to know I'm here for you." Concern knits Sarah's brow. "And there are options."

"I'm not so sure."

"God, Willa. Maybe not around here, with Doc Maro. But we could go somewhere—"

"First of all, that's not exactly the road trip I was hoping we'd take together. Besides, I've already told Kenny. My parents know too. It's no longer so cut-and-dried."

"You'll get through it. *We'll* get through it."

A shadow falls across the tabletop. Willa looks up and sees Dean Kramer standing there. He towers above them, lean and tall in his paint-spattered jeans and button-up with the rolled-up sleeves. His dark hair hangs low over his eyes. "Hey, Willa."

"Hey."

"Hey, Dean," Sarah says, smirking. "I'm here too, you know."

"Oh, hi, Sarah." Dean's face flushes. "Sorry."

"No worries." Sarah wiggles her shoulders and pops another piece of bacon into her mouth. Her expression, even as she chews, is one of amusement born of understanding.

"Uh, mind if I join you?" Dean asks. His voice is smooth and deep and hesitant.

"Yeah. Of course," Sarah chirps before Willa can respond. She slides out of her seat, her amusement dancing on her lips. "In fact, I just remembered I need to run a few errands. You keep Willa company. Just make sure she gets home safe and sound, all right?"

"No problem."

He slides into the seat across from Willa as Sarah reaches over, squeezes Willa's arm.

"Sarah, wait—" Willa starts to protest, but Sarah simply winks before flouncing to the front counter to pay the tab, then out the door.

Dean clears his throat. "Hey."

"Um, you said that already."

"Yeah, I guess I did."

"So . . ."

"So, hey."

"Hey."

Dean shifts uneasily in his seat. There are unspoken questions in his eyes, on his lips. Willa fidgets with the edge of a paper napkin, nervous energy knotting in her stomach.

"Haven't seen much of you this summer," he says.

"Yeah, I know. It's been busy."

"Same, same." He draws in a breath. "Still, feels a little weird."

It does feel strange. It has for a while now. The two had been playground friends in their youth. Tag and red rover and hopscotch. They'd sat under sprawling, majestic oak trees, some said to be hundreds of years old, and concocted stories of ghosts and pirates and treasure buried on the island.

In their middle school years, they'd drifted apart, pulled away by differing interests, differing friend groups, by circumstance. Their paths rarely crossed for a time, and they honestly didn't really miss one another.

Then, in just the last year, they'd had two classes together—calculus and English. Sitting next to one another in each class, their friendship was rekindled. More time spent together, picking up where they left off. Except no more hopscotch. More like stealing kisses under those old oak trees. And then Kenny came along, and that just about broke Dean's heart.

Now they sit across from one another, their on-again, off-again, on-again friendship, the changing nature of their connection, hanging between them. Dean's eyes betray a vulnerability that pulls at Willa's heart, reminding her of the kid he used to be, of the reasons she's been drawn to him despite years apart, reminding her of why she kissed him under the boughs of that ancient tree.

So right now, all of this is weird.

"You know how it is," Willa says. "But here we are now."

"You been okay?"

A lump swells in Willa's throat as she mutters, "Yeah." The question is not some sort of auto-response—Dean really cares. She tells herself not to cry, not in front of him. "How about you?"

"I've been good, keeping busy, I guess. I got a letter."

"Okay?"

"An acceptance letter. To an art school in New York. For the fall semester."

"That's great!" Willa feels herself circling a drain, congratulating Sarah, congratulating Dean. "You deserve it."

Dean shrugs. "I don't think I'm gonna go."

"What? Why not? Why wouldn't you?"

"Honestly, I don't even remember applying. I mean, I'm sure I did, just to appease my mom."

"Maybe she applied for you?"

"Maybe. I feel like she's trying to get rid of me."

They share a laugh for a second, then Willa turns serious. "But really, Dean, why not?"

Dean stares at her in silence for a second or two.

Oh, please, no. Don't let him profess his love to me. Don't let him say he wants to stay because of me. She forces the thoughts through her brain. Even though her heart beats a little faster thinking that might be what he says.

"Can I show you something?" he says.

"What is it?"

"Not here. Come with me. To the gallery."

Never before has he invited her to his sacred place. He's talked about it plenty. But he's always kept it to himself.

"All right," Willa says.

"Now?"

"Uh, sure. Where else do I have to be?" She takes one of the napkins, wraps her toast in the paper, before she stands to follow him. "For the birds."

CHAPTER TWENTY-TWO

DEPUTY ERIC REED'S REFLECTION PLAYS across the glass of the driver's-side window in his patrol car. His fingers flex on the steering wheel. The air conditioner cools his skin in the morning heat. Even without the AC, though, he imagines he'd feel cold.

Beyond the window, beyond his own haunted reflection, is the gravel parking lot for the Wilson Island Marina and Fishing Center.

Cars are parked outside the line of motel rooms. The doors to the dozen rooms are emblazoned with jumping dolphins. A family, the father lugging a cooler, the kids carrying beach towels, unloads one of the vehicles, heading toward the promised EVERY ROOM HAS AC cool.

The weather-beaten, salt-stained, two-story marina is similarly painted in blues and whites. Boats of all shapes and sizes—practical fishing boats, small recreational yachts, sailing vessels—are docked along sturdy, meandering wooden piers. Other boats sit atop trailers, being backed down the concrete ramp into the oil-swirled waters.

The scent of fish and seaweed, mingling with the sharp tang of gasoline, lingers in the air, coming through the cruiser's AC vents, coming through Eric's memories.

Surrounding the motel and marina is a sandy beach (not really suitable for swimming—sorry to the beach-towel-laden kids entering Room 6—thanks to the oil that swirls eerily on the surface of the water), swaying sea grasses, and sun-cooked palms.

Behind the motel, surrounded by pines, an RV park plays host to a dozen or more motor homes and towable campers.

Eric takes it all in, surroundings he's seen nearly every day of his life. Now, though, it all looks different. Wrong. Everything seems unfamiliar. The cruiser presses in around him. The uniform he wears feels scratchy and ill-fitted. His own thoughts twist without heeding his direction, circling back to—

Barry Hadley sprawled on the floor, eyes staring, mouth agape, dark holes in his flesh.

Allison Hadley on the bed, the covers soaked in blood, her organs cruelly removed.

Both of them, hollowed out.

The darkness within the room, within their wounds, draws him down into a place where he can't breathe, can't speak, and all he can smell is his own puke, and all he can hear over the thundering rush of his own blood is Deputy Keene, her voice high and screeching, shrieking at him. *Walk the walk! Walk the walk!*

A sudden tap at the passenger window startles him—like a fish yanked from the depths—back to reality.

Standing at the window is Rachel Lang. She wears a bright-yellow sundress, her long dark hair drawn back into a ponytail. Her vivid green eyes are locked on him. She pulls at the door handle, finds it locked, then shrugs at him as if to say, *Are you gonna open up or what?*

Eric thumps a button with his forefinger. The lock disengages, the door is pulled open, and Rachel slides into the passenger seat with ease. She's done this many times before. As with her every movement, her comfort and confidence are a subtle acknowledgment of her control in every situation, every relationship, every dynamic.

Especially theirs. No need to test boundaries. Forget the uniform, forget the badge. She's in charge. And she knows it.

It's been that way since they were in middle school, long before Eric became a sheriff's deputy, long before Rachel became the sole investigative reporter, editor, and ad sales specialist for the area's weekly newspaper, the *Wilson Island Gazette and Examiner*.

"What have you got?" she asks expectantly.

"It's nice to see you too," Eric grumbles, trying to reestablish a bit of control.

"Sorry."

There's an amused smile on her lips, but she's all business. She might conceal that from most people, but not Eric. He's known her for too long. He's fallen prey to that disarming smile too many times.

She's on the hunt.

It's never mattered what she was after. Student body president. The lead in the school play. The Miss Wilson Island pageant title. The most popular boy in school (who, by the way, had *not* been Eric). Her current job. She chased her desires with a cold ruthlessness.

A faint scent of jasmine mingles with the sterile smell of the car's interior.

She hasn't changed her choice of perfume in all these years, Eric thinks. *She's nothing if not relentless. And stubborn.*

"How've you been?" she asks, conceding in a manner that in no way admits defeat.

Eric fights the urge to spew—he winces at the thought—everything he's seen, everything he's experienced and felt. He knows if he doesn't rein it in, he'll babble insanely and end up weeping, here in his patrol car, all over his fucking uniform, right in front of the girl he's loved since seventh grade.

Walk the walk.

"I've been all right." It's all he can manage without risking the avalanche.

"I don't believe you."

Eric looks to the rearview mirror, avoiding her eyes for his own. Another truck towing an expensive fishing boat pulls into the lot. "I don't know."

"Long night?" Rachel asks, a hint of genuine concern breaking through her usually composed exterior.

"You might say that."

"You know word's already on the street, right? I was getting texts at two a.m., three phone calls before six. There are already a bunch of weird rumors online."

"Just rumors," Eric says.

"Until they're not."

"Sounds like you don't need me," Eric scoffs.

"I'd rather know exactly what's going on. The truth. Not speculation."

"The sheriff wouldn't want me talking to you."

"No?"

"Not about this."

"Of course not. He'd rather the community spiral out of control in a whirlwind of whispers and rumors. If he wanted to keep everyone calm, he'd let people know what's going on."

Eric hesitates, knowing the risk, the line he's about to cross. But as he looks into those eyes filled with a mix of determination and vulnerability, his survival instincts, at least when it comes to Rachel, wither on the vine. The truth is a heavy burden, one that could endanger them both. But there's no turning back now. She's always had a way of drawing whatever she wanted out of him. And despite everything, he finds that he doesn't really care about the rules anymore. Not when it comes to her. The consequences seem distant, unimportant.

On the steering wheel, his fingers tremble.

He pulls his hand away, squeezes those fingers into a fist.

He starts to speak, but his throat feels rough, like he's taken in gulping mouthfuls of the sand on the beach. He swallows, the truth constricting the words as if it's a tangible thing, fighting, scraping and clawing, to keep itself hidden.

"All right." Rachel can barely sit still. "How bad are we talking?"

"*Really* bad."

CHAPTER TWENTY-THREE

A BRIGHT-YELLOW SMILEY FACE PERFORMS ITS sacred duty from its emblazoned place upon a coffee mug. The black coffee within has gone cold, but it's bitter and strong, the way the doctor likes it. He takes a sip, lets the liquid sit in his mouth for a moment, and swishes it around before swallowing it down. The mug trembles in Doc Maro's grip.

For nearly forty years, Doc Maro has practiced medicine, right here on Wilson Island, right here in the same building, right here where he'd grown up and lived most of his life.

And he has never seen anything like this.

The beaming face smiles from the mug. *Half empty? Half full? All a matter of perspective.*

Sitting at his desk, the doctor tugs open a drawer. Among a few loose ink pens and notepads, a bottle of whiskey rolls out from the shadows. The cheap stuff. It's been in there for years. He can't remember who gave it to him. One of his old friends. More of a gag gift than anything, a remembrance of the "good old days" when he used to steal bad booze from his old man's liquor cabinet. Those days are behind him now. He hasn't had a sip in . . .

Thirty years.

He snatches the bottle from the drawer, twists the cap to break the seal, and splashes a healthy pour into his mug.

Just like that, the mug is full again.

How's that for optimism?

He takes another drink of cold coffee. This time it burns.

The smiley face leers at him. He doesn't bother putting the bottle away.

Who would judge him for having a drink? Who would judge him for having a *couple* of drinks? If they had seen what he'd seen, they'd join him in trying to wash away the vile images burned into his skull, seared against the backs of his eyelids.

Barry and Allison.

Working in a small town, treating almost everyone who lives in the vicinity at one point or another, Doc Maro has grown accustomed to death. Desensitized to it. Sooner or later, everyone reaches the end of the line, strangers and friends alike, and as he himself has gotten on in years, he has seen people he's known for a good long while pass on from this world and into the Great Beyond. He's always met such events with the calm respect and dignity that such a significant moment deserves.

But Barry and Allison aren't just dead.

They hadn't been taken by illness. They'd been mutilated.

Just down the hall, in the small examination room, lie the bodies of a man and a woman Doc Maro has known almost his entire life. The woman had been killed quickly and efficiently.

God help me, I hope there wasn't much pain.

After she'd died, but before her body had cooled, she had been opened with an almost surgical precision. Her skin peeled back, the tissue folded away, the organs sliced delicately from the surrounding flesh.

Barry's body, though, tells a different story, one of savagery and anger. Where Allison's wounds whisper of meticulous intent, Barry's scream of frenzy and panic and confusion.

Barry, the stubborn old bastard, fought back. Not that it changed anything.

Their organs—their hearts, their livers, their kidneys, their intestines— had been removed.

And now they are in his examination room, cooling in plastic tubs.

Rugged knuckles rap against the door, cracking through the silence. Sheriff Buck stands just outside, looking pale, looking weary, worn thin like the clinic's hall carpet. He holds two paper cups, wrapped in insulating sleeves, in his hands. Little tendrils of steam rise from under the plastic to-go lids.

"Thought you could use one too," the sheriff says, raising the cup in his left hand. His eyes settle on the mug on Maro's desk, and he shrugs. "Guess not."

"Come on in," Doc Maro says, his voice low, measured, and calm. "Sit down."

The chair creaks, complaining under his weight, as the sheriff settles into his seat. He places the two to-go cups on the desk and eyes the bottle of whiskey. His eyes catch Maro's own, and he almost asks a question. Then he shrugs again and lets any judgment he might hold wither on the vine.

"What the hell have you brought me?" Doc Maro asks. The question hangs heavy in the air.

The sheriff shifts in his noisy chair and swigs his coffee. "I was hoping you could tell me."

"The wounds," Doc Maro says, "are starkly different between the two victims. The woman—"

"Allison," the sheriff says.

"—her wounds show a surgical precision. They're careful. The killer took their time. The man's wounds are more chaotic, frenzied, haphazard."

"You can call them by their names."

"I'd rather not."

"Fair enough. The wounds, then. The differences. What do you make of that?"

"The way the woman was killed, it's almost as if she was an experiment, whereas with the man . . . it seems like more of a personal attack. I think he fought back. I think he rattled the killer, made him angry."

"Who the hell would have done something like this?"

"Both the victims were well liked in the community."

The overhead lights hum.

"The first attack was made with precision," Doc Maro says again, his voice low.

"Like a doctor might do?" the sheriff asks.

Maro sighs, his breath stinking of booze. "No. I was thinking—especially after the second attack—someone more like a butcher."

CHAPTER TWENTY-FOUR

"**C**AN YOU IMAGINE?" **MRS. CREWES** says. "Rats?"

Slim and Bo, decked out in their khaki Surefire Pest Solutions uniforms, stand on the front stoop. Each of the men tugs plastic baggies over his boots.

"I mean," Mrs. Crewes continues, "nothing like this has ever happened to me. I keep a very tidy home."

"We've been getting lots of calls lately," Bo says. "Plenty of folks reporting infestations just like yours. You did nothing wrong."

With a quick shake of his head, Slim warns his partner not to use words like "infestation" because it tends to spook clients.

Mrs. Crewes fights to maintain her polite *Please don't judge me* smile. "I appreciate you coming to see me in such short order."

Not like we had a choice, Slim thinks, *not after you called Li'l Winslow for a favor.*

"I'm so glad there was an opening in your busy schedule," she says.

And that *sounds a bit too condescending for my liking.*

"Let's see how bad your *infestation* is," he says.

Mrs. Crewes blanches at this, and swings the door open as she steps back, allowing them entry.

"Don't worry, ma'am." With his feet covered in crinkling plastic, Bo steps across the threshold and into the house. "We'll have this issue cleared up in no time at all."

Her home is beyond very tidy—it's immaculate, the kind of place that whispers of Sunday dinners and fresh flower arrangements. The living room couch and love seat are covered in protective plastic. The throw pillows have been freshly fluffed. The area rugs show the tracks of a recent vacuuming. It reminds Slim of his grandma's house back in Wilmington. So neat and orderly.

A place for everything and everything in its place.

Of course, Grandma had pests too—those damn mice, especially when it rained. And she had cats, which Slim also considered pests, to catch the mice. A never-ending cycle.

The pine and lemon scent of cleaning products hangs in the air. The floors have been freshly swept and mopped, maybe more than once. Every wooden surface gleams from a recent polishing. The morning sun shines through spot-free windows.

This, too, reminds Slim of Grandma. When she so much as glimpsed one of those rodents on a rainy day, she went into a cleaning frenzy, pushing the broom and mop, slinging Pledge-soaked rags, until the house looked like a model home, as if that might drive the little critters away.

Slim tosses a glance in Bo's direction. They both know from experience that the "rats" are more than likely cute little puffballs that will make the mice in Grandma's house look ferocious by comparison.

Of course, they still have to die. You call the Death Request Line, and death is what you get.

"Let's take a look around," Bo says, "see what we're dealing with."

"Well," Mrs. Crewes notes, "it's rats."

"Yes, ma'am."

Slim hasn't partnered with Bo often. Usually he goes out on calls with Barry. But Barry never showed up for work, never called in either. Maybe they should swing by the old man's house on their lunch break, see if he's okay.

Bo's gaze sweeps from the meticulously dusted baseboards to the shadows lurking behind heavy pieces of furniture. He crouches, running a gloved finger along the floor, inspecting for telltale droppings or gnaw marks.

Mrs. Crewes follows, watching over the exterminators, her hands clenching and unclenching.

"Anything?" she asks, hopeful.

"Not yet, but we'll find them." Bo surveys the room with the practiced eye of a pest war veteran. "We're just trying to get an idea of the extent of the problem. We'll set traps along these paths. And we'll leave some poison too. Rats'll take it back to the nest and share it with the others. Kill them where they live. It's strong stuff. Efficient."

In the same way, Slim thinks, *that a nuclear bomb is efficient*. The poison Bo likes to use isn't just lethal, it's a goddamned show of force.

Not to mention, if the nest is too close to the wall, the decaying rat smell will be ungodly for a couple of weeks. But Bo doesn't mention that part.

"It cuts down on the population quickly," Bo says proudly, "not just here but in the community as a whole."

"Well, I'm less concerned about the community," Mrs. Crewes says in a syrupy-sweet voice, "than I am my own home."

"Yes, ma'am."

"My husband, God rest his soul, would have been so ashamed of rats in our home."

"It happens."

"Not to me," she replies, straightening.

"Yes, ma'am. Like I said, you did nothing wrong."

Kneeling, Slim slides his cell phone from his pocket and shines its flashlight, the beam slicing through the dimness under a large china cabinet.

He rises, shakes his head. *I got nothing*.

"Back here," Mrs. Crewes says. Eager to prove she's not imagining things, she moves toward a closed door at the end of the hall. "I've seen them back here a few times. I've been keeping the door shut tight, trying to keep them from getting into the rest of the house. Not that it's done any good." Her hand lingers on the doorknob, her fingers tracing the cool metal with a hesitant touch. She swallows hard.

Wow. She's really shaken, Slim thinks. *Well—time to meet Mickey and Minnie*.

The door swings open. A pungent stink plumes from within, doing battle with the pine and lemon freshness. Bo leans past Mrs. Crewes, reaching into the room to flip the light switch.

A rat, wet and filthy and the size of a small dog, sits on the toilet. It lowers its head. Hisses.

The floor, the sink, the bathtub are covered in fat, greasy rats. Dozens of them, darting back and forth, squirming over each other. Rat shit covers every surface.

"*Jesus Christ Almighty!*" Bo exclaims, stepping back.

A horrified gasp escapes Mrs. Crewes's mouth.

Slim simply sucks at his teeth.

With the door open, the rats now spill out of the bathroom, a wave of furry bodies scurrying and darting and slithering over one another. They squeak and rasp, their sharp nails scraping the hardwood. The vermin surge through the doorway, a frenzied mass of fur and tails scuttling past Slim's plastic-covered boots, an unending stream pouring out of the bathroom like water breaking through a dam.

The rats dash and dart down the hall, escaping into the living room, the kitchen, the den.

"Oh!" Mrs. Crewes shouts. "*Oh no!*"

Bo stands rigid. He looks over his shoulder, in the direction the rats are headed. He doesn't give chase, though. Instead, he steps forward into the bathroom, his plastic-covered feet crushing pellets of feces underneath.

"Aren't you going to do something?!" Mrs. Crewes shrieks. "Aren't you going to *kill* them?! They're all over my house now!"

"Don't worry," Slim replies. "We need to figure out where they're coming from. That's more important right this second than killing the ones that've slipped past us."

In the bathroom, Bo crouches, his knees popping. He pulls his Maglite from his breast pocket. Bo leans down, his eyes narrow, his nostrils flaring, as he aims a powerful beam of light behind the toilet.

"Would you look at that?" he says, speaking to no one other than himself.

A hole, maybe a foot across, gapes in the wall behind the toilet. Chunks of plaster lie scattered on the floor, chewed and ripped up and thrown aside. A smell of mildew and rot and shit and filthy fur oozes from within.

Slim steps closer, cranes his neck for a better look.

"What is it?" Mrs. Crewes asks.

"Ma'am, please stay back right now," Bo says. "It's all right. Just give me a little room."

He leans closer, hooking his fingers around the edge of the hole, tugging ever so slightly.

The rotting wood crumbles under his fingers, the hole expanding by several inches.

"Oh my word!" Mrs. Crewes says.

"Don't worry," Slim tells her. "You were gonna need to replace that section of the wall anyhow."

"Maybe this entire wall," Bo says.

Now that he has a little more room, he shines his light into the gaping hole—

—and then jerks back, slipping and falling on his ass on the feces-covered floor.

From the shadows, an army of cockroaches emerges, their glossy carapaces clicking and hissing against each other. They dart this way and that in meandering patterns.

Mrs. Crewes screams.

A trio of long, pale centipedes slithers out among the roaches, their elongated bodies coiling and uncoiling as they join the insects in their exodus.

An involuntary shudder runs down Slim's spine. The sight of them—legions upon legions of writhing antennae and segmented bodies—is enough to unsettle even a seasoned exterminator.

He can't help it—he involuntarily begins stomping at the insects, crushing them underfoot.

"Jesus—you ever seen anything like this?!" Bo says, voice raised.

Slim hunkers down, trying to avoid kneeling in rat shit, his pulse quickening as he peers into the hole in the wall. Into the abyss. He half expects more rats—more roaches, more centipedes—to come spilling out, but there's only a deep, resonant silence. With a steadying breath, Slim leans closer, straining his eyes to make sense of what lies beyond.

There's movement down there, too subtle to be another horde of rats.

Something else is in the darkness, something alive—and watching.

"What the fuck . . . ?"

Slim's voice is barely a whisper, but it echoes in the darkness beyond the hole in the wall, bouncing back at them.

. . . What the fuck . . .

. . . What the fuck . . .

. . . What the fuck . . .

CHAPTER TWENTY-FIVE

THE TIRES OF THE BATTLESHIP crunch across the gravel lot as Sarah pulls up to the gas pumps. An old-timey bell clangs a couple of times. Inside the Gas-N-Go, the clerk waves but doesn't leave his seat within his kingdom of cigarette cartons. The bell is a leftover from the days of full service, which has long given way to pay-at-the-pump self-reliance.

Which suits Sarah just fine.

Killing the engine, she hops out of the car, unscrews the fuel tank cap, slots the nozzle in, swipes her credit card, and sets the pump to auto-fill. While the numbers on the pump's aged digital display climb steadily, Sarah fishes her phone from the back pocket of her worn jeans. Her thumb swipes across the screen, bringing it to life.

She scrolls to her contacts, finding her favorites, and almost sends Willa a text, just to check in. Almost.

Willa's a big girl. She can take care of herself. And if there's one person on the island Sarah trusts to look out for Willa—one person besides *herself*, of course—it's Dean.

Definitely not Kenny, that fuckhead.

Sarah never understood what Willa saw in that guy. Good-looking, sure. Popular, nice enough . . . well, maybe in mixed company. But he always rubbed her the wrong way. In matters of the heart, though, Willa was not one to be swayed. *And look where that landed her.*

Sarah leans against the side of the Battleship. The metal is warm upon her backside. She scrolls through photos. Mom, smiling and drinking a latte, foam on her nose. Sprocket rolling on the floor, his belly exposed for petting, who's a good doggie. A burger with all the fixings that she grilled herself and deemed worthy of immortalization. The cheer squad. She stops at an image of her and Willa taken just last summer. Their smiles are wide and the world around them is radiant and alive and full of possibilities. In the photo, Willa's hair is green, Sarah's purple.

What were we thinking?

With a *thump*, the pump handle releases, dragging Sarah kicking and screaming back to the present. She slides her phone back into her pocket, replaces the nozzle, and screws the gas cap back on. Looking past the pump, she gazes across the street.

There, Denny Finn Danvers, called "the Warlock" by kids who wouldn't be caught dead calling anyone that, hurries along, dressed in boots and jeans and a leather jacket, all far too warm for summer, but hey, Denny's got a style to maintain and, as Sarah likes to say, game recognizes game. He keeps his head down, not making eye contact with anyone as he walks.

Nearby, Mrs. Keats sweeps the sidewalk outside Mermaid's Crossing. Her little shop's windows are filled with nautical souvenirs. Glass fishing floats. Tangles of old nets. Bits of coral and sand dollars and horseshoe crab shells. Wooden models of sailing ships and sandpipers. The old woman has been peddling her tchotchkes for as long as out-of-towners have been visiting the island.

She hurries back into her shop as Milt Grandland strolls along the sidewalk.

Sometimes Milt forgets his swimsuit.

Not in an *aw, hell, I left my trunks at home* kind of way, either. Sometimes, when Milt ambles down from his elevated beach house to go for a brisk swim—his "morning constitutional"—he forgets to wear pants at all. Or underwear, for that matter.

The islanders are used to him. They rarely give him a second blushing look.

Today Milt wears nothing but a pair of boxers boasting only a few stray threads precariously holding them together in certain spots.

Gravity, friction, and faith.

Milt is a town peculiarity. He's just . . . always been there, odd and half naked at least. Or at most. Depends on your point of view. Whenever he goes on his little walks, he never bothers anyone, except for the occasional near or complete nudity. Folks around Wilson

Island just accept him as one of the many strange salty dogs who call this place home.

A slick, clean SUV pulls up alongside the curb a couple of doors down, right outside the Taco Shack. Scraps hops out, a parcel wrapped in brown paper under his arm. He spits a stream of dark-brown tobacco juice to the street, wipes his mouth with the back of his hand, then jogs to the door and glides inside. Not a minute later, he reemerges, no longer carrying the package. Scraps works for Willa's dad, running all sorts of errands, some unseemly, some seemly.

Or, *at least, seemly-lite.*

Ride-or-dies though they may be, Sarah and Willa almost never talk about Willa's dad. Willa isn't stupid. She knows she is a gangster's daughter. Or, at least, the daughter of a Wilson Island gangster, which probably isn't all that bad. But Sarah learned a long time ago that it is best to just let Willa ignore what she wants to ignore.

As Sarah turns back toward her sticker-covered car, she catches sight of a familiar pickup rumbling into the parking lot. The truck is ancient, like the Battleship, probably a few years older. There's not much keeping the old junker running.

Once again, gravity, friction, and faith hard at work in the universe.

The bed of the truck is filled with coolers and buckets and netting. On both sides of the pickup, in spray-painted stencil letters, are the words:

BENNINGS SHRIMP
GOOD EATING
GOOD BAIT

The truck chugs to a stop, the door screeches open, and an old man sloughs out of the vehicle. He's rail-thin, his skin tanned dark, dirt forever set into the deep wrinkles of his face. His coveralls and tattered baseball cap are stained with grease.

"How-do, Sarah?" he says, tipping his hat.

"Hi, Mr. Bennings," she replies, matching his friendly tone. "How's tricks?"

"I don't reckon complaining'll do me a bit of good." He talks fast, and his words are thick with island brogue. He's a "high-toider." Old Ocracoke stock. "Plenty of folks coming in to fish, and all of them need bait. Sold out whistle-quick this morning."

Coming in from out of town to fish, one of the first sights one is likely to see when crossing the Walters Memorial Bridge is Roy Bennings's truck parked alongside the road, the old man sitting on the tailgate, coolers filled with plastic grocery bags of shrimp on ice. He sells them—"the best bait for these waters"—hand over fist during fishing season.

"Getting another pack of smokes or three 'fore I head out to scoop some more bugs."

"Well, you take care now."

Mr. Bennings taps two fingers to the brim of his filthy hat and heads inside for his cigarettes.

Sarah wonders if he even realizes they've had this exact conversation at least a half dozen times. Maybe he does, and just enjoys the comfort and security of habit.

She climbs into the Battleship and cranks the engine. Through the window, she watches townsfolk meander along the sidewalks, in and out of various businesses, carrying on with the routine and contentment of their day-in-day-out existence. They're blind to the chains that drag them down, oblivious to the anchors that tether them to a life of simplicity and sameness.

And now, she thinks, *Willa has become one of them.*

Fuck.

CHAPTER TWENTY-SIX

WAVES HISS AND RUMBLE, SMASHING against jagged black rocks. Sea spray mists Willa's skin, leaving a sheen on her cheeks and bare arms, dampening the crumpled paper sack she holds at her side. The air is brisk, and it carries the tang of salt and seaweed. The wind tosses her hair as she walks along the pebble-strewn shore.

Dean walks beside her, a canvas satchel slung over his shoulder and hanging at his side. The worn fabric bears frayed seams and spatters of multicolored paint.

Up ahead, a towering wall of limestone, frocked with trees clinging precariously upon craggy cliffs, rises from the beach. A mouth opens in the center of the rock wall, and great chunks of stone lead up to the opening, as if the cave had spat the rocks out so that it might yell back at the tumultuous ocean.

Above, a cloud of seagulls wheel and cry, riding wind currents, watching Willa and Dean with cocked heads and vested interest.

Willa opens the bag, pulls the napkins away from the toast she took from the Red Eye. Tearing a piece from the bread, she tosses it skyward. One of the gulls swoops down, snapping up the morsel in midair before it can hit the ground. The bird's victory triggers a frenzy among the other seagulls, and soon Willa and Dean stand in a storm of flapping birds darting in and swooping low. The wind from their wings buffets Willa's face as the gulls fly all around.

"Remember the Tasty King," Dean announces.

Willa laughs as she tears several more pieces of toast apart and flings them out over the wet rocks.

The screeching cloud surges after the treats.

In town, the Tasty King stands empty. Once upon a time, it had been a hopping burger and ice cream stand. As a kid, Willa had been quite a fan of both their chili burger and the banana split. Open only during the summer months, Tasty King was a landmark of seasonal fun. And then, if you believed the urban legend, the seagulls found it. All it took was one customer offering up a scrap of hot dog. The Tasty King, the birds quickly learned, was where plenty of food could be found. Over the course of a couple of weeks, the gulls swarmed the place, growing bolder and more aggressive, Hitchcockian, sometimes snatching burgers right out of the hands of hungry customers. They roosted there like gargoyles in the night, only to plume into the air in ravenous fury at the sign of the first customer of the day. Bird shit fell with abandon from the sky. A few customers were even attacked. Over time, it became just too much of a hassle to grab a bite at the Tasty King. The burgers and soft-serve within went unsold, and the business eventually closed.

Abandoned to the seagulls. A real heartbreak.

The birds still flocked to the place, though, wreathed it like a crown of gray and white, waiting, waiting.

That, of course, is the story locals tell.

"Oh, come on, the Tasty King didn't close because of seagulls," Willa says. "Mr. Ward retired and he didn't want anyone else running his business into the ground."

"Nevermore," Dean croaks.

"Ha. Quoth the Raven."

She holds a scrap of toast high, and a gull swoops in, snapping it from her grasp.

"That," Dean says, "is a good way to lose a finger."

"Can't help it. I've always loved feeding them. My dad used to take me out on our little fishing boat or to the end of Drummond's Pier, and we'd throw bread to them. They remind me of, I don't know, better times?"

As she flings the last scrap into the air, the frenzy intensifies, wings beating as the birds screech and shriek and batter at one another for position.

"I don't think we want to be out here when your adoring fans realize you've run out of snacks." Dean takes her gently by the elbow. "Come on. Let's find some cover."

"They'd never turn on me!" Willa says in mock defiance.

"They'll pick your bones clean!"

They laugh, and the seagulls seem to laugh with them. Dean grabs Willa's hand to help her navigate the polished rock pathway leading to the cave.

"Careful," he says. "They're slippery."

The cave yawns around them, wide and tall, the floor littered with jagged bits of stone, glittering pebbles, and scattered seashells. The rock walls amplify the hiss-and-rush sound of the surf against the beach, the chattering of the gulls, the hum of the wind. The salt air mingles with the musty scent of damp stone. The tunnel stretches into the distance, into darkness.

"I haven't been here in ages," Willa says.

"This was always my favorite spot on the island."

Old graffiti covers the rock walls around the entrance.

> CORY ~~LOVES~~ BONES TOM
> SAVE THE FUCKING LIGHTHOUSE
> MAMMON WILL RETURN
> KEEP OUT
> SEX ROCKET WAS HERE

Willa smirks at Dean. "Hah. Your work there, Sex Rocket?"

"No, not me." Dean blushes. "But it did sort of inspire me, I guess."

Dean moves ahead, the shadows rushing toward him like the hungry seagulls, drenching him in their embrace. Reaching into his paint-stained satchel, he retrieves a small candle and some matches. With a faint scrape and a flare, the candle blazes to life.

Then another.

And another.

Dozens of partially melted candles are placed around the cave—on the floor, in craggy crevices in the walls, on natural ledges. As the soft glow of candlelight expands, a makeshift art studio fades into view. A small folding table is laden with tubes of colorful oil paints, jars of brushes and murky water, and a palette. The floor is a vast kaleidoscope of intermingled colors from spatters and drops and spills.

The walls, seeming to shift and move in the trembling light, are covered in paint. A scenic reflection of the beach on a stormy day, lightning dancing in the sky over the ocean. A shot of Wilson Island, looking picturesque and inviting. Close-ups of those omnipresent seagulls. The night of the meteor shower, depicted with streaks of luminous paint that make the stars seem to dance, one of them streaking from one side of the cave, across the ceiling, and down the wall on the other side. A simple, almost prehistoric cave painting of horses, charging across the rock and changing into colorful and lifelike images of wild equines galloping the length of the wall. Flowers and waterfalls and rivers made of cascading, vibrant light.

Here and there, old graffiti is absorbed into the paintings, messages left long ago incorporated into and almost hidden by the beautiful artwork.

"Dean . . ." Willa starts, her voice echoing slightly off the walls. "This is insane. You've made something incredible here."

She reaches out to touch one of the paintings, then hesitates, her fingers a few centimeters from the stone.

"Go ahead," Dean says.

Willa lets her fingertips trace the rough rock canvas beneath the paint. She blinks, allowing her eyes to adjust to the dimmer light, where the flickering glow of the candles just barely lights the rough walls. The paintings seem to go on forever, swallowed up by the recesses of the cave.

"How long have you been coming here?" Willa asks.

"A couple of years."

"You know . . . you should let others see this."

"I'm letting *you* see it."

"You know what I mean. Dean—this work could be in showcases, exhibits, galleries."

"Eh—I like it here. I just feel like . . . I don't know . . . it means something more, maybe? It's not about recognition. It's about creation. That probably sounds really corny."

"Yeah . . . maybe a little."

But she likes it. Corniness only goes so far.

Dean stands quiet, and his eyes, those deep pools of thought, remain fixed on the paintings as if they speak to him in ways words never can. Willa sees it then—the way his art is inseparable from this hidden grotto, his soul interwoven with the cave's damp walls. It's as if he pours a part of himself into the stone with every brushstroke, leaving behind a piece of his essence that no gallery could ever contain.

She understands, yet a part of her yearns to see Dean rise beyond this self-imposed confinement. He certainly deserves it.

She takes another few steps, then stops, looking up at a face on the wall staring back at her. The portrait is rendered in swaths of bright colors—colors that should clash and yet somehow come together in a way that works. The expression is a little sad. There's a faraway look to the eyes.

"Is that . . . me?" Willa asks.

Dean stands in the shadows behind her. "Caught you in a moment."

She imagines Dean here, in solitude, brush in hand, tirelessly bringing his inner visions to life. The thought of him painting by flickering candlelight, alone with his art and the sound of the sea, envelops her. He must have spent countless hours here.

Turning away from him and the intensity of his gaze, Willa lets her eyes wander down the tunnels branching off from the main cavern. They stretch into darkness, their depths unknown, beckoning to the part of her that craves exploration. The shadows seem to pulse with potential, each curve of the rocky walls an empty canvas waiting for Dean's touch.

Standing at the edge of the candlelight, Willa stares down the nearest tunnel into the blackness beyond.

"How far have you gone in this place?" she asks.

"Quite a ways, actually, but not the entire cave system by any means. Not sure why I would paint anywhere else. I'll never run out of canvas. These tunnels stretch all over the island. There are miles of them."

She imagines Dean, alone in this hidden world, creating vibrant paintings that come alive under his brush, stepping deeper and deeper into the cave with every new painting. Not wanting to leave this place for art school or anywhere else.

And she feels a hint of sadness, thinking that one day he might just paint his way into nothingness and never return.

Not nothingness. One day, he might paint his way into—

"Forever," she whispers.

CHAPTER TWENTY-SEVEN

THE *JILLY-BEE II* CHOPS THROUGH the cresting waves, froth slamming against the hull, sea spray dusting the air. The boat bounces upon the water's surface, rising and falling, rising and falling. The passengers—a fishing party out of Tennessee—hoot and holler and laugh every time the vessel takes air and slams down. They hold on for dear life, doing their damnedest to keep their longnecks from spilling and their lunches from coming back up.

"To the hunt!" A flush-faced man—"King Dave," as his friends call him— raises a frothing bottle in a sloppy toast.

His companions, a handful of men and women who are all at least as drunk as he is, lift their bottles of beer and red Solo cups filled with vodka and grapefruit juice sloshing over the side.

Upon the deck, wet with water and oozing blood, are a dozen sizable Spanish mackerel and twice as many bluefish, gleaming silver in the sun. When they reach the island, Kenny knows the fishing party will spend a while taking photos of the day's haul, posting them proudly to social media and to make their friends and family jealous, later printing off the pictures and framing them for their desks in their real estate and banking and human resources offices. Once the photo shoot comes to an end, Larry Smythe will offer— for a modest fee, of course—to clean and fillet all the fish and pack them in ice.

From a cell phone connected to Bluetooth speakers, a playlist— almost certainly put together specifically for this trip—spools endless songs about endless summers. Sandy beaches and piña coladas and margaritas, saltwater air and carefree days, in a loop as limitless as the horizon. Some of the passengers sing along, out of sync and out of tune and out of fucks to give regarding how bad they sound.

At the helm, Kenny's dad throws a nod toward his son. He brings in a thousand dollars a day on these fishing charters, sometimes more if the fishing parties do well and decide to tip. At the moment, though, he's not too concerned about money. He's also, thank goodness, not worrying about paying for damages to the truck. He can be a hard man, damn cold. But right now, he's just happy to have his kid along.

One day, Kenny will leave Wilson Island. He won't see his father often after that. And he knows he'll regret not spending more time with his old man while he could.

Or maybe this is where I'll be from here on out.

"I'm pregnant."

Willa had slapped him in the face.

She had hooked him, yanked him out of the water, gaffed him, and hauled him onto the deck, leaving him there, flopping and leaking blood as his gills flexed open and closed, open and closed.

How the hell did she expect me to react?

The fishing group continues their cheerful banter, punctuated by laughter, oblivious to the labor of their hosts. As he absently coils rope or slings fish or cleans up empty bottles—dead soldiers—Kenny listens to these drunken men and women, their privilege and social standing and class status coming through loud and clear.

"Did you hear about the merger?"

"Now's the time to buy!"

"I don't know. I lost a bundle. But hey, hell, it's only money!"

"Vacation homes feel like a bad investment."

"We're doing this again next month, right?"

Kenny eyes the boat—the totality of his own family's wealth—a twenty-five-foot center console fishing vessel. The *Jilly-Bee II*, named after his mom.

His mom, who always wanted to get off the island but managed to fall in love with a guy who bled salt water.

His mom, who got knocked up at a young age and sealed her fate.

His mom, who always had this sad, faraway look in her eyes, especially when she thought no one was watching.

His mom, who yearned for Kenny to leave Wilson Island and make something of himself, if for no other reason than to live vicariously through him.

His mom, who died without ever seeing Kenny realize his (and her) dreams.

Kenny's gaze drifts to the horizon where sea meets sky—a line as unreachable as the lives these passengers lead. A pang of envy surges within him, followed closely by a deep-seated resentment. It isn't just their money or their freedom that stings—it's the reminder of his own stagnant existence, anchored to Wilson Island by invisible chains forged from obligation and circumstance.

Because Willa got pregnant.

He knows it's unfair, that it's not her fault. But—he can't help it—it *feels* like her fault. And he feels even worse for conjuring that feeling.

Music drifts across the deck, the tinny soundtrack to the party's end, Jimmy Buffett and Kenny Chesney, but they fail to lift his spirits. Instead, they underscore the vast gulf between the life he leads and the one this entire charter takes for granted.

What does Kenny Chesney know about Kenny Smythe's life?

As the *Jilly-Bee II* navigates along the shore of the Shelby Banks, the old Cape Jordan Lighthouse comes into view, a silent sentinel, once used to help ships navigate the banks, now slowly crumbling, the sea sneaking up on it, hungrily eroding the shores. One day, Kenny imagines, it will simply vanish, toppling into the waters and becoming just another coastal legend.

Kenny moves about the deck, securing gear and prepping to dock as laughter vies for position among beachy melodies. He watches the fishing party sway, some with the rhythm of the music, others with the roll of the sea underfoot, yet others with the dizziness that comes with too much to drink.

Just as they did on the way out, the fishing party *oooohs* and *aaahs* at the wild horses roaming the tall grasses along the banks. Kenny's dad slows the boat for them, letting the passengers enjoy the view and snap a few pictures. Locals say the horses have lived there, unbridled and free, for hundreds of years, having swum to shore from sinking British ships.

Soon the marina, surrounded by its rocky shoals, meandering

piers, and docked vessels, comes into view. Seagulls watch from barnacle-encrusted dock posts. Pelicans bob lazily in water churning with colorful slicks of oil.

The fishing party hoots and hollers anew, signaling its victory.

As the chugging boat nudges against the dock, Kenny springs into action, coiling rope, tying the boat off. The first to disembark are a couple of women, slightly unsteady from the motion of the ocean—or perhaps all the alcohol. They're both in their forties, and they're both, as far as Kenny is concerned, knockouts. One is blond, the other brunette, and they obviously spend time in the gym. They laugh a bit too loudly as Kenny offers his arm for support, his athletic build steady as a rock against their teetering steps.

"Thanks, handsome," one slurs. "Always nice to have a strong man around."

"Part of the service," Kenny replies.

"Too bad we can't take you home with us," the other woman chimes in, winking as she steadies herself against Kenny's broad shoulder.

"Maybe next time," he says.

He watches them saunter away, their laughter trailing behind as the men join them to pose with their haul and chant "Fill the boat! Fill the boat! Fill the boat!" And for just a fleeting moment, he imagines what it would be like to leave with them, to sail away from Wilson Island and its small-town chains. But the dream dissolves as quickly as it formed, and Kenny's left standing on the familiar wooden planks of the dock, the echo of beach music fading into the evening air.

Kenny loops the weathered rope around the cleat, securing the vessel to the dock as the last of the late-afternoon light plays across the water. His father gives a curt nod of approval from the helm before disappearing into the cabin. The reverie of the sea is a siren song, but Kenny's feet are planted firmly on the planks beneath him, each knot a reminder of his rooted existence.

"Kenny?"

His name, spoken by an unfamiliar voice, pulls his attention away from the task at hand.

He straightens, turns, and finds a woman standing on the docks. He knows her. He's seen her many times around town. He's even been interviewed by her several times after a game. Rachel Lang. She runs the local paper.

A newspaper, in this day and age.

Hell, Kenny has been getting text messages all day about the accident and the rumors surrounding it. His buddy Charlie has sent pic after pic of raw hamburger and anatomy charts and slasher movie posters.

Real funny guy.

But word hasn't spread to everyone.

Not yet.

The fishing party, for instance—King Dave and his loyal subjects—hadn't heard about last night's strangeness. Or, if they had, they didn't give enough of a shit to let it ruin their vacation.

People on the island still rely on the *Gazette* for their grocery store coupons, yard sale advertisements, and local gossip.

Kenny wipes his hands on his shorts. A pang of worry crosses his mind. He knows why she's here, and her presence signals a ripple in the calm waters of Wilson Island life. He braces himself for what might follow as she says:

"Mind if I ask you a few questions?"

CHAPTER TWENTY-EIGHT

WITH ONE HAND, SLIM GRABS a plastic-wrapped sandwich—chicken salad on spongy white—from the refrigerated shelf at the back of Rudy's Mart. With the other, he holds his phone, trying to call Barry one more time. And, one more time, there's no answer.

Sauntering down the aisle toward the front counter, he eyes Doritos and Cheetos, Oreos rolled into tubes, Slim Jims, and Sour Patch Kids. He passes them all by. He's never been one to worry about hunger all that much, which is how he earned his nickname. He only eats one meal a day at most. Sometimes that meal is one of these recently considered bags of chips or a sleeve of cookies. Today it's the prepackaged chicken salad sandwich grabbed at the convenience store as he drives across town to check on his friend.

An instrumental version of—

Is that fucking "Copacabana"?

—plays from an old-school boombox behind the counter.

Rudy, the shop's namesake, sits at the cash register. He's forty years past his prime and forty pounds overweight. Balding and sweating, he watches the store with dead eyes peering out from behind smudged glasses. He's owned Rudy's Mart and sat at the cash register since Slim was a snot-nosed kid.

Thinking twice, Slim checks the expiration date on his sandwich. He's been burned before by an outdated Rudy's Mart chicken salad. This one, though, has a week to go before it becomes questionable.

Any *more* questionable.

"That all for you?" Rudy asks, already punching the price into the register, which is also old-school, like the boombox.

"That's it," Slim says.

The price appears on the register's screen, and Rudy looks at Slim without speaking. Slim digs money out of his pocket and slaps it on the counter. With a nod and a curt smile, he grabs his lunch and ducks out the front door.

His Surefire Pest Solutions truck waits for him in the parking lot. Pristine white. The company logo and phone number are emblazoned on the side. A cartoonish fiberglass bug perches on the roof, a smile on its lips, two X's where its eyes should be.

The ridiculous-looking bug seems to be directing that smile at Slim. And he flips it off.

He thinks about the crumbling hole behind Mrs. Crewes's toilet, about the rats and the centipedes and the roaches that spilled out of it, about the ensuing slaughter that took place as they chased the fleeing pests through the house, about the lie they told the old woman as they closed the door to the bathroom and hustled the living hell out of there.

"We've killed as many of the pests as we could, laid out poison, set traps. It'll take time for an infestation like this to die off. We'll check back with you in a couple of days. Re-treat the area as necessary."

But no smiling, X-eyed bug in the world is a match for the nasty nest in that house.

If it were me, Slim thinks, *I'd move.*

Yeah? And go where?

Slim climbs into the truck, unwraps his sandwich, and takes a bite. Even though he scrubbed and scrubbed, the acrid scent of rat poison clings to his fingers, mixing with the bland taste of the chicken salad in a nauseating combination. He changed out of his uniform—covered in rat shit and crushed insect goo—as soon as he returned to the office. He keeps a spare in his locker for just such an occasion. But the stink of the clothing, stuffed into the back of the truck, lingers in his memory. He takes another bite, throws the truck into gear, and pulls out of the lot. He's grown accustomed to the smell, along with the realization that he'll never get the poison stink off his skin.

From the radio, some upbeat surfer shit plays. A strumming ukulele and a thrumming bongo. Slim grimaces, his disgust more pronounced for the music than for the smell of mayonnaise, pickles, and strychnine. With his half-eaten sandwich in hand, he flips the station, finding some pop nonsense dedicated to grinding his nerves to dust and turning his brain into nosebleed gray matter running from his nostrils.

One day, he thinks. *One day.*

He daydreams about playing Europe and Ratt and Def Leppard and Metallica and Led Zeppelin on his own station. Buying the Cape Jordan Lighthouse and broadcasting from the tower. *"Playing the greatest hard-rock hits of all time—as we crumble into the ocean!"*

People will love him for his efforts.

A sudden movement catches his eye—something skittering across the dashboard. Slim's heart races as he swerves, nearly hitting a parked car. When he looks again, nothing is there.

Get it together, he chides himself. *You're losing it.*

The truck crawls to a stop outside Barry's modest single-story house. The last bite of chicken salad sandwich Slim is chewing turns to mush, unswallowed, in his mouth. Slim blinks in disbelief at the yellow police tape stretched across Barry's front door.

Slim sits there, staring, the truck idling. He wants to go up and knock, double-check his phone to see if he has the right address. Make another call that he knows will go unanswered.

Something darts across the dashboard, this time for real.

One of those goddamn greasy roaches from Mrs. Crewes's house. Somehow it escaped, probably hitching a ride on Slim's pants leg.

Slim slaps a hand down on the insect. He closes his fingers around it, then unrolls the window and, without taking his eyes off Barry's barricaded house, tosses it out to freedom.

Not now—I'm on break, he thinks.

Maybe he shouldn't have spared the nasty little fucker.

He watches the police tape snap and dance in the breeze.

And he doesn't feel like bringing any more death into the world at the moment.

CHAPTER TWENTY-NINE

"TO BARRY!"

Surrounded by shelves of traps and plastic poison containers, breathing deep of air that reeks of insecticide, Slim raises his coffee cup.

The rest of the crew—Bo, Duncan, Jerry, and Matty—raise their own mugs, glasses, and jars—a motley collection acquired from desk drawers and cabinets. Their beverage containers clink, but there isn't a drop of joe to be found. Barry, after all, isn't around to coax the ancient, grumbling Mr. Coffee to life. And this isn't quite the occasion, anyhow.

"To Barry!"

Slim tilts his head back and lets liquid fire slide down his throat.

The other men on the team grunt or grimace or try to suppress their reactions to the whiskey burn, just as they have to the news of Barry's . . .

Passing? Death? Murder?

Bo is numb, no emotion on his face.

Duncan tries to tamp down a morbid giggle.

"Booze is a kind of poison, you know," Jerry the philosopher notes. "We're poisoning ourselves, just like we poison rats. There's some irony in that, don't you think?"

Matty stares into his cup, as if hoping to find some answer floating atop the whiskey within.

"First in," he says, remembering Barry's drive and determination. "Last out."

And Slim—

The phone rings. No one moves to answer.

"Fuck it. It's after hours," Jerry says. "Just let it go to voicemail."

Their ritual of mourning affords no interruption.

On Barry's desk is a photo of the man, surrounded by mismatched, flickering candles and a can of his favorite beer, unopened and now warm. He would have liked that, especially since dearly departed Allison wouldn't let him drink the stuff anymore.

"To Allison," Bo says somberly. And the others join in the toast. Many of them had never met Barry's wife, but they all felt like they knew her because of the stories. More like Barry's grousing. But none of them doubted that Barry loved his wife, that he would have been completely lost without her.

The phone rings again, a shrill cry. No one moves. Tonight, the rats can wait in their squalor, the termites can gnaw their way to fat-bellied glory, and the roaches can plot their dominion over the earth.

The Death Request Line will, for once, go unanswered.

"Those rats," Bo says, never looking up from his cup. "At the Crewes' place. Shit, man. I've never seen anything like it."

"Roaches too," Slim says. "They came right up out of the floor."

"They chewed their way up from underground," Bo says. "This is one for the goddamned books."

None of them has ever seen Bo look . . . haunted before.

But he damn sure looks haunted now.

Like he'll never shake the memory of the vermin boiling up from below.

"Something drove them up," Bo says.

"Is it just me," Matty asks, "or does this job get more batshit crazy every day?"

"It's you *and* the job," Slim says, trying to break the tension. "You're *both* getting more batshit every day."

They laugh at that. All of them except Bo.

"Wonder how Barry would have handled the situation?" Jerry asks.

Only Slim notices, but Bo grumbles under his breath and grimaces, and it's not from the whiskey. He and Barry always had a bit of a rivalry when it came to pest control. Of all things to measure dick sizes over: Barry with his decades of experience, Bo with his love of exotic (and often concocted on the fly) pesticides. The two men might have respected each other, might have even liked each other, but they lived in a constant tug-of-war to determine who was the best at what they did.

"Remember that time he tried to outsmart the raccoons? Those elaborate traps?" Matty asks, a small smile tugging at the corners of his mouth.

"'Elaborate' is one word for it," Jerry replies. "'Insane' might be another."

"He rigged Brenner's whole backyard like some kind of wildlife obstacle course," Matty says. "Snares, deadfall buckets, pits."

"Ended up catching himself more times than the raccoons," Jerry says.

"At least he got rid of them," Slim says.

"They just got tired of hearing his fussing and complaining," Bo says. "They moved on to quieter backyards!"

They all laugh at that. Then just as quickly the room falls into somber silence.

The telephone sounds off again, and no one moves to answer it. By the third ring, Li'l Winslow is yelling from behind his office door.

"Who the hell is catching all these fucking phone calls?"

Slim picks the handset up, then carefully places it back in the cradle.

"If I ever get my hands on the sicko who did this," Matty growls, his voice low and menacing, "they're gonna wish they'd never crawled out of their fucking hole."

"We don't even know exactly what happened," Jerry says.

"We know enough, goddammit. Murder is murder."

"Whoever did it," Bo says, "they ain't finished."

"How do you know that?"

"Just do."

"Maybe we're talking about one of those traveling serial killers," says Jerry, who watches too many true-crime documentaries. "He—or she—might've already skipped town. Could be halfway to Timbuktu by now."

"If you're moving along," Slim says, "an island is the last place you'd come."

"*This*," Matty agrees, "is the end of the line."

The group falls silent once more.

"Well," Slim says at last, "fuck."

"Here's to that," Bo says. Mugs and glasses and jars clink together once more.

The back-office door swings open. The toasts abruptly end. The boss, Li'l Winslow, steps out and into the center of the gathering, all five feet of him. His fresh, smooth face flushes red. He looks to each of the men in his employ, but doesn't give two seconds of attention to the makeshift shrine to Barry.

"You boys gonna tie one on, I guess."

"Already there," Bo says.

"Well," Li'l Winslow says, "you might want to put a pin in that plan."

Slim, caught mid-sip, sets his drink down with a *clack*.

"We're getting swamped with calls," Winslow says. His lips quirk into what could be mistaken for a smile. "More than we could handle even with Barry on the job. I'm gonna hire some new faces, get some new blood. Until we get 'em hired and trained, though, I'm instituting mandatory overtime for each and every one of you."

Dissatisfied, halfhearted groans bounce around the room.

Grumblings about "union rights" and "decent working hours" are muttered but unheeded.

"Can't say I'm thrilled about missing my weekend," Jerry pipes up, his tone threaded with sarcasm as he pours another glass of cheap bourbon. "But I guess the roaches won't exterminate themselves."

"Rats neither," Slim says, and he looks at Bo, sharing a dark thought.

"Right, then." Winslow's statement hangs heavy, shutting down any further discussion. "So maybe cut back on the hard stuff then, huh?"

"You want to have one with us, boss?" Slim asks, a cup in hand, holding it out to him.

A kind of challenge. Or maybe a simple dare.

Winslow looks at the cup for a moment, then turns back toward his office. "I don't want y'all hungover tomorrow, get me?"

The door slams as he storms back into his office.

"Barry would've loved this," Matty remarks dryly.

"Hah. He would have hated it," Slim says. The men raise their glasses in agreement. "But he might have appreciated that it was all because of him."

"Something tells me he's laughing at us right now," Bo says.

"Eh. Who gives a fuck what that little gremlin says," Jerry quietly remarks, chucking his chin in the direction of Li'l Winslow's office. "I'm getting lit tonight."

"Let's just hope," Matty says, "we don't get so drunk that we accidentally end up exterminating each other tomorrow."

The Death Request Line trills anew.

From behind the closed office door, Li'l Winslow yells, "Somebody *answer* the fucking phone this time, *please*!"

"Will do, boss!" Slim calls back. He picks the phone up off the cradle, then quickly replaces it. "Right after one last drink."

It's a futile act of defiance against the night and against the ever-present buzz on the line. But for a brief moment, the laughter is genuine, and Barry's there among them, laughing the loudest of all.

Slim doesn't want to believe Barry's gone. Almost refuses to, but knows it's true, as there isn't any coffee in the pot, the thought of which is instantly depressing as shit.

CHAPTER THIRTY

THE NET PLUMES OVER THE shallows like a blossoming flower, then falls with a whisper into the water.

Roy Bennings wraps the nylon line around his elbow as he drags the net back through the mud and wet grasses. He then hauls the dripping net out of the water, examining his catch. Four shrimp, tangled in the nylon, twitch and kick. He plucks the shrimp—bugs, he likes to call them—from their captivity and tosses them in his bucket. He draws deep on his cigarette, breathes out a billowing cloud. His eyes scan the shallows, watchful for telltale signs of movement beneath the surface.

He hurls the net out again. It arcs through the air and hits the water with a soft splash. Then he drags the net back. A half dozen shrimp come up this time, trapped and twitching in the woven fabric. Into the bucket they go, and Bennings casts the net once more.

Near about every day, he parks his old truck—BENNINGS SHRIMP, GOOD EATING, GOOD BAIT—in the pine forest, just off the main road. He hauls out a couple of buckets stuffed full with his nets. He hikes down the sandy path to the mud bottoms. And he gets to work.

The routine is automatic. Cast the net. Drag it back. Pluck the shrimp. Toss them into the bucket. Take a drag on the cigarette. Repeat.

He slowly paces down the bank with every throw, the wet fibers of the net scratching at his weathered and calloused hands. Just a little ways from here is an oyster reef. *That's* where the bugs'll be more plentiful.

No sense, though, in wasting a throw. The net sails out over the water.

Walking the sandy path through the woods, pacing the muddy banks, smoking his cigarette, Roy Bennings is at peace. He's happy.

He's been coming out this way since he was a boy. Back then, he ate all the shrimp he caught. Now he sells them—GOOD EATING, GOOD BAIT. What he's always loved about shrimping is the solitude. He relies on the out-of-towners, the *dingbatters* his old man would have called them, for his living, but over the years, Wilson Island has just gotten too damned crowded for his tastes. Too many tourist sportsmen and drunken fools. Out here, though, along the mud bottoms, he's alone. Can actually hear himself think. Or not, for that matter.

He drags the net back.

This time he catches another four shrimp, but also drags up a pair of flat-bodied flounders. Not too large, but big enough for supper. A good deal if there ever was one. He tosses them in the bucket too, already planning on frying them up when he gets home.

He casts the net out. And realizes that he's not alone after all.

Several yards away, a figure stands at the water's edge. He's backlit by the setting sun, bathed in shadow, and Bennings can't see him clearly. Something about his stance, though, makes the old man uneasy. This figure—this man—is not facing the water.

He's turned directly toward Bennings. A cold sweat prickles at the back of his neck.

He knows it's just another fisherman, a shrimper like himself maybe, or possibly a hiker enjoying the wetlands. But he's pissed all over Bennings's beloved isolation.

Bennings raises a hand—to wave, yes, but also to shade his eyes so he might see a little more clearly. The figure doesn't return the gesture, doesn't move at all. For a second, Bennings wonders if someone has raised a scarecrow or something on the water's edge.

There's something about the stranger's face that just doesn't sit right.

Bennings casts the net into the water. Hauls it back. Plucks shrimp from the netting. Tosses them in the bucket. Casts the net.

For a moment, he watches ripples play across the water's surface. Then he draws the cord, feeling the resistance of his catch. The net emerges, heavy and writhing with life. Jackpot. Shrimp sparkle, tiny jewels in the wet mesh. Bennings dumps the abundant catch into his bucket.

Then—only then—does he look back down the bank. The figure still stands there, motionless, watching.

"Hey there!" Bennings calls out, friendly. "What are you up to over yonder?"

The figure doesn't respond. Doesn't move.

Bennings casts the net, hauls it back, clears it of shrimp. He glances, sidelong, down the bank, eyeing the motionless figure.

He casts the net, drags it back through the mud and grass, empties the catch into the bucket.

He raises his eyes again to look toward the motionless figure. Who is now running—

—as fast as he can—

—right at Bennings.

The stranger is hunched over, keeping low, charging. His booted feet splash in the mud. Now Bennings can see that he wears jeans and a gray button-up shirt, but also a black leather apron and black rubber gloves. Around his waist is a belt laden with swaying, glittering, sharp blades. His face—something is *wrong* with his face—he wears a mask.

Bennings is frozen, numbed, and the net slips from his fingers to fall into the mud at his feet. Then instinct and adrenaline kick in, and he takes a step back. He turns—

Just as the masked figure slams into him.

The sudden force knocks the wind right out of him, his cigarette flying from his lips. The world spins, and Bennings sprawls backward, toppling. He splashes into the shallows. He gasps for air, struggling to regain his senses. His hands clutch at the grass. Mud cakes his palms, his face. His legs slip and kick, knocking over his bucket. Dozens of shrimp spill across the slick ground, scurrying for freedom.

His attacker is now on top of him, straddling him, grabbing him with a gloved hand and forcing him onto his back.

"Please," Bennings chokes.

He gazes up and sees no mercy . . .

. . . sees no *eyes* . . .

Holding Bennings down with one mud-slicked, gloved hand, the faceless stranger raises his other hand. Something sharp gleams in his fingers. It comes down once, twice, three times, punching again and again into Bennings's throat. The old man feels warmth spatter his face, but no pain, at least not at first, and it takes him a second to realize he's been stabbed, that his throat has been ripped open, his flesh gouged up from the wound in his neck.

Panic sets in, and it serves no purpose.

His hands claw feebly at the grass, seeking leverage where there is none, and they're growing weaker. He thinks maybe he's wet himself.

His killer, panting and out of breath, stands up and steps back, watching as Bennings bleeds out, red slowly mixing into the muddy waters.

A cold numbness creeps up Bennings's limbs. Panic flutters away, replaced by throbbing, pulsing pain. And even that fades quickly.

In these last moments, time stretches, each second elongated. Bennings's thoughts scatter, memories flickering past: the warmth of the sun on his back, the salty spray on his face, the laughter of friends long gone. Then those fragments slip away, leaving him adrift.

Bennings looks up at his murderer, standing over him, panting roughly, wearing that strange eyeless mask with the writhing, swinging breathing tube, and a calmness settles over him.

Nearby, flopping in the mud, are the two flounders he just caught. They leap and gape, their gills spasming open and closed, open and closed.

Bennings rolls his eyes once more to the killer. His own mouth opens and closes. Opens and closes. No sound comes out.

The killer, though, seems to sense Bennings's distress. He turns his masked face toward the fish dancing in the mud. With the toe of his boot, he nudges both the flounders toward the water until they splash into the drink and swim away.

After that, darkness swallows Bennings down into nothing.

WEDNESDAY

SPREADING WORD GIVES BIRTH TO FEAR, BUT NO ONE UNDERSTANDS THE TRUTH.

CHAPTER THIRTY-ONE

WILLA WINCES AGAINST THE STRANGE luminescence bathing her face. While she was in the cave, in Dean's gallery, the world has turned a sickly and swirling puke green. An unnatural color. Green clouds billow, rolling through the sky. The ocean, too, roils in its greenness. The waves come in grand undulations, smashing against the rocks. They are silent, though, as if someone has hit reality's mute button, the sea itself closely guarding its secrets.

Sound off for the apocalypse.

Brushing a stray strand of hair behind her ear, Willa regards the transformed landscape.

A congregation of seagulls perches on the jagged, rocky, sea-sprayed outcroppings. They, too, are silent, unwilling to share their chaotic and frenzied call. Silently they peck and tear at a shared meal of pale, translucent, wriggling abominations.

With a deep breath that does nothing to steady her nerves, Willa shifts her gaze from the gulls' abhorrent feast back to the dissonant but weirdly silent seascape. Then she looks toward the entrance to the cave.

"Dean?"

Yet even as she hears her words echoing in her skull, she's unsure if she's made any sound at all.

She turns her head, assuming Dean has emerged from the cave with her, that he's standing a step or two behind her, that—any second now—he'll place a comforting hand on her shoulder and tell her it'll be all right. But he's not at her side. Instead, he stands in the cave mouth, gray-green in the shadow, a wide-eyed, puzzled look on his face.

"Dean?" she says again, louder now, even though she's still uncertain if she's actually made a real sound or not.

Dean's expression never changes as his eyes lock on to Willa's. His mouth opens. Closes. Opens. He's speaking, saying something, the same short phrase over and over, but no sound escapes his lips.

The silence is smothering. Willa steps toward him.

A distortion ripples in the air behind Dean, like heat waves over asphalt, and something unseen latches on to him, yanking him back forcefully into the deep darkness of the cave.

He keeps on speaking in urgent silence, even as he's swallowed by nothingness.

Willa takes three more steps, then stumbles to a stop, her muscles tense.

Dean is gone.

She must force herself to remember he was ever there at all.

A step. She edges toward the cave's gaping mouth. He *was* there.

The air shifts, billowing out, warm and thick, across her face, then whooshing past her, sucked back into the darkness. Like the cave is breathing.

He was here.

Who?

Dean.

Dean was here.

He's still somewhere in the cave.

Who?

Dean.

A shudder passes through the ground at Willa's feet, and it feels as if the sand beneath the black pebbles and seashells has gone fleshy. She takes another step.

He was here.

Dean.

He's still in there.

In the dark.

Something moves deep in the cave, beyond the gallery of paintings. Something scrabbling and slithering and writhing and oozing in the blackness. Something foul and stinking and pale spilling toward the entrance—toward Willa—in the silence.

Willa can barely breathe as she spins on her heels. Her bare feet pound across the pebbled sand, each step flinging gritty particles against her shins, cutting into the bottoms of her feet.

Where are my shoes?

The sky above stretches out in an oppressive canopy of green, taunting her with its unnatural hue.

She feels a clawing pain in the pit of her stomach. Wet warmth running down her inner thighs. She glances down, her breath catching in her throat as she sees dark rivulets snaking down her legs, blood painting a crimson trail across the beach behind her. She puts a hand across her stomach, and feels something—

Scrabble.

Slither.

Writhe.

Ooze.

—inside her.

The sky's sickly green pallor is broken suddenly by a flurry of white and gray. Willa barely registers the incoming shapes before a cloud of seagulls descends upon her. They dart and swoop in with beaks snapping.

A tear across her cheek. A rip across her arm. Hair shredded from her scalp. A gash across her forehead. Blood rushes into her eyes.

She has to get back to—

The truck.

Whose truck?

Who brought me here?

A gull snaps at her face, grabbing her lower lip in its beak, trying to tear it away.

Willa flails.

Sound floods into her ears, breaking the enveloping silence. It's deafening, like being punched in the face with noise. The seagulls are screaming at her, but it's not their usual sound of crying out for leftover food, begging for scraps or toast or bits of Tasty King burgers. These shrieks belong to hungry, wailing babies.

She stumbles, swatting at the gulls as they dive and peck at her. But there are too many of them, and she's hopelessly outnumbered. One bird grabs on to her hair, pulling it out by the roots. Another bites into her arm, drawing blood.

A sudden jolt of pain in her stomach brings her back to reality. She looks down in horror as something writhes under her shirt. She can feel it moving inside her, trying to break free.

I've gotta get out of here.

I've gotta get to the truck.

Whose truck?

She's unsure how she got here, who brought her.

With a surge of determination, Willa pushes through the swarm of gulls, and her bloodied legs propel her away. Panting, eyes stinging with blood and tears, she knows she can't stay upright, knows she is going to fall, knows the gulls will descend upon her and pick her bones clean.

Her legs give out, and she pitches forward.

Into the arms of a waiting figure.

A man in a black leather apron, black gloves, and a mask that twitches and wriggles on his face.

CHAPTER THIRTY-TWO

WILLA JUMPS UP IN BED, her legs kicking the sheets away. She sits upright, leans forward, trying to catch her breath. Her fingertips fall to her chest, her heart pounding under the fabric of her tank top. She keeps her eyes closed for a few gasping breaths, then looks around the room.

There, in the morning light streaming in around the curtains, is her cozy chair. There's Bigsby Bear. There are her guitars, her amp. There are all her photos dangling from strings of glittering LED lights.

These things are real.

That puke-green sky, the pale and fleshy thing moving in the cave, the squirming horrors the seagulls mutilated with their beaks—those were all just part of some fucked-up pregnancy dream.

A pregnancy dream, sure.

One tainted by blood and body parts in the street.

The man, though, the figure in the leather apron and gloves and—

—that featureless, wriggling mask—

—seemed real enough.

The echo of his shape, like a wraith, lingers in the bedroom.

Staring at her without eyes.

This is a dream.

And no dream lasts once its illusion has faded.

Willa should be waking.

The eyeless figure remains, though, even as the dream begins to come apart like smoke. He's solid against a background of phantasm. He clings to existence as the dream crumbles around him.

Somehow, Willa thinks, *he's real.*

The ghost-echo begins to fade.

Did I somehow dream him into existence?

CHAPTER THIRTY-THREE

"**CAN YOU BELIEVE THIS** total shit?!"
The newspaper smacks to the desk hard enough to rattle ballpoint pens in their mason jar container.

Sheriff Buck leans back in his chair, the springs groaning under his weight. The muscles along his jaw clench tight. The walls of his cramped office—covered in framed commendations, photos with the governor and at prize-winning barbecue competitions and of the sheriff smiling next to huge game fish on display—seem to be closing in, trapping him in the space with the headlines.

DOUBLE HOMICIDE ON WILSON ISLAND
EYEWITNESSES DETAIL GRUESOME MUTILATION

And right under the headline is a photo, obviously hastily snapped with a cell phone.

A bloody trash bag in the street.

The sheriff himself standing nearby, hands on his hips, looking down toward the street.

Looking lost.

"Can you believe this total horseshit?!" he almost yells this time, to no one in particular.

The sheriff looks at his fingertips, expecting to see them stained with black ink. They're clean. Printing techniques have improved over the years. But whether you can see it or not, the ink is still going to leave a stain.

They didn't waste any fucking time rushing this to press, did they?

The *Gazette and Examiner* has been coming out every Wednesday for years, but it usually doesn't get distributed until a little later in the day. Today it hit the streets before the break of dawn. Rachel Lang must've been working overtime to—

Fuck with my entire day.

"It's been on their website since yesterday evening." Tessa Kendry stands in the door to his office, her knitting needles in hand, yarn trailing back to her desk where's she's been working on her scarf or mittens or blanket or whatever she's making to kill time. She was likely, Buck imagines, a knockout in her youthful years that had passed her by at least thirty years prior. She stands just over five feet tall, with a slim frame. Her eyes are bright blue behind her horn-rimmed glasses, and her curly hair is overdyed an unnaturally red color. "There was no way to keep this quiet, and you know it."

A vein throbs in Buck's temple.

The *Wilson Island Gazette and Examiner*, published once a week, delivered every Wednesday, chock-full of weather updates and fishing news and articles about the Little League and coupons for fifty cents off ground beef at the fucking Save-a-Ton.

And detailed reports on brutal fucking murders.

On my watch.

Every word, every sentence, might as well have been a wad of phlegm hawked up into his face, a blatant affront to Buck's authority, a challenge to his ability to keep the town safe.

Standing, his back groaning and creaking every bit as loudly as the chair, Buck paces. He circles the desk, every step measured, a consideration of how he navigates the waters ahead, how he manages to course-correct before it all spins out of control.

"Sheriff," Tessa says, "you need to take a breath. Your heart isn't built for this kind of stress anymore."

He locks eyes with Tess. She cocks her head slightly, a warning, wordlessly telling him to gauge his actions—especially with her— carefully. The mix of maternal worry and professional caution takes the sheriff aback.

"Whatever you do," she says, "don't check social media."

Buck steps toward Tess, puts a hand on her shoulder, and gently moves her aside. Stepping across the main station room, he stands over Eric's desk. Papers lie scattered, piled on top of folders and paper clips intended to wrangle the clutter. The guy has never been much for organization. An empty coffee mug bearing the faded image of Garfield the cat sits on the edge of the desk.

I'D LIKE MORNINGS, proclaims the mug, IF THEY STARTED LATER.

"I know what you're thinking." Tess shifts her weight, her fingers tightening around the knitting needles. "But Eric wouldn't—"

"Please don't finish that sentence." Buck's teeth grind together. "Not unless you really believe what you're about to say."

Tess falls silent, letting the implications hang between them.

"There's gonna be a panic," Buck says. "Folks are gonna lose their shit over this."

"They already—" Tessa catches herself, swallowing her false words of comfort and falling silent again.

News of this will spread like wildfire through dry grass. The sheriff knows what comes next—doors will be double-locked, curtains drawn tight, neighbor eyeing neighbor with suspicion usually reserved for strangers. And every damn one of them condemning Buck for letting a goddamn murderer into their midst.

"Well," Tess says as she shuffles back to her desk, "if everyone else is losing their heads, we've got to do our best to keep ours."

Sage advice, as always.

"Do me a favor, will ya, Tess?"

"Anything you need."

"Radio Eric and tell him to get his ass back here." He glances at his own desk, at the newspaper lingering there. "Now, if you don't mind."

CHAPTER THIRTY-FOUR

EVERY MORNING, GRACE COTTON, OWNER of the Island Boutique, loves the five minutes leading up to the opening of her shop. She savors those fleeting moments of solitude before the hustle and bustle of the daily grind. Not that she minds the customers. She enjoys helping people and loves meeting new people.

But there's nothing wrong with a moment of peace.

She walks past the sundresses and blouses and skirts on display, running her fingertips over the fabric. The walls of the boutique are sky blue. Decorative seagulls stand atop every display. Light music—almost like the sound of wind chimes—plays from overhead speakers. Aaand . . . there's already someone standing at the door.

But it's not a customer—it's Mrs. Peterson, who owns Island Properties. She's dressed prim and proper—purchased from Grace, of course—but looks nervous and ill at ease, her face drawn tight. She clutches her cell phone in her left hand as she taps incessantly on the glass with her right. She presses the screen of her phone against the door, trying to show Grace something. But the phone has reverted to its lock screen, showing only a photo of Mrs. Peterson's three cats.

Grace moves to let the woman in. Before she unlocks the door, she pauses to flip the SORRY, WE'RE CLOSED sign to YES, WE'RE OPEN.

Oh well, might as well get the day started a minute or two early.

The door flies open as soon as it's unlocked, Grace staggering back to avoid being clobbered. Mrs. Peterson, looking over her shoulder as if she's afraid of being followed, bursts into the boutique.

"Oh, hi there," Grace manages to get out. "Is everything okay?"

"No, no, no." The older woman's eyes dart nervously up and down the shop. "Everything is most definitely not okay. It's . . . it's awful. I don't know what we're going to do. We're going to be ruined by this. Me, you, everyone!"

"What are you talking about?"

"Haven't you heard?" Mrs. Petersen shoves her phone into Grace's hands.

"This is just a photo of—"

Shaking her head, Mrs. Peterson yanks the phone back, punches in her passcode, and swipes her screen.

"A killer! Here, right on Wilson Island!" She holds the phone up to a news article about murders on the island. "Who's going to want to buy a dress, let alone a beachfront condo, with a murderer on the loose? He's going to put every last one of us out of business!"

...

Sitting at the breakfast table, the newspaper spread out next to her cup of morning tea, Margie Kindt dabs at her eyes and speaks in a hushed, confused, and frantic tone.

"I . . . I can't believe it. We just saw them at Beach Bingo. And now they're gone."

Across from her, his eyes lingering on the article, Kyle shakes his head. "I don't know how anyone could do such a thing."

"They were such lovely people." Margie's shoulders shake as she suppresses a sob. "I've known Allison since middle school."

"This kind of thing doesn't happen here," Kyle says.

"It does, though. Don't you see? It does now."

...

Oblivious to the shocked whispers, Milt strolls down Main Street. His tan, leathery skin glistens with sweat. Today, at least, he wears faded, too-tight swim trunks. Longtime residents of Wilson Island know that this might change at a moment's notice. The old surf-bum, after all, has a knack for leaving his clothing in the darndest places.

A couple of local kids, pimply-faced teenagers in bright polo shirts, white shorts, and boat shoes, guffaw as Milt passes. One of them whistles.

"Better watch out, Milty!"

"There's a killer on the island!"

"A slasher!"

"He sees a hot little thing like you, who knows what'll happen?"

Milt turns, puffs his weathered chest, and smiles. "I'd take that," he says, his voice syrupy sweet, "as a compliment."

...

"Come on, kids!" Lloyd Danvers calls. "Who wants ice cream? I'm buying!"

Of course I'm buying, he thinks. *I'm always buying. Who the hell else would be?*

Cheering with delight, his kids hurry down the boardwalk to where Lloyd waits by the ice cream and cookie stand. Hannah is eight, Claire six, and Danny five. They're all dressed in T-shirts pulled over swimsuits, and already darkly tanned, even though their annual vacation only started four days earlier. They all order ice cream cones—pistachio and chocolate and strawberry-dipped—as their father pays.

"You want anything, hon?" Lloyd calls out to Sue.

Standing a few yards away, looking uncomfortably out across the water, Sue says, "Nothing."

Two days earlier, she'd been all smiles and laughter. Now she carries the attitude of someone who just wants to go home as quickly as possible.

As the kids race off with their treats, Lloyd walks over to Sue. "It's going to be all right," he says.

"You don't know that." Sue doesn't even look at him. Together, with or without kids, they've been coming to Wilson Island for over a decade, swimming in the same waters, eating at the same restaurants, chartering the same boats, renting the same beach house for three weeks at a time. Now, though, she looks out across this once-familiar place like she doesn't recognize it at all. Sue turns her head suddenly, panic on her face. She looks at her children, laughing, their faces smeared with ice cream. "Kids! Don't wander off so far!"

Lloyd touches her arm.

"Look, it was awful," he says, "but I'm willing to bet it was an isolated incident. The cops are going to catch this guy in no time. Everyone's going to be fine."

He almost says, *Don't let this ruin our vacation*, but he knows he'd sound like a callous asshole.

Sue forces a smile—on the surface if not in her heart.

Good enough, he thinks. *I've sunk a lot of cash into this trip. Can't let it go to waste.*

•••

Madhouse Quinn, standing next to a wire trash can on the edge of the beach, clutches the newspaper in trembling hands. The headline boasts of recent murders. The article names victims, names witnesses. It even names the killer—the Wilson Island Ripper—in an almost nonchalant way. The piece goes so far as to discuss the killer's methodologies and to speculate on motivations.

"This," Quinn mutters, "is not your story to tell."

With a sudden, violent motion, he crushes the paper into a ball and shoves it into the trash receptacle with all the other garbage.

"This will not do."

CHAPTER THIRTY-FIVE

DEPUTY ERIC REED DUCKS HIS head into Buck's office.

"You wanted to see me, Sheriff?"

Buck looks up and drums his fingers on his cluttered desk. He lets his eyes linger on Eric's, waiting for the younger man to break contact. When that happens—less than a minute later—the sheriff rises, grunting with a bit of effort, and hitches his belt.

"I reckon I did," he says.

On his desk is today's edition of the *Wilson Island Gazette and Examiner*.

Well, Eric thinks, *fuck*.

Eric catches Tess's eye, but she quickly looks down, breaking eye contact with him even more quickly than he did with the sheriff. The phone trills loudly, and she snaps it up mid-ring. "Sheriff's department," she answers, and Eric hears a shade of relief in her voice. She wants no part of whatever's about to happen.

The sheriff brushes past Eric, moving through the office.

"Why don't you walk with me?" he asks.

Eric's guts turn to jelly—boiling jelly at that—but he follows Sheriff Buck as the man walks straight out the front door.

The Fredericks County Sheriff's Department, with its large window, bench, and snapping American flag, is nestled among the post office, the Volunteer Engine-and-Ladder Company, and a handful of quaint shops and eateries. The good folks of Wilson Island—the residents as well as a few touristy types—bustle about, getting started with their day's activities, work for some, relaxation for others.

Thumbs hooked on his belt, Buck takes a deep breath of the salty air.

"Take a goddamn look around, Eric."

Eric does as he's told.

A few passersby eye the sheriff and deputy as they walk along the sidewalk. Some keep their heads down. A few have phones in hand, scrolling through lurid details of the murder. A couple of people hold newspapers rolled in their hands.

"What is it that you see?"

"People."

Buck grumbles, "People, *sir*."

"Yes, sir. People, sir."

The sheriff saunters away from the station. Eric, feeling a bit like a dog brought to heel, follows.

"What *about* these people?" Buck asks.

"I'm sorry?"

"Use those 'excellent observational skills' you mentioned on your job application."

"I guess . . . well, some of them might look a little on edge or something."

"On edge?"

"Nervous. Scared, maybe."

"Scared of what?"

"The killer."

Buck watches the sidewalk ahead. A young couple hurries past, nearly stepping off the sidewalk to get out of the sheriff's way.

"The murders have everyone on edge," Eric remarks. "There has been a lot of chatter online. Some folks have even posted pictures from the night of the accident."

"I thought"—Buck's irritation is bullhorn-loud—"we were keeping a handle on photos and the like that evening."

"We were, sir, but there's only four of us. We couldn't keep an eye on everyone."

Another group of townsfolk huddle around the recently painted bright-blue mailbox outside the post office.

Eric can't hear what they're discussing. Might be the weather. Might be fishing. Or it might be . . .

". . . *they don't have a single lead* . . ."

". . . *how could this happen here* . . ."

"... *how could they let this happen ...*"

"Who are they scared of?" the sheriff asks.

"Sir, I—"

"You already know the answer," the sheriff says.

"They're scared of *us*."

"That's right."

"But—"

"They're scared we won't or can't do our job. They're scared we can't protect them."

"I-I didn't mean—I—" *Stop stammering. Stop it. Walk the walk, even when you're getting chewed out.* "I didn't mean to cause all this trouble."

"And yet, here we are."

"I thought I was doing the right thing."

"You weren't thinking about right or wrong and you know it."

"Excuse me, sir?"

"The only thing on your mind was whether or not sharing a few big, bad secrets might put you in Rachel's good graces. You thought maybe, if you gave her a big story, she might let you take her out to dinner, might let you slip your hand up her skirt."

Eric flinches. Buck's not necessarily wrong. But he doesn't like anyone—the sheriff or otherwise—talking about Rachel like that.

"She's got you wrapped around her pinkie finger," the sheriff continues. "And she knows it."

Again, no lie detected. "Sheriff ... sir ... she told me getting the story out, getting the truth out, would help."

"Help who exactly?"

"The town. The people who live here. Us."

Buck holds up the pinkie of his left hand, mimes wrapping a thread around it tightly with his right.

"So, are you gonna fire me?" Eric asks. "I fucked up, sir. I realize that. It won't happen again."

"I considered letting you go, yeah."

Eric knows that was likely the case. Still, hearing it out loud stings.

"Now, though, is not the time. I need everyone out there trying to find the person who butchered Barry and Allie."

The Ripper. That's what Rachel called him in the article. He doesn't say it, though. He values his un-kicked ass a little too much.

"But the next time you start to thinking about what might be right or wrong, I want you to come to *me* first. Those kinds of decisions are officially *way* above your pay grade. Understand?"

"Yes, sir."

"And do yourself a favor. *Please*. Find some other girl to pine after."

"Huh?"

"You keep letting Rachel Lang string you along, sooner or later that thread's gonna slip off her finger and get around your throat. You hear me?"

Eric doesn't want to answer, but he knows a verbal response is expected. "Yes, sir. I get you. Loud and clear."

CHAPTER THIRTY-SIX

THE AC IS ACTING UP again, chugging away but doing little to cool the trailer, and the breeze coming in through the cracked window is warm and stale.

"Too fucking hot!"

The Warlock strips out of his leather jacket and Chucks and jeans, leaving the clothing on the floor amid all the other dirty clothes. Wearing only a Megadeth T-shirt and boxers, he sprawls sweatily on his bed, spiral-bound notebook and leaking ballpoint in hand. He stares at the ceiling and tries to dream up a dark and dangerous catacomb filled with giant spiders and yugoloths and gibbering mouthers. The pen lingers on the paper, aimlessly scratching out interconnecting squares and rectangles and circles representing rooms and corridors—

That no adventurer will ever explore.

Tightly wedged in among his *Monster Manual*, *Fiend Folio*, and *Deities and Demigods* are dozens of notebooks similar to the one he now clutches. Each one bursts with meticulously crafted adventures, detailing room after room, cavern after cavern, all thoughtfully planned with intricate plots and dangerous foes and vivid settings. The pages are filled with scribbles and sketches pulled from his imagination, waiting to be brought to life at the gaming table.

And all so very pointless.

From down the hall, the Warlock hears Uncle Terry snoring noisily in his recliner. The steady sound lulls the Warlock into a sleepy state, and his eyelids flutter. Much like how a yawn is contagious, the rhythmic snoring makes him crave the embrace of a nap.

Still his pen works, jotting down ideas.

Perhaps he'll gather a new gaming group, a band of fresh faces eager to roll dice and weave stories together. He doesn't yet know *where* they'd play, not just yet, but he'll figure it out. For all he cares, they can play in the vacant lot behind Rudy's Mart. They can play in the old school, which kind of resembles a dungeon, breathing in asbestos as they battle dragons and demons. They can even play on the beach, rolling dice in the surf and sketching out maps in the sand.

He closes his eyes—just for a second—and darkness engulfs him. In the abyss, vivid visions unfurl:

Muscle-bound monsters with gnarled claws and menacing maws.

Deadly pitfalls and traps springing as nimble shadows leap clear.

Fiery explosions erupting from spell-weaving fingertips in brilliant, scorching plumes.

He sees Madhouse Quinn, smoking a joint, preaching to no one in particular.

He sees the faceless entity standing eerily outside his window.

He sees . . .

Blood-dripping blades.

Not the noble weapons of gallant adventures. Not a sword like the many-named blade. Not a mighty battle-axe of some dwarvish lord.

Instead, he sees a butcher's knife, a finely honed scalpel, and a rough-edged fish scaler.

All smeared with oozing gore.

He jumps, his eyes snapping open.

"What was that?"

He'd heard whispers this morning when he wandered out in search of a Cheerwine to start the day. He had seen the headlines on the front page of Uncle Terry's newspaper draped over the arm of the recliner. He knows a murder took place. He knows the killer has not been apprehended. Now the news is worming its way into his daydreams.

Maybe, he thinks, he should capitalize on the story. It's on his mind, so why not? Maybe he can craft an adventure centered on a cunning serial killer on the loose. A slasher in a fantastical medieval world filled with castles and knights. Now, *that* concept truly intrigues him.

He returns to his notebook—only to discover that he has filled the entire page.

He doesn't recall writing so much, but there it is: a tapestry of scribbles and doodles covering the paper. At the top of the page is the map he'd been drawing, followed by notes on encounters associated with each chamber. After that, the writing becomes increasingly chaotic. Tangled thoughts spiral out, barely connected, leaping from one random musing to another. Scattered among the words are doodles of tiny swords, their blades sharp. Each element, whether word or drawing, seems to converge and direct attention toward a single focal point.

The image haphazardly sketched at the bottom of the page resembles the barbed shell of a massive crustacean surrounded by hundreds of whipping tendrils.

Along with the surrounding swords—all pointed at the strange shape—is the same phrase scrawled over and over, the letters jumbled together sloppily.

THECALLERTHECALLERTHECALLERTHECALLERTHE CALLERTHECALLER

The Warlock blinks. Why did he draw that? Why did he write that? And . . . when?

He strips the page out of the notebook, crumples it up, and flings it across the room.

A chilling sensation seeps through him, not from the outside world, but from within, from his bones.

He suddenly and inexplicably regrets ever complaining about the heat.

CHAPTER THIRTY-SEVEN

THE AUTOMATIC DOORS OF THE Save-a-Ton open with a *swish*, a tad too slow for Sheriff Buck's tastes. A series of musical chimes sounds overhead, announcing his entry. His boots tread on the worn linoleum, the sound muffled by the soft hum of refrigeration units lining the walls. The fluorescent lights cast a sterile glow over the grocery store. The aisles are packed with out-of-towners gathering supplies for camping trips and stays at Airbnbs and fishing expeditions.

Price check on Beanie Weenies and dried ham, he thinks, remembering his own excursions out on the open water when he had time once, fishing for flounder and cobia and whatever else his hook might snag. Today, of course, he's fishing for something else entirely, and it makes his stomach turn.

Behind the counter, the cashier, Mildred Fairway, runs rolls of paper towels and boxes of instant coffee over the price scanner. A middle-aged woman with tired eyes, she smiles mechanically at a customer while making change. Her movements are practiced, automatic, and disinterested.

At the end of the conveyor belt lane, one of the Save-a-Ton's two bag boys plies his trade. He's lanky with shaggy brown hair that falls into his eyes. He wears a red apron over his jeans and a name tag that reads JUNIOR. His hands move quickly as he stuffs groceries into paper sacks and hoists them into a shopping cart. As Junior finishes bagging an elderly woman's groceries, she smiles at him and thanks him for his help. He mumbles a polite response before turning to help another customer.

Sheriff Buck makes his way over to the register. Mildred gives him a small, tight smile as he approaches, but she eyes the next three customers in her line, their shopping carts loaded down and waiting.

"Busy day?" Buck asks her.

Mildred sighs. "No busier than any other day this time of year," she notes with a hint of exhaustion in her voice.

"I'll have to come back for my essentials another time, then," Sheriff Buck replies with a chuckle.

"You here on official business?"

Buck's eyes fall to the copies of the *Gazette* displayed along with the magazines, crossword puzzle books, and gossip rags. The headline—**DOUBLE HOMICIDE ON WILSON ISLAND**—glares back at him.

Buck suppresses a growl, tips his hat, and walks toward the back of the store. He can feel the eyes of every customer, every employee, following him.

Light, meaningless music plays throughout the Save-a-Ton, instrumental versions of once-popular country songs. It's the kind of music that gets stuck in your head for hours, but you can't remember the lyrics or who sang it. And you can't be troubled to look it up.

Nearby, Henry Owens, the produce manager, meticulously arranges apples in a perfect display of reds and greens, oblivious to the world beyond his crates of fruit.

Making his way to the back, Buck passes the deli counter where a young girl takes orders and prepares sandwiches. He thinks her name is Bowie or something ridiculous like that. Her parents are part-time islanders, just coming in for the summer months. That means she doesn't need to work, but does so at her parents' insistence or from her own desire to keep the hell away from them. She has long blond hair tied up in a messy ponytail and a bright grin on her face as she chats with customers. He forces a smile at her in passing, but she doesn't seem to notice him.

Farther down by the refrigerated section, several tourists mutter among themselves about the exorbitant cost of milk and eggs. Their accents are out of place here. One of them, a wiry man in a garish Hawaiian shirt, gesticulates wildly with a carton of half-and-half.

"Can you believe these prices?" he complains to his companion, a woman with sunburned shoulders peeking out from under a spaghetti-strap tank top. "Highway robbery, I tell ya."

Tourist town. Tourist prices. What do you expect?

But as Sheriff Buck nears them, their complaints dry up into the chilled air.

Complaining about prices ain't a crime, folks.

Buck offers a curt nod as he moves past them.

The scent of raw meat surrounds the butcher's counter, metallic and unnervingly familiar. Under the harsh light, the glass display cabinet is full of beef, pork, and chicken, each piece artfully arranged.

Buck's stomach gives a sickening kick.

Each marbled piece of meat reminds him of the body parts strewn across Killdeer Avenue. He imagines Doc Maro dealing with Barry and Allison Hadley, piecing them together like some grotesque jigsaw puzzle on the steel table in his back-room morgue.

"Morning, Sheriff," Grady Weeks says. His white butcher's apron is stained with blood. He's tall and broad, eyes too small and too close together for his melon-shaped head. He has a cleaver in hand.

Jesus. You paint one hell of a picture.

"Morning, Grady," Buck replies, his voice level despite his unease. He leans against the cool glass of the case, eyes not quite focusing on the neat labels declaring cuts and prices, his hands gripping the top of the cabinet.

"Anything I can get for you?" Grady asks, setting his cleaver aside and wiping his hands on his bloodstained apron.

"Not today," Buck says, purposely keeping his eyes away from the meat display.

"Well, I'm guessing this isn't a social call."

"Actually, I'm guessing you probably heard about the spot of trouble we had Monday night."

Grady shrugs, leaning back against the stainless steel countertop. "Heard some, sure. Just whispers. Someone got hurt, right?"

"That's right. Barry and Allison Hadley."

"That's a damn shame."

Buck looks down at the cuts of beef, the sirloin, the KC strips, the slabs of rib. He imagines Barry and Allison, split open, their organs harvested.

"Did you know them?" he asks, not bothering to raise his eyes, trying to be casual. He eyes the meats as he waits for Grady to answer.

"Barry and Allie? No. Not really. Allie came in from time to time. Barry too, when he had a mind to grill. That's about it, though."

Buck nods, still not meeting Grady's eyes. "You don't live too far from their house, you know," he says.

"That a fact?"

"Just a couple of streets over, actually." Now Buck raises his gaze, meets Grady's eyes.

"Never realized that."

"Well, it's a small island."

"I suppose we all live close to each other out this way. Ain't that right?"

"You didn't happen to notice anything unusual Monday night, did you? Anything out of the ordinary on your street?"

"Buck"—Grady mugs and shakes his head slowly, deliberately, like he wants to make sure Buck sees the act clearly—"if I'm being honest, this conversation we're having right now is just about the most out-of-the ordinary thing to happen to me in a minute."

"Sorry. I'm just trying to put the pieces of a puzzle together, I reckon." *The way Doc Maro put Barry and Allie together.*

"Is there a reason you're asking me and not anyone else?" Grady asks.

"It's like I said." Buck shrugs. "You live near them."

"Can't say that I noticed anything. After a long day, I draw the blinds, sit in my easy chair for a bit in front of the box, then hit the sack."

"Quiet night at home, then?"

"Yup, just me and the missus. Didn't step out once. Thought about going out to the Tugboat but decided to just stay in."

Buck slaps his hand lightly against the countertop a couple of times. "All right, all right. Good to know."

"I feel like"—Grady cocks his head slightly, rubs the palms of his hands down the apron—"you ain't telling me something I should know. You ain't asking something you want to ask."

Buck's hand hovers over the glass before pulling back. The marbled red of the rib-eyes feels too close to the carnage he so recently witnessed, but life on Wilson Island grinds on regardless of his discomfort.

He clears his throat, an attempt to dislodge the unease sitting heavy in his chest.

"Nah, it's nothing. Hey, tell you what—I'll take two steaks," he manages to say, voice firm despite the turmoil brewing inside him. "The rib-eyes."

Grady grabs the steaks, wraps them, and weighs them.

"Grilling out tonight, Sheriff?"

"Something like that," Buck responds, though the thought of eating twists his stomach into more complicated knots. "Much appreciated. See you around."

Back up front at the register, he waits in line with the rest of the patrons. He pays Mildred with cash as Junior bags up the steaks. Then he shuffles out the automatic doors that slide open far too sluggishly.

Warm, salty air chases away the chill of the grocery store. Looking back into the store, Buck can no longer see the meat counter. He can no longer see if Grady is watching him. He looks at the bag of wrapped steaks he's carrying, and his stomach turns once again.

He tosses the steaks in a curbside trash can and continues on his way.

CHAPTER THIRTY-EIGHT

IN LOW, LATE-AFTERNOON LIGHT, a pair of shadows slip through the tall grass bordering Aldo Renner's property.

Jimmy and Lewis Cooper hunker down near a woodpile overgrown with weeds. They're covered in a sheen of sweat and breathing hard, and can barely suppress their giddy laughter. Jimmy, the older of the siblings, tightly clutches a BB gun.

From his hiding spot, Jimmy takes aim, lining up a shot with one of the unsuspecting chickens pecking about in Mr. Renner's yard.

"Bet you can't hit the one with the weird tuft on its head," Lewis whispers, eternal mischief in his eager voice. He nudges Jimmy with an elbow, watching the slender boy's finger hesitate on the trigger.

"Watch me," Jimmy replies.

His finger tightens. With a soft *pop*, the BB pellet zings past its intended target and pings harmlessly off the metal roof of the nearby chicken coop. The chickens scatter in every direction, a squawking flurry of feathers.

Lewis laughs. "Is that what I'm supposed to be watching?"

With a curse, Jimmy passes the gun to his brother.

Lewis shoulders Jimmy out of the way and crawls, soldier-style, into a shooter's position in the weeds.

Just as he's about to take his shot, the back door of the farmhouse bangs open. Aldo Renner steps out onto his stoop, brandishing not a BB rifle, but a real shotgun.

"I see you, you little bastards!" the farmer yells.

Jimmy and Lewis scramble to their feet.

The shotgun booms. The brothers don't look back, but Jimmy will later swear he felt buckshot whiz past his head. Still, as the Cooper brothers burst into the safety of the surrounding trees, they howl with laughter.

・・・

Butler leans on the pier's railing, finishes off his Natty Boh, crumples the can, and flings it into the water.

"Shouldn't litter," Nelson says, half snorting, not really believing it, just saying it to needle his buddy. He leans with his elbows against the railing, his feet kicked out and crossed.

"This pier is my dad's property," Butler says. "That means the water is my dad's property too. And *that* means I can do what I want."

"I don't think that's how it works," Lee says. He sits on the warped, creaking wood, his legs dangling over the side of the pier.

"I'm fucking bored," Nelson whines. "We should hop in that Trans Am of yours, man, cruise the streets, find some beer and some chicks."

With the side of his foot, Butler nudges the cooler full of Natty Bohs they've dragged out here with them.

"Fine," Nelson says. "Then let's just find some chicks!"

"When have we ever just gone out scoping girls?" Lee asks.

"I'm boooooooorrrrred," Nelson says.

Some mosquitos buzz about, dive-bombing Butler, and he absently swats them away.

He looks out across the tributary, the water sparkling in the fading sun, the reeds undulating softly. The water's the same. The beer's the same. The company's the same. This is how it goes: Summer after summer, Butler, Nelson, and Lee drag their asses out to Wilson Island between semesters. He knows he's holding on to the past, to nostalgia, to his friends, to the good times they used to have, to the beer they used to drink when they were kids. And he's not complaining.

This summer, though . . .

"How many more years do you think we've got out here?" he asks.

"The way the skeeters are biting," Lee says, "I only have a couple more minutes."

"I'm serious," Butler says. "One year? Two? Once we graduate, there's no chance we can spend our entire summer on the island."

"We'll do vacations," Nelson says.

"Yeah, yeah." Butler grabs another can of beer and cracks it open. "A weekend here and there, but how long will that last?"

Nelson and Lee exchange looks but offer no answers.

"Now," Butler says, "with this maybe being one of the last times we can all get together like this, we've got some sort of psycho killer—"

"*Qu'est-ce que c'est*." Lee snickers, speaking the only French he ever bothered to learn.

Butler acknowledges the joke with something close to a growl, gulps his beer down, and flicks the can—without crushing it—into the water.

"What if we caught him?" Nelson asks no one in particular.

"Who?" Lee asks.

"The killer. What did they call him in the news? The Ripper."

"Now, that," Butler says, "would make for an epic summer."

...

"Behold the sizzle!"

Rich Gingham, king of the grill, grins, his deeply tanned skin crinkling around his eyes. He flips a burger, pushes a couple of hot dogs across the grate.

"If you keep cooking like this, we'll need to invest in a bigger camper," Lilly jokes, watching her husband work within the billowing smoke.

"It's not the cooking that expands the waistline," Rich says proudly. "It's the eating!"

Theirs is not the only grill flaming and smoking in the small, shaded RV park behind the Wilson Island Marina and Fishing Center. A dozen RVs are parked behind the hotel, shaded by tall trees, just a hop, a skip, and a jump from the water. Among the recreational vehicles, Lilly spots at least four grills and Big Green Eggs and fire pits being put to good use. Other campers gather outside their homes-on-wheels, sitting under awnings, gathering around picnic tables, listening to beach tunes, cracking beers, laughing as they enjoy the cool breeze running off the water.

Neighboring campers, drawn by the scent of grilled delights, saunter over with curious smiles. "Something smells good over here," one calls out.

"Back!" Rich calls, laughing, brandishing his barbecue tongs like a sword. "Back, you scavengers! Back!"

As dusk settles like a soft blanket over the campground, laughter and stories begin to weave through the air, mingling with the twinkle of fireflies.

CHAPTER THIRTY-NINE

THE DOOR CRASHES AGAINST THE WALL.

Storming into the house, he tosses the crumpled envelopes he retrieved from the mailbox onto the cluttered countertop. He doesn't bother to riffle through the pile. He knows what he'll find. More bills. More demands. More threats of property liens and black marks on credit reports. More reminders of a piss-poor mundane existence.

An existence he only wishes he could embrace.

The bills lie forgotten as his gaze shifts back to the peeling wallpaper, the cracks in the linoleum floor, the rust around the faucets, the water stains on the ceiling.

Wouldn't that be something special if he could worry about such trivialities?

He slams the door as forcefully as he threw it open. He paces the kitchen—back and forth—a caged animal unable to find rest. He wants the house to shake with every footfall. His teeth grind together, bone grinding against bone.

The sheriff.

He came right into the grocery store.

Right into my place of business. Just strolled in like he owned the place. And he was looking for something.

For someone.

He was asking questions.

He crashes out of the kitchen, another door bashing against another wall, and stands in the dimly lit living room. In the aftermath of his rage, the silence punctuates his shallow, frustrated breaths. The furniture casts long shadows that seem to creep closer, to grab at him, to claw at him.

He contemplates an ending to his misery.

That's what you did, Dad. You gave up. You turned your back on your responsibilities.

This isn't something he asked for. This isn't something he wanted. This is a responsibility that was thrust upon him.

And I was too weak to refuse. Too scared?

He closes his eyes, savoring—just for a moment—the thought of surrender. But the tranquility is fleeting, ripped away by a deeper compulsion that refuses to be silenced. It gnaws at his conscience, an insatiable drive that demands he keeps working.

Demands he keeps harvesting. Demands he keeps killing.

His hands tremble as he fights the internal battle, the yearning to find peace warring with the darker forces that drive him onward. His eyes open and fixate on the ancient wallpaper, the mundane sight grounding him momentarily. Yet the question lingers—should he just stop?

But I can't.

I won't.

And it's not weakness. It's not fear. It's strength.

This isn't what he wanted. He didn't want to hurt anyone. He didn't want to kill anyone. And he damn sure didn't want the police sniffing around his job.

The Wilson Island Ripper.

That's what the newspaper calls him.

But that's not my name.

No one else could do what he does. No one else *would*. A shiver travels down his spine.

What if they catch me? What if they lock me up?

If they do that, who would take care of—

"Mama?"

His words seem too loud in the quiet of the house.

He rushes up the stairs, two at a time, and throws open the door to his mother's bedroom. She's there, in bed, snuggled into the folds of her blankets. Her eyes, clouded with confusion, lift to meet his as he enters the room. The corners of her mouth curl into a sweet, childlike smile that belies the depth of her fragility.

"You came upstairs," he says.

"I couldn't rest downstairs. Not with the scratching. Not with the rats."

"We don't have rats."

"I heard them."

"Climbing the stairs by yourself. Mama, that's dangerous. If you fall again . . ."

"Your father's here with me."

But he's not. He hasn't been here for weeks.

"He wouldn't let me fall," she says.

He hesitates. "I just worry about you," he says.

He watches the smile on her lips falter, replaced by the worry that perpetually haunts the lines of her face. "I know you do. I heard a loud noise."

"It was nothing."

"I think it was Mr. No-Face."

There it is. That's *my name*.

"I'm going to go downstairs," he says, "make some supper."

She opens her mouth, but the terrible shrieking sound that emerges from her lips is not hers.

It's inhuman.

"Hungry!" she shrieks. "Hungry! Hungry! *Hungry! HUNGRY!*"

CHAPTER FORTY

WILLA SLIPS ON HER FADED denim jacket, the one with the frayed cuffs that, thanks to her "classic rocker" phase, is covered in dozens of patches. Bon Jovi. Ratt. Mötley Crüe. Savatage. Her tastes in music have changed drastically over the years. Now she prefers punk and blues-infused folk rock and even country. But the patches remain. She likes them. They remind her of who she used to be.

And, frankly, I kicked ass back then.

She's paired the jacket with a black top, black jeans with just the right amount of strategically placed rips and tears, and a pair of Keds. She gives herself a once-over in the mirror.

I still kick ass.

There's a bounce in her step as she descends the stairs. It's been a while since she felt that little thrill, the buzz she feels at this moment. A hint of guilt nibbles at the edges of the buzz, sure, but she squishes it down. She can feel guilty tomorrow. Tonight she wants to have a little fun.

"Going out again?" Her mom's voice floats from the living room. She's curled up on the couch with one of her books, a throw over her legs but not her bare feet. The piano—the one Mom plays sometimes when she's lamenting her own glory days—sits in the corner. The large window looks out across the perfectly manicured lawn, the drive, the quiet and well-lit neighborhood with houses that aren't too close together.

"Yeah, just for a bit." Willa barely skips a step, breezing past the doorway as quickly and nonchalantly as possible.

"You look cute," Mom calls after her. Her voice is bright, cheery, but tinged with concern.

"Thanks," Willa says, though the compliment takes her by surprise.

"Are you seeing Kenny?"

Willa sighs, stutters to a stop, and slowly wheels toward the living room, because she knows she's not getting out of the house without at least some discussion.

"No. Sarah's picking me up," Willa says, her tone light, attempting to assuage her mom's worry. "We're going to meet Dean, get a bite, go mini-golfing."

She doesn't mention that it was Dean who asked her to go out and she asked Sarah to be a third wheel because it made her feel a little more comfortable. If her mom thinks Sarah and Dean are a couple and that Willa's tagging along, well, so be it.

"Dean?" Mom puts her book aside and leans forward. "Huh. Haven't heard that name in a bit."

"Yeah," Willa says. She fiddles with a turquoise ring on her finger, a habit when her nerves kick in or when she feels cornered. "We ran into each other earlier and thought it might be fun to catch up."

"But no Kenny?"

Willa suppresses an eye-rolling instinct. Sometimes she forgets that her mother's not an idiot.

"No," she says. "Kenny's . . . He's got a lot on his mind right now. I don't think he wants to see me at the moment."

And I don't really want to see him.

Mom pushes the throw from her legs and slips off the couch. Willa senses the tension in her mother's stance, her protective instinct, tripped up with genuine worry, manifesting physically. "You need to talk to him, you know."

"I will."

"Be careful, okay?" It's less of a request, more of a gentle command.

"I will," Willa says again, even though she doesn't feel it. She kind of wants to do anything but be careful, even if it's just for a night.

"Extra careful, Willa." There's a tremor in her mother's voice. "It's not safe out there, especially now."

Willa looks back and, for the first time, notices the newspaper on the coffee table, the headline proclaiming that there's been a murder on their little island.

"I know, Mom." A reassuring smile graces Willa's lips despite the anxiety that flutters in her chest. "Sarah will be with me. And Dean. I'll be okay. Safety in numbers, right?"

Her mother shrugs an agreement that lacks conviction.

As Willa reaches for the doorknob, a creak from Dad's office catches her attention. The door eases open just enough for her father's figure to come into view. He stands there, framed by the glow of his desk lamp, his gaze fixed on her. His eyes, usually so full of warmth when he interacts with her, now offer no readable emotion. His silence speaks volumes. Willa meets his gaze, searching for the words he doesn't say, the warnings he doesn't voice. He knows she must walk her own path, make her own mistakes.

And, boy oh boy, have I made them.

She steps over the threshold, closing the door on her mother. There's a chill in the air, and Willa pulls her jacket tighter around her. For a moment, she's alone. No sign of Sarah. Her parents in the house, seemingly thousands of miles away, completely cut off from her.

She's both a little sad and relieved when she hears the Battleship's horn tooting from down the street. Headlights slice through the darkness. Sarah's old station wagon slides up to the curb. Through the veil of stickers, Willa sees Sarah behind the wheel, leaning over, looking toward her. Willa rushes out to the car.

Sarah calls out, "Get in, loser! Don't you know there's a murderer on the loose?"

As Sarah puts the car into gear and they pull away from the house, Willa lets out a breath she didn't realize she'd been holding.

CHAPTER FORTY-ONE

TAKING AIM AT THE RAGING gorilla's mouth, Willa steadies herself.

Neon lights flash. Miniature windmills spin. Putters clack against colorful golf balls. Golfers cheer and groan and laugh in equal measure. Bells ring and bumpers clack from a bank of vintage pinball machines. Somewhere, lost in a maze of old-school arcade cabinets, *Space Invaders* missile launches, and *Moon Buggy* jumps, Pac-Man *waka-waka*s his way through an armada of ghosts before warbling out his own piteous death cry.

Beach Bum Games and Family Fun is a throwback. The open-air arcade and mini-golf course has occupied the same spot for decades. Even though it's changed owners half a dozen times over the years, the hot spot hasn't evolved all that much. Embracing the simplicity and charm of nostalgia, Beach Bum has managed to avoid the ticket-for-prizes business model. Instead, it offers a glimpse of the beach boardwalk arcade of old, salty air, sandy floor, and all.

Willa shoots her shot, the orange golf ball racing across the green, banking into the two-by-four siding, and spinning across a banana-shaped bridge toward the gaping mouth of—

"Ugh! What's this fucking monkey's problem?!"

Helplessly, Willa watches as the ball strikes one of the gorilla's animated hands and bounces off course.

"He hates us." Sarah places her own golf ball on its mark and putts. The ball, batted away by the gorilla, joins Willa's in oblivion. "I think that's his job, why he's been put on this earth."

Since she was a little girl, Willa has been locked in a life-or-death feud with the simian guardian of Hole 10, courtesy of the course that meanders around the central arcade hub. The gorilla, his paint in a constant peeling state, climbs from a hole in the center of the green, his hulking arms rising and falling to protect his mouth, which is open in a silent roar. Not once has Willa conquered the ape, nor has she ever seen anyone else succeed without cheating.

Par four, my ass.

Dean, too, fails to feed the gorilla a golf ball, and they all decide to just mark the max number of strokes on the scorecard and move on. The gorilla, they all agree, should be the final hole, the ultimate challenge, but rhyme and reason don't really have a place at Beach Bum Games and Family Fun.

Crossing curved wooden bridges and navigating artificial waterfalls, they play through rounds punctuated by bizarre themes, from an underwater adventure complete with a spongy octopus hazard to a haunted graveyard where skeletons pop from behind tombstones, their jaws unhinged in silent laughter. Cement dinosaurs loom over a mushroom garden populated by ceramic gnomes. A garish fiberglass dragon, whose scales have faded from bright red to a dull and peeling pink, climbs a volcano at the heart of the course. Every hour on the hour (assuming the current owners remembered to fill the tank) the volcano erupts in a cloud of dancing bubbles.

Willa's glad the place hasn't changed, happy to see that the video games—a quarter of which are adorned with SORRY, FOLKS! IT'S BUSTED! signs—are relics of the past, that the ridiculous decorations are still on display, even that the gorilla is still unbeatable. Everything else—especially her plans and dreams—changes at a breakneck pace. It's nice to have a single bastion of normalcy standing lighthouse-tall at the center of madness. She's pleased to be here with Dean and Sarah, getting swept up in nonsense, even if it's just for a couple of hours.

The next obstacle is the windmill—a staple of mini-golf courses worldwide. The blades turn slowly in the middle of a field of bobbing firefly lights. Willa steps forward and, despite the lunacy of the surrounding fantastical landscape, focuses on lining up the perfect shot. She knows from experience that the windmill can smack a golf ball across the fairway with the skill of a professional hockey goalie defending the net. The shot has to be timed . . .

. . . just . . .

. . . right . . .

With a crack, the ball zooms across the green, zips between the windmill's blades, and clatters into the hole.

"Whoa!" Dean exclaims. "Hole in one!"

"Nice!" Sarah starts clapping, and a few other onlookers cheer as well.

Willa knows it's dumb, but she feels pride. Redeemed, almost.

Sure, sure. She'd been defeated by the ape-lord of Beach Bum Games. But so has almost everyone else who ever held a putter. And, while one obstacle had beaten her, she had conquered the next.

There's probably a lesson in here somewhere. Who knew Putt-Putt could be therapeutic?

Dean stands next to Willa as Sarah plays through. He's close, almost touching his shoulder to hers. With a half step, she could close the distance and brush up against him. She considers doing so as Sarah takes her first swing, her second. On the third swing, the windmill's blades narrowly clip the ball. On the fourth, Sarah sinks the shot. The moment passes, and Dean steps away to try his luck.

"Are you . . . blushing?" Sarah asks, smiling, as she slips up beside Willa.

"I'm not. It's just warm out, is all."

"Not really."

"Shut up."

It takes Dean three shots to bypass the windmill. They mark their scores, Willa taking the lead, and move on to a hole surrounded by cement mermaids and sharks. The mermaids, lounging in neon coral and faux sea-foam, grin sheepishly. The shark's painted eyes have a goofy, goggling look that renders him more comical than menacing.

"So," Sarah says. "Real talk."

"Oh no."

"Should we be worried?" Dean asks.

"Probably," Willa says.

She holds her breath in anticipation of what Sarah might say.

"Do you think there's a chance"—Sarah gestures with her putter, pointing from a family of four to a couple of teens eating pizza to some kids playing pinball to the guy renting out golf clubs and scorecards—"that there's a killer lurking amongst us?"

"Come again?" Willa asks.

"Think about it," Sarah says. "All these people, all these locals, all these tourists, all these smiling faces. Any one of them could be a murderer—*the* murderer. They might be blending in, but also be scoping out their next kill. Any one of them could be a wolf in sheep's clothing."

"A slasher," Dean says, "in dad shorts."

"Exactly!" Sarah snaps her fingers and points at Dean. "Yes. Adds a bit of excitement to the game, doesn't it?"

"You're weird," Willa says, trying to sound annoyed, but at least a little relieved that Sarah isn't playing some sort of embarrassing matchmaking game.

"And?" Sarah asks. "The paper said—"

"Oh, come on. You didn't read the paper," Willa interrupts.

"No." Sarah shrugs. "But I'm pretty sure I can infer the gist of it. There's a killer right here in our sleepy little town, cutting folks up and harvesting body parts. Everyone is a suspect. If shitty horror movies have taught me anything, it's that the quiet beach town is the perfect breeding ground for such a thing."

"You're thinking sharks," Dean says. He pats the head of the roaring cement shark. "Sharks aren't slashers."

"They're monsters," Sarah says. "Same difference."

"Can we talk about something else?" Willa asks. "Please? Anything else?"

Sarah peers behind Willa, rolls her eyes, and says, "I think you're about to get your wish."

Before Willa can react, she hears Kenny's voice.

"Hey, Willa."

Her heart sinks. All the fun she's been having rushes out of her body, a retreating wave, and when the surf comes crashing back, it's full of stress and responsibility and difficult decisions.

Willa turns as Kenny crosses the miniature greens without regard for the game or other players. His shoulders are broad but a little slouched. His tousled hair looks like it has wrestled with the sea breeze and lost.

"Jesus, Kenny," Sarah huffs. "Watch the course."

"Didn't realize we were playing on sacred ground," Kenny says.

"There's a path right there," Sarah says, her tone sharp as she gestures toward the designated walkway.

Kenny notices the path, dismisses it, and looks back toward Willa. Then at Sarah. Then at Dean.

"What is all this?" he asks, his gaze lingering on Dean.

"What does it look like?" Willa steps closer to him, wrenching his attention away from Dean. "We're playing mini-golf."

"I see that," Kenny says, "but what's *he* doing here?"

"What's it matter?" Willa's eyes tick to Sarah, then to Dean. "He's my friend, isn't he?"

"Apparently."

Did the temperature just drop?

"Can we help you with something, Kenny?" Sarah asks. Her knuckles are on her hips. She's small but fierce.

Kenny never takes his eyes off Willa. "Just thought I'd have a word with my girlfriend."

"Thought you two broke up," Sarah shoots back.

"Look," Dean says, "we're just trying to blow off a little steam, you know? Maybe now's not a good time."

"I bet." Now Kenny turns toward Dean, closes the space between them in a couple of steps. "I just bet it's not a good time. For you. Sorry if I interrupted your date or whatever this is."

"Leave him alone," Sarah says, sliding in between the two young men.

"Mind your own business," Kenny says.

Several people around the course now look toward the group. They pause mid-swing or in the middle of blasting *Galaga* space insects. In tight little circles, they whisper to each other, some of them hoping to witness a fight, maybe others muttering, *"There he is, the kid who almost ran over a murderer, the kid who found body parts spilled all over the street."*

"Kenny." Willa gently grabs his arm, pulls him a step back. "Why don't we go talk somewhere else, all right?"

Kenny's eyes are fixed on Dean, but after a tense moment he growls, "Fine," and turns away.

Willa exchanges a look with Sarah, whose expression is a mix of relief and frustration and maybe even a little annoyed amusement.

A standoff amid gorillas and flamingos and cartoonish sharks is, after all, more than a little ridiculous.

Willa guides Kenny down the designated path this time, past the mermaids and monkeys and sheet-metal UFOs, past the stares, the whispers, and the giggles of the other golfers. Her hand rests on his arm, the touch meant to pacify and assure. The parking lot is well lit, crowded with cars and with Beach Bum Games patrons either leaving for the night or just arriving. They finally stop next to Sarah's car. On the cracked pavement between them is a dropped ice cream cone, the cone also cracked, the chocolate-vanilla swirl melting and oozing.

"All right," Willa says. "You wanted to talk. So talk."

"What did I stumble on to here?" Kenny asks. "Are you on some sort of date with him?"

"No. We're just all hanging out."

"Okay, sure. Whatever you say. You're just hanging out with the guy who's been chasing after you, like, forever."

"No, he hasn't."

"Don't try to tell me that bullshit, all right?"

Willa only answers with a shrug.

"That's what I thought," Kenny says.

"Stop it." Willa's tone is sharp. "This isn't about Dean."

"I'm not so sure."

"What is that supposed to mean?"

"For all I know, maybe he's the one who knocked you—"

"Finish that sentence, and you're gonna get dropped right on your ass, I fucking promise you."

Anger seethes behind Kenny's eyes, but he's not foolish enough to challenge the threat. He knows her too well. She's not bluffing by a long shot.

"I thought," Willa says, "maybe you wanted to talk things out."

Kenny scoffs. "I don't know what I was trying to accomplish."

"How did you find me anyhow?"

"I wasn't stalking you, if that's what you're asking. Charlie Grimes and Jay Biggins clocked you, gave me a call."

A sleek black pickup is parked across the street. It shines, freshly waxed, under the streetlights. Across the top is a row of floodlights.

Willa notices the truck, recognizes it, and watches it for a second or two.

"Hello?" Kenny asks.

Willa tries to focus on Kenny.

"Sorry," she says.

"Am I boring you?" Kenny asks.

"I said I was sorry."

But she glances toward the truck again. She knows it's probably nothing. Wilson Island isn't that big. It's not that unusual to spot a vehicle you know. But something isn't sitting well with her about the—

"What do you keep looking at?" Kenny asks, following her line of sight.

"Nothing," she says.

Willa forces herself to look Kenny in the eye, but she can't force herself to talk. And Kenny returns the favor of silence.

What is he waiting for? she thinks. He *owes* me *an apology.*

She knows she's not going to get it.

Kenny has already spat out every word he has to say on the matter of Willa's grand designs to ruin his life, his facial muscles ticking like the hands of a clock wound too tight.

"What now?" he asks.

"You tell me," Willa says.

"This is all really messed up."

"Which part?"

"I'm not ready to be a father."

"You don't have to tell me that." Willa can't help herself. "You proved that the other night."

Kenny rocks back on his heels as if slapped. His eyes widen, then narrow. Willa winces, wishing she hadn't spoken so quickly. She didn't mean for her words to be so sharp.

Or did I?

Either way, she hadn't expected Kenny to be so stricken by what she'd said.

"You know what? Fine," Kenny spits out, bitterness lacing his tone. "If you don't think I can handle this, if you don't want me around, why'd you even bother saying anything? Just handle it on your own and leave me out of it."

He storms off.

The parking lot lights flicker, casting elongated shadows that dance after him, trying to lure him back, maybe in the way Willa should be trying to bring him back. She knows they're not finished, there's more they need to talk about, but she says nothing, makes no move to stop him. Soon enough the shadows give up their chase too as Kenny trudges into the night.

Willa sighs, looks up to the stars, then back across the street.

Now a figure stands next to the truck. Silently watching.

She takes a step toward the figure.

"Hey!" she calls. "You need something?"

The figure moves quickly, hopping in the truck, revving the engine, and speeding off.

CHAPTER FORTY-TWO

"**H**OW DID *THAT* GO?" Sarah asks.

"Oh, it was just lovely, trust me."

Willa walks past a bank of retro video games—*Battlezone* and *Mat Mania* and *Satan's Hollow*—to join Sarah and Dean at an umbrella-covered picnic table. Their putters lie across the table, acting as paperweights for scorecards. A trio of paper plates, loaded with Beach Bum's "famous" (for all the wrong reasons) "New York slice" pepperoni pizza, sit nearby, as do fountain sodas. One of the pizzas is little more than crust and pools of orange grease. Another is half eaten. The final slice is untouched.

"We got you some." Sarah tilts her head toward the pristine plate and the seat directly across from her. Next to Dean.

"I was gonna give you five more minutes," Dean says, wiping his mouth to conceal his smile, "and then all bets were off."

Willa sits and pulls the pizza and soda closer. "Thanks."

"Don't thank us yet," Sarah says, reaching out to slap the scorecards. "You lost."

"I didn't even play the last four holes," Willa says.

"That's right," Sarah says, "which is why you lost."

"Fair enough."

All around, families play golf, kids feed quarters to machines, boyfriends win teddy bears from claw machines for their girlfriends, teens throw clattering Skee-Balls up ramps or whack moles with padded cudgels or smack air hockey pucks back and forth at one another as music thumps in the background.

Life goes on, Willa thinks, *even when it's crumbling to pieces.*

Each of those quivering, pulsating, blood-spewing chunks of the existence that came before, the existence that has been shattered, keep on living, at least for a time. And if it's your life that's collapsed into the mess, only you can figure out which piece to pick up in your trembling fingers, which piece to nurture while the others wither and die and rot.

"Whatever you're thinking about"—Sarah leans across the table and touches Willa's wrist—"cut that shit out. Now."

"Sorry," Willa says.

She picks up her slice of soggy pizza, forces herself to take a bite. The cheese is thick, greasy, and chewy. The pepperoni is a little burned around the edges. The sauce is lukewarm and tangy. A just-okay slice overall, not quite on the level of trash pizza, at least. She swallows and coughs, covering her mouth with the back of her hand.

"The garlic," she says, "is strong with this one."

"Should've warned you," Dean says.

"Who cares?" Sarah takes a bite of her own slice. "I'm not planning on kissing anyone tonight. Are *you*?"

Instantly, Dean looks down at the crust on his plate.

Under the table, Willa kicks Sarah's shin. "Ow!" Sarah jumps in her seat.

And the three of them laugh, letting a moment of joy seep into the cracks running between the chunks of Willa's broken life, filling them like glue, and Willa thinks that if she can just hold it all together, just keep from moving and from letting go while the glue dries, she might be able to salvage her existence. She laughs a little too long, a little too loudly, and the laughter turns like milk left in the sun. She feels her mouth twitching into a frown, her eyes burning with tears.

Dean puts a hand on her shoulder, squeezing gently. "Hey," he says, and he's going to follow it with mawkish words of comfort.

It's going to be all right. We're here for you. You're not alone in this.

But when Willa turns toward him, when their eyes meet, he lets whatever he was going to say remain unspoken.

"Hey yourself," Willa replies, her smile twitching back against the frown.

For a moment, the three of them sit in silence, which expands into something bigger and deeper. It drowns out the sounds of video games and air hockey and music and golf. It fills the space between them.

"So," Sarah says at last. "What's next?"

"Next?" Willa asks. "I'm not sure. I'll figure something out."

"I'm not talking about what comes next in *life*," Sarah says. "I'm talking about tonight. You guys want to get out of here?"

"And do what?" Willa asks.

"I heard about a bonfire party on the beach," Dean says halfheartedly.

"Oh. Who's throwing it?" Sarah asks.

"Not sure. Charlie Grimes and Jay Biggins, I think."

"Ugh, no. Fuck that," Sarah says, shutting the suggestion down.

Dean lets out the breath he was holding.

"Nobody cares," Willa says, "do they? There's been a murder. The killer hasn't been found. They're still out there. And everyone carries on like everything's just fine."

"It'll get worse," Dean remarks.

"Hoo boy, you two are just rays of light in the cold, dark night," Sarah says. "Come on. Let's at least go for a walk along the waterway. If I sit here any longer, this pizza grease will congeal in my stomach—I might solidify completely and they'll just put me out as another golf course decoration."

Chair legs scrape against concrete as Willa, Sarah, and Dean push away from the table. Even amid the music and bells and whistles and digital laser blasts, the noise seems loud and grating. Ditching their plates but keeping their sodas, they head out the front gates and walk along the sidewalk bordering the parking lot. Willa watches the street, head on a swivel.

"Relax," Sarah says. "I think Kenny probably went home."

"I'm not worried about Kenny," says Willa.

"Most refreshing thing you've said all night."

The concrete path, lined with thick chains painted black and posts painted white, borders the waterway. Several luxurious yachts are docked along the path, silent, dark, gently rocking in the water. Painted on transoms are names like *The Simple Life* and *My Other Car* and *High Roller*. A few clusters of seagulls float quietly on the water. Distantly, the buoy bells ring in the night.

Willa glances over her shoulder, watching the path behind them.

"Seriously," Sarah says. "What are you looking for?"

"Earlier, I saw someone watching me. Kenny and me."

Sarah turns to look down the path, dramatically craning her neck for a better look.

"Well, there's no one there now." She looks to her companions. A mischievous smirk plays across her lips. "You know what? I'm gonna take a restroom break."

"Wait—" Willa starts, realizing she's being set up for some alone time with Dean.

"Nature waits for no woman!" Sarah says as she hurries across the lot toward the public restrooms. She looks back playfully before stepping through the door.

Willa and Dean look out across the moored boats, out across the water, as they wait.

And wait.

Sarah is sure taking her sweet time.

After a few minutes of awkwardness, Dean speaks. "Can I see you again?" The question hovers between them. "I mean, can *we* see each other again?"

"Dean, I—" Willa hesitates. *Just say yes, dummy.* The voice in her head sounds a lot like Sarah.

It's not that simple. There it is, her own voice, echoing in her skull.

"Let's . . . let's talk about it another time," she finally says.

"Another time," Dean repeats, looking down and nodding as he steps back.

"Things are just . . . complicated right now."

Dean stands before her, his brow knitted in concern—or is it confusion? "You want to talk about that, then?"

"Want to? Yes."

"But you're not going to."

Willa's laugh is short, humorless, more a hiccup of hysteria than anything else. "No. Not yet."

"I get it," Dean assures her, though the crease between his brows deepens. "Take all the time you need."

Sarah finally saunters back to their gathering. "You two get this figured out yet or what?"

Willa and Dean look at each other. "Or what," they say, speaking as one.

CHAPTER FORTY-THREE

*M*AYBE, KENNY THINKS, *I SHOULD* have just fucking apologized.

He stomps down the street, away from Beach Bum Games and Family Fun, past the bicycle and boogie board rentals, past Java Joint. His hands are shoved into his pockets, his shoulders hunched.

That's why I went looking for her, isn't it? To apologize.

He'd intended to tell her he was sorry, that he was an asshole, that they would figure everything out, that their lives would still work out.

But, hell, she was on a *date*.

She could deny it if she wanted, but he knew better. Dean Kramer's been sniffing after her for years. Always waiting to swoop in like a pelican scooping fish from the sea. He must've sensed their argument, felt it in the ether, and jumped in as soon as he saw an opening.

Not a pelican. A fucking vulture.

...

Mr. No-Face watches.

He hangs back, wrapped in the shadows. His vision is blurry under the milky, opaque mask, but his eyes follow Kenny's every move. Anger sharpens his vision.

Kenny fucking Smythe.

There are several people on the shit list.

The sheriff, for asking questions at work, hunting for him.

Barry Hadley, dead or not, for fighting back, for taking him by surprise, for putting him off his game.

Why couldn't he just lie down and die quietly, with a little dignity?

His own father for saddling him with the bloodletting, with the harvest, with such gruesome and crushing responsibility.

Why couldn't he have just carried through on the promises he made?

He placed himself on the list too, for making so many mistakes, letting his nerves and unease get the better of him.

Why am I such a fuckup?

Kenny Smythe had earned *his* shit list position for nearly running Mr. No-Face over, making him drop his harvest, and drawing unnecessary attention to his important work.

His important work.

My important work.

Work passed from father to son, like a holy rite. Kenny's interference, intentional or not, was almost blasphemous.

It's Kenny's fault Mr. Bennings had to die.

His fault. Maybe.

But the knife was in my hand. And whose fault is that?

Sherrif Buck. Kenny Smythe. Barry Hadley. Mr. No-Face's father. Mr. No-Face himself.

Two of the people on the shit list are already dead.

One poses too much of a threat. One—himself—still has a job to do.

That leaves only Kenny.

And he certainly, one hundred percent deserves to die.

Aside from Kenny, the street is empty. Mr. No-Face could slip out, rush up behind him, slap a gloved hand over his throat, stab a razor-sharp blade into the small of his back, and drag him into the alleys to finish his bloody work.

One second he would be there, the next he would be gone.

Mr. No-Face clenches his fists, feeling the urge to run after Kenny and make him pay for what he's done, for ruining everything, for sowing so much pain and anguish over the years.

...

Kenny kicks a half-crushed soda can down the sidewalk. The metal scrapes along before coming to a fitful stop. He comes up behind it and kicks it again. The irony.

Kenny feels like, now more than ever, he's just pointlessly trying to kick life into his relationship with Willa, into his own forward trajectory, into his plans to get away, but everything keeps skittering to a pathetic, crushed-can ending. After the fourth kick, he leaves the can in peace.

I shouldn't have said that about Dean.

The accusation, unfinished and lingering in the air, may have been a nail in the coffin of his time with Willa. At the very least, it's going to take a lot of work to make that up to her. And he isn't sure he has the energy to try.

...

Mr. No-Face's fingers slip around the handle of one of the many blades hanging from his belt. His grip tightens, the leather gloves creaking. The muscles in his legs tense.

Kenny will be missed. His death won't go unnoticed. This might be kicking the hornet's nest, seriously tempting fate.

But with everything spiraling wildly around him, he wants to grab the steering wheel and take control again.

I'm in charge, he tells himself. *And killing Kenny fucking Smythe will prove it.*

A sleek black pickup cruises down the street, and Mr. No-Face stops in mid-step and reverses course, reeling backward into the concealing darkness of the alley. The truck moves slowly along, keeping a good distance from Kenny but definitely keeping pace.

Could it be one of his friends? Or someone with a beef against him? Whoever it is, they aren't necessarily hiding. They don't care if Kenny spots them.

Maybe they want him to see?

Mr. No-Face watches from a safe distance, still concealed, as Kenny and the truck turn a corner and disappear from sight. The moment of hesitation was all he needed for clarity of purpose to sink back into his skull. He can't risk any more mistakes, or invite additional trouble into his life.

Back to the original plan.

There are plenty of other people on Wilson Island no one will miss. He should know. He is one of them.

...

The moon hangs overhead, a pale, watchful eye, and one full of judgment. Kenny's shadow stretches out, distorted, before him. The silhouette, he thinks, doesn't look like it belongs to him. Just like the life he's living—the breath he draws—doesn't feel like his own anymore. It's a caricature. Misshapen like the drawings one might commission from any artist on the pier during a Saturday afternoon.

Kenny hears footsteps coming from somewhere behind him. He turns his head, half expecting, half hoping to see Willa chasing after him. The sidewalk, though, is empty. Willa's gone back to her date/not-date.

He's alone.

Only, he hadn't imagined those footsteps, had he?

He snorts at the thought. He would just about dare anyone to follow him, to step up on him, to start static. The way he feels right now, he'd welcome it.

Or so he tells himself.

He quickens his pace, trying to outrun the nagging feeling that he's *not* alone.

Willa's dad is not someone to fuck around with. Kenny knew it when he started dating the man's daughter, and that knowledge is a white-hot poker in his brain now that they've broken up. If Wade Hanson caught wind of everything that's happened—

Why wouldn't he? He knows everything else going on around the island.

—what would stop him from sending one of his guys to "have a word" with Kenny?

Fuck.

For all he knows, Willa might have actually *wanted* her dad to send that big bearded gorilla to knock some sense into Kenny. Or, more likely, just knock the shit out of him.

He glances back once more.

A black pickup cruises past, moving slow, and the driver watches Kenny.

Kenny almost yells a warning or a threat.

He swallows it down, though.

Maybe, just maybe, he sees a shadow, as twisted and warped as his own, pull back into the darkness of an alleyway.

Shrinking away from the passing truck, just like him.

He tries to laugh it off.

Accompanied by the soft scuff of his shoes on the sidewalk, Kenny moves along. His pace is brisk.

The streetlights, buzzing overhead, flicker and gutter.

...

Just a few blocks away is the Tugboat Saloon.

Mr. No-Face hangs out in the alley, where all the drunks who can't wait for the restroom come to piss and puke. It reeks here of stale beer and urine and vomit. Silently, he curses himself for not going after Kenny Smythe as he'd planned, curses himself for letting self-doubt and cowardice get the better of him.

Every few minutes, the doors of the Tugboat swing open and patrons spill out, accompanied by the sounds of yacht rock or country music. Mr. No-Face leans against the wall and lowers his head as the drunks amble past. If they happen to notice him, they might dismiss him as one of their own, losing his battle to keep his supper and drinks down for the night.

A handful of bar-goers stumble out.

Then another.

And another.

When Grady Weeks finds his way out the door, Mr. No-Face is almost at the end of his patience. He has anticipated this moment, though. After working with the man at the Save-a-Ton for so long, he knows his habits fairly well. Grady frequents the Tugboat a few times a week, more when he's feeling especially stressed. And today, after the sheriff's ham-fisted questions, well, he's bound to be on edge.

As Grady staggers past, Mr. No-Face slips out, grabs him, and yanks him back into the alley.

Grady's no small fry, and to ensure he doesn't fight back, not like Barry Hadley, No-Face jams a scalpel four inches deep into the man's temple. Grady's eyes roll around in his head, one up, one down, both blooding over. The alley serves its purpose well, because Grady does piss himself and upchuck down the front of his shirt.

"I'm really sorry about this, Grady," Mr. No-Face says.

If Grady can hear him, though, it will only be a muffled gargling sound.

Mr. No-Face likes Grady, but he's a perfect candidate for sacrifice. The sheriff suspects him. At least, it seems so based on the questions asked at the store. Grady knows it himself. He bitched about it all afternoon. And if Grady vanishes, the sheriff might very well think he skipped town to avoid getting caught.

Lowering Grady—who is kicking weakly and fitfully—to the ground, Mr. No-Face quickly searches the man's pockets for his car keys. He'll grab his vehicle, throw the body in the back, and find someplace secluded to do his work.

"What do you want from him?" he asks.

His voice is still muffled, but he knows that this time he will be understood.

"What should I take?"

Nothing.

The answer startles him.

"Aren't you hungry?"

I don't want this one.

"A body's a body."

This one was for you, *not me.*

He looks the corpse over, trying to figure out why he is being refused. He can't understand. She's never been so picky before. Except for when it came to—

His father.

And he knows damn well how that turned out.

CHAPTER FORTY-FOUR

THE HEAT OF THE BONFIRE washes across the Warlock's back as he leaves the chatter, the laughter, and the hip-hop music behind. The kids pay him no mind. They've almost forgotten he was ever there. The cases of beer, the bottle of Jack, and the joints must have, in their minds, just magically appeared. And his hand sliding a wad of crumpled bills into his jeans pocket, that's just the way the Warlock likes it.

That's what he tells himself, anyhow. *I mean, they could have invited me to stay.*

Trudging across the beach, feeling the sand pull at his boots, he winds his way through the tangles of pale, scattered driftwood.

He knows most of those little scumbags by name. Evan and Kyle. Rob and Alexandra. Lisa and Megan. There were a dozen others, some he recognized, others most likely out-of-towners the group picked up like pilot fish. If they'd asked him to share a drink and a smoke with them, he might have considered it.

When he finally looks back, they're nothing but shadows, moving around a great ceremonial flame.

They're not concerned with death. Not in the moment, not at the hands of a murderer. Not ever. Safety in numbers.

But the Warlock, as always, is alone.

Slipping and shuffling up the slope, he finds his way to the crest of a dune. Looking to his left, he gazes out across the vast, black, whispering expanse of the ocean. The Undersea, he calls it, named after one of his favorite Dungeons & Dragons settings. To his right, packed sand stretches out before him, dotted with more gnarled driftwood and marked with crisscrossing tire tracks. The Point, where kids park to hook up. He refers to it as the Deep Dark Lie, named after a mix of his own uneasiness with all things related to love.

No one is parked here tonight, though. A group of kids partying around a raging bonfire is one thing while a killer is on the loose. A pair of kids peeling each other out of their panties and boxer briefs in the back of a Ford Fiesta . . . well . . . that's the stuff of organ-harvesting urban legends.

The Warlock faces the open water and plops his ass down on the shifting sand. He watches the dark abyss seething before him, stretching into forever, and the hiss of the surf sounds like whispered promises. Digging into his jacket pocket, he drags out a plastic baggie filled with weed, paper, and a light. He rolls a joint with ease, flares up, breathes deep, and tries to decipher what the Undersea is telling him.

Smoke roils up around him, and he stares through the veil, letting his mind drift. "What secrets do you hold for me tonight?" he mutters into the dark.

And the Undersea replies, *I got nothing, bro.*

But there is someone moving out there, isn't there? A single figure, standing on the water's edge.

So still it might be a crooked piece of driftwood in the roiling surf.

Sea spray paints the figure in mist.

A ghost.

A phantom.

Maybe it's just Madhouse Quinn. He's been out here before, right? But . . .

. . . when?

Silently he mouths the name—*Madhouse*—and expects the figure to sense him, to turn in his direction, shamble this way, and bum a drag from him. The phantom doesn't react. There is no reply save for the unceasing crash of the waves.

A sudden sense of familiarity rattles him. He knows what's happening. As sure as he knows the kids at the beach party, and Madhouse Quinn, as sure as he knows all the names he's given his sword hanging on the wall back in his bedroom. He's been here before. It's déjà vu, writhing like the smoke that rings his head, squirming through his mind, setting his nerves to twitching.

"Hey!" he calls out, letting his voice bounce across the sand. "What're you doing out there?"

The figure doesn't respond, just stares out across the darkness.
"What are you looking at?"
No answer.

With another pull on the joint, the Warlock rambles to his feet, patting the omnipresent grit off his clothes. His boots sink into the sand as he slide-shambles down the sloping dune. Regaining a steady stance at the bottom, he squints in the direction of the figure.

It's a man.

He knows it now.

He's seen him before.

In that very spot.

The Warlock shuffles toward him. "Hey, man. What are you staring at out there?"

He looks to the darkness of the water, sees nothing.

Can he not hear me over the surf?

Waves roll in and recede, frothing around the man's feet.

He doesn't react. Doesn't move.

The sand is wet under the Warlock's feet. He looks across the water again.

And when he glances toward the shoreline once more, the figure is gone. He looks up and down the beach, but sees no sign of the man, no sign of wet footprints.

It was driftwood, along with the effects of the weed. Must have been. Pulled away with the tide.

Shells roll in with the foam, clicking together like tiny bones in a flooded graveyard. The Warlock watches them, eyes tracing their aimless dance, and this is familiar too.

CHAPTER FORTY-FIVE

FOR THE FIRST TIME IN almost a year, Willa plucks at the strings of her old acoustic guitar. She sits in her comfy corner chair, the teddy bear exiled to the bed to act as an audience. She strums out a fragmented melody, a song she was writing before her world went belly-up. She hums lyrics she doesn't quite remember how to sing.

Sharp, sudden pain lances through Willa's stomach, traveling through her muscles, up her spine, down her arms, and through her hands. Her fingers twitch on the string, ending the half-formed song on a jarring note. She gasps and doubles over. The guitar clatters to the floor.

"What—"

She presses her hand against her belly as she struggles to her feet. Her legs feel weak, like they might buckle. Her vision goes blurry with the pain.

Only it's not pain. Not exactly.

It's hunger.

I'm starving.

Only it's not Willa who's hungry. Not exactly.

Leaving her guitar on the floor, leaving her bear on the bed, Willa wobbles out of her bedroom. She keeps one hand over her stomach, the other gripping the handrail, as she descends on shaky legs.

Kenny sits at one end of the kitchen table, Dean at the other. They bore holes into one another's eyes, like they're having a staring competition, and don't blink when Willa enters the room. Silverware and dishes litter the table, but they're covered with dust.

Only it's not dust. Not exactly.

"Something's wrong," Willa says, her voice little more than a whisper.

The emptiness in her stomach sucks at her. She feels like she might collapse into herself. Her legs finally give out in three unsteady steps toward the refrigerator. She falls against it, knocking magnets to the floor, leaning against it, her cheek pressed against the cold stainless steel.

Kenny and Dean never move, don't even look at her.

Willa grabs the fridge handle and yanks the door open. Cool air hits her face. The nothingness that's inside her stomach expands and contracts, palpitating in excitement.

There, a plastic container of leftover chicken—she tears off the lid and plunges her fingers into the cold meat. She shoves handful after handful into her mouth, biting her lower lip a couple of times in her fervor, barely chewing before swallowing.

Not enough.

She reaches deeper into the fridge, knocking over the ketchup bottle and cans of soda, pulling out a package of raw ground beef. The packaging leaves a ring of congealing blood on the shelf. The logical part of her mind screams in protest, but it's drowned out by the deafening roar of her hunger. With her teeth, she tears the plastic wrapper from the meat, and wolfs down mouthful after mouthful of bloody beef.

Still not enough.

She drops the Styrofoam plate that held the beef. Her fingers, the back of her hand, are sticky with cold, nearly jellied blood. She regards her hand, pale and trembling. She turns it over, looking at it curiously. It's the same hand she used to play her nearly forgotten song earlier, but now she barely recognizes anything. Drool spills down her bloodied chin.

Kenny and Dean continue to stare at one another.

Willa raises her hand to her mouth.

And now Kenny and Dean are drooling too, their saliva dripping to a tabletop covered in—

The dust of bone.

Willa sinks her teeth into the meat of her hand, ripping the skin, tearing the muscle away.

...

Willa's eyes snap open.

She stares at the ceiling for a few seconds. Then she tries without success to blink away the memory of yet another bad dream.

Gently, she runs a trembling hand over her stomach.

She wonders if these increasingly intense nightmares are trying to tell her something. Or maybe all the news about the killer—the Ripper—is kicking itself around in her head while she sleeps. Could she just be trying to make sense of it all?

Whatever the case, she wants nothing to do with the message. She just wants a good night's sleep for a change.

The worst part, one that's not imaginary? She's *so* hungry.

THURSDAY

THE NIGHT BELONGS TO THE MEAT PUPPETS.

CHAPTER FORTY-SIX

TALL PALMS LINE THE STREET where Sheriff Buck parks in the shade. He leans back in the leather seat. The windows of the county-issued SUV are rolled down a few inches to let the breeze from the waterfront roll through, but he still has the AC blasting. Through mirrored aviators, he watches as morning life on Wilson Island gets underway.

A family of tourists parades past, sporting wide-brimmed hats and bright and comfy attire, loaded down with bags full of towels and sunscreen and bottles of water. They pause to take photos with the miniature Cape Jordan Lighthouse replica, then hurry on their way, probably going to grab breakfast at DeeDee's Waterside or catch a ferry tour of the banks.

A heavy-duty pickup chugs past, hauling a massive, gleaming fishing boat. The boat, the sheriff notes, is a late model, worth probably three times the truck's value.

Farther along, several bronzed local teens amble by, surfboards either tucked under their arms or carried on their heads. Buck knows them—maybe not by name, but he recognizes them just the same. A bunch of surf-weasels who've whiled away the morning hours riding waves and are now heading back in to spend the day drinking beers, getting high, and napping.

An RV trundles down the street, heading away from the half dozen or so RV parks on the east side of town. Moving on to someplace else. Buck's always thought that maybe, when he finally retires, he might get one of those big recreational vehicles for himself, roam the countryside.

Maybe he'd even find someone to take the ride with him. He does have his eye on someone. But that's a concern for another time.

He wonders if these campers are leaving town because of the murders, the threat of a killer in their midst.

The dispatch radio crackles. *"You there, Sheriff?"* Tess's voice buzzes over the airwaves.

Buck snaps up the mic. "Where else would I be?"

"Very funny. Listen, Anita Weeks has been calling all morning, says she really needs to talk to you. Grady's wife. I told her you'd return her call when you got back to the office later, but she says it can't wait."

The butcher's beloved, calling with some urgency, just a day after Buck visited him in the Save-a-Ton.

"Text me her number," Buck says, "and I'll call her back right now."

"Will do."

Fingers drumming on the steering wheel, Buck waits for the number to pop through.

Outside the SUV, folks watch boats of all shapes and sizes cruising the waterway. Others take a load off on the covered swings lining the sidewalk. Still others pop into the Deepwater Dive Shop or Island Cupcakes or Smith Brothers Cigar and Pipe. A teenager skateboards down the sidewalk, wheels clattering on pavement. An elderly couple strolls arm in arm, their pace slow and measured.

His phone chimes, and Anita Weeks's number appears on the screen, along with an all-caps message from Tess.

SHE SOUNDS WORRIED.

Buck's thumb presses the underlined number, and the call screen springs to life.

Anita answers the call on the first ring. *"Hello?"* Her voice is anxious, expectant, and eager.

"Anita, it's Buck. I hear you've been trying to reach me."

"Oh, thank you for calling. It's Grady."

"What about him?"

"He didn't come home last night."

"From work?"

"From the Tugboat. He goes there to meet some of the guys every Wednesday. But he's usually home by ten. I tried calling him, but he's not answering. I don't know where he is. I'm worried sick."

Buck frowns. He shifts in his seat, trying to do the impossible and find a brief moment of comfort. He looks at the phone, trying to will his incredulous look across the line to Anita Weeks.

Vanishing without a trace, right after I nudged him with a few questions? Have to say, more than a little suspicious.

But Buck doesn't *have* to say it, not at this moment, not while Anita is in such a frenzy. So he holds his tongue and saves his self-righteous ah-has for later. *I'm not a total asshole.* "You think maybe he tied one on? Maybe he caught a ride with one of his friends, bunked down with them."

Three teenage girls in sunglasses and sundresses saunter by. They carry shopping bags from the boutique down the way, laughing and gossiping as they flounce along.

"Getting drunk like that is not his style. I called everyone I know he hangs out with. They said he left the bar on his own, near about nine forty-five or so, just like always."

"Well, I'm sure there's a simple explanation. All right? I don't want you worrying too much."

"Buck, with all the talk—"

"I know, I know, but this is nothing until it's something."

"I'm not sure that makes me feel any better."

Pat Neely, all of eighty years old, wearing only headphones, Speedo shorts, and roller skates, rockets past, doing a spin in the parking lot. His dark, wrinkled skin glistens with an overabundance of tanning oil. He wiggles his fingers as he zooms past the SUV.

"Let me ask you this, Anita. Was . . . well . . . was Grady acting like himself before he went out? I mean, he wasn't acting unusual or anything, was he?"

"No."

"If there was anything out of the ordinary, it might be worth knowing."

"He said you came to talk to him at the market."

"Yes, that's right."

"He said you were asking him about Barry and Allison, about the killings."

Buck holds on to his words for a second, then says, "Yup. Just idle conversation. Doing my due diligence."

Denny Danvers, that drug-dealing burnout shithead the local kids call "the Warlock," shuffles along the sidewalk, head down. He looks up, spots the sheriff's SUV, and quickly turns to walk the other way. *Good, keep on walking, fuckhead.*

"He just thought it was a little odd, I guess. He said you asked where he was the night it happened. That you thought he might be involved or something."

"Just routine questioning, Anita."

"Well, coming to him was ridiculous. He was home, with me, the whole night. And even if he hadn't been, there isn't anyone on the island who would ever think he had something to do with anything like that, not in a million years. So that was uncalled for."

"He was upset, though . . . with me coming by?"

"Maybe a little, but who wouldn't be, under the circumstances. I told him he was just being foolish."

"Anita, tell you what: I'm going to start looking into this. I'll drive by the Tugboat, ask around. You sit tight and try not to worry, all right?"

"*Thank you, Sheriff.*"

Buck disconnects the call and tosses the phone onto the dash. Maybe he'd struck a little too close to home during his conversation with Grady. Had he gotten spooked? Skipped town until things cooled down a little? Shit.

Buck throws the SUV into gear and pulls away from the shade of the palms, thinking.

CHAPTER FORTY-SEVEN

ONE LAST WALK ALONG THE sandy beach trail, one more quick loop around the park to say good-bye to their transient neighbors, and then Rich and Lilly Gingham will hit the road.

The next stop on their journey is Roanoke Island, a little under four hours away, farther up the banks. Rich has booked space at a fifteen-lot RV park, another spot with laundry facilities, showers, biking and hiking trails, and canal access for canoes and kayaks. This one will also have a nice pool, where Lilly plans to spend most of her time.

Rich may not know how to thoroughly enjoy a relaxing retirement, what with his grilling and canoeing and biking, but she most certainly does.

Of course, Rich already has plans to visit the Lost Colony at Roanoke.

For as long as Lilly has known him, her husband has been an avid history buff. One of his favorite stories is the legend of the Lost Colony. In the late summer of 1587, more than one hundred English settlers arrived on the coast of what is now North Carolina. Just three years later, those settlers had completely vanished. The only clue to their fate was the word *Croatoan* carved on a wooden post near their settlement.

Lilly's a little surprised this wasn't the first stop on their journey, but never really brought it up. When Rich had suggested the Outer Banks, she knew what he really meant was the Lost Colony. Maybe he's trying to save it for as long as possible, let his anticipation build.

Some part of her husband, Lilly knows, clings to a childlike belief that *he* will somehow be the one to solve the great American mystery. He'll take one step onto Roanoke Island and all the pieces of the puzzle—every clue that historians and scholars and archaeologists and tens of thousands of tourists have missed over the years—will fall right into place.

She loves him for his delusions. Maybe she's delusional too, because a part of her hopes he will indeed solve the mystery.

As the sun rises over the horizon, the campground stirs. Temporary residents emerge from their RVs and tents, stretching stiff limbs and breathing deep of the brisk, salty air. Coffee brews in electric pots. Pop-Tarts and crackers with peanut butter are munched with abandon. Eggs and bacon sizzle over sputtering campfires or upon propane stoves.

Rich and Lilly have spent the morning prepping the RV for the road. Campsite clutter is cleared. Dishes are washed and securely stored. Doors and drawers are latched. Tanks are emptied. Water lines are disconnected. With the chores completed, Rich and Lilly leave the vehicle in the shadows of their secluded spot—a location Rich has been quite proud of—and walk the site to say their farewells.

Ray, a retiree, devoted camping enthusiast, and golfer with whom Rich shared beers a couple of nights ago, waves and walks in their direction.

Not even 8 a.m., and he's already got a cold one in hand, Lilly muses. *I've really got to up my retirement game.*

"You two heading out?" Ray asks.

"Yeah, I guess this is it," Rich replies.

"Sorry to hear that. It was damn good meeting you. Hopefully we run into each other again somewhere down the road. Let me give you my number and email so we can keep in touch, yeah?"

"You better give it to me," Lilly says.

Rich knows better than to argue. He's never been good at keeping in touch with anyone. Lilly plugs Jack's information—and that of his wife—into her phone. They shake hands and trade hugs.

Maybe they *will* see each other again. There are a lot of roads, yes, and plenty of RV parks, but there's always the chance they'll somehow travel in the same circles.

Heading back to their RV, they wave and call good-byes to the community of campers:

"You two take care of each other out there."

"Sure nice meeting you."

"If you're ever in our neck of the woods, you've got a place to stay."

"Take my word for it, you've gotta try Granite Hot Springs. It'll change your life."

Returning to their "home on the road," Lilly pulls the door open and takes one last look around the campsite. The morning air is crisp and filled with the scent of pine and dew. The other campers—the ones who aren't sleeping in—are busy with their morning rituals. Some are brewing coffee over small camp stoves, while others are folding up their tents or chatting quietly in the soft glow of the rising sun. They've exchanged their farewells, knowing they're almost certainly never going to cross paths with the Ginghams again. Their vacationing lifestyle is temporary and transient and fleeting, and so are the "friendships" they've formed. As soon as someone drifts out of their orbit, they are replaced by another traveler, each new face erasing the memory of the last.

At least, that's how Lilly sees it.

It makes her a little sad.

Rich takes the driver's seat, wiggles a bit to ensure his comfort. Lilly grabs her iPad from the couch, tosses it on the dash, and takes the passenger's spot. Rich reaches over and gives her knee a squeeze.

"Next stop—"

A gloved hand clamps down on Rich's forehead. A hooked knife tears across his throat. Blood jumps from Rich's throat and cascades down his shirt.

Her husband begins kicking and spasming. His fingers slide to his throat, feeling feebly at the warm, gushing blood, at the tattered meat of his skin. A gurgling rasp escapes his lips.

Lilly tries to scream, but the sound catches in her throat and comes out as a wheezing gasp. She turns in her seat, pressing her back against the passenger-side window, trying to push herself as far as possible from—

He has no face!

He has no face!

He has no face!

Where their attacker's face should be is a pale, bony covering, chalk white, with ridges and contours that create only the vaguest outline of eyes and a nose. A long, segmented tube, also made of a bone-like material, hangs where his mouth should be, the sections clacking together. The faceless man pulls his hand away from Rich's head, the knife away from his throat. Shredded skin clings to the blade.

Rich's fingers flex on the steering wheel, and to Lilly it almost looks like he's typing, his fingers jumping in weird patterns. He slides down in the seat, his legs twitching.

Now the scream starts to free itself from Lilly's throat.

Quiet and rasping and feeble at first but building.

"Ahh—"

Grunting, the faceless man springs toward Lilly, clamping his hand over her mouth, slamming the back of her head against the glass, driving the point of the blade into her left eye.

Once, twice, three times.

He stabs so deep, his knuckles crunch into her orbital bones, and he twists the knife to silence the scream building beneath his gloved hand.

Lilly's thoughts turn to mush.

There's something in my eye!
There's something in my . . .
There's something . . .

And then, even though her body twitches, her thoughts still.

Mr. No-Face grabs the now-dead man by the shoulder and yanks him out of the driver's seat. He lets the body fall next to the passenger seat, by the dead woman. With a bloody, gloved hand, he hooks his fingers under the seam of his mask and tugs it off. He gags and retches. He slides behind the wheel, noticing a pair of cheap plastic sunglasses and a faded ball cap on the dash. He grabs both items, puts them on. He throws the RV into drive and pulls away.

By some miracle, the other campers haven't even looked in their direction.

Next stop: anywhere but here.

CHAPTER FORTY-EIGHT

TWENTY-FIVE YEARS AGO, THE *Wilson Island Gazette and Examiner* was printed on-site, in the ill-lit back room behind the main offices. The chunky, clunking, wheezy press worked day and night, churning out page after page. The walls were covered in thick, sootlike ink. Old newspapers were stacked haphazardly on every surface. The air smelled of grease and a faint burning scent.

And it was just the way Rachel's dear old dad liked it.

Of course, back then, the paper came out five days a week—Sunday, Tuesday, Wednesday, Thursday, and Friday—without fail.

Her dad used to bring her to the office with him, letting his secretary look after her while he worked, acting as publisher, editor, and sometimes reporter. Rachel barely remembers all that, though sometimes, when she wanders around the empty offices, she catches hints of sounds, of smells, that take her back.

Now the printing press is silent and still, an old, bulky relic, the grease long gone thick with dust. No darkroom in the back, reeking of chemicals. No layout table with X-acto knives and glue and rulers to help position articles and headlines.

These days, only one employee runs the show—Rachel herself, acting as publisher, editor, reporter, and delivery manager.

The *Gazette* comes out only once a week, with supplemental materials posted online as time allows. Usually the paper is printed in Morehead City. Uploaded by 3 p.m. on Tuesday, delivered to the offices by 5 a.m. the next morning. Deliveries still work pretty much the way they once did, only it's Rachel herself who makes sure local businesses and the handful of loyal subscribers receive the latest issue every Wednesday morning.

She's like a kid with a paper route.

This week, though, she put in an express order, rushing a slightly abbreviated edition of the paper to press, and she hired a few local teens to help her run her deliveries, ensuring everyone got their copies early.

She had spent most of the night posting to the *Gazette*'s website and social media too, forgoing sleep in order to spread the good (or downright awful) word, but she didn't feel tired at all.

Maybe it's morbid.

Maybe it's twisted.

But Rachel hasn't felt this excited about running this place and continuing her father's legacy since the day she walked through the doors and started the paper anew.

Thank you very much, Wilson Island Ripper.

She sits at her desk in the front office where her father once plied his trade. From the big picture window, she can see the street outside. Right now, though, she's focused on composing a piece about public opinions concerning the murders.

> "It's just awful, really awful. My husband and I have been coming here during the summer since we got married. We bring our kids with us. They love it. It's hard to believe something so terrible could happen."
> —Meredith Finch, 35, Chapel Hill, North Carolina

> "I guess it's scary, yeah, but what isn't scary these days?"
> —Oswald Lucas, 65, Goldsboro, North Carolina

> "I don't expect a decline in business, if I'm being honest. In fact, the shop is doing better right now than it was at this time last year. I don't feel like tourists are really paying attention to the stories."
> —Brenda Ferris, 46, Wilson Island, North Carolina

Fuck off, Brenda.

She almost deletes that one. After all, she has dozens of quotes from various residents and visitors. Sure, she might have worked her ass off to coax the comments from those she hastily interviewed. Sure, some of them weren't even aware, at the time of questioning, of the murders. But she had done her best to make sure they were well informed in the three to five minutes she spoke to them. In the end, she decides to keep Brenda's words in the article.

Truth in journalism. And it'll be nice to see Brenda eat her words.

A flicker of movement catches her eye, and she looks out the window. Across the street, leaning against the faded red brick of the old post office, stands a disheveled figure in a dark trench coat, a tattered stocking cap, and fingerless gloves. He stares in the direction of her office, looking back at her. She knows him well. Owen Quinn, dubbed "Madhouse Quinn" by the locals, a fixture of the community, something of a Wilson Island curiosity.

One of many.

And Rachel has not yet asked him his opinion of the Ripper.

Grabbing her phone and slipping her feet into her shoes, discarded under the desk, Rachel hurries out the door. She waits as a Jeep with a pair of surfboards lashed to the roll bars zips past. Then she dashes across the street. Instinctually, almost reflexively, her thumb moves across the screen of the phone in her hand, opening the voice recorder app.

Madhouse never takes his eyes off her.

Like he's been waiting for me. Expecting me.

Rachel is ten paces away when she speaks. "Hi, Mr. Quinn."

"Hi yourself," he mutters.

"I wondered if I could ask you a few questions."

She reaches out, holding her phone toward Quinn so she can pick up his every word.

"I reckon so."

"It's about the recent murders. I'm guessing you're aware—"

"I'd reckon near about everyone is. You made sure of *that*, didn't you?"

"Well, I'm very interested in hearing your thoughts about how these events affect our community."

Quinn looks at the phone, raises his eyes to meet hers, says nothing.

"Mr. Quinn?" Rachel asks, taking a step closer.

"The impact"—he leans in, speaking directly into the phone—"has *yet to be seen.*"

"So—you don't think the murders were an isolated incident? You think the killer might strike again?"

"You don't know the whole story." He moves a step closer. He's dressed far too warmly for the weather. He smells of sweat and urine and old, wet cigarettes. "You're so busy chasing shadows, but you don't see what's blotting out the light."

"I'm not sure I understand."

"They got you dancing on strings like a marionette."

"And who would that be?"

"I've seen the puppeteer."

He's living up to his nickname. "What does that mean, Mr. Quinn?"

"Meat puppets."

Is he really crazy? Or is this all for show?

Then he says something that piques her reporter's interests. "You'd best hope he's not done."

"The Ripper?"

"If that's what you want to call him."

"It almost sounds like you have suspicions about his motivations, maybe even about his identity."

"Not suspicions. It's not your story to tell, but you're telling it just the same, ain't you?"

"I'm reporting the news," Rachel says. "People have a right to know what's going on in their community. I'm sure you agree."

"Well—you weren't there."

"Where's that?"

"You weren't chosen."

"Chosen for what?"

"To spread the gospel."

"Ah." Rachel's thumb slides across the phone's screen, ending the recording. "Thank you, Mr. Quinn."

For fucking nothing.

Readers might enjoy a little craziness from time to time, but this was a bridge too far.

She gives him a halfhearted, pitying smile, and turns away. Across the street, she sees the offices of the *Gazette*, the local paper she's been struggling to keep alive, the rag that sold out this week thanks to recent violence, the publication that might very well get national attention soon. If Rachel plays her cards right.

"I can show you the truth," Quinn says.

Rachel stops . . . waits for him to explain.

"There's something you ought to see, something that will change the story, for you, for everyone you tell."

What did her father like to say? *Some reporters have a knack for sorting the wheat from the chaff, lead-wise. The rest of us, we chase every lead. We pull at every thread till our hands bleed. Sometimes we get nothing but bloody hands. Other times the blood spatters onto the page and tells one hell of a story.*

She opens the recording she's made, rolling it back a few seconds, hits play.

"*It's not your story to tell,*" Madhouse Quinn's voice says.

The homeless man eyes the phone. He's still chewing on the inside of his cheek, most likely working the taste of his own blood into his mouth.

"So—you want to know the whole story or not?" he asks.

"All right. I'll nibble."

"I'll show you if you like."

"Okay."

"Tonight, then—meet me at the Golden Dunes."

CHAPTER FORTY-NINE

No matter the *smuggle-stolen-goods, run-bootleg-blu-ray, make-high-interest-loans, peddle-guns-to-people-who-shouldn't-have-guns, hide-someone-who-doesn't-want-to-be-found, break-the-leg-of-someone-who-doesn't-want-a-broken-leg* project Willa's dad cooks up, Scraps and Bear are there to do the dirty work. The two men—she doesn't even know their real names—are the closest thing to a friend group her father has. He trusts them with all his business dealings—the ones Willa knows about and otherwise—and they are well paid for that trust.

Scraps is tall and lean, his hair shaggy, his face always unshaven. He has a kind of feral look about him.

Bear, on the other hand, is big and broad, bearded, with deep-set, haunted eyes.

On at least a couple of occasions, Willa has heard the term "leg breaker" muttered in regard to Bear. Only when he's nowhere within earshot.

The men step out of her dad's office as Willa approaches. Scraps pulls the door closed behind him, an act of habit rather than a gesture of denial.

"Hey, Willa," he says in his low, nasally voice. "We're done here, so you can go right in."

"Thanks," Willa says, wrinkling her nose in an exaggerated fashion. "I live here, you know, so I don't need your permission."

Scraps steps out of her way, holding his hands up in mock surrender, while Bear lets out a hearty snort of laughter.

Willa shoots a snide look at Scraps as she slides into her father's office. She widens her eyes and playfully gasps as she slams the door shut in his face.

"Dad, I need to ask you something." Willa tries her damnedest to sound like an adult. "And I need you to answer me honestly."

"Honesty," her father replies, "is my only excuse."

"I appreciate that."

Her father stands at the bar, cleverly concealed in a faux-antique nautical globe, and pours himself a drink—bourbon, neat, as usual. His sleeves are rolled up. The top couple of buttons of his dress shirt are undone. If he'd been wearing a tie, which he does every now and then, the garment has been cast aside.

"Should I be standing for this?" her father asks. "Or should I sit?"

"I don't think it's going to rock your world or anything." If the last few days haven't rattled him, then nothing will.

"All right, then." He sips his drink without taking his eyes off his daughter. "Hit me with it."

Willa doesn't sit either. Her hands clutch the back of one of the armchairs facing the desk. "Well, I kind of want to talk about—"

"I thought you were going to ask a question. This sounds like a statement. What are they teaching you kids in school these days? See? Now, *that* is a question."

Willa rolls her eyes. "I'm getting to it."

"Sorry. You know, in a few years, I won't get the chance to annoy you like this. So I've got to seize the opportunity when I can."

"Were you trying to annoy me when you had Scraps following me last night?"

"Ah." The simple, short utterance hangs in the air, heavy and bloated.

"That's not really an answer."

"Can you blame me for wanting to make sure my daughter isn't the next *Gazette* headline? Humor me, Willa. There's literally a killer on the loose."

"I can take care of myself."

"Of that, there is no doubt." Her father shrugs. "Would it make you feel better to know that it wasn't you he was following?"

"Kenny, then? I'd rather you just leave him alone."

"What am I supposed to say?" Her father pours himself another drink. "I don't like the guy."

"If it's any consolation, I don't like him much right now either."

"Excellent. And they say teenagers and their parents never see eye to eye."

"Look, Dad," she says, and lets the words hang in the air just a beat too long. "I get it. You're worried. I appreciate it. It means more than you know, but the whole espionage act doesn't do much for me."

Her dad rolls his chair away from the desk and plops into it. "Okay. Noted," he says, and he seems to deflate a little.

"And if you're trying to be secretive or whatever, Scraps is your absolute worst bet. He sticks out like a sore thumb."

"Maybe I wanted you to see him. Not so much you, really, as Kenny."

"Seriously. I can handle myself, at least when it comes to Kenny. The last thing I need is someone lurking around."

"What if I got someone a little more inconspicuous?"

"Maybe you just . . . don't. How about that?"

"Fair enough, as long as you don't hold it against me that I worry."

"Deal," Willa says.

CHAPTER FIFTY

SHE'S IN MY DREAMS. The thought is not his own. *And I'm in hers.*

He hears his mother's voice in his head, weak and weary, raspy and wretched. Even then, the words are alien.

Blood slicks his gloves as he works, his blades slicing flesh, his fingers peeling fatty folds of skin away, his hands drawing the organs from their housing of tissue and muscle and bone.

The stomach, yes.

With every kill, a different harvest is demanded.

The eyes.

The tongue.

The lips.

There is no rhyme or reason. He does only what he's told. And he casts the rest aside.

And now, apparently, sometimes she doesn't want what he brings her at all. Like with Grady.

"That one was for you," he says again, the words sounding different, tasting different, on his tongue.

That's not true! He didn't want to hurt Grady. *It was necessary.*

He'd briefly considered, when he pulled the RV out of the park behind the marina, just driving his happy ass as far from Wilson Island and his responsibilities as he possibly could on whatever gas was in the tank.

The idea was beautiful, for all of three minutes. That's what his father had done. Just gave up, almost as soon as his offerings were rejected . . . as soon as the demands became too great.

To turn back now, to stop, would just mean someone else would be saddled with the responsibilities. Or not. And that was so much worse.

So he'd made his way to the old Haney farm on the outskirts of town, overgrown and crumbling and forgotten, lost down a long and winding dirt road. No one bothers coming out this way anymore. Kids once traveled here to party, but those days are over. Ghost stories did some of the job of running kids off—along with almost anyone else. The growing population of hungry, diseased rats did the rest. He'd parked the RV in the dilapidated barn, where only the rats could see.

And that's where he commenced his work.

He dragged the bodies into the back of the RV, laid them out on the floor. He now takes his time with them, honoring their sacrifice, honoring the harvest. When he's done, he'll leave the RV here. Maybe he'll leave the doors open so the rats can feast on the remains. Either way, no one will find it, not before he has a chance to finally dispose of the vehicle properly a few towns away.

If I ever get a goddamn chance to slip away, even for a day or so.

Other mutilated bodies he's sunk in the drink or left deep in the woods. But he's running short on time of late.

His father had it easy, tossing the leftover animal carcasses out at Golden Dunes, where only a bunch of crazy hobos would see.

She's growing more demanding, more agitated, more—

Hungry! Hungry! Hungry! The voice rings in his head.

Almost forgot the teeth. He reaches to his belt of blades and tools, takes up his pliers, and sets about pulling them, one by one, from the mouths of his sacrifices.

He can't view them as people. To have sympathy for them risks everything.

It takes him longer than he expects—the work is strenuous. When he's finally finished, his clothing is drenched in sweat and blood. He pants under the eyeless mask, his breath like a furnace. A bloody pile of teeth, some with dark fillings and ligaments dangling from the roots, is on the floor.

"Is this enough?" he mumbles under the mask.

For now, Mother says.

Shit. She isn't satisfied. She never is . . . even when she only demands specific pieces.

And he's not sure if these thoughts are his. Or hers.

What do we do about the girl? she says.
"What girl?"
The girl in my dreams. The mother.
"I don't know."
Yes, you do.
"It's too dangerous."
She's too dangerous.

He realizes he's talking to himself, like a dialogue with his own reflection in a mirror, carrying both sides of the conversation.

"You know what you have to do."

CHAPTER FIFTY-ONE

ONE THING BUCK LOVES ABOUT the Red Eye: they pour their coffee damn strong.

He drains the mug and motions to Kayla that he needs a top-off. She hurries to the table, smiles kindly, and fills it to the brim.

"I'm guessing," she says, "this is a keep-'em-coming kind of situation."

Buck returns the happy face as best he can and says, "That must be some of that ESP working for you, huh?"

Kayla cocks her hip to the side, puts the knuckles of her free hand at her waist, and winks. "Don't need to be psychic to recognize a man in need." She taps her fingertips on the table a couple of times, gives Buck a look that says, *I'll keep my eye . . . or my third eye . . . on you*, and hustles off to handle her other orders.

With everything weighing on his mind, with a town on the verge of panic, potential suspects missing, a killer walking the streets, and the meeting he's about to take right here in this very diner, Buck almost forgets to admire the view as Kayla walks away. Almost. But to do anything less than watch her jeans work to keep up with that saunter would be an insult to manhood, to Kayla, and to Mother Nature herself.

He sips his coffee and, for a fleeting moment, enjoys the view.

Kayla's a hippie, with dainty seashells and threads of gold woven into brown hair streaked with gray. She wears tie-dyed T-shirts during her off-hours. Buck's seen her in one that says KEEP AUSTIN WEIRD from time to time, and he guesses that's where she's from, even though he doesn't hear much of an accent when he speaks to her. Today she's in a deliberately torn tank top that shows off a tattoo on her back just above her left shoulder blade, a coiling dragon with butterfly wings.

She reads tea leaves and tarot cards and star patterns and the like, from what he's heard around town, and she's proud to tell anyone who listens that she has premonitions.

Maybe she can help me with this case. Like in the movies.

Only, Buck doesn't believe in card reading and mind reading and the like. What's more, he doesn't want to drag someone like Kayla into business this nasty. What he *would* like to do, as soon as this nightmare blows over, is to ask her out on a real honest-to-God date. Dinner, drinks, the whole nine yards. And he genuinely believes that, even though she's probably ten years younger than him, she might just say yes. So, something to look forward to.

The bell above the door rings, and Wade Hanson steps inside the Red Eye. He's dressed in khaki jeans, leather deck shoes, and a darkblue polo shirt, and carries himself with the self-assured confidence of a man who closes more business deals before he gets out of bed in the morning than most people dream of in a week. He looks across the room, spots Buck, and heads that way.

As he weaves through the aisles, a few patrons eye him, a mixture of easy-to-spot fake smiles and genuine expressions of happiness on their faces. Everyone who calls Wilson Island home knows Wade, and it's better to exchange pleasantries and be on his good side than the alternative.

Admiration and fear. Maybe a bit of both.

And Buck doesn't like to think about where he might fall on that indicator.

Wade smiles as he greets friends and neighbors.

"Morning, Wade!" Kayla calls from the back of the restaurant. "I'll be right with you!" Her voice sounds bright, cheery, excited to see him. Now, that one stings a bit, and Buck slurps his coffee in frustration.

"Morning, Sheriff," Wade says, his voice as smooth as the polished shoes he wears. He slides into the booth seat across from Buck. "I appreciate you meeting with me like this. I know you've got a lot on your plate right now."

"Figured you wouldn't have asked to meet if it wasn't important."

Wade looks around the diner, eyeing both familiar and unfamiliar faces. "I guess not."

Kayla approaches with her ever-ready pot of coffee, and Buck decides it's better to discuss more lighthearted subjects until she's out of earshot.

"Saw that girl of yours playing at the Kite Festival a little while back. She's got some talent."

"Doesn't get it from me. I never really had a gift for music."

Kayla swings by with smiles and fresh coffee, then moves along to let them talk.

"I saw her again," Buck says, "just a few nights ago." Wade looks across the table at him. "But I reckon you already know that."

"She hasn't said much about it. Maybe she's got too many other things on her mind. I think, though, I've got the gist of it."

"You come to tell me how I ain't doing my job?"

"No. It's not like that."

"Oh. What's it like, then?"

"I know the resources you have at your disposal."

"I reckon you do."

The hint of animosity, of accusation, plays between the two men.

"I wanted to see about . . . helping you out," Wade says. "I've got people who work for me, people who owe me favors, and I thought maybe you could use a few more boots on the ground."

Buck drains his cup again. "Yeah, thanks, but I'll pass."

"Hear me out."

"I don't think I need to, do I?"

"I live on this island, same as you. My *family* lives here. And now we've got someone running around hacking people up?"

"And you want to make sure we catch him."

"Of course I do."

"Before someone you love gets hurt."

"You can't fault me for that."

"Before our little town attracts the attention of someone besides local law enforcement—say, someone federal?"

That takes the wind right out of Wade's sails, puffs it back in his face like secondhand smoke, and shuts him right the fuck up. Admittedly, Buck didn't think that would be the case when he said it. But, goddamn, he savors this small victory while he can.

"Wade—I don't like the idea of a bunch of . . . people who owe you favors, a bunch of loose cannons, running up and down the island, looking for trouble."

"I'm just talking about a handful of trusted personnel."

"Vigilantes, you mean. Sorry—pass," the sheriff says again. "Sorry. I'm good."

Wade swallows down a frustrated grumble. The way he twists his head, it doesn't go down easily.

"I've got a handle on this," Buck continues. "I'll get it wrapped up, *without* your help. Then, maybe, I can turn my attention to other matters."

Wade chuckles in response, a forced, fake, warning sound.

"Didn't think you'd find that so funny."

"What's funny, Sheriff, is that you think I'm asking permission."

Buck stiffens in his seat.

"My crew hits town this evening," Wade says.

"Dammit, Wade—"

"Relax. They're not going to get in your way. They're here to help you, to support you. That's the way I see it. And . . . that's the way the mayor and the rest of the town council see it too."

Ohhh, you fucker. Buck leans forward, but before he can get the words out, Kayla approaches the table.

"Sorry, fellas," she says. "I didn't mean to interrupt."

"It's fine," Wade says. "I think we were just about done here anyway. That sound about right to you, Buck?"

Buck's eyes narrow as he answers. "Not hardly."

Kayla, not needing ESP to sense the tension at the table, wheels away to tend other customers.

And Buck isn't all that sorry to see her go, not with how overly friendly she was when she greeted Wade Hanson in the first place.

"Why do I feel," Wade says, "that you're trying to make this more difficult than it needs to be?"

"Not at all," Buck replies. "I just don't appreciate you, your shady business, your dirty money, your pompous attitude, or your non-negotiable offer to swoop in with street trash and somehow save us all."

A few other customers fall silent, mid-chew, and look in Buck's direction.

Fuck discretion. And fuck them.

"I most certainly don't appreciate your ulterior motives," Buck says. "But if the mayor wants your help—and you can be damn sure I will be checking in with him about that—then he can have it. I won't stand in the way."

"That's good to hear," Wade manages to reply.

"I'm a little surprised, though." A satisfied snarl twitches across Buck's face. "A man with your 'business' acumen ought to see when something's about to blow up in his face. This manhunt of yours, these armchair bounty hunters you're bringing into *my* town? You're asking for a world of headaches, heartache, and hurt. And I, for one, can't wait to see how you and the mayor and the city council handle it."

The surprised look on Wade's face is just about as pleasing as Red Eye coffee. The man isn't used to anyone standing up to him, to anyone "talking back," especially not in public. Buck will live large on this meal for days.

The sheriff rises, thumps a couple of fingers on the tabletop, and winks.

"Thanks for the fucking coffee."

CHAPTER FIFTY-TWO

HE WATCHES HIS MOTHER SLEEP.

The painted wooden chair, usually reserved for an old Raggedy Ann doll, creaks under his weight. The doll, tattered and yellowed with age, sprawls across the floor. He always hated that doll, felt creeped out by its dead black eyes. Quietly he slides his booted foot across the floor, eases his toes under the doll, and sends that floppy bitch sailing across the room. She hits the far wall with a soft *thump* and topples to the floor.

The curtains are drawn, and the dim light of a bedside lamp casts shadows across the bare hardwood floor, along the faded and peeling wallpaper.

His mother breathes unevenly in her sleep, her frail and age-spotted hand clutching the patchwork blankets, pulling them up tight around her body.

"Mama?" He whispers at first, not sure if he really wants to wake her. Then, louder: "Mama?"

Her lips tremble, a question forming in her sleep. She shifts slightly. Her grip on the blankets tightens, the trace of color in her knuckles flushing out, leaving her thin skin stretched taut and white. With a moan of exertion, she opens her eyes. At first her vision is unfocused, her eyes darting around, trying to gain purchase on—

Anything.

Then she finds him, stares at him. "What?" she asks. But that's not the word she's looking for. "Who?"

"It's me, Mama." He leans forward, letting the feeble light spill over his face.

"I . . ."

She's weak.

No.
Sick.
No.
Suffering.
No.
One.
Will.
Miss.
Her.

She reaches out, fingers spasming open and closed. He takes her hand. Her skin is delicate, her bones brittle in his gentle grasp. He pushes the thought—the notion of putting her out of her misery, of taking her below—from his mind.

Her eyes widen as she looks at him.

"I . . . don't know you."

"Don't say that, Mama." His throat closes up. "Please."

"You shouldn't be here My son will be home soon. He doesn't like when people bother me. I should be resting."

"I'm right here."

She stares at him with a mix of confusion and fear. He can almost see the wheels turning in her skull as she tries to pin him down in her mind, to remember who he is. "This . . . isn't the face your father gave you."

He blinks, uncertain. Ever since he was a little boy, everyone—including his mother—has told him how much he favors his father, how he was almost the spitting image of the man. He always took it as a point of pride, at least up until the point when Dad went gaunt and pale with the weight of his responsibilities.

Her fingers slip from his grasp, and her hand goes to his face, fingertips brushing his chin, his lips, his nose, his forehead.

"Your face is all wrong." She pulls away, her fingers suddenly drawing back into a claw. "You look like your mother."

"You mean I look like you."

She turns away from him.

"You know that's not what I mean."

CHAPTER FIFTY-THREE

DEAN'S BRUSH SLIDES ACROSS THE damp stone wall, leaving a streak of color in its wake. An electric lantern pushes the darkness back. He's moved deeper into the tunnel now, his work on the unseen exhibit expanding. He pauses and steps back to observe the painting that has occupied his last five hours.

Or longer. Sometimes he loses track of time in the gallery. When he's painting, hours can feel like minutes.

On the smooth cave wall, an undulating, cloudlike colony of seagulls looms above the crumbling gray ruins of the Tasty King. Through the windows, the terrified faces of fry cooks and front-counter workers scream, begging anyone who will listen to help them escape the squabbling birds. People on the street, though, pay them no mind. They wear bright bathing suits, sunglasses, hats to protect them from the sun, but each one has the oversized, gawking, screeching head of a seagull.

Not his usual style. But he wasn't really feeling his usual self today.

Wiping sweat from his brow with the back of his hand, he feels a dab of paint smear across his forehead. He grabs his phone from his work table, careful to keep it paint-free. Before switching to the camera mode, he checks—

Nothing.

No messages. No calls. This despite the good reception he gets in this place.

He scans the walls leading back to the cave mouth, sees the portrait he painted of Willa, thoughtful and a little sad.

I caught her in a moment.

He snaps a couple of pictures of his latest work, attaches them to a text message that reads **Looks better in person**, and sends them Willa's way.

He feels a pang of sadness. He imagines she's never going to see the painting in person. *Because, let's face it, she's never coming back here to the gallery.*

He's not sure why he feels that. Maybe it's the uncertain way they left things. Did he come on too strong? Or is he just feeling sorry for himself?

Something scrapes across stone.

Dean looks toward the entrance of the cave again. Beyond the painted walls, the cave opens to the beach, where the whitecaps rumble.

He knows, though, that sound bounces in here.

It didn't come from outside the cave. It came from *deeper* in the darkness.

Dean holds his breath. Listens. There it is again, clear even over the rush and hiss of the ocean—a definite scraping, like a furtive footstep across stone. Somebody is moving back there. Walking. Coming closer.

"Hello?" he calls out.

The only response is an echo of his own voice.

It shouldn't surprise him that other people might be exploring the caves. He isn't the only person to ever paint on the walls. Of course, his works are projects of love and effort, art even, while the other markings are phrases spray-painted by, among others, someone calling themselves Sex Rocket.

"Hello . . . ?" he calls again.

For a second, the ominous sound dies down, and Dean hears nothing but the ocean, the distant cry of seagulls, intruding into the gallery from the outside.

Then, hopefully, he says: "Willa . . . ?"

And now his call *is* answered. He hears voices. People talking. He can't tell what they're saying. They're too far away. But he hears laughter too. And—

A dog barking.

Grabbing his lantern, Dean ventures farther into the cave, his feet slipping on a slight, wet slope. He ducks his head to avoid a low overhang, winding around a corner.

Still the sounds of talking and of laughter and of barking ring out.

Then, a scream. Dean's own.

Bouncing off the paintings of Wilson Island and of horses and of seagulls. And of Willa's sad, thoughtful face.

He screams for a long while before finally falling silent. And that utterly frightful time for Dean doesn't pass quickly at all.

CHAPTER FIFTY-FOUR

*T*HIS, ERIC THINKS, *is going to be a shit show.*
   A lifted pickup roars past, its bed filled with camouflage-clad men clutching rifles. Behind the truck, a sleek sports car weaves recklessly through traffic, bass thumping from its speakers, followed by a trio of SUVs, their passengers hidden by shadow and tinted glass. A squad of rough-looking bikers, their leather vests adorned with menacing patches, growls along the streets.
   What in the name of God has Wade Hanson brought down upon us? Wade Hanson and *Sheriff Buck.*
   The sheriff could have put his foot down. He could have stopped this. Instead, he just bent over and took it. Now he expects Wilson Island to bend over too.
   It isn't just Hanson and the sheriff to blame, though, is it? Eric understands that he himself bears some of the blame. *Me and Rachel. Funny, everybody to blame, except the killer.*
   "Dispatch, this is Reed." Eric speaks into his radio, voice steady despite his racing heart. "We've got a goddamned parade coming into town. I'm guessing three dozen out-of-towners, maybe more. I can't handle it all myself. I'm gonna need some backup."
   "*The out-of-towners,*" Tess replies, "*are meant to be backup.*"
   A convertible full of fraternity bros speeds by, music blaring. The horn blasting over and over like a fanfare trumpet signaling a charge.
   "What am I supposed to do here?" Eric asks.
   He climbs back into his patrol car, already knowing the answer. Hears it clear as a bell. But it's not Tess's voice responding over the airwaves. It's Keene's, echoing in his skull.
   Walk the fucking walk.

CHAPTER FIFTY-FIVE

THE ABANDONED HIGH SCHOOL RISES before them. The place closed down years ago, thanks to an asbestos problem. Scraps, who attended here, wonders how much of the stuff he breathed in over the years, how much of the shit burrowed into the tissue of his lungs, waiting to turn into cancer. Tonight, though, as he stands on the tailgate of his truck and looks out across a sea of grizzled faces, anxious and impatient—

Jesus.

—faces covered in war paint like it's Sunday-Sunday-Sunday at the college ballgame, he knows he's got more important matters than asbestos to worry about.

Wade really called out the dogs of war.

Thunder rumbles in the distance, as if in agreement. Gray clouds mask the night sky overhead.

The parking lot, cracked and overgrown with weeds though it is, is packed with a dozen or more cars, trucks, SUVs, and motorcycles. Scraps recognizes some of the men and women gathered before him. More than half are ex-cons, petty criminals, and ne'er-do-wells who Wade has bailed out over the years. Others are college- and high school–age kids looking for a thrill. And still others are sportsmen and hunters, here to hunt something other than turkeys and rabbits and deer. While most of the crowd is composed of out-of-towners, there are more than a few locals in the mix. They're armed with an assortment of shotguns and rifles, baseball bats and golf clubs. There's even a pitchfork in the crowd to really complete the angry mob aesthetic. They hoot and howl and laugh, calling out challenges to one another, placing bets on who's going to bring the Wilson Island Ripper to justice first.

Gotta hand it to Wade. He knows how to bring in one helluva crowd. Men. Women. Young. Old. Rich. Poor. Bikers. Roughnecks.

Burnouts. Career deadbeats. Career criminals. Sportsmen. Brawlers. Preppy frat boys.

Reprobates.

Jackasses with something to prove.

If pure chaos walked out of the closet wearing leather vests and trucker caps and Oakleys and polo shirts with the collars turned up, it would look a lot like this crew milling outside the high school. Who says people can't put aside their differences? All they needed, it seemed, was someone to hunt.

Bear, standing next to the truck, bellows: "Listen up, you sorry bunch of degenerates!"

The crowd cheers back at him.

"I said, listen *up*!" Bear yells.

This time the clamor dies down into uneasy and expectant mutters. Bear looks up at Scraps, signaling *Go ahead*.

"You all know why you're here," Scraps says to the crowd. "We've got ourselves a killer on the loose, and Mr. Hanson wants him found ASAP."

Several members of the mob stomp their feet and cheer. *I'm surrounded by idiots*, Scraps thinks.

"Some of you," he says, "well, I guess you're here out of a sense of civic duty."

A few locals clap and shout.

Once again, Scraps fights to keep from laughing in their faces.

"And some of you owe Mr. Hanson a debt. Consider this your chance to repay it."

A few mob members nod in silent acknowledgment. Scraps can appreciate their sentiment. He's right there in the mix with them, after all.

"Some of you want to earn Mr. Hanson's appreciation," Scraps continues, "so you can turn that into a favor at some point down the line."

Fair enough, he thinks.

"Some of you," Scraps says, "are out here looking for a little fun."

The thrill-seekers whoop with excitement. *And we've circled right back around to idiocy*.

"Well," Scraps says, "I don't really give a good goddamn *why* you dragged yourselves out here. Good for you, whatever your reasons. The only thing Mr. Hanson cares about, and therefore the only thing *I* care about, is keeping Wilson Island safe."

Several voices rise from the crowd.

"If I find this bastard, I'm gonna skin him alive!"

"We'll make him sorry he was ever born!"

"Let's get him!"

"Kick his ass!"

A siren barks out, short and loud, and the red-and-blue lights of a sheriff's patrol car wash over the crowd. Scraps and Bear look in the direction of the disturbance. Faces turn angrily to see who's interrupted their fervor.

Deputy Eric Reed stands at the open door of his car. "That's just about enough of that!" he calls out.

He walks through the crowd, eyeing each and every one of them, and he doesn't so much as miss a step when a burly biker or gruff hunter or cocky college kid gets in his way. He stands tall and makes them step aside.

"This isn't about vigilante justice," Eric says as he approaches the truck, raising his arms to address the mob. A low grumble of dissatisfaction can be heard.

Still standing on the tailgate, Scraps crouches down to share a word with the deputy. "Son," he says, "these activities have been agreed upon and sanctioned by the sheriff."

Eric turns his head, fixes Scraps with a cold glare. "Oh, that's a load of horseshit, and you know it." Eric addresses the crowd once more. "Listen to me. You need to think of yourselves as something more like a neighborhood watch. You see something, you say something. If you do happen to come upon the suspect, we do *not* want you to engage. You report it and stay the hell out of our way. Is that understood?"

Scraps stands and scans the array of faces before him. "You heard the deputy, right?"

The crowd laughs and yells snide comments.

"So, get out there and find this bastard!"

CHAPTER FIFTY-SIX

LOVINGLY, MR. NO-FACE PULLS THE thin blanket over his mother's frail form. He leans down, pressing his forehead against hers. Her skin is cool and damp. She reeks, needs another bath, for all the good it does. Soap only covers up the stink of decay and death for so long.

"I've got to go out," he says, "just for a little while. You get some rest."

Her eyes flutter toward him, focusing. She raises her hand, her cool fingers sliding down his cheek.

"I don't like this," she says.

"I know. I don't either."

"Mr. No-Face."

He flinches back from her touch, but her eyes are fixed on his. He's not wearing the mask.

Or—

He reaches up, touches his own face, his skin hot where his mother's was cool. He touches his eyelashes, his nose, his lips.

No.

His fingertips linger on his lips. His eyes focus on his mother's mouth. He's not wearing the mask.

Yet.

"Mama?" he breathes.

"I don't want to dream about her anymore." But it doesn't sound like his mother. Not his *real* mother. The thing in the bed smiles, her dry lips cracking and oozing oil and blood. "You understand, don't you?" she asks.

He starts to shake his head, then stops himself.

"She'll ruin everything."

"I won't let her," he says.

I want my mask. If he had it, he might not be able to see his mother clearly, might not see her sleeping peacefully, even as he has a conversation with her.

If he had the mask, he wouldn't be able to touch his own face. He wouldn't know that it was his lips moving as his mother spoke with a voice that was not her own.

CHAPTER FIFTY-SEVEN

SOME DAMN FOOL HAS ACTUALLY brought bloodhounds.

The dogs race toward the forest, straining against their leashes, pulling their owners along, sticking their noses to the ground or to the sky as they bray loudly.

What scent have they caught? Who are they chasing? They're just running to run.

Sitting in his truck, parked along the stretch of Eastwood Road cutting through the woods, Scraps grumbles in contempt as he sends a text message to his boss.

Nothing to report.

Short, sweet, to the point.

Unrolling the window, he spits a stream of dark, sticky tobacco juice into the tall grass beside the road.

Along the road, a line of trucks and cars stands silent and empty, their drivers and passengers charging into the woodlands, as eager as the bloodhounds. The dogs have vanished into the dense forest, but he can still hear their barking. The beams of a dozen or more flashlights cut erratically through the trees. Soon enough, those will disappear from sight too.

Scraps never much cared for hunting. His old man used to force him to hunt deer and ducks and rabbits. Always said he wanted to teach him to live off the land. Said it would toughen him up.

Even as a kid, Scraps recognized such a notion as bullshit. Hell, he lives off fast food and microwave TV dinners, and he is and always will be the toughest bastard around. *Next to Bear, maybe.*

As a kid, though, he went along with it because that's what he was supposed to do. It was the only time he ever really spent with his father. And he pretty much hated every second of it.

Scraps always felt a little guilty about that. His old man died more than a decade gone by. His ticker had given up the ghost while he was out hunting on his own. *How's that for a messed-up bit of irony?*

Now Scraps is out hunting again, this time for Wade Hanson.

In the passenger seat, Bear leans forward and gazes up at the night sky. Clouds blot out the stars. Lightning flickers. It hasn't started thundering just yet, but it's coming.

"We ain't getting out in this, are we?" Bear asks.

"Get out in what?" Scraps asks. "It ain't raining."

"It's gonna."

"When that happens, about seventy-five percent of these jackasses are gonna hightail it home. If they ain't caught the Ripper by then, well, we might just have to get out in it."

"What was Wade thinking?" Bear asks. "Sending a bunch of dumbasses out to track down a killer."

"He wants to drive the Ripper out into the open. Doesn't need skilled hunters for that. Just needs bodies."

"You think that's gonna work?"

Scraps rolls up his window, puts the truck into drive, and pulls away from the grass. Back in town, a bunch of other would-be vigilantes are almost certainly patrolling the streets. He figures he should check on them too. He doesn't know if one of them will find the killer or not.

All he knows for certain is that he damn sure isn't chasing after a bunch of dogs through the fucking woods, especially when it's about to rain.

...

Deputy Eric Reed sits in his cruiser, his window down, watching the empty street. Calico Drive. Home to a couple of thrift stores, a boxing gym, and the White Sands Christian Fellowship. He's alone. It smells like it's going to rain. Every now and then, thunder grumbles in the distance, lightning fidgets through the clouds. It's the kind of night when anyone with a bit of sense would just stay inside.

A battered truck rounds the corner. Assorted locals squat in the back, some with rifles or baseball bats or crowbars. Eric recognizes the driver, Everett, and the front passenger, Frankie. Cousins who are almost always up to no good. He knows most of the men in the back too. The truck slows as it passes the cruiser. Eric leans out his window and offers a three-fingered greeting.

"Seen anything?" Everett asks.

"Nothing worth mentioning."

In the passenger seat, Frankie leans forward. "Well, thank the good Lord we've got you on the case, huh?!" he yells loud enough that the men in back can hear.

They all laugh.

With swollen knuckles, Everett punches the ceiling of the truck's cab three times. The truck pulls away.

The men still laughing all the way down the street.

...

"There goes some more of them!"

Wally stands at the neon-illuminated window of the Tugboat. He takes a swig of his bottled beer, the cheap stuff on special every Thursday night, as he witnesses car after truck after motorcycle roar down the street.

"Must be a hundred of them out there."

"Not that many," Delores says. She sits at the bar, peeling the label off her own beer bottle.

"I been counting," Wally says without looking away from the window.

"They're circling the block," Delores says. "You're counting them over and over."

Ignoring her, Wally leans closer to the window. "So damn many," he says, his breath frosting the glass.

Delores looks up from her label ripping, sees herself reflected in the mirror behind the bar. Written on the mirror in gold letters is the tavern's name and motto.

THE TUGBOAT
WE'RE NOT A STRIP CLUB

Behind her, seated in the shadows that grow thick in the joint, are a handful of the regulars, all of them nursing their own beers and shooters. She sees them in here all the time, but doesn't really know any of them, doesn't know what kind of trouble they might be up to when they think nobody is looking.

"A hundred of them," Wally remarks, "all looking for just one man."

•••

"What in the fuck do we have here?"

Braydon flexes his fingers on the steering wheel. He's got the Jeep's ragtop down, enjoying the summery night air. He's blasting Rage Against the Machine. Old-school shit. Braydon likes the thrashing beat, but he's never bothered listening to the lyrics.

His bros—Carl, Merv, and Pete—are with him. They usually come out to Wilson Island a few times a summer, but never for something like this. Still, they're a little high on edibles, which is tradition for them on their getaways.

"What in the fuck do we have here?" he says again.

His friends notice what he's looking at. They shift eagerly in their seats. Carl, in the front, stands up, gripping the roll bar.

"That's a fucking pervert if I've ever seen one!" he yells.

Walking along the sidewalk is a tall, thin man. He's old, with long gray hair. His skin is deeply tan, and all of it can be seen, because he's stark naked.

The bros cry out to the man as the Jeep swings up to the curb.

"Hey, asshole!"

"Hey, perv!"

"What the fuck's up, Ripper-man?"

The naked man turns, shocked, and staggers back from them.

The bros leap from the Jeep, surrounding the old guy, not waiting for his response, not giving him a chance to escape. They punch. They kick. They shove him to the ground and kick him some more. Even when the old man stops squirming, even when he stops mewling for help or mercy, when he stops trying to defend himself and goes limp . . .

. . . they keep right on stomping.

There's blood on the street when they're done.

Blood on their fists. Blood on their shoes.

Panting, they stand in a circle around the naked man's still form.

"Did we just kill this guy?" Merv asks.

"Check his pulse," Carl says.

"I ain't fucking touching him!"

"He was a pervert, right?" Pete timidly nudges the guy with the toe of his shoe. "He was probably the Ripper."

"He doesn't even have a knife," Merv says.

Braydon looks away from the naked man's body, checks the street to see if there's anyone else around, makes sure no one is recording them.

"Come on!" He scrambles for the Jeep. "Let's get the fuck out of here!"

CHAPTER FIFTY-EIGHT

SITTING ON THE COUCH, THE Warlock stares at a cold-in-the-middle slice of bake-your-own pizza. Orange oil from the slice soaks into his paper plate. In his recliner, facing the static-filled screen of the television, Uncle Terry tears into his own slice as lukewarm grease dribbles down his chin.

"You hear about that murder?" Terry mumbles through a mouthful of pepperoni, cheese, and tomato paste. "Whole town's in an uproar."

"You mean from a couple of days ago?"

"Whenever it was." Uncle Terry plots his next bite, chomps into his pizza, and speaks with a full mouth. "It was in the paper."

"Yeah," the Warlock says. "Of course I heard."

"Probably some dope-smoking pothead. Probably one of *your* customers."

"Maybe."

"Paper says the killing's ritualistic. You know what that means? *Occult*."

"I know what 'ritualistic' means."

"If I was one of you D&D freaks, I'd watch my step."

"You *are* one of those D&D freaks."

"Not anymore."

"That's only because no one wants to play with you."

"You heard about what Wade Hanson's done? He called in the fucking cavalry. He's got people coming in from all over the state."

"Where did you hear that?" the Warlock asks. *All you ever do is sit here in this trailer.*

"I got a call," Terry says. "I know people."

"Who?" the Warlock asks. *Who would give enough of a shit to tell you anything?* "You know what? Doesn't matter."

"He's called up an honest-to-God mob. They're gonna find that guy, burn him down."

"Sounds like a disaster waiting to happen, if you ask me."

"Serves them right," Terry continues. "Serves the killer right. Serves the town right. Folks round here getting too high and mighty. Persnickety. Too comfortable. Too damn proud for their own good."

The Warlock tosses what's left of his pizza slice onto the plate.

"You all right?"

"Fine," the Warlock says. "Just . . . not hungry."

"Suit yourself." Terry shrugs, reaching for another slice. "More for me. And don't expect me to save any leftovers for you."

Without another word, the Warlock rises from the couch. He strides down the hall to his bedroom. In this special place, his books and magazines and dice and miniatures welcome him. On the wall, his many-named sword awaits.

A disaster waiting to happen.

For some reason, though, he wants to be part of it. Part of something. Part of *anything*.

He grasps the sword's hilt, closes his eyes as he imagines power flowing from the metal into his fingertips.

He takes the weapon from the wall, holds the many-named sword out, looks down its length. The blade gleams.

"This," he says, "you can trust."

Wielding the sword, the Warlock makes his way back down the hall. Uncle Terry, his mouth full of pizza, stiffens in his seat when he sees his nephew. His eyes grow wide when he notices the weapon.

"What the hell do you think you're doing?" he asks, his chin covered in orange grease.

"I'm going out."

Terry laughs. "You walk around carrying that thing, and somebody might think *you're* the Ripper!"

The Warlock looks down at the blade painted with dozens of mythical names, and instantly knows his uncle is right. He considers leaving it behind, going back to his room and whiling away the hours painting miniatures he'll never use in a game and planning out Dungeons & Dragons adventures he'll never run. Instead, his grip tightens on the hilt and he steps out of the trailer, down the creaking steps, and into the night. He doesn't bother closing the door behind him.

"If you don't get yourself killed," Terry calls out, "bring me back a carton of cigarettes!" His uncle's laughter follows the Warlock into the night.

CHAPTER FIFTY-NINE

HEADLIGHTS FLOOD ACROSS THE ENTRYWAY sign of the Golden Dunes subdivision. Rachel's hatchback—the same one she uses to deliver bundles of papers around town every Wednesday—rolls past concrete slabs, empty walls, and skeletal remains of unfinished houses. Putting the car into park, Rachel sits there in the comforting glow of the dashboard lights, letting the radio play softly as she watches the abandoned subdivision for signs of life.

The last time she was here, it was in the middle of the day. There were still a few contractors and trucks and pieces of heavy equipment to be found.

She'd snapped a photo with her phone that graced the front page of the *Gazette* and got a little play on socials: a lone construction worker, orange vest slung over his dirtied white T-shirt, hard hat in hand, head hanging low in defeat. Behind him, a backhoe, silent and still, the arm low, the shovel as dejected as the worker's head. And behind that, a landscape of unfinished framework.

She's always had a good eye for photo composition, for telling a story without words.

The buildings, some draped in flapping opaque plastic sheeting, haven't changed much in the years that followed. There are no machines now, though. No trucks. No workers.

And definitely no streetlights out here.

The moon and stars are concealed behind clouds.

When I cut the engine, I'll be in near-total darkness.

She digs her phone from her purse and turns the flashlight on, letting harsh white light burst around her.

Turning the key, Rachel lets the car's lights dim and steps out. She slams the door loudly, letting anyone who might be listening, or waiting, know she's there. She squints into the shadows, searching for a sign of movement. There are figures huddled in the nooks and crevices of the forgotten development, watching her silently, unmoving.

Golden Dunes has been claimed by those who would otherwise have no homes.

"City of lost souls," Rachel murmurs to herself.

That might make a decent headline. **CITY OF LOST SOULS: HOPELESSNESS OR RESOURCEFULNESS?**

When this business with the Ripper is finished, maybe she'll devote a little energy to telling the story of the people currently living in Golden Dunes. It wouldn't move as many papers as a "murderer in our midst" story, but it might get some attention outside the community.

"There you are."

Though she prides herself on keeping her cool and not startling easily, she jumps, and her heart rate spikes. She whirls around, aiming the light of her phone, and finds Madhouse Quinn standing behind her.

"You almost gave me a heart attack," she says.

He regards her with glimmering eyes.

"Hello?" Annoyed already, Rachel shrugs, not really wanting to make idle chitchat with the man, but unwilling to wallow in silence. "You wanted me to come out here. And . . . what? Now you've got nothing to say?"

Quinn turns away from her, motioning for her to follow.

She's only half convinced that he's not wasting her time, but her pulse quickens as she follows him into the subdivision, wending between the silent hulks.

"A storm's coming," Quinn says. He doesn't bother looking at the clouds overhead.

"I know," Rachel says. "Foul weather's been forecast for a few days. I wrote about it in this week's paper."

"You think anyone noticed a weather report in your paper this week?"

"Probably not."

"A lot of rats are gonna drown," Quinn says.

"You find that tragic?"

Rachel follows Quinn deeper into the ghostly subdivision, her phone's flashlight bathing the man in light. She can already feel the storm brewing, the air thick and heavy with humidity. Lightning flashes in the distance, illuminating the outlines of half-finished houses.

"They don't have anyone to tell their story," Quinn remarks.

"I'm sorry?"

"The rats."

"Oh yeah. Right. Can't say they'll be missed."

"*You* ought to do that."

"Tell the story of the rats?"

Now Quinn looks back, nodding.

"I feel like there are more important stories to tell."

"They're not yours."

"O-kay-a. Look. I don't know what this is all about, Mr. Quinn. But, frankly, none of the stories I write are mine. I'm a journalist. My job is to tell the stories of *others*. Otherwise, they don't get told at all."

"You weren't there."

"For what?"

"You weren't chosen."

This isn't the first time he's said as much. "What does that even mean?" she asks.

This is a bad idea. The realization floods her senses.

She looks back toward her car, but she's already lost sight of it behind the framework structures.

"Only five of us were there that night. Only five of us were chosen, and each of us is meant to walk a different path. I was chosen to tell the story to spread—"

"The gospel," Rachel says.

"So, you *do* understand." Madhouse Quinn blinks. "You *do* realize what you're trying to take from me."

"I don't preach, Mr. Quinn. I don't spread the gospel. I just report the news."

His face goes cold once more. "Over here," he says.

Rounding a corner, they pass a cluster of makeshift tents constructed of old blankets and tarps and fabric scraps and carpet remnants. Several people gather around the tents, watching them. Madhouse Quinn doesn't bother acknowledging them. As discreetly as possible,

Rachel swings her flashlight/phone in their direction and snaps a couple of photos.

"Where are you taking me?" Rachel asks.

"We're almost there."

At the outskirts of an empty lot, Madhouse Quinn shambles to a stop.

The air smells of decay. The earth is littered with the carcasses of animals, some months old, some much more recent. Dogs, cats, rats, even birds. They are scattered in the dirt, a few almost devoid of flesh and skin, some crawling with maggots.

"What the hell is all this?" Rachel asks. She covers her nose with the sleeve of her jacket, trying without success to block out the stink.

"End of the line," Quinn announces.

Silently, the field of the dead stares back at her, eyes pale white orbs, eye sockets empty, or bloated with wriggling maggots.

"Animals come here to die," Quinn says.

"What are you talking about . . . ? What are you saying? Are you trying to tell me this is some sort of elephant graveyard scenario?"

"I'm saying"—Madhouse Quinn stares out across the field reverently—"they come here to die."

"I don't—"

"Or they're brought here."

With that, Rachel's senses snap into focus. The animals, each and every one of them, have been ripped open. "*Who* brought them here?"

"He was chosen."

"Oh my God. The Ripper. *He* did this?"

No response.

"You've . . . seen him, haven't you. You know exactly who he is."

"You want to put his name in your paper?"

Yes, she thinks, but instead says: "I want to take his name to the police."

And then she sees it, beyond the scattered bodies of dogs and cats, animals who more than likely grace the MISSING PET signs that clutter nearly every telephone pole in town. A larger figure, sprawled in the dirt, rotting like the rest.

"I keep sayin' and you aren't hearin' me: This isn't your story to tell," Quinn says.

"Who did this?"

"His father was the one who brought the animals out here, tossing what was left of them across this field. He brought them by the sackful, especially after she started rejecting the offerings."

"Who's *she*?"

"He stopped bringing his gifts. We thought he was done with this place. Turns out, he just wasn't cut out for it. Couldn't hack it. So . . . he passed the torch. Unwittingly, of course. But . . . passed it just the same. His son does the work now, but he doesn't bring the leftovers out here."

Quinn definitely knows the murderer, can identify the person. And if she can get him to tell her, she can be the one to bring the killer to justice, saving who knows how many lives.

Who am I kidding? Catching the killer, rooting them out, getting them off the street, sending them to prison—that's all well and good. But Rachel's self-aware enough to know that's not why she's following Madhouse Quinn through the dark. A story like this pays big dividends in terms of profile, clout, and reputation. Instead of the publisher of a rinky-dink island rag, she'll be recognized as a real journalist on a national level. Interviews, job offers, book deals, and maybe even a ticket out of this town are just within her grasp.

"Who did this?" Rachel asks. "Who killed those people?"

"This is sacred ground."

"Sacred to who?"

But she's just starting to notice the shadows gathering around them, the people shuffling in from all sides. They keep their distance, there in the darkness. Rachel swings her light toward them, but the beam doesn't quite reach their features. There's something wrong with them, though. Their shadows are all wrong, especially around their heads.

"Stories are alive," Madhouse intones. "They breathe, they grow, and some . . . some are carnivorous. Some are *hungry*."

The flesh at the back of Rachel's neck prickles. Suddenly she's not worried about the story, or readership, or the paper. Nor clout or reputation. She's not even worried about the dead animals or the body in the field before her. Right in this moment, she only cares about her own safety.

Madhouse Quinn's hand darts from the shadows, a glint of steel in his grasp. Rachel's eyes barely register the blade before it buries itself into her stomach. She gasps, doubles over. Her knees buckle beneath her. She tumbles forward, sprawling into the carcass-filled lot, hands scrabbling against the dirt, her fingers brushing against fur and decay. The killing field welcomes her, embraces her. Her breaths come in shallow hitches, a cruel mimicry of laughter at the absurdity of her predicament. Rachel wheezes, a bubble of blood bursting on her lips.

The weird figures watch, silent, unmoving, as Madhouse Quinn stands above her.

"Story's over."

CHAPTER SIXTY

FOR HOURS, THE SKY HAS threatened to unleash the storm. Clouds seethe, flickers of lightning illuminating their depths. Wind goes from still to whipping to still again in the blink of an eye. Those who know the island, who have lived through countless hurricanes and tropical storms, watch the signs with a kind of held-breath reverence. When the sky finally fulfills its promise, it does so with no additional preamble, no sprinkles of rain, no building thunder. Buckets of stinging rain come down all at once, drenching anyone who's out and about. Gusts of wind rush past, picking up debris, threatening to rip hats from heads, tear shingles from roofs, and uproot trees from the earth. Jagged, writhing lightning crackles and sizzles across the blackness of night.

Like witch's fire.

CHAPTER SIXTY-ONE

*I **LOOK LIKE A FUCKING IDIOT**,* the Warlock thinks.

And honestly, he does.

He treads through the downpour, bucket cap pulled low over his brow but doing little to keep his long hair from getting soaked, just like his Ravenloft T-shirt, his ratty jeans, and his boots. The fingers of his right hand are wrapped tightly around the hilt of his sword. The heaviness of the weapon is strange. Every name painted along the blade—*Frostmourne, Glamdring, Blackfyre, Excalibur*, among others—weighs the sword down.

It is laden with purpose.

"Now," he mutters in the pouring rain, "once more, I must ride with my knights to defend what was, and the dream of what could be."

I sound like an idiot too.

Any other night, a guy walking down the street carrying a blade painted with the names of mythical swords might raise a few eyebrows, even inspire a few calls to emergency services. Not tonight, though. There aren't many people around in a storm like this, not while thunder booms, lightning sizzles, wind howls, and rain lashes the island in phantom-like sheets. Those who *are* out and about are looking for trouble. The Warlock has seen a couple of baseball bats, a tire iron, a shotgun, and even a fire axe in the grips of unknown figures patrolling the night.

Pitchforks and torches. Swords. The mob. Hunting the monster.

His eyes dart from side to side as he walks along. He tenses every time he passes a darkened alley, wondering if this is the moment when he'll meet his destiny, if this is when a knife-wielding madman—the Ripper—will leap out of hiding to strike.

Wondering if he's ready, or if he's made a terrible mistake being out here.

Engines roar in the storm, and the Warlock turns toward headlights diffused by the rain. A truck rumbles along the street. Three shadowy, huddled figures in the cab, four more—all soaking wet, irritated, and armed to the teeth—in the back. He knows the truck, knows the men. Marcus Derry, Cliff Ryan, and their sons. All mean-spirited, angry, the kind of guys who go fishing and hunting not for food, but in order to kill something.

They wake up every morning and choose violence. This just gives them an excuse. Me, I'm more like a tourist.

Only, the Warlock's not seeking violence, at least not for the sake of it alone. He braves the storm and the rowdy mob, even the potential encounter with a murderer, for something more. Something bigger than himself. A spirit, an entity, an angel, a demon, or a fucking repressed memory has lured him out, given him a sense of meaning and purpose he hasn't felt in . . .

. . . well . . .

He's actually *never* felt such purpose before.

And the heavy rain can't drown that out.

Big tires cast a lashing haze of water across his face as the truck races past.

There are other vehicles cruising the streets. Unfamiliar ones, sleek and black, with windows tinted. Like sharks hunting a meal. Out-of-town "talent," brought in to bring a mad dog to heel with cold, detached efficiency.

A Trans Am hydroplanes to a stop along the curb. The doors open, and three young men pile out into the maelstrom. He knows them too. Butler, Lee, and Nelson. They've all moved away, gone off to college, but they're back home for the summer, trying to recapture their youth. Two of them are armed, Lee with a bat, Nelson with a hammer. Surely Butler has a weapon stashed inside the car, next to the driver's seat. The Warlock takes a step back and tightens his hand on the sword's hilt.

"You—what are you doing out here, Warlock?" Butler asks.

"Tonight's not exactly a night for pushing weed," Lee says.

"I don't know," Nelson remarks. "I think I could use a little. What have you got, man?"

"I don't have anything," the Warlock replies.

"What good are you, then?" Nelson says.

"Look at him," Butler says. "Look at his sword. The fucking nerd's out here like the rest of us, looking for the killer."

"I guess I am." He nods toward the car. "You got room for one more?"

The three guys howl with laughter.

The rain has soaked their clothing and matted their hair. Butler wipes his face, like he's trying to change his bemused and mocking expression into something even more cruel.

"Come on, man!" he says. "This ain't a movie!"

The Warlock tries—and fails—not to scoff at them. Butler and Nelson used to roll dice and slay dragons with him a couple of times a week. Traitors.

"We're dealing with real dangerous shit!" Nelson says.

"I know that," the Warlock replies, raising his voice to be heard over the downpour.

"Do you?" Nelson asks.

"I can help you," the Warlock says.

"We don't want your help," says Butler.

"Clear heads, man," Nelson says. "Clear heads and steady hands. That's what we need."

"Really. Weren't you just asking me for weed?" the Warlock notes.

"Why?" Nelson asks. "You got any?"

They laugh again.

"Just go home, man," Butler tells him.

They hurry back into the car, slamming the doors, cutting off their laughter. Wheels spin on wet pavement, and they speed off into the night, taillights painting the asphalt in red.

The Warlock continues on his way.

He looks at the sword, turns it over in his hand. Water runs down the steel, across the names—*Andúril, Graywand, Doomgiver*—and drips from the blade.

He still thinks he sounds like an idiot.

CHAPTER SIXTY-TWO

WILLA'S PHONE CHIMES.

SARAH: You been washed away yet?

Her message flashes across the screen, the latest in a long chain of texts dating back five years. The girls have been communicating for what feels like forever, and neither one of them has the heart to clear out the threads. The back-and-forth conversation illustrates a long evolution covering subjects such as music and sleepovers and boys and schoolwork and college and hopes and fears and dreams.

And now torrential storms.

Wind rattles the windows. Rain blasts against the glass panes. The lights flicker overhead, cowering at the crashing thunder and blossoming lightning, then surging back, brave again until the next cataclysmic boom.

Willa sits cross-legged on what they all call "Dad's chair" even though her father spends almost no time whatsoever in the living room. Her phone glows in her hands, her thumbs dancing across the screen.

WILLA: It's not too bad.
SARAH: Maybe not for Fort Hanson. Our roof springs one more leak and we officially live in an aquarium.

Three little dots bounce at the bottom of the screen, Sarah still writing.

SARAH: How's your mom holding up?

On the couch, Willa's mother is curled up in a medicated slumber, a knit blanket pulled up to her chin. The rhythmic rise and fall of her chest is the only sign she isn't another piece of the furniture.

WILLA: Coma state.

Storms do not sit well with her mom. They are, in fact, panic-inducing. It took weeks for her to get over Hurricane Helene. As soon as she recovered, her dad had driven Mom directly to Doc Maro's office, where he prescribed a bit of pharmaceutical peace of mind for just such an occasion.

Her mom wasn't always afraid of storms. Willa remembers that when she was little more than a toddler, they used to go for walks in torrential downpours. And they loved it. She doesn't know what changed. She guesses people don't need any major trauma to develop new stress-induced anxiety.

Sometimes fear just slips in uninvited.

SARAH: She's missing the apocalypse.

Willa can almost hear Sarah's voice in the messages. It's like she's right here in the room, even though she's across town, holed up with her own family, battening down the hatches against the intense storm. It comforts her.

WILLA: BRB. Gotta pee.
SARAH: I don't rate bathroom texts? I thought you loved me.

Chuckling, Willa abandons her phone on the chair's armrest. She pulls herself to her feet and quietly crosses the room, trying not to disturb her mom. Her bare feet sink into the plush carpet.

The door to her father's office is open a couple of inches, and Willa peeks in as she walks past. Dad paces back and forth before his desk. He sits in his office chair about as frequently as in the living room one. In one hand he clasps his phone, looking at it expectantly. In the other he holds a glass of bourbon.

He's sent out the alarm—calling in loyal employees and old friends, working the network of people who, when he proclaimed jump, did their very best pogo impersonations. He has rounded up a posse to track down a killer, the figure the local paper is calling the Wilson Island Ripper. Based on his demeanor, though, the posse has yet to yield the desired results.

Willa pushes the door open another inch or so, looks in. "No luck?" she asks, already knowing the answer.

Dad looks at her, curtaining his worry behind a smile. "We'll find him."

"And what happens when you do?"

"We'll make sure he doesn't hurt anyone else."

"For some reason, that's not comforting."

"You don't need to worry."

Easier said than done.

Willa loves her father dearly and knows he's a good man, intent on protecting his family. What he does for a living doesn't change that. Yet she's aware that others in town carry a hint of fear toward him.

Sometimes she feels that fear too—not because of anything he's done, but because of what she imagines he might be capable of, should he choose to act on it. That's something she has never witnessed. He has rallied a crowd to hunt down the killer. She wonders—if they succeed, if they catch him—

Will I see that side of Dad?

And was there any coming back from that?

Drumming a good-bye upon the door, Willa backs away, leaving her father to his own devices. Now she moves a little more quickly, on her tiptoes, toward the downstairs bathroom. She doesn't bother closing the door. Funny, she didn't want to bring her phone and Sarah along with her, but she's also not too hung up on perfect privacy. Dad's not leaving his office, and Mom's not leaving the couch. Complete isolation from her family doesn't feel all that great anyhow. Cutoff shorts around her ankles, she sits on cold porcelain and contemplates important matters at hand.

The Wilson Island Ripper. That name kind of sucks. What would she call the killer if it was up to her? No clue.

But she's almost certain she can come up with something better. And she knows perfectly well that Sarah probably already has a half dozen new noms de guerre in mind for Wilson Island's very own murderer.

And that, she decides, will occupy the next couple of dozen text messages at least.

Do I know how to ride out a storm or do I?

Finishing up and washing her hands, Willa hurries back down the hall toward the living room. She isn't scared or nervous, with the weather battering the house, but she doesn't really feel like being alone either.

The lights sputter out as she reaches the living room, welcoming her. Beyond the big picture window is a blur of wind and rain. The scene draws her across the room. Forgetting her phone for a second, she looks out at the world. Rain whips against the glass and lashes the yard. Trees bend to the whims of the gale. Leaves and debris skitter across the lawn.

Willa presses her fingertips to the cool glass, tracing the rivulets that race each other down the pane. The sky falls before her, but there is a strange kind of beauty to the whirling, wild tumult. It's untamed and unbridled and doesn't give a damn about nightmares or pregnancies or asshole boyfriends. She looks at her reflection on the glass and wishes she—

Only it's not her reflection.

A figure, conjured by the ferocity of the storm, has materialized in front of her.

The man—or what should be a man—is shrouded by the deluge, dressed in dark coveralls, clad in a leather apron, wearing heavy gloves, girded with a belt of mismatched blades.

And he has no face.

Something opaque and pale and featureless—save for a long, bony, segmented trunk—covers his head.

Water sluices off the mask, runs down his apron, drips from his fingertips.

The man without a face tilts his head, as though curious or perhaps amused by the girl looking back at him.

Somehow, Willa knows exactly who she's looking at. This is the Wilson Island Ripper—the murderer her father is hoping to catch.

Willa backs away from the window, slowly at first, one step.

"Dad?"

Then another. Two more.

"Dad!"

Her breath catches in her throat, a strangled gasp clawing its way out as she looks to her mom, sleeping on the couch, to the partially open door of her father's office.

"*Dad!* He's here! The killer! He's right—"

She expects to see that eyeless face at the window. He's gone, though. Swallowed up by lashing sheets of rain.

The office door crashes open and her father bursts into the living room, looking to and fro, clutching a pistol in his hand. "Where?!" he demands.

"The window . . . he was just—"

Words fail Willa. She can't get past her brief encounter with the faceless man.

Dad moves to the window, standing close to the glass, craning his neck, looking left, then right, trying to catch a glimpse of the intruder.

"I didn't get a good look," Willa says, "but I'm pretty sure it's him."

On the couch, Willa's mother stirs. Her eyes open, confused, blinking. She reaches out, as if she thinks she's in bed, as if she'll find her husband next to her. Then, realizing she's on the couch, she pushes herself up.

"Wade?" Her voice is thick.

"It's all right, Sue. Just stay where you are, okay? Give me a second here."

He crosses to the foyer, and Willa follows him. He unlocks the front door, pushes it open to invite the storm inside.

"Stay behind me," he says.

"Dad, be careful."

Her father steps outside onto the porch, letting the stinging rain glaze his face. Mist roils in front of him, a writhing cloud. A flash of lightning brightens the yard, casting elongated, twisted versions of the familiar onto the wet grass.

Behind him, Willa watches, every muscle tense.

She registers the movement before he does. A quick flash. A shape detaching itself from the shadows, darting past the front window, coming in fast from the side.

"Dad—!"

At the last second, her father turns his face away from the movement. A blade arcs out, catching the flash of a crackling stroke of lightning. Arching up, the blade strafes across his face, ripping skin like tissue paper, tracing the outline of his cheekbone.

If he hadn't turned—

Her father hunches over, his hand instinctively rising to cover and protect his injury.

And the man without a face strikes again. The blade comes down, tearing across the back of her father's protective hand.

Blood curls and twists in the water that slicks the painted boards of the porch. Like thunder, the gun booms in the dark.

The planks at her father's feet explode in a shower of splinters.

The Ripper—the name doesn't seem so ridiculous now—kicks Willa's father, raises his booted foot, and stomps the gun from his fingers. The weapon spins across the rain-slicked porch, sliding over the side and into the bushes. Another kick, this one to a buckling knee, drops her father to a kneeling position. Dismissively, the killer reaches out with his gloved hand, grabs Wade Hanson by the hair, and yanks, rolling him down the front steps and into the mud.

A deafening clap of thunder shakes the house's foundations.

Seeing her father being attacked in such a brutal manner, Willa feels an unexpected desire to glimpse his dark side—the aspect she worried she might one day witness. She wishes she could muster some of it herself.

The killer turns his obscured face toward the door, toward Willa, the strange tube—if that's what it really is—swinging back and forth under his blank face.

How can he see me?

The Ripper steps across the threshold. Dad kicks and squirms and groans in the mud behind him. A silent *No* on her lips, Willa backs away from the door.

Stepping into the foyer, the Ripper reaches out, his gloved fingers twitching, water dripping from his fingertips. Rain sweeps in behind him.

Willa takes three more steps, then turns, knocking knickknacks from side tables. She sprints down the hall, chancing a look into the living room. Her mother still sits there, sort of slumped forward, blinking, in a fugue state, her mind not registering the events unfolding around her. On the arm of the chair—her father's chair—Willa's phone chimes, the screen flares. Sarah is sending her messages. Willa can imagine what they say:

How long does it take for you to pee?

The killer chases Willa—if he sees her mom, he doesn't react to her. Willa wants to keep it that way.

She wants to lure him away from her dazed mother, lead him away from her injured father before he returns for round two.

Back door.

Dodging furniture, she takes great, leaping steps down the hall, throwing herself through the kitchen. If she were thinking clearly, she might have grabbed a blade for herself from the block of knives. But she's devoid of thought, of survival instinct other than the back door—and she leaves the knife.

Just like she left her phone.

Her dad. Her mom.

She bursts through the back entrance, the night swallowing her whole, the wind lashing against her face as if nature itself is trying to push her into the house. She doesn't touch the steps, her bare feet slapping against the wet grass.

She glances back.

At first she only sees the open door to the kitchen, the light spilling out into the night. She almost stops, because she's afraid that instead of leading him away, she's allowed the killer to ply his trade within, focusing his attention on Mom and Dad. Then he appears, tall and dark and faceless, standing boldly in the door to face the storm. He holds the same knife used to cut her father in his right hand.

He flies down the steps after Willa.

She screams, running toward the wet street, into the storm. Water rushes in churning rivers along the curb. Her legs pump hard, pushing her ahead.

She doesn't look back.

She knows the Ripper is there, hot on her heels.

CHAPTER SIXTY-THREE

RAW FEAR FUELS WILLA'S ESCAPE. Her heart hammers in her chest. Her side aches as her breath blasts raggedly from her lips. Her bare feet sting against the pavement. Her clothes are soaked through, sticking to her skin. Her hair is heavy with water, curling bangs hanging in her face.

Around her, the neighborhood is a corridor of homes, some dark and silent, others illuminated but the curtains drawn.

The Ripper is right behind her.

Through the downpour, she can hear him now, his booted feet slapping through puddles on the street, his own angry grunting beneath his mask.

Gaining ground. Getting closer.

She can't seek refuge at one of the neighboring houses. If she runs across the yard, beats against a locked door, the Ripper will be on top of her in an instant, stabbing and slashing at her with his blades.

Willa screams for help, her throat raw, but she knows the people inside those houses cannot distinguish her over the rain and wind and thunder that shrieks right along with her.

A hand snaps out, seizing her wrist with a gloved hand, yanking her back, almost pulling her off her feet. She whirls and finds herself staring into the blank nightmare that passes for the Ripper's face.

"No!" She twists her arm, trying to pull free. "Let go!"

She reaches out with her free hand and scratches at his masked face. She digs trenches in its surface. It feels like wet wax beneath her fingernails.

It twitches like gooseflesh.

What the fuck?

The Ripper refuses to let go. He pulls, dragging her toward him. She sees beads of blood welling up along the scratches she left in the mask, washing away in the rain, oozing down the curve of the featureless face. The long, segmented tube whips back and forth. A smell like rotted meat suddenly hangs heavy in the air.

What the fuck?

Willa's eyes dart toward the nearby houses. No one is watching. No one is coming to save her.

As lightning spiderwebs across the sky, a sword slashes out, glinting in the sudden, bursting glow. The tip of the blade arcs toward the killer's face, missing him by less than an inch, and only then because the faceless man releases Willa and hops back, almost slipping and falling on the wet pavement. Spattering rain, the sword whips back, raised high, and comes down again, clanging against the pavement. Along the length of the blade, like graffiti, names are painted in various colors.

The Warlock . . . ?

Drenched to the bone, panting, teeth bared, Wilson Island's nerdy weed dealer brandishes an honest-to-God sword.

Willa can't help it. The night's mantra bounces through her skull once more.

What . . . the . . . fuck?

The Ripper's face can't be seen, but he's certainly surprised, recoiling, cocking his eyeless face to the side, summing up the surreal situation before the fingers of one hand squeeze on the handle of the knife, before the fingers of the other hand pull another blade from the jangling belt at his waist. The momentary confusion passes, and the Ripper moves in, his blades now stabbing and slashing at the Warlock.

Weapon or not, Willa realizes, the Warlock is not some sort of natural sword-wielding hero.

His eyes go wide. A startled gasp reshapes his mouth from a fury-filled grimace to a fright-filled O. He shuffles back, almost tripping over his own feet, to avoid the slashing arcs of the Ripper's blades.

When he came out tonight, Willa thinks, *when he took that sword from his wall or closet or toy chest or wherever, he never expected to really put it to work, to be in a real clash of steel.*

Metal strikes against metal as the Ripper advances, arms like pinwheels, striking again and again at the sword as the Warlock backpedals, as he parries the attacks. Every time the Ripper strikes, a vibration shudders through the Warlock's arm.

Watching the battle—a man with a replica sword the only thing standing between her and a murderer with no face—Willa has no clue what to do next.

Do I help? Go get help? Check on Mom and Dad? Run for my life?

The Ripper slashes at the Warlock, and he ducks to the side, the deadly blades slicing through his jacket at his shoulder, drawing blood. The Warlock brings the tip of his sword down, letting it scrape the street; then, almost falling back on his ass, he rapidly brings the blade up. A lucky strike—the tip clips the bottom of the featureless mask with a hollow *crack*.

The Ripper grunts and flinches as the mask is knocked from his face, flying upward, tumbling through the air.

Dropping his knives, turning his head wildly, looking for his mask, the Ripper's face is a blur for only a moment before he looks toward Willa and the Warlock, angrily snarling.

"Junior . . . ?" The name slips from the Warlock's lips, a whisper almost lost in the downpour.

Hunched over, panting, water dripping from his face, her attacker roars in horror and frustration and fury. Blood rings his face, tiny cuts and scrapes running across his forehead, down past his ears, around his chin. His lips are horribly chapped and cracked.

Willa recognizes him too. Junior Simms, who bags groceries at the Save-a-Ton, who cares for his aging mother, who was picked on mercilessly by guys like Kenny and his friends. The pieces of the puzzle don't fit. How could *he* be the monster who's been terrorizing Wilson Island?

On the wet street, the faceless mask—

—twitches.

A trick of the light, maybe, an optical illusion caused by the rain or the rushing gutter water, but Willa swears something just moved around the edges, and the long, segmented tube descending from the bottom now slithers like a coiling snake, writhing back and forth.

"Junior?"

The Warlock says the name again, almost pleading, begging for the unmasked murderer to explain what is happening.

Junior, still panting with rage, raises his eyes to meet the Warlock's. His lips pull away from his teeth in disgust. The blood ringing his face oozes in the rain, curling down his neck. If he recognizes his name, he doesn't respond.

Emboldened, the Warlock draws his sword back, raises it high, ready for another swing.

"What are you doing?" Willa demands.

"What the fuck do you mean?! He just tried to hack us to pieces!" the Warlock says, nearly screaming.

"It doesn't matter!" Willa grabs the Warlock's arm, tries to force him to lower the sword. "You can't just kill him! Hey! You can't just . . . fuck, what are you doing?! You can't just chop his head off!"

The Warlock hasn't planned this far ahead—that much is written all over his confused face. He looks to Willa for some guidance in this real-life cosplay gone awry, but he doesn't lower the sword.

A gunshot rings out in the storm.

The Warlock flails backward, falling hard to the pavement, his sword rasping as it spins away from him across the street.

"*Willa!*"

Her father, no more than a hazy outline in the rain, races down the street, gun in hand.

Shivering, both from adrenaline and the chill in the air, Willa blinks rain from her eyes.

Oh my God, he shot the wrong guy. He saw the Warlock. Saw the sword raised high. He shot the wrong guy.

Junior Simms springs to his feet, surging forward. His shoulder slams into Willa's stomach. She cries out, slips, falls to the street, gasping.

"*Willa?*"

Another gunshot explodes in the night.

Now curtains are being pulled away from windows in some of the nearby houses. Front doors are opening, neighbors peering into the gale.

They don't see Junior Simms, though. He's already vanished.

Into the mist.

Into the curtain of rain.

Willa's father crouches next to her, helping her sit up. He keeps the gun trained on the Warlock. Willa places a hand on her father's arm, pushes the gun down.

"No! No, Dad. Not him! He saved my life!"

The Warlock, clutching his shoulder, squirms on the ground, wreathed in a pool of blood that undulates in the water.

"Fuuuuuuuuuck!"

Painfully, the Warlock picks himself up off the street. Blood oozes from between his fingers as he tries to keep pressure on his shoulder.

"Junior . . . ?" he asks.

"I don't know!" Willa says. "He's gone!"

"Where is—"

Willa nods in the direction of the Warlock's painted, many-named weapon. "The sword's over there."

"Not the sword," the Warlock says. "The mask. Where's his *mask*?"

CHAPTER SIXTY-FOUR

*T**HIS,* **JUNIOR THINKS,** *must be how the people I killed felt.*
Frightened, confused, unable to catch a breath, helpless. Hunted. Alone.

His sodden clothing clings to him, heavy, slowing him down. The belt of ritual blades at his waist jangles and jingles. Rain hammers him, lashing against him in relentless sheets. Drenched and disoriented, Junior lurches through alleys, through backyards, empty lots. He avoids the main streets as best he can. There are too many cars around, tires rasping on wet pavement, headlights washing away the darkness. There are new people on the street, roused by Wade Hanson, calling out to one another, searching for him, patrolling with flashlights and guns and bats.

I can't go home. They'll be waiting for me there. They know who I am now.

I want my face back. My no-face.

He reaches up, protecting his eyes, nose, and lips, gloved fingertips twitching over the skin as if trying to solve a puzzle. The ragged punctures ringing his features throb and ooze. His throat burns with all the agony of a raging strep infection.

Worst of all, he can no longer hear her. Mother has gone silent.

Lightning forks across the sky and the world around him goes white. Holding his breath, he shudder-steps to a stop, turns in place. He is out in the open, exposed. Naked without his mask. The storm mocks him. Plays with him, like a cat with a wounded mouse. The tempest conceals him and the mist and shadow, but only until it doesn't, only until it decides to illuminate his surroundings in a burst of—

Witch's fire.

As darkness rushes back in around him, he pushes ahead, tripping over a chunk of old tire, flailing forward, sprawling in the mud and pooling water. The collapse jars every muscle in his body. He bites his tongue and tastes blood. A sob catches in his sore throat. Up until moments ago, he had been the hunter, the predator, the killer, the horror movie slasher.

Mr. No-Face.

Now, though, he is the hapless victim, running for his life, tripping and falling while the walls close in around him.

Now he's just an ordinary man—one who falls in the mud, who misses his mask, who worries about his mother, who is deathly afraid.

The mask had been more than a disguise, more than a connection to Mother. It had made him feel . . . *apart* from everyone else.

Detached. Invincible.

Looking up, he sees a small, rain-drenched dog before him.

It's Buster, watching him curiously.

The dog backs away, mud spattering the hair of its legs, then turns to run. Buster takes a couple of steps, looks back at Junior, and barks. Then he hops past mud puddles and continues on his way. He stops again after a couple of yards, looks back, barks again, and waits.

He wants me to follow.

Struggling to his feet, Junior chases after the dog, this weird little animal he almost killed on the night Kenny Smythe nearly plowed into him with his truck, on the night he screwed up so royally, on the first fateful night he had taken a person's life.

Undeterred by the storm, Buster hurries on his way. The tags on the little dog's collar jingle, keeping rhythm with the knives and peelers and scalers on Junior's belt. Junior follows, unsteady and unsure, lurching along after the dog.

Buster stops at the end of an alleyway. His tail wags excitedly, expectantly. Junior steps closer, almost moves past Buster, but the dog growls a warning, and he pauses. A truck full of armed men in rain slickers blasts past, casting a spray of water from under the tires. Once it's gone, taillights tracing a path as it peels around the corner, Buster sets out once more.

Rain pelts the two as they hurry along the deserted streets. Their feet splash through water-filled potholes. Buster leads Junior past darkened buildings, down alleys and side streets, always keeping a safe distance between them and any signs of life.

They pass another patrol of armed citizens, flashlights sweeping across the buildings and area. Junior ducks behind a dumpster and holds his breath. He lowers his head, not wanting one of the beams of light to wash across his all-too-human face. When he looks up, Buster is patiently waiting for him.

The dog, Junior realizes, is a harbinger. *A guide.*

But where is this dog leading him? And why has it taken such an interest in him?

By the time they reach the deserted lot behind Rudy's Mart, the rain is finally starting to let up.

The little dog turns to look at him before darting into the nearby woods.

Junior follows cautiously, trying not to make too much noise as he pushes through branches and steps over fallen logs. His feet squelch in the wet sand. He hears rustling in the bushes around him.

They move deeper into the woods, away from town and any signs of civilization.

Junior and Buster soon emerge from the woods, the trees parting to reveal a suburban subdivision. Rows of unfinished houses stand silently, their windows dark and their doorways gaping or boarded up.

Junior knows this place well.

The Golden Dunes subdivision, location of the killing field, home of dozens of transients, one of whom lost her life upon Junior's blades.

Buster had been here with him when he killed the homeless out-of-town girl, too.

Like some sort of witness.

Silent homes, some little more than framework skeletons, loom on either side of the street as Junior shuffles along. If the development had been successful, the houses might have been filled with laughter, with tears, with moms and dads and children, with family dinners. Kids might have ridden bikes in the street or played basketball in the driveways or jumped on trampolines in the backyards.

We don't always get what we deserve.

The dog leads him to the end of the street, and he recognizes this place. This is what Junior calls the Field of the Dead, where the bodies of animals are scattered across the ground like an offering to—

A figure stands in the center of the field, shrouded in the rain, arms cast out to the sides.

Deific.

"Daddy—"

The word slips from his mouth unbidden, and Junior once again wishes he were wearing his mask.

His No-Face wouldn't allow him to speak, to say something so stupid. Because this isn't Daddy.

The figure lowers his arms and steps forward. A crackle of lightning reveals his weathered, bearded face.

Buster whimpers at his approach.

"You don't belong here," he says. "You never did."

Madhouse Quinn.

"Th-they're after me," Junior mutters.

"Why?" Madhouse trudges across the wet carcasses of dozens of animals, their brittle bones crunching underfoot. "Why would they give a damn about you?"

"You know why."

Madhouse steps so close Junior can smell his body odor. As witch's fire flickers through the blackness, he looks deep into Junior's eyes, trying to find a seed of recognition. He traces rough fingertips across Junior's face, as if trying to coax a memory from the young man's skin.

"I lost the mask," Junior says.

Madhouse studies his face for a moment.

"You weren't there that night." Madhouse Quinn pulls his hand away from Junior and stretches his grimy fingers out wide. "You are not one of the five."

"Five?"

"You were not chosen."

Figures peel away from the darkness now, shuffling out of the shadows, surrounding Junior, pressing in close.

Their faces are covered, each and every one of them. Some wear cheap, dirty Halloween masks or simple cloth masks, while others have elaborate creations that cover their entire heads. Handmade disguises. Rotting mockeries of human faces constructed of skin and fur and feather and bone harvested from dead animals. Taken from the offerings his father had made.

They close in around him. They do not speak, but Junior hears their voices just the same.

"Not chosen."

"Not chosen."

"Not chosen."

They speak with Mother's voice.

More masked figures emerge from the darkness, taking their places among the others.

Junior backs up, feeling a surge of terror as he realizes that these are not just masks. They're *real* faces, contorted by madness.

And they all seem to be looking at him with hunger in their eyes.

The little dog watches from behind Junior's legs, curious but wary. It knows something is not right here.

The crowd closes in around Junior, reaching for him with dirt-caked hands and gnarled fingers. They want something from him, something he doesn't understand. As they press in upon him, Junior's legs buckle. He falls to his knees on the street.

Yipping, Buster flees into the shadows.

A glow washes over everyone. Headlights.

The masked figures recoil, pulling away from Junior, their various disguises thrown to the ground.

A gleaming black pickup truck rumbles ominously down the center of the wind- and rainswept street, its engine growling like a restless beast. Floodlights across the top of the cab blaze in the darkness.

Those gathered nearby hesitate, some shielding their eyes from the glare of the light reflecting off the truck's polished surface. The pickup's doors swing open with a metallic clank.

"Step back!" Scraps shouts as he leaps from the vehicle, his voice sharp and commanding. "All of you!"

"You heard him!" Bear echoes, his tone leaving no room for defiance.

Scraps grips a tire iron in his hand. Beside him, Bear cradles a shotgun. A more intimidating weapon for a more intimidating man. He pumps it, ratcheting a shell into the chamber.

The crowd fully retreats, giving the two men a wide berth.

Bear aims the shotgun at Junior.

"Hands where we can see them!" Scraps barks. "Right now!"

Junior rises unsteadily to his knees, hands raised in surrender.

"If he moves," Scraps tells Bear, "just blow his fucking head off and we can be done with it."

Scraps moves in close, searches Junior, stripping him of his blade-laden belt, passing the weapons to Bear.

"You . . . you can't do th-this," Junior stammers.

"Oh yeah? I bet we can do just about whatever we want." Scraps uses the tire iron, lengthwise, to give Junior a shove. "You're just lucky I'm in a kindhearted mood."

Bear hoists Junior to his feet with one arm and marches him to the truck.

Junior casts a final glance over his shoulder. The residents of Golden Dunes remain, silently observing. Their masks lie discarded on the glistening, rain-slicked street.

And with a sinking feeling in the pit of his gut, Junior understands that their masks did not abandon them.

CHAPTER SIXTY-FIVE

SHERIFF BUCK, ALONG WITH HIS three deputies—Reed, Keene, and Fines—wait outside the station in the pouring rain. Each droplet weaves a trail down their slickers. They look like gray ghosts in the dark.

"Look at that," Scraps says as he pulls his truck to a stop. "You're famous."

"Probably just what you wanted when you started cutting people up," Bear says.

At Bear's feet, the blade-adorned belt oozes water onto the floormats.

"N-no." Water drips from Junior's hair as he shakes from the cold. "I was trying to help."

"Uh-huh. Tell that to them." Scraps eyes the cops. "I, for one, don't like the rain. I don't like you dripping all over the inside of my truck. And I don't like being this close to the sheriff's department. So we're just gonna hand you over and be done with your sorry ass."

Bear shoves his door open and hauls Junior out by the arm. Something in Junior's arm pops, and he groans in pain. Scraps comes around the front of the truck and takes Junior by his other arm, and they march him—this grocery store bag boy, this mama's boy, this near shut-in, this killer—toward the station.

As they drag Junior from the truck, Sheriff Buck grumbles in his direction. "We're never gonna hear the goddamned end of this."

The deputies move through the curtain of rain to meet Scraps, Bear, and Junior.

"We caught him," Scraps says, raising his voice so he can be heard over the downpour. "We might as well walk him through the door."

The deputies exchange uncertain glances with Buck.

"Just get him inside," the sheriff says.

Scraps nods as they saunter past.

"His knives are still in the truck." Bear winks at the sheriff. "Might want to grab those. You know. For evidence."

"Reed," Buck says, "haul yourself out to Golden Dunes. Sweep the area. Keep an eye out for anything unusual or noteworthy before the rain washes it all away."

"Yes, sir," Reed says.

Junior Simms's legs are rigid, stiffening with exhaustion, but he offers no resistance as Scraps and Bear escort him into the station. They flank him, each firmly grasping one of his arms. Bear's grip is so tight it seems he might rip the arm clean off and use it to batter Junior into submission if he put up a fight. A wet trail marks their path across the floor.

Tessa Kendry, sitting at her receptionist's desk, phone pressed to her ear, pen in hand, watches Junior with her mouth agape. She's known him and his family for years, used to babysit him when he was little.

Junior averts his eyes. He can't stand the look of disgust on the woman's face.

Sheriff Buck follows, his slicker dribbling water, beads of rain on his plastic hat covering, with his deputies close behind. He carries the jangling belt of blades. He tosses it onto the desk and rubs his fingers together as if he can somehow feel blood and gore on them.

"Put him in a cell," Buck says.

"You don't want a statement?" Fines asks.

"We ain't gonna get anything useful from him tonight," Buck notes, and nothing else.

"What about Doc Maro?" Tessa asks. "Maybe we should have him come over and take a look at those wounds. His face—"

"The doctor can see him tomorrow."

The two deputies take over from Scraps and Bear, who lose no time heading back to their truck. "This way." Keene tugs his arm, steering him toward a dented and scuffed door of cold gray steel.

Fines releases Junior, just for a moment, and uses one of the keys on his belt to unlock the door.

Junior looks back over his shoulder at the sheriff. "My mother," he says.

Will she be all right? Will she be worried? Will she even know I'm not home?

There's anger in Sheriff Buck's glare.

"We'll look in on her," he snaps.

Keene shoves Junior through the door. Here the flooring changes from linoleum to concrete. The walls are lined with cells, all of them empty. Harsh fluorescent bulbs flicker overhead. At the last of the cell doors, Fines fumbles with the jangling keys again. The lock turns with a heavy *chunk*. The door groans on its hinges. Keene ushers Junior into the holding cell with another shove.

The door slams shut with the crash of metal on metal.

The deputies watch him for a bit. He understands the confused looks on their faces.

They're trying to figure me out. Trying to understand how I could do what I did.

Giving up, Deputies Keene and Fines head back down the hall. The cellblock door slams behind them

They don't understand that they've just killed everyone.

CHAPTER SIXTY-SIX

MAYBE IF HE HADN'T BEEN shot in the first place, the Warlock might have felt bad about bleeding all over Willa Hanson's kitchen.

They're both soaked to the bone, wrapped in blankets, sitting across from one another at the kitchen table with cups of hot chocolate before them. Between the mugs, the Warlock's painted sword stretches across the table. Willa looks down at her phone, her thumbs typing out a message to one of her friends. The Warlock clutches a blood-soaked towel to his shoulder. Patches of smeared, bloody footprints trail across the tile floor.

"Can't fucking believe your dad shot me," the Warlock says, not for the first time since they came in out of the rain.

"It only grazed your shoulder," Willa replies.

"A *bullet* grazed my shoulder. From a *gun*. From a gun fired by your *dad*. Which means, your dad *shot* me."

"In his defense, you were swinging a sword around his daughter."

"I was saving your life."

"With a *sword*."

"How the hell else was I supposed to save you?"

They suddenly laugh at the ridiculousness of it all, at the bloody floor and the soaked clothing and the patchwork blankets and the sword and the fucking hot chocolate. Most of all, they laugh because they're both still alive.

Somehow. Miraculously.

"Seriously," Willa says, sobering for a moment, "thank you. I would've been dead if you weren't there."

The Warlock looks down awkwardly, and grabs his cup of hot chocolate. He drinks it in three gulps. Setting the cup back on the table, he rolls his injured shoulder. "Ow. Dammit."

Willa touches the sword on the table. "What's with all the names?"

"It's stupid, I guess."

"What's stupid?"

"In all the books I've read, all the movies I've watched"— the Warlock shrugs—"um . . . the swords, at least the important ones, always had *names*, and the names gave them power. I thought it was cool, I guess . . . and I wanted this sword to have power too."

Willa eyes all the words painted along the blade.

Excalibur. Stormbringer. Sting. Mourneblade. Glamdring. Andúril. Blackrazor. Graywand. Scalpel. Doomgiver.

"A lot of names. A lot of power."

"Not really," says the Warlock. "I just never settled on any one name. None of them ever really mattered anyhow."

"What's this one?"

"That's from *Lord of the Rings*."

"And this one?"

"*Game of Thrones*."

Her fingers touch the blade, moving toward another name.

"That's from the Elric books. Stormbringer. That's his soul-stealing sword. This one, Mourneblade, is from Elric too. It's his cousin's sword."

"Hm." Willa isn't really paying attention; he can tell she isn't all that interested. "What about this one?"

"Witch's Fire," the Warlock says. "Not from a book. Just thought it sounded cool. It's what my granny used to call lightning on stormy nights."

Almost on cue, lightning flickers outside.

"'Granny?'" Willa asks.

"Yeah. Why, what do you call your grandmother?"

"Nana."

"Is that any better?"

"You just don't seem like the 'Granny' type." Willa shrugs. "What about for you? Why do you call yourself Warlock?"

"*The* Warlock."

"Sure."

"Why not?"

"Don't you think it's a little . . ."

"Dumb?"

"I was going to say 'a little dorky,'" Willa says. "Who knows, though? You saved my life. My dad's not gonna forget that. He'll probably even offer you a job."

"Seriously?"

"Knowing my dad? Yeah. And when he does, you'll fit right in with all his other nonsensically named employees."

Willa's phone chimes, and she looks to the screen, her thumbs typing out a message.

"Who are you talking to?" the Warlock asks.

"Sarah. My friend. I think she's freaking out."

"Aren't you?"

Willa looks up from her phone. "Not right now."

"Good for you, I guess."

"Are you? Freaking out, I mean."

"Uh, hello? That was only Junior fucking Simms."

"You know him?"

"*Yeah*. Everyone knows him."

"I guess so."

"I used to play D&D with him," the Warlock says. "Uh. Dungeons and Dragons."

"I know what D&D stands for."

"Just making sure."

"The dungeons are calling," Willa says absently.

"What's that?" The Warlock sits up in his chair.

"It's just the name of a song."

"Yeah. From Savatage. *You* know Savatage?"

"Indeed. We're all full of surprises."

"Just like Junior Simms, huh? I never expected anything like *that* from him. I mean, he *killed* somebody. A few somebodies, I think. He tried to kill you."

"And my dad."

"Did you also know," the Warlock says, grinning, "that your dad shot me?"

"So I've heard." Willa rolls her eyes, playing along. "Once the storm clears, we can get you to the doctor if you want."

"I'll be all right." The Warlock flexes his shoulder. "Doesn't really hurt all that bad now."

The phone rings in Mr. Hanson's office down the hall and he answers. Though the Warlock can't make out what he's saying, his tone sounds excited.

"What was with that mask anyway?" the Warlock asks.

"Creepy, right?"

"No, I mean, where'd it go? When I knocked it off his face, it fell to the street. Then it was just . . . gone."

"The rain must've washed it away."

"Come on. How is that possible?"

Mr. Hanson enters the room. His phone is in his hand at his side. "Who was it?" Willa asks.

"Scraps." Excitement and relief bubble in his voice. "They got him, Willa. Junior Simms. They caught the bastard."

And just like that, the rain stops pelting the house.

CHAPTER SIXTY-SEVEN

"LISTEN TO ME! PLEASE! YOU need to let me out! Please!"

Drool runs down Junior's chin. He sags against the bars of the cell, presses his face against the cool metal, screaming for all he's worth.

"*Please!* You gotta let me *out*!"

His voice ricochets off the cinderblock walls.

"If you don't let me out, *you're all gonna die*!"

He holds his breath, waiting for a response, but none comes.

"*You're not listening!*" Junior hollers, pressing his face between the bars, spittle flying from his lips. "Something bad's gonna happen! You've got to listen! You've got to understand! You've gotta believe me!"

No one bothers to hear him out.

"This isn't about me! This is bigger than you can imagine! I didn't want to hurt anyone! I didn't! But she isn't going to wait! She's hungry! She expects to be fed! If she's not . . ."

At last he quiets down. Gives up.

Junior shuffles away from the bars, regarding his surroundings, the concrete floor and walls, the sink, the toilet, the small bed. The air is damp and heavy, the rain from the world outside pushing in, seeping through the pores of the cinderblocks and his soaking wet clothing. The chill of the floor rises through Junior's feet and legs, up through his gut, and into his chest. He sits on the mattress, feeling the old springs bite into his ass.

His face hurts. The lacerations and gouges ringing his features are swollen and leaking and throbbing. He wants to touch the tiny cuts, but dares not.

He clutches his hands—freed from their ritual gloves—together. He studies the backs of his hands, his palms, his fingers, the tiny scars from old cuts, the length of his nails, the hairs on the backs of his knuckles. He squeezes his hands together, watching the color drain from his skin. The way he presses them, it looks like he's praying. He closes his eyes.

Hungry.

The voice echoes in his brain so loudly it makes him jump.

His eyes snap open wide. He looks around for the source of the sound. He's alone, though.

Hungry.

A glow spills across the hallway, ghostly and cold, chasing shadows into corners. The light is pale, translucent, tentative, as if it might vanish at any moment. It crawls across the walls like a spreading patch of ice.

Junior shifts uneasily on his mattress seat.

A female figure, pale and angelic, glides along the hall. She is too tall for a human being, her legs too long, jointed like an animal's, her arms bending in too many places, in too many conflicting directions, her fingers—only three of them on each hand—too long and spindly. She is naked, but her flesh hangs from her overlong bones in draping, shawl-like sheets. She has no hair, but a mane of wriggling, squirming tentacles hangs from the back of her elongated skull. She has no nose to speak of, no lips, and her lidless eyes are large and bulging and black.

Junior's mouth falls open.

He never wants to look away. He wants to stare at her forever.

But he glances toward the wall-mounted cameras at the end of the hall, the red light glittering, and he wonders if the deputies, the sheriff, at their desks and in their offices, are witnessing what he sees. *Do they understand now?*

"*Do you know why I am here?*" she asks.

Her mouth does not move.

"Yes," he says, his voice trembling.

"*Why?*"

"Because I fucked up," Junior says. "Because now there's no one to help you. To feed you. Because you're hungry."

She stares at him with those overlarge black eyes.

"No," she says, her mouth unmoving. "*I was never all that hungry in the first place.*"

CHAPTER SIXTY-EIGHT

*R*ACHEL WOULD LOVE TO BE HERE, Deputy Eric Reed thinks. *Here at the scene of the Wilson Island Ripper's capture. She should be here to report on it.*

But he damn sure isn't calling her.

He considers it, yes, but leaves his phone untouched as he explores the empty buildings and unfinished streets of Golden Dunes. He likes his job, and already has the boss's evil eye looking in his direction. So if she finds out about the arrest, it won't be from him.

Walk the walk.

He's supposed to take statements, but the people who call this area home avoid him. They have cast aside their odd, monstrous faces and vanished into the night. Various masks litter the deserted streets, silently jeering and laughing and roaring in the glow of his Maglite. Eric doesn't know what the hell that was all about. Maybe some sort of weird vagrant/pagan nonsense.

Golden Dunes is now a ghost town. And Eric, wearing his clear plastic rain poncho, looks a bit like the Grim Reaper.

Ghosts steer clear of the Angel of Death.

He shines his Maglite and spots a couple of figures slipping past, dodging through the shadows as he approaches. He lets them be. What could they tell him that he doesn't already know?

He sees a few more people darting between empty houses.

And that's—

Rachel's car . . . ?

The little hatchback is tucked out of the way behind one of the hollow, graffiti-covered houses.

Is she here? Already? Has she been here this entire time . . . ?

Eric circles the car, pointing the Maglite through the windows.

The doors, he sees, are not locked. The tires have crushed a track through beach grasses.

The last few droplets of rain patter against his poncho.

"Rachel?" he calls, moving his light into the darkness surrounding him on all sides.

A hint of worry tickles in the back of his brain. Now he grabs his phone and dials her number. He presses it to his ear, under the hood of the poncho, and hears—

Ringing. Here in Golden Dunes. Not far from where he's standing.

He follows the sound.

The call goes to voicemail. *"Hi, it's Rachel Lang with the* Wilson Island Gazette and Examiner. *I'm busy chasing down leads and writing stories. Leave me a message and I'll get back to you as soon as I can."* He disconnects. Dials again.

The ringing brings Eric to the edge of an abandoned, weed-choked lot.

A lot filled with—

Dozens of animal carcasses litter the ground—cats and dogs in various states of decomposition. Some look relatively fresh, others little more than fur-covered bones. Eric's hand trembles as he sweeps the light across the field.

And not just animals. The rain-drenched body of a young woman is sprawled here.

The body of—

"Rachel . . . ?" His voice is timid and shaky.

Her skin is pale. Her blouse is soaked in blood. Her phone, still illuminated and ringing, is clutched in her rigid fingers.

He still presses his own phone to his ear as her voicemail picks up once more.

"Hi, it's Rachel Lang with the Wilson Island Gazette and Examiner. *I'm busy chasing down leads and writing stories. Leave me a message and I'll get back to you as soon as I can."*

Rachel's eyes are open, staring, looking right back at him.

Turns out she *has* been here all this time.

CHAPTER SIXTY-NINE

WILLA SQUIRMS AND KICKS UNDER her sheets. She wants to sleep but can't get comfortable. Every time her eyes begin to flutter closed, some twinge of discomfort snaps her back to wakefulness.

Her legs ache. She rolls to her right side. She flops to her left. She turns her pillow over and over again, trying to find a cool spot to lie on. Finally she rolls again to her back, staring at the ceiling as she huffs out a breath, blowing stray hair away from her eyes.

A nasty stinging sensation radiates from her feet, not like they are asleep or numb.

The opposite.

Her nerves are on fire, and lances of pain shoot up from the balls of her feet.

Brow furrowed, Willa glances toward her covered feet. She wiggles her toes, hoping to chase the pain away. It's insistent, however, nagging and—

Hungry.

Propping herself up on her elbows, Willa peers toward the foot of the bed. Moonlight streams in through the window. The stars, she thinks, must have burned away the clouds with the storm's passing.

Burned them . . . like witch's fire.

Still, it's too dark to see clearly. The pale moonlight creates impossible shapes from the shadows, shapes that cannot be there, furtive movement that cannot exist. So she reaches for the lamp on her bedside table. With a click, light floods the room.

But the surreal shapes and movement remain.

Her feet, shrouded under the sheets, look misshapen and swollen. Too large.

They move, even though she is no longer wiggling her toes.

They turn red.

A flower of blood blossoms across the white sheets, spreading out from her toes, crawling across the fabric, expanding in a meandering pattern.

She must have cut herself while running in the streets. *But why didn't I notice before now?*

Hesitant, afraid of what she might see, she lifts the sheet, pulls it up so she can look down at her feet.

A woman—at least something that vaguely resembles one—stares back at her. It's crawling up over the foot of the bed, hunching over Willa's feet. Its skin is bone pale. Its eyes are large dark orbs. Its hair—if that's what it is—appears fleshy and squirming. It pulls itself away from the bloody remains of Willa's feet, lipless mouth slathered in red. It hisses, revealing tattered flesh between needle-sharp teeth.

One of Willa's toes is stuck between its fangs. Yet Willa feels no pain.

"Jesus!"

Willa hurls the covers away, the fabric fluttering in the air, and pushes herself back, away from the devouring woman, her back pressed against the headboard.

Willa's left foot is completely gone, a shattered bone jutting from the chewed-up, blood-pumping stump. Her right foot remains, but it hangs from her leg only by a few strips of flesh and sinew, her ankle bitten all the way through.

The woman-creature holds Willa's leg almost tenderly, lovingly, as it lowers its head and continues to feed.

Willa recoils, throwing herself sideways from the bed, landing on her stomach, falling into the tangle of bedclothes. Pushing herself up, clawing at the floor, she feels the warmth of her own blood on the sheets.

Pain that was absent until now lances up her legs as, shakily, she rises.

How—

She stands on the bloody stumps, her cracked bones scraping at the floor, blood spreading in a pool around her. Her right foot hangs from her ankle, the toes still twitching.

The foot-eating creature rises from the bed, impossibly tall, and the strange, undulating sheets of pale flesh peel away from her spindly arms, reaching out, tracing along the walls. Blood—Willa's blood—drips from her chin.

She doesn't make a sound. But Willa understands.

She's not done eating.

The room spins around Willa, a carousel of shadows and moonlight, but her focus narrows to the bloody path she paints as she propels herself forward, the raw edges of torn flesh and exposed bone grinding against the unforgiving surface beneath her.

Willa stumbles toward her bedroom door, her legs almost buckling, like part of a strange dance, the bones of her ankles scrabbling against the floor. The pain in her stomach blossoms with an intensity that threatens to buckle her knees. Sweat mingles with tears. The fabric of her tank top is stained red. Every step sends agony up her legs.

She'll eat. And eat. And eat. Until there's nothing left.

Then, abruptly, the world falls away.

...

Willa wakes.

This time she doesn't move, but lies in bed, staring at the ceiling, trying to remember what's real and what's a dream.

She'd thought the dreams were a by-product of the Ripper's—of *Junior's*—killing spree.

She'd thought that the nightmares would stop now that he was in custody and couldn't hurt anyone else.

Fuck. This isn't over yet.

CHAPTER SEVENTY

"**Y**OU . . . LIED?" JUNIOR ASKS.

"*I told you,*" says Mother, "*what you needed to hear.*"

Somehow she's in the cell with him now, the bars unable to contain her. She stands before him as he sits on the edge of the bed, and he looks up at her.

She's hurt him. But he adores her just the same.

She is beautiful and terrible, radiant and ghastly. This is how she's meant to look. This is what she looked like before she fell to earth, before Junior's father found her and started the ritual. She regards him curiously, the way a child might view a forgotten plaything.

It's not pity in her black eyes. Or love.

Is it mercy?

She is cold in her etherealness, in her eerie grace and majesty, in her angelic—deific—presence.

"You said you were hungry," Junior quietly remarks.

"And I was." Her lipless mouth does not move as she speaks. "I still am . . . in a fashion."

"You said you needed me . . . needed my father . . . to hunt for you."

"I was weak."

"We brought you what you needed."

"*Hunger was something you could understand.*"

"We were helping you."

"*Caring for another was something you could understand.*"

...

Dripping wet but shrugging out of his poncho, Deputy Eric Reed bursts through the station doors. His jaw set, his eyes blazing, he races across the office.

Tessa rises from her desk. "Eric?"

He doesn't acknowledge her.

"Is everything all right?"

Eric strides to the door that leads to the holding cells. He fumbles with the keys, jams one into the lock. Metal screeches as the door swings open. Eric steps into the hall and closes the door.

In the room behind him, he hears Tessa. "Buck?! You better get out here."

...

"*I have lived on this world for thousands of years,*" the Mother says. "*I have watched empires rise and fall. I have been worshipped as a god.*"

"Yes," Junior says. Her divinity has never been in question.

"*I did not want to be here,*" the Mother says. "*Not then. And certainly not now.*"

"You promised not to hurt anyone else if we kept you fed."

"*Did you think you could keep me satisfied?*"

"I thought—"

"*I know what is waiting for me,*" the Mother says, "*and I tried to escape.*"

"You were almost dead when my father found you."

"*I leapt away from this world.*" She raises her head, looking toward the blankness of the ceiling. "*I sprang toward the stars. I almost succeeded.*"

"Almost."

"*Gravity took hold, dragged me back to this world . . . back to reality.*"

"You fell."

...

Eric stands at the cell door. *The motherfucker is talking to himself,* he realizes, *muttering back and forth, having a conversation, using two different voices.*

Junior Simms, the bag boy at the Save-a-Ton, the Wilson Island Ripper, sits on the edge of his bed and stares up, as if looking into the face of a tall someone that only he can see. If he knows Eric is standing there, he doesn't react to him.

"The flames of reentry seared the flesh from my bones," Junior says in a deep and resonant voice.

Eric unlocks the cell door and steps inside. He steps right in front of Junior, directly in his line of sight, right in the space seemingly occupied by his phantom visitor.

"If I had not fallen into the ocean," Junior says, "I might have been burned to nothing but ash."

Is this even the same person? Eric wonders. *Is this the man who—*

"You fucking killed her," Eric says.

"What happens now?" Junior says, using his normal voice.

For a second, Eric thinks he is talking to him, but then the killer responds to his own question.

"Your work is now done," switching again to that deep tone.

Eric can't help himself—he draws his fist back, strikes Junior across the face. Junior's head snaps to the side, and he sprawls back, his skull smacking against the concrete wall behind him. Blood from a busted lip spills down his chin.

Bet that *gets your attention.*

"You have done everything I asked of you," Junior merely states, speaking in his other voice.

•••

"*Almost everything*," the Mother adds.

"Willa," Junior replies.

"*Yes—the girl. She lives still.*"

"I tried to kill her."

"*You have failed me.*"

"I know."

"*A mother for a mother.*"

"What about the town? If I'm locked up in here, I can't feed you. You promised, though. You said if we kept you fed, you'd leave everyone here alone."

"*A bargain,*" the Mother says, "*yes. That remains in place.*"

"I was only trying to protect the town."

"A bargain against the inevitable is something else your human mind can comprehend all too well. A prayer. And unanswered. This was easy for you to accept."

How many times had he prayed? By himself or at his father's side? How many times had he prayed with his mother? How many times had he begged God to heal his mother or, if not, strike her from the earth?

"Ah, I see. You thought you could be a savior," the Mother says, almost mocking him.

"No," Junior says. "That's not it."

"You thought you might feed God and be blessed in return."

"You promised, though."

"And did I not honor our accord?"

"Yes."

...

With both hands, Eric grabs Junior by the shirt, yanking him to his feet.

"Look at me!" Eric says. "Knock this shit off! Talk to *me*."

"But now you're trapped," Junior says, deep-voiced. "Now you cannot feed me, and our pact has been broken."

Eric shoves Junior to the floor, hunkers down over him, punches him. Once. Twice. A half dozen times.

He feels Junior's nose crumple, his cheekbone crack.

He punches him again and again, until blood gushes from his nostrils and spills down his chin.

"Please," Junior says, his words slurred.

Eric drives his fist into Junior's face. His knuckles are covered in blood and spit and even one of the Wilson Island Ripper's teeth. Before he can hit the man again, his loss of self-control overwhelming, he feels a vise close around his wrist.

"That's *enough*!" Buck says, gripping his wrist. "Hey—Eric!"

Eric looks at the sheriff, blinking in surprise, panting.

Junior, his face a crimson mask, lies on the floor, breathing bloody bubbles.

"Don't leave me," he says weakly.

"I no longer need you," he answers himself, and now his words are clear once more, deeper.

"Don't kill everyone," Junior says, his words muffled. "Please."

"It is too late to beg," he answers lucidly in the deep voice, as if he feels no pain at all, as if he's completely unaware of his current surroundings or circumstances. "But do not despair. You have failed, yes, but I never thought you would succeed. What is now to come... is inevitable."

CHAPTER SEVENTY-ONE

"**S**HERIFF'S DEPARTMENT."

Deputy Keene drums her knuckles against the front door. The dark-red paint, peeling from years of neglect, flakes off, some of it sticking to her skin, some of it falling to the porch.

"Maybe nobody's home," Deputy Fines says.

"Junior's mother never leaves the house," Keene says. "She's in there."

"What about his father?"

"I've been thinking about that." Keene doesn't take her eyes off the door. "Back in the station, Junior was begging for us to check in on his mother, but he never mentioned his father."

"And?"

"Might be nothing."

"You think his father's dead?"

"You seen him around in the last few weeks?" Keene asks. "Can you think of seeing him even once?"

"So what?" Fines asks. "I don't keep tabs on everybody in town. Neither do you."

Keene answers by knocking on the door once more.

"You think the mother knew?"

"About the killings?" Keene asks.

"Yeah."

"Who knows? Tell you what: If it had been *my* mom, she would have figured something out. She has an intuition about things."

"Mine too. We called it her sixth sense."

"Right. So maybe Mrs. Simms didn't know exactly what her son was doing, but she almost certainly knew that something was off."

"Junior might just be real good at hiding things."

"He's a fucking bag boy."

"Bag boys can be sneaky."

"Not Junior Simms. I know him. He's . . . not that bright."

Keene knocks on the door again, waits, but there is still no answer.

"Maybe Junior killed her too," Fines notes.

"Nah. He wanted us to check on her."

"You heard the guy. He's raving like a lunatic. For all we know, he's been cuddling a jar filled with her bits and pieces, pickled in vinegar."

Keene wraps her hand around the doorknob—

—just as the door opens.

Both deputies shuffle back, surprised, as Mrs. Simms greets them. She is small, frail, jaundiced, wrapped in a ratty, stinking house robe. Her gray hair hangs down in clumps over nearly dead eyes.

"Junior . . . ?" she asks.

"No. No, ma'am," Keene replies. "I'm Deputy Keene. This is Deputy Fines. We're with the Fredericks County Sheriff's Department."

"I thought I called the exterminator."

"Maybe so, Mrs. Simms. That's not why we're here. May we come in?"

Without a response, the old woman turns away from the door, moving stiffly into the house.

"Junior told me he'd handle the bugs," she says.

Keene and Fines exchange unsure looks, then step across the threshold.

The paint on the walls is chipped and faded, revealing layers of grime and dirt underneath. Piles of clutter crowd every surface, leaving barely any space to navigate around rickety furniture. The windows are filmed with dust, blocking out the outside world better than any curtain might.

"Ma'am," Keene says, "we're here to tell you that your son has been arrested."

"Arrested?"

"Yes, ma'am," Keene says. "I'm afraid so."

"The charges are significant," Fines adds.

A musty odor permeates the thick air, hinting at the dampness within the walls, rot in the floorboards, and animals lurking in hidden spaces.

Mrs. Simms lowers herself onto the couch, sits silently, letting the idea roll over and over in her head.

"Do you have any idea why we might have arrested your son?" Keene asks.

The old woman looks up at them. "That wasn't my son you arrested."

"Excuse me?" Fines remarks.

"It was Mr. No-Face. First he took my husband. Then he took my son."

"Your husband," Keene says. "Where is he, Mrs. Simms?"

"He's gone."

"Did Junior hurt him?"

"Don't be silly." Mrs. Simms watches her hands as she flexes her arthritic fingers open and closed. "Junior *loved* his father. He wanted to carry on his work. That's how Mr. No-Face got him too."

Deputy Fines speaks in a gentle, urgent tone. "Mrs. Simms . . . we really need to talk about your son."

The elderly woman looks up from her feeble hands, her eyes rheumy and distant. "You stopped him."

"Yes, we did," Keene says.

"Stopped him . . . from completing his father's work."

Keene and Fines exchange shrugs.

"Ma'am," Keene says, "I'm sorry, we don't know what that means."

As they speak, a strange sound permeates the surrounding silence—a scuttling, then a chittering, like insects whispering secrets in the dark.

"Did . . . you hear that?" Fines asks.

"I always hear it," Mrs. Simms replies.

The chittering grows louder, more insistent, as if something in the house senses the presence of the deputies, of intruders. Intermingling with the insectile racket, a whispering human voice can be heard, its words indiscernible.

"Where is your husband?" Keene asks, and her hand falls to the butt of her firearm. "Is there anyone else in the house with you right now?"

"That all depends."

"Really. You mind if we take a look around, Mrs. Simms?" Deputy Fines asks.

"Go ahead," she replies, "if it suits you."

The chittering grows louder, then fades. The whisper too grows frantic, then quiets.

"Mrs. Simms," Keene says, "if it's all the same to you, I'd like you to stay right where you are."

"Where else would I go?"

Fines leads the way. Dust motes dance like specters in the dim light. The floorboards creak. The faint smell of mildew and rot seems to blossom from the old wood.

"Look at this place," Fines says. "Jesus. Ought to be condemned."

The scraping sound, the whispers, come from behind a swollen door nestled in the corner of the dilapidated, cluttered, filthy kitchen. Dishes that haven't been cleaned in days fill the sink. Moldy food festers, green and black, upon plates on the counter. Still, the nauseating stink coming from behind the door is worse than anything else the kitchen has to offer. Keene leans close to the door, trying to hear a little more clearly. Instead she gets a deep whiff of rot and decay. She flinches away, almost gagging.

"Pantry?" Fines says.

"Maybe a laundry room," Keene replies.

"You don't think that's his kill room, do you?"

Keene draws her pistol.

Fines pushes at the door. At first it resists. Dampness has cemented it to the frame. With a grunt and a shove, though, the deputy forces the door open.

The putrid odor washes over them. Keene puts a hand over her nose as she steps up next to Fines to get a look.

It might once have been a walk-in pantry, cramped, lined with shelves of canned food. But the floor has been ripped up, the linoleum peeled back in mildewed sheets, the floorboards pulled away and piled in the corner. The ground below has been dug out, dirt and rock scattered around the perimeter of the massive wound in the earth. A shovel and a pick are propped in the corner.

The house groans around them. Settling.

Structural damage.

Suddenly Keene doesn't want to be in this room, doesn't want to be in the house at all.

Fines steps to the edge of the hole, pulls his flashlight, and shines the beam down into the darkness. The light doesn't reach the bottom but it reveals jagged rock walls, and the smell—that godawful stench of rotten meat and mildew—wafts up from below.

"How deep do you think it goes?" he asks. "Looks like it leads into a cave or something."

Keene's gaze traces the edge of the hole, the remaining floor speckled with red-brown stains.

"Yeah, look—this is likely where he took his victims," she says. "He probably threw their bodies down there."

"Victims? You think there were others? Besides Barry and Allie?"

"I don't know."

"How many?"

"I don't *know*."

Clicking and chittering rise from the depths of the pit. Along with a strange yowling and growling. Those human-sounding whispers.

Instinctively, Keene's hand tightens around the grip of her service pistol.

"Keene." Fines draws his gun too. "My God, there's somebody down there."

"Steady," Keene says through gritted teeth.

The maw at their feet erupts like a geyser. A volcano of bone and meat.

A nightmarish horde of screeching, howling, and chittering abominations tumbles up from the abyss.

They might have been insects with rugged exoskeletons and clicking mandibles.

They might have been spiders with twitching legs reaching for anything in their path.

They might have been oversized house centipedes with segmented bodies and spindly feelers.

They might have been crustaceans with serrated and snapping claws.

Tattered skin and dripping, bloody flesh dangle from pallid shells made of misshapen bone. They scuttle on spasming legs, snapping viciously at the air with a multitude of claws. They lash out with an excess of bone-like, serrated blades. Thorny, chitinous tentacle antennae whip back and forth in frenzied aggression. They leap, crawl, and slither over one another, scrabbling over the pit's edge. The creatures are a chaotic assembly of mismatched horrors, as if nature herself has gone mad, piecing together twisted Tinkertoys without care for the right parts. Some are small, the size of rats, while others are as large as cats or dogs.

But that's where any resemblance to real-world animals shatters into obscene turmoil.

Keene fires her gun into the swarm. One of the creatures recoils, its shell cracking, ichor spewing across the ruined floor. The thing gurgles and screeches, though it has no apparent mouth. Keene clamps her other hand on Fines's shoulder and yanks him back. Together they stagger out of the tiny room and she pulls the door closed as the creatures batter against the waterlogged wood.

And alongside that, human voices can be heard from behind the door.

A young woman's voice. A man's voice.

There's a back door to the house, just a few steps away, but Keene moves toward the living room.

"What are you doing?!" Fines yells, following her.

"Mrs. Simms! We can't just leave her here!"

The floor beneath Keene's feet shudders, a low rumble accompanying the shift. Dust cascades from the ceiling as hairline fractures spread across the plaster.

In the kitchen, the pantry door bashes open. The unearthly creatures—dozens of them, maybe more—screech.

Framed pictures fall from the wall. Knickknacks topple from shelves. The room groans. Timbers creak overhead.

"It's a fucking earthquake!" Fines yells.

He's not right, but not exactly wrong either. Keene feels a vibration travel up through the soles of her shoes. It races up the surrounding walls, a jagged crack lancing toward the ceiling, which quickly splinters, chunks of wood and plaster raining down.

All the while, the creatures hiss and yowl and shriek in the kitchen, spilling out into the hall, into the living room. Hundreds of them.

A support beam above Keene gives way with a shuddering crack, and a section of the ceiling crashes down. She throws herself against a wall, pressing flat. Fines dives clear, a huge chunk of the floor from upstairs missing him by mere inches. Dust plumes like smoke around them.

Keene loses track of her partner in the detritus cloud. "Fines?" she calls. "I'm . . . I'm here!"

His shape moves through the chaos, his arm sweeping back and forth, trying to clear his vision.

"Over here!" Keene calls. "This way!" She thinks she remembers the way out. Where they left Mrs. Simms.

Pale shapes skitter through drifting dust, their legs scraping against the heaving, buckling floor.

Keene fires her gun, but she can't be sure if she hit any target.

Fines stumbles to her side. His face is sweaty, dust turning to muddy rivulets on his skin.

"Something's moving under us!" he shouts.

"We have to find—"

Mrs. Simms emerges like a specter from the ruins. The old woman stands before Deputies Keene and Fines, swaying slightly, unsteady. A pale mass clings to her face like a mask. But it has no eyes. What looks like a length of spinal cord hangs from the mask, lashing back and forth, like a breathing tube made of gristle and bone.

"Jesus!"

Fines raises his pistol. But before he can pull the trigger, the creature clinging to Mrs. Simms's face twitches. As if sensing danger, it detaches with a wet, sucking sound, and falls to the carpet. Looking like a pale horseshoe crab, the beast skitters away, zigzagging across the floor on dozens of bloody legs.

It takes Mrs. Simms's skin with it. The old woman's wide eyes stare out from a canvas of glistening crimson where her features once were.

Fines fires his service weapon and Mrs. Simms flies into the dust, vanishing.

Keene gapes at Fines. "What the hell did you just do?!"

Holding his gun, panting, Fines looks into the cloud, watching the vague shape of the woman he just shot, like a memory in the dust, slowly closing in on itself.

Wood splits and cracks. Glass shatters. The floor buckles. More dust and debris cascade from the ceiling.

My God. We're going to be buried here, Keene thinks.

"Keep moving!" she yells.

Fines follows as Keene pitches toward the front of the house. The floor sags beneath her, crumbling, promising to gobble them down, to swallow them whole and condemn them to whatever—

"Keene!"

—waits below.

Fines shrieks as several of the monsters—*Yes, exactly what they are*, Keene thinks—skitter out of the wreckage to grab at him, claws snatching his ankles, wrenching him off his feet. He falls hard to the floor. The creatures slash through the deputy's uniform as if it were mere paper. Blood blossoms across the fabric. Keene reaches for him, but the pit creatures yank him back, dragging him into the cloud as he screams and claws with one hand at the quaking floor. Fines fires his gun at them, over and over, but he's still screaming in the rubble long after he's out of bullets.

Keene moves to follow, but another section of the ceiling slams down to block her path.

Coughing, she wheels toward the door.

Something heavy smashes against the back of her head, and her gun flies from her fingers.

She sees stars. Almost falls. She reaches the threshold just as the rest of the ceiling caves in behind her. With a final burst of effort, she throws herself through the doorway and tumbles onto the wet, unkempt lawn. The night air hits her like a shocking slap.

Gasping for breath, Keene rolls onto her back.

A blanket of clouds covers the sky, but she still sees stars, firing, one after another, through her eyes.

The house trembles and buckles, folds in upon itself, and collapses with a booming, cracking, groaning crash.

The pit greedily consumes the structure.

The pit grows.

CHAPTER SEVENTY-TWO

DUST PLUMES HANG IN A writhing cloud over the wreckage of the Simms house. Jagged cracks ripple through the earth, leading back to the unseen, hungry sinkhole beneath the ruined structure.

Deputy Keene crawls across the lawn, grunting with exertion. Blood mixes with sweat running down her face in a sheet, cutting a swath through the grime. The blood soaks into the collar of her uniform. Unable to stand, she continues, like an infant, away from the debris field. She fumbles at the mic clipped to the front of her shirt. Her fingers sting, grit-crusted and covered in tiny cuts, a couple of fingernails snapped down to the quick. Clutching the mic like a lifeline, like her most prized possession, she presses the button, holding the speaker close to her mouth, her lips brushing it.

"Dispatch."

Her throat is raw, shredded from screaming she doesn't remember.

But, of course, she did.

"Dispatch . . . this is Keene." She looks back at the ruins. "I'm at the Simms place."

Crackling static answers.

Her mind races, spins wildly, trying to piece together exactly what the fuck has just happened.

She and Fines had knocked on the door. Met Mrs. Simms. Heard something odd scuttling in the house. Heard someone whispering. And when they investigated—

Her memory doesn't hold. It collapses, comes apart like the house.

Flashes of light fill her vision.

She reaches back with unsure fingers. There's blood there, yes, oozing through her hair. But that's not the worst of it. Her head feels . . . misshapen . . . dented, partially caved in. There's no pain.

And that's what scares her. There *should* be pain. If it was just a cut, wouldn't it sting?

Is her skull pushing down on part of her brain, shutting down her pain receptors?

"Dispatch, this is Keene," she says, louder this time, her voice gaining some semblance of control. "I need backup. There's an officer down. Fines has been—"

Eaten alive.

The memory stitches itself together. Her partner screaming as those things crawled over him, cutting feelers working across his skin, taking him apart. Dragging him into the dark. Back toward the pit.

The static hisses back at her.

Behind her, something moves in the rubble.

Deputy Keene presses the transmit button on her mic, stanching the grating static.

"Dispatch, this is Deputy Keene," she says again. "We've got an officer down at the Simms place. I'm . . . hurt. Bad, I think. Need backup immediately."

She releases the button, listening for any sign of life over the radio. The hissing static mocks her.

On the street, the police cruiser awaits. *Move. Walk the walk, for real.* Keene pushes herself up. Staggers weakly toward the vehicle. *There's something under the house.*

She has to warn someone.

She almost falls, once, twice, before she reaches the car, slamming against it, bracing herself. She catches a glimpse of herself in the window, but turns away before she gets a clear look. She sees the blood. The hair-covered skin hanging down one side of her skull. Sees that there's something missing.

"Oh God," she chokes.

I'm dead. There's no way I live through this.

She presses the button on the mic once more. "Something's here," she says. "Something attacked us. We need—"

The radio sputters to life for a moment, only to drown her out with more abrasive static. With every crackle, Keene feels the frayed edges of her world unraveling further.

"Please," she whispers, not into the mic. Not into the static. Who is she pleading with? *God?*

The mic crackles, and a voice—Tessa—finally speaks to her.

"Keene? Is that you?"

"Yes. It's me. We've got an officer down. We need backup."

"Keene? There's something wrong with your signal. I can't make out what you're saying."

"We've got an officer down at the Simms place."

"Keene . . . ?"

She opens her mouth to speak again, and a gush of blood spills out. Something fat and wet flops onto her chin. Her tongue.

Tessa can't understand Keene because her tongue is hanging by a few threads from its roots.

And her brain isn't working right, no it isn't, not letting her realize how badly she's hurt, not letting her understand that she can't speak clearly, can't walk the walk.

Keene looks back at the pile of wood and stone where the Simms house once stood. She watches for any sign of life in the debris. A subtle shift catches her attention—a stirring within the ruins that teases a sliver of hope.

"Fines?" she says. But the name is just a mangled grunt.

From the wreckage of the house, dozens of hellish creatures burst forth, sprinting, lunging, and skittering in every direction, a frenzied horde of razor claws, gnashing and snapping mandibles, and bladelike legs and feelers.

On twitching legs, a pair of the monsters zero in on Keene, scurrying toward her with shocking speed.

Instinct takes over as Keene fumbles with bloody fingers at the car door's handle. Her fingers slip and fall uselessly away. She rips the mic from her shirt, holds it close.

"Backup—"

But anyone listening on the other end hears only an unintelligible scream.

CHAPTER SEVENTY-THREE

SOMEONE MIGHT THINK, IF THEY weren't paying attention, that the creature scurrying down the middle of Main Street is some sort of oversized crab. It certainly crawls in such a herky-jerky fashion, sideways, on numerous hooked and barbed legs. It's red, too, the way some crabs have the same pigment. And it boasts a kind of hard shell and serrated, clawlike appendages.

That, though, is where the similarities to a crab—or anything else, really—end.

The creature's shell is actually made of pale, rigid, strangely formed bone. Its crimson coloration is thanks to the raw, oozing, rotting meat and skin that stretch across its carapace. The twitching movements are caused by contractions and palpitations of bloody tendons, causing the ill-jointed legs to spasm and tremble.

The creature skitters to a stop. It has no eyes, but it stands at attention, sensing something.

It does have lips, though. Human lips, raggedly stitched across its back.

The lips convulse.

"*Walk the walk,*" it chitters, using the voice of the dead.

Dozens of voices . . . dozens of screeches . . . dozens of howls . . . respond.

Hungrily.

...

In his cell, Junior Simms speaks in a voice that is not his own.

"*Go forth.*"

CHAPTER SEVENTY-FOUR

RED AND BLUE LIGHTS STROBE across the crumbled ruins of the Simms house. The entire structure has caved in upon itself, collapsing into the gaping, cracked earth below. All that remains is a chaotic pile of twisted and splintered wood.

The other houses in the neighborhood stand eerily silent, their intact structures a stark contrast to the rubble in their midst. If the sinkhole beneath the Simms house were to expand, the homes on either side might topple into the darkness like dominoes. In several nearby houses, windows are shattered and gaping. Some doors hang awkwardly on their hinges.

What happened here?

Deputy Eric Reed sits in his cruiser, both hands on the steering wheel. His knuckles are raw and swollen and bruised from the brutal beating he gave Junior. He thinks he might have broken a couple of his fingers.

If he gets his hands on Junior again, he'll gladly break the rest.

The sheriff had dispatched Eric to the Simms house . . . far from the station . . . far from Junior Simms himself . . . to check on Keene and Fines.

Sure enough, Keene's patrol car is parked at the curb in front of him, but there is no sign of Keene.

Or Fines, for that matter.

The Simms house itself is all but gone.

The sheriff's true intention, of course, was clear: to remove Eric from the station and from Junior's presence, to distance him from the object of his unbridled rage until Buck figured out exactly what was going on and exactly what he should do next.

Until he could decide Eric's professional fate.

Eric already knows his career in law enforcement is over.

In truth, it ended the instant he confided in Rachel about the murders.

Rachel.

He'd toyed with the idea of defying Buck's commands, had considered returning to Golden Dunes to retrieve her corpse from that forsaken killing field. He'd never even mentioned what he'd found. In his rage, in his desire to punish Junior, he hadn't called it in or filed a report. It wasn't anyone else's business. No one else gave a damn about Rachel, not like he did. He couldn't bring himself to go back out there, though. He couldn't bear to see her like that again. So instead, he'd followed orders, played the part of a dutiful deputy.

And now here he sits, blinking at the scene unfolding around him.

One house completely wrecked. Others looking as though they have been ravaged and looted by a roving gang.

Wade Hanson's crew?

Maybe, now that Junior Simms has been caught, the gathered mob is venting its misplaced rage on the town itself.

That'll be a helluva story for—

His shoulders shake as he laughs and weeps at the same time.

A sudden, heavy *thump* reverberates through the car. Jolted aware once more, Eric wipes away the tears, directs his disoriented gaze toward the window.

Perched on the hood is a bizarre . . . animal.

About a year ago, Eric and his buddies had netted an enormous blue land crab, its shell spanning the size of a dinner platter. It was the largest any of them had ever seen. A real freak of nature.

The creature now perched on the hood reminds Eric of that colossal catch. This one, though, is bone white, its shell decorated with ragged, bleeding strips of bloody skin and meat. Unlike a crab, it sports three arms, and three claws instead of two.

Even though his muscles don't want to obey him, Eric shoves the car door open. He steps out, hand on the butt of his firearm. He rounds the hood, looking at the crab-beast.

The creature turns in place on the hood, watching.

A meandering crimson trail glistens on the sidewalk, leading toward the remains of the house.

Keene.

She was dragged into the house.

There are similar blood smears, similar patterns, all along the street. Several people were dragged away.

By what?

Creatures like this one?

Down the street, several figures—about the size of the horrid thing on the hood, but definitely differently shaped—scurry back and forth across the pavement.

Eric hears screams from the crumbled ruins of the Simms house. *"Nothing to see here, folks!"*

That's Fines's voice.

"The Gunrunners rule!"

A woman's voice, one he can't quite place.

Someone is alive in there.

Giving the creature on the hood of the car one last look—

There are dark holes in its shell that might conceal eyes. It stares back at him without moving.

—Eric rushes toward the wreckage, scanning in a panic-stricken search for an entry point, for any sign of life.

"I'm . . . I'm here!" he shouts, his voice cracking. "It's Eric Reed! Deputy Reed!"

He's a law enforcement officer again, even if it's just for a moment, even if he'll be relieved of duty once and for all when he returns to the station.

A voice responds, commanding: *"Walk the walk, Eric. Walk the walk."*

Keene.

"Just hold on!" Eric falls to his knees, starts throwing debris aside, tossing two-by-fours and sections of drywall into the yard. "We're going to get you out of there!"

Another voice calls to him:

"I'm busy chasing down leads and writing stories."

"Rachel?"

His heart clenches tight. It can't be.

Can it?

Junior Simms killed her. Eric saw her lifeless body. Didn't he?

Eric glances down at his battered knuckles.

"Where are you taking me?"

Rachel's voice rings out again, clear as a bell, barely muffled by the debris.

"I'm coming! Rachel! I'm coming!" He screams his throat raw, hoping—praying—she can hear him.

He wrenches aside the shattered frame of a window, revealing a small opening in the rubble, just large enough for a person to squeeze through.

"Rachel!" he calls out.

He maneuvers through the narrow passage, dust cascading from above, splinters biting into his skin as he crawls forward.

Rachel's voice reaches him again, echoing in the confined space.

"How bad are we talking?"

He knows it can't be her. He knows she's dead.

But he's also always known that he's never been one to listen to reason, not when it comes to Rachel.

Eric pushes a hand deeper into the tunnel he's created. He grasps at bits of wood, grasps at dirt. Grunting and panting and sweating, he drags himself along. Exposed nails and bits of jagged wood tear at him, ripping into his skin.

Rachel's voice repeats from below.

"How bad are we talking?"

So much closer now.

Something sharp and serrated tears into his flesh with a nasty crunch. Bones snap like brittle wood.

This time, it isn't an exposed nail or a sharp piece of lumber. This time, something with jagged teeth bites down on him.

Bites down and begins to chew.

Eric instinctively jerks his hand back, but the unseen creature has a viselike grip and refuses to let go. With an inexorable pull, it drags him down, down, down, deeper into the cloying darkness, down where Rachel—or at least something that sounds like her—waits for him.

The first snapping mouth is joined by another.

And another.

And another.

He feels his flesh stripped away. Muscle pulled from bone.

For the life of him—which only lasts a minute or so longer—he can't tell which of the biting mouths is the one speaking with Rachel's voice.

CHAPTER SEVENTY-FIVE

"**YOU DID IT, MAN!**"

Charlie Grimes lets out a triumphant yawp as he stands shakily atop the mildewed and weather-stained couch that adorns his sagging back porch.

With a beer can in hand, ready for a pitch, Charlie takes careful aim at a teetering pyramid of similar cans stacked on the weathered patio table. He flings the can across the patio. The pyramid clanks and clatters apart, collapsing across the untreated planks.

"You survived!"

But Kenny doesn't feel like he's survived much of anything. His head pounds with freight train force. His stomach turns. One beer had made his time hiding out at Charlie's place go by quickly enough. Two eased his mind, even as the overhanging patio roof sprang a couple of dozen leaks. After he watched Charlie's dogs—a pair of overgrown, smelly mutts who had no intention of getting out in the rain—compete in the championship of *Let's see who can leave the biggest pile of shit right here on the deck even though the yard is only a couple of feet away*, he decided to throw caution to the wind and have half the case. Now he is paying the price.

"Wade Hanson can't kill you!" Charlie says. "How's that feel?"

"Like I'm gonna puke," Kenny replies.

"Puke bucket," Charlie says in a faux English accent, "is in the corner, m'lord."

Somewhere during the night, Kenny had convinced himself that Willa's father had orchestrated this frenzied mob of lunatics not with the intention of hunting down a murderer, but solely to punish him.

For getting Willa pregnant. For breaking up with her. Just for fucking up so hard at life.

"They caught the guy," Charlie says, squinting at the dim glow of his cell phone screen. "I've been getting text messages for the last hour. Signal's bad. They're just popping through now. Either that, or I was too fucked up to notice. You're in the clear now."

Perhaps he'd been mistaken.

"You know," Charlie continues, "the way you were so adamant about laying low out here, I almost thought you might *be* the killer."

"And yet you still let me stay."

"What good are friends if they won't get wasted with you while you hide from an enraged mob? So, like, you know . . . you are safe . . . sound . . . Get the fuck off my porch and go home."

"Whatever, asshole."

He knows Charlie's kidding. The two have been crashing at each other's cribs since they were in grade school. But the night is getting long in the tooth, and if he isn't going to be mistakenly—

—or purposefully—

—murdered by a mob of stark raving vigilantes, his old man expects him on the boat.

First, though, he has to stand up.

He plants his feet, grips the spongy arm of the mildewed couch, and pushes himself up. He sways a little, finds his footing, then turns to bid Charlie good night.

Charlie sags into a metal chair, his head tilted back, his mouth agape, his cell phone clutched protectively to his chest.

Kenny offers a silent salute and stumbles across the yard and out the gate.

Charlie's mutts raise their heads and chuff at him, but they don't get up.

Kenny feels a slight clarity creeping in, as if the fog of inebriation is beginning to lift, while he staggers through the dew-drenched grass of Charlie's front yard. Moisture seeps through the soles of his shoes, soaking his socks. Maybe, he muses, he'll be halfway sober by the time he finally reaches the familiarity of his own doorstep.

Work awaits him in a few hours. And the long, winding walk across town.

...

Dragging his painted sword behind him, the Warlock marches through dark but familiar lands.

Ambercast, where the wealthy elite dwell in their castles.

The Plaza of Lies, where businesses ply their trade.

The Ashen Court, the cinderblock duplexes where the masses dwell.

The Behemoth, the poisoned, forgotten school.

On his way to the Warren, where he nests like a rat.

For the most part, the streets are quiet and still. Every now and then, a truck or jeep streaks past, flashing lights and honking the horns. The killer—the Ripper—has been apprehended, and the citizens celebrate the way they might celebrate the Devil Dogs winning a national championship.

He doubts anyone will stop and talk to him, but he imagines how it might play out if they did.

Who are you? the traveler might ask.

I am the Warlock, he would say.

And what role, pray tell, did you play in the night's events?

I did battle with the Ripper himself, he will tell them, *and I did smite him to the ground. I have saved the maiden, Willa, and earned the admiration of her father, the baron!*

You know, he thinks, *maybe I should have let them drive me home.*

...

Instead of his head clearing, Kenny feels as if the thundering train in his skull is growing louder, rattling around in his skull, bouncing violently from brain to bone. He trudges along Appleton Street, where the houses are black as pitch. The streetlights are out too, leaving just the hint of the moon peeking from behind cloud cover to light his way.

Storm must have knocked out power here and there around town.

He hears the gurgling of rushing water from within the sewer drains lining the street.

Unsure what time it is, he digs his phone from his pants pocket. The phone indicates that it's closing in on eleven, but he can't get a signal. Cell service is just as spotty as electricity. At least Charlie had managed to receive messages revealing that the killer had been apprehended.

Kenny wonders if it's someone he knows. *Maybe it's Dean.*

He notices movement across the street. Next to one of the sewer drains, a possum wiggles and squirms. Its movement is weird as hell, like it's inchworming backward into the darkness of the gutter. He approaches the animal, shining the light of his phone, and spots a trail of black blood on the moonlit street.

It reminds him of the blood on Killdeer Avenue.

The possum is dead. Its eyes vacant and lifeless and opaque. Its mouth open, its tongue jutting out from between sharp teeth. Its fur is matted with blood.

Something tugs the dead animal into the drain.

Drunkenly, Kenny kicks the possum like a football, sending it sprawling into a nearby yard.

Something . . . else . . . emerges from the drain. Its legs scrape and clatter against the sidewalk, producing a sound that echoes in the still night. It resembles a grotesque mass of shell or bone, with interwoven tendons stretched taut over its body. A long, sinewy appendage, reminiscent of a vein-covered spine, waves back and forth where its neck and head might be, ending in a snapping claw.

The creature twitches on the pavement for a second, then rushes straight at Kenny.

•••

An unfamiliar feeling uncoils in the Warlock's chest. Hope. He isn't sure if he likes how it feels or not. Willa had said her dad would want to repay him for saving her life. And why not? The girl would be dead if he hadn't raised his blade in her defense.

Whatever rewards await . . . whatever XP bonuses are in store for him . . . he has earned them.

He wonders what Uncle Terry will think when he tells him. Maybe he won't bother saying anything at all.

He tries to hold on to that thought. Tries to banish the others that say, *You'll blow it. You'll blow it, just like always.*

Maybe Mr. Hanson will offer him a job, like Willa suggested. A loyal retainer, maybe, tasked with guarding the royal family. The many-named sword is ready to serve in this capacity.

He laughs at the implausibility of it. But still, he boldly swings the sword through the air.

Wade Hanson is, from what the Warlock has heard, the secret power running the show on Wilson Island. His business interests aren't necessarily legal, but they're obviously profitable. And people around town like the man. Or at least respect him. If the Warlock starts working for him, maybe he'll earn a little of that respect too.

This might be his chance to make something of himself. To stop dealing to dumb teens behind Rudy's Mart. To get out from under Uncle Terry's thumb. Maybe finally get his own place. Then, by God, he could start up a new D&D campaign! He'd have people lining up to play!

He's so lost in his thoughts that he almost misses the sound of a roaring engine. A Trans Am speeds around the corner, spraying mist up from under the tires. The car sways to the side, fishtails, straightens, and bears down on him.

Instead of diving out of the way, the Warlock holds his sword out before him, as if trying to warn the charging beast away.

His legs don't want to work. This feeling is more familiar than hope. More comforting.

He's fucked, and he knows it.

...

Kenny's not sure of much.

But he knows he's fast.

He pours on the speed, leaving the weird creature behind, darting through yards, hopping fences. From every direction come the sounds of screams, of shattering glass, of car alarms blaring incessantly, of gunshots.

What the fuck?

He feels as if the weird creature he saw, the surrealness of it all, was a starting bell for something impossible. Maybe Charlie'd slipped something in one of his beers. *Wouldn't put it past him.*

It would be a big, stupid joke, Kenny Smythe tripping balls, seeing monsters, hearing the world coming down around his ears while he ran screaming through the streets.

Am I actually screaming?

He doesn't know, doesn't care. Worrying about such things diverts focus.

Kenny shuts out the sounds for fear of drowning in them. He keeps his arms and legs pumping, eyes on the prize—getting home, finding his father.

When he reaches his house, when he wills his arms and legs to stop moving, when he slows down for half a second and takes a big, panting lungful of breath, he sees his dad standing in the front yard, swinging one of Kenny's old baseball bats at a half dozen monsters.

They look sort of like the drain-dwelling possum-eater he encountered, but not exactly—close enough that they're obviously related. *Like inbred cousins.*

Kenny sprints across the street and into the yard, hopping a ditch. Larry Smythe is twenty feet away, fifteen, then suddenly right there, drenched in sweat, fighting for his life, but giving out—fast. Leaping over one of the creatures, Kenny reaches his dad's side. His dad stumbles, almost falls. At his feet is a cooler, knocked over. Its contents—canned food, bread, peanut butter—spill across the yard.

He was packing for a bugout.

"We need to move!" Larry says, gulping down air, shoving Kenny toward his old truck.

More of those creatures pour into the yard, moving in zigzag patterns. One of them is the original possum-eater.

Kenny wonders if they've been chasing him all along, if they've been in hot pursuit while he was so focused on getting home.

He wonders—

Was Dad going to ditch me?

The creatures come from under the porch, from around the rotting bulk of the *Jilly-Bee*, from out of the goddamn trees.

Kenny grabs the bat from his father's weakening fingers.

"Let's go!" he says.

He leads the way, battering the oncoming creatures aside. Their shells crack under the impact of the bat. They topple through the air. A single. A double. A foul ball. A home run.

When they hit the ground, they get back up and throw themselves into the fight once more.

A large, bony, crablike thing leaps at Kenny. He draws the bat back, swings, and strikes it right out of the air. The bat snaps in half in a shower of splinters. Kenny's fingers go numb from the impact. What remains of the weapon falls from his grip.

They reach the truck, pull themselves inside, and slam the doors closed, Dad behind the wheel.

The creatures throw themselves against the pickup, trying to break through, get to the delicious, meaty center protected by the metal and glass casing.

"What are they?" Kenny can't catch his breath. He can't feel his fingers. "Where the hell did they all come from?"

"They're everywhere," Dad says, "every goddamn where."

The truck surges forward before Kenny has time to brace himself.

Kenny looks over his shoulder, out the back window, into the bed, where gas cans roll about, bouncing into coolers and cases of bottled water and six-packs of beer.

He was going to leave me.

Not that it matters now. Now they are together. "What are we doing?" Kenny asks.

His father grips the steering wheel with white knuckles.

"We're getting the fuck off this island!"

...

The Warlock freezes as the Trans Am speeds toward him.

At the last second, the car skids to the right, narrowly missing him, jumping the curb, tearing through a white picket fence, digging muddy trenches in a wet yard before grinding to a stop.

The Warlock, clutching the sword like a fighter on an epic quest, thanks the stars he didn't just shit himself.

He knows the Trans Am. He saw it a little earlier in the evening. It's Butler's ride.

He follows the car across the sidewalk, through the soggy yard. He cranes his neck, trying to get a look inside.

"Hey," he says. "Are you guys all right in there?"

The passenger door springs open. And the Warlock hops back. Once more, thanks his bowels for holding their own.

A body spills out, ravaged and twisted, the clothes dark with blood. "Jesus!"

He can't tell who it is. Maybe Nelson. Lee? The body kicks and squirms in the mud. Whoever it is, they aren't dead. At least, not yet. *Close enough.* He hates thinking that way, so callously, but it's true.

Then the driver's door opens. The driver staggers out of the car. It *must* be Butler, but the Warlock can't be a hundred percent sure.

His face is covered by a . . . mass . . . of bony tissue. It almost looks like a facehugger in *Aliens*. It looks—

Like the mask Junior wore.

Butler—if this *is* Butler—wears a shirt drenched in blood. He moves blindly in faltering steps. A sound—half gargle, half scream—comes from beneath the mask.

A living mask.

Blood gushes out from under it, and the Warlock doesn't want to think about what it is doing to the face beneath.

But he can't help it.

The flesh is being cut away, rearranged, and *shape-shifted* into something else. When the mask, a disguise itself, falls away, the face underneath will be completely different than it was before.

It's worse than that, though.

It's so much more terrible than the weirdness he might have written into a D&D campaign.

He sees it pulling pieces of flesh out from under it. Sees it weaving the threads of tissue. Sees it sewing the meat onto its own shell.

Butler jerks in his direction, moving toward him, reaching out.

Can he see me?

Butler draws closer.

He's being eaten alive.

The Warlock grips his sword, and he drives it forward, drives it deep into Butler's chest. Butler shrieks under the bony creature. He grabs the Warlock's shoulder, his fingers tightening, then his grip relaxes and he topples into the mud.

The Warlock looks to the passenger who fell out of the car. He is still.

He looks back to Butler—

And sees that the thing that was on his face is gone, leaving a red, leering skull with its passing.

Where the hell is it?

More of the creatures fall out of the car, each one a different shape and size, each one covered in bits of twitching flesh.

One tumbles out. Then another. And they keep on coming. Like macabre circus clowns out of a tiny car.

How many are there?

He doesn't wait around to find out.

He thinks—and this surprises him—about his uncle, worries whether the man is safe in their trailer.

He sprints for the Warren.

For home.

CHAPTER SEVENTY-SIX

MRS. ABERNATHY SHUFFLES ONTO HER back porch, the boards groaning beneath her slippered feet as she descends to the patio. In her weathered hands, she clutches a dented tin bowl, the sound of kibble rattling within. "Here, kitty-kitties," she calls.

With each moment that passes without an answering meow, her heart sinks. She gives the kibble bowl another shake, a little more vigorously this time. The storm must have frightened what few strays remained into hiding for the night. She's just about to give up when she notices furtive movement in the brush at the garden's edge.

A meow answers the summoning of the kibble.

"Ah, there you are," Mrs. Abernathy says.

But what crawl into her backyard are not grateful, hungry kitties.

No two are exactly alike. Some are barely bigger than mice. Others are the size of cats . . . or dogs . . . or even small humans. What eyes exist are human or animal and sometimes a mix of the two. Some have mouths or toothy orifices that might as well be mouths. Puckering, bleeding blowholes. They are hard-shelled, gore-coated things, many-legged with snapping, scissorlike claws and blades. The muscle and tissue and skin and fur that's stretched across their shells throbs and jerks.

Nearly screaming, Mrs. Abernathy stumbles, the backs of her ankles striking the edge of the lower step. She falls onto her house robe–covered ass.

The creatures swarm toward her. Hungry, yes. But definitely not her beloved kitties.

...

The wet thicket crunches and squelches underfoot as Lewis and Jimmy Cooper creep along the edges of Old Man Renner's farm.

Last time they were caught trespassing, the farmer had chased them off with a warning blast from his shotgun. But tonight, bathed in the silver glow of a half-eaten moon, they've returned with a yearning for payback in their hearts and their father's revolver tucked in the waistband of Jimmy's jeans.

"Keep it down, will ya?" Lewis whispers, his voice sharp, his eyes watching the farmhouse as they approach. They're not going to hurt anyone. Maybe a couple of chickens, yeah, but not Mr. Renner himself. They just want to scare him a little, to remind him that the Cooper brothers are not to be fucked with. If they wake the old guy up too soon, though, if they don't take him by surprise . . . well, certainly all bets are off. "Try not to breathe so damn loud. You sound like your heart's about to pop. And, I don't know, maybe stop stepping on every goddamned stick you pass."

"Shut up," Jimmy says, his standard comeback when he has nothing else of value to add to a conversation. He reaches down, touches the handle of the pistol, grips it for assurance.

"Be careful with that," Lewis says. "Damn, Jimmy. You should've let me carry it. You're gonna shoot your pecker off."

"Shut up."

"If the sheriff catches us," Lewis says, "it's our ass."

"Sheriff ain't gonna catch us," Jimmy says, "because he's got his hands full with everything going on in town. Killers. Vigilante justice. We're the last couple of dickheads on his mind."

They reach the corner of the dilapidated barn, crouch together in the shadows, and watch the farmhouse for any sign of life. Even though the porch light burns in the night, the house is dark and silent. The yard is littered with the bloody bodies of chickens. Tufts of feathers carpet the ground. More feathers drift lazily through the air. This just happened, moments ago.

"Someone . . . or something . . . killed his chickens—" Lewis says.

A shotgun blast booms in the night. A bright flash fills the house. Aldo Renner, backpedaling, bursts out of the front door, reeling onto the porch, weapon of choice in hand. At first the brothers think he's spotted them again, he's unloading that gun of his at them. But no—he's not facing them. He's shooting at something inside.

The shotgun roars again, and Old Man Renner breeches the weapon, clumsily fishes more shells from his shirt pocket, and loads up. The whole time, he's shrieking like a madman at something in his own home.

Lewis grabs Jimmy's shoulder, squeezes.

"We should—"

But before either of the brothers can process their next move, an awful swarm of hideous things bursts out of the house. Twisted spider/crab creatures, bone and blood and wet and red tissue, too many skittering legs and too many snapping claws.

"What are they?" Lewis shrieks. "What are they? What the fuck are they?"

"How the fuck—" Jimmy cries.

But he doesn't know how to finish the sentence.

He's never seen anything like the awful horrors spilling out of Old Man Renner's house. They skitter and crawl and hop and squirm in a jerking, spasming fashion. Aside from the skin and meat pulled taut over pale and misshapen bones, no two are alike.

Jimmy draws the revolver. He takes aim with a trembling hand, pulls the trigger.

The shot goes wild, striking Old Man Renner in the back of the neck. He stiffens, wheels around, his eyes large and wild. The shotgun falls from his hands. He takes three steps before his legs give out under him and he collapses, toppling off the porch and onto the muddy ground.

"What the fuck?!" Lewis gasps.

Jimmy looks at the pistol in horror. "I didn't mean to—"

The creatures from the house immediately scurry over Mr. Renner's body, ripping and tearing at his flesh. Their sharp, bony legs are soon slathered in blood.

"Come on!" Lewis yells, but his voice is drowned by grotesque chitters and hisses coming from the creatures crawling all over now Dead Man Renner and also from the surrounding woods.

Lewis grabs the gun from his brother's limp hand. "We've gotta get out of here!"

The Cooper brothers scramble into the so-called safety of the forest, where more of the creatures wait for them.

Five more gunshots echo in the night.
They might as well be shooting chickens with BBs.

...

"I think," Mrs. Vaughan says, "it's probably safe to go home."

The office wall clock ticks well past closing hours, well past bedtime. Just to double-check the time, Doc Maro looks at his wristwatch. He'd promised the sheriff that his offices would stay open tonight. Just in case. With dozens of good-old-boy vigilantes on the streets, all of them looking for trouble, the possibility of bodily harm was high. Having the good doctor ready to bandage scrapes and set bones just made sense. Better to have it and not need it than need it and not have it.

In this case, thankfully, it had not been necessary. No distraught calls. No injured not-quite-weekend warriors staggering bleeding through his door with accidental self-inflicted wounds.

Doc Maro and Mrs. Vaughan had used the downtime for filing and organizing and tidying up.

Now, though, as Mrs. Vaughan stands in the door to his office, it's time to call it a night.

"Anything else you need?" Mrs. Vaughan's exhaustion comes through loud and clear.

"No, thank you." Doc Maro smiles. "Appreciate you sticking around with me. Have a good evening."

"Eh. What's left of it," Mrs. Vaughan says. She disappears into the hall, her footsteps fading into the silence of the empty clinic.

The doctor turns back to his filing cabinets, slipping the last folder into place with all the others. Paper slides against paper, the medical histories of hundreds of patients over the years, and the drawer rolls shut with a metal *clunk*. Maro takes a breath, then—

A scream—Mrs. Vaughan's—shatters the stillness.

Doc Maro moves, shakily but quickly, out of his office. Looking down the hall, past the lobby and waiting room, he sees that the front door stands open. Mrs. Vaughan is on the floor, on her back, kicking and squirming. Something crawls across her body. The size of a football, like a malformed skull, it drags itself along on a cluster of spidery legs. From its underside, another mass of twitching near-legs lances and slices and stabs at Mrs. Vaughan's flesh, ripping skin and tissue and muscle. Some of the cuts are precise and almost delicate, Doc Maro sees, while others are vicious and nasty.

As if it's harvesting her, he thinks with a clinical detachment.

Then the lizard brain part of him takes over, and Doc Maro feels the scream bubbling up his throat. He stumbles back toward his office. With one last look down the hall, he sees a half dozen more of the horrible creatures darting through the door and into the clinic. They zigzag, chittering, and screeching, and—

Is that laughing?

He slams the door to his office, throwing his weight against it as he feels one of the creatures leaping against the door. And another. And another. They batter against the wood. The door cracks. The frame splinters.

The creatures are indeed laughing. It's a distinctly human sound. And the door doesn't hold.

CHAPTER SEVENTY-SEVEN

"**IT'S LIKE I'M RIDING SHOTGUN** through the goddamned apocalypse!"

Bear braces one hand on the truck's ceiling as Scraps guns the engine, swerving, crunching over three of the crab-spider-insect things scurrying across the streets. The truck bounces, crushing them.

All around them, Wilson Island is coming undone.

Windows smashed. Cars wrecked, some overturned, some burning.

Power lines down, sparking and sizzling and dancing like living serpents on the asphalt.

Bloody corpses in the street.

Everywhere they look, they see the strange creatures. Skittering about. Hunting.

With a *whumpf*, a plume of fire blasts into the sky, and heat washes across the black pickup. The pumps at the Gas-N-Go burst into flames, rocketing debris into the air and across the road. Bits of falling metal pelt the truck like smoldering hail. The fireball sends a pack of the bone-and-blood critters rolling like tumbleweeds, some of them ablaze.

"Oh, shit!" Bear exclaims.

Scraps veers hard to the right, narrowly missing a man who runs, flailing, out in front of them. Three of the creatures crawl on his back, digging their clawed legs into his shoulders, neck, and face. They cling to him like ticks on a dog.

Might have been an act of mercy if we had run him over, Scraps thinks.

The truck bounces again—over God knows what this time—as they speed past several cars crashed together like a kid's Matchbox collection spilled into the street. Smoke curls up from the cars. More awful creatures perch on the demolished vehicles. One of the monsters holds up a large flap of human skin, waving it like a victory flag.

"What the hell is this?" Bear says.

"Fuck if I know," Scraps answers, keeping his eyes on the road. "Maybe the storm washed these things up."

"There's so damn many of them!"

The truck swings around a corner, gliding through a puddle, sending a spray of water through the air.

They whip down the main drag, accelerating past the Red Eye Diner. The windows are either shattered or slathered in blood. A woman—maybe fifty years old—runs down the middle of the street, pursued by a half dozen of the scuttling, hopping, zigzagging creatures.

"Where are they coming from?" Scraps mutters.

"You *know* where they're coming from," Bear says.

Scraps and Bear have discussed theology on many occasions, usually while on long road trips, sometimes over shots of whiskey. Scraps has never really believed in any all-powerful beings. No God. No Devil.

Bear, on the other hand, grew up as a Faith Free Will Baptist, and while he long ago turned his back on every Sunday school lesson he ever heard, the sermons and prayer sessions come back to haunt him from time to time.

"They've come up from hell itself," he says.

"Oh, please. Ain't no such—"

"Look out!" Bear stiffens in his seat, presses his right foot against the floorboard as if he has a set of brakes on the passenger side dedicated to him.

Scraps slams the brakes so hard it feels like the truck might flip bed over hood.

A family of five—a mother, father, and three kids—runs across the street in front of the truck. They're holding each other's hands, the dad in the lead, the mom in the rear. They are dressed in bright summer clothing, their skin darkly tan. They're not locals.

This is their vacation.

The father screams something repeatedly as he leads the group. The kids and the mom are all weeping.

The father squeezes the hand of his son, who might be five years old, as he guides them past the truck. All three of the kids—two girls and a boy—look right through the truck's windshield, right at Scraps and Bear.

They plead with their eyes. *Help us.*

Several of the bony monstrosities, eager to catch up to the procession and cut it to pieces, scurry after them.

"Aw, hell," Scraps breathes.

Bear shoulders open his door.

"What the fuck—" Scraps says.

"I ain't watching those kids die!" Bear shouts.

The truck shudders and rocks as the big man leaps out. He leaves his shotgun behind, knowing it will be of little use, not unless he wants to risk cutting the members of an innocent family in half as he blasts away at the attacking horrors.

That, too, might be a fucking mercy, Scraps thinks.

The family keeps moving, Scraps finally making out what the father's yelling at them. "Don't look back! Don't look back! Don't look back!"

The pursuing creatures snip at the mother's legs. She's wearing white shorts. The backs of her lower legs have been slashed open several times. The wounds gape, and blood runs down to her shoes.

"Claire!" she cries. "Danny! Hannah!"

Like she's trying to remember the names of her kids in her final moments.

The father nearly falls. The boy's hand slips from his grasp. The father regains his footing, grabs the kid by the arm, and keeps on keeping on. He sees his wife at the rear of the group, a look of hopelessness passing between them.

In five long strides, Bear closes the distance between them. For a big fucker, the bearded man moves fast. He kicks one of the creatures, sending it sprawling across the road.

He stomps another, cracking its shell.

But several more of the things, noticing the big man's presence, now scurry his way.

Scraps pounds the dashboard several times with his fist. "Shit, shit, shit!"

He makes the decision. "Wait for me, dammit!"

Scraps throws his door open, hops out, takes a step. He stops himself, returns to the truck, and grabs the tire iron that he always keeps handy. *Just for emergencies.*

Bear charges the monsters, stomping and kicking another one of them. A sickening crunch cuts its screech short.

The father looks back at him.

"Where the fuck are you going?" Bear shouts.

"Our van!" the father answers.

Across the street and several yards away, a blue minivan is parked.

"If we can just get to—"

"Just move your asses!" Bear bellows.

Scraps swats at a couple of the monsters as he races into the fray. The tire iron catches one of them midair as it leaps for his face. He smashes another as it stabs at his leg with a long tail that looks like a spear made of jagged bone.

Reaching Bear's side, Scraps notices that the creatures Bear crushed are actually working to stitch each other back together, using tiny appendages like knitting needles to weave and twist flesh and muscle, cinching broken bone back into new formations.

Calling Dr. Hell Beast.

The family reaches the minivan. The father lets go of his son's hand, starts furiously digging in his pocket for the keys. He checks one pocket, then the other.

"Are you fucking kidding?" Scraps yells.

"I've got them!" the mother says, holding the gleaming keys overhead, then tossing them.

The father catches the keys, almost drops them, then shores up his grip and unlocks the minivan. He yanks the door open and moves aside as his family dives past him. The mother and son throw themselves into the front passenger seat. The two little girls hide in the back. The father pulls himself into the van, slams the door, and looks back in the deepest thanks at Scraps and Bear.

Bear's too busy stomping monsters to see. But Scraps notices.

The father jams the key in the ignition, gives it a turn. Minivan sputters, stalls. The mother, clutching her son to her, sobs and shakes with terror. Then the engine catches. The vehicle lurches forward and barrels down the street, pulping a couple more creatures, leaving Scraps and Bear in its wake.

The bone-and-meat horrors converge on the pair.

"Back to the truck!" Bear says.

"No shit!" Scraps says.

Another wave of monsters charges. Scraps wheels around, teeth bared, and takes the lead in a mad rush back to the truck. He sweeps the tire iron back and forth, knocking the creatures away, clearing a path. Bear follows, barreling through the monsters, even as sharp claws rip into his legs.

As they reach the truck, they see another creature sitting in the passenger seat, its shell covered in tightly stretched skin from which a pair of goggling eyes stare wildly. Three arching arms, each ending in snapping bone claws, rise from the thing's body.

Without hesitating, Bear reaches in, grabs the creature, and hurls it to the street.

They climb into the cab. Bloody, beaten, sweating, panting, but alive.

Scraps slumps against the steering wheel, trying to find air to gasp.

Bear's head hits the back of the seat.

For a moment, the world is just the sound of their ragged breathing and the thump of their hearts.

"Jesus. What now?" Bear asks at last.

"Wade," Scraps says. "If these things are all over town, he's gonna need us."

He throws the truck into gear and slams the gas, even as a new trio of the bloody, flesh-and-bone horrors scrabble onto the hood.

CHAPTER SEVENTY-EIGHT

SCABROUS LEGS SCRAPE AGAINST THE outer walls. Window glass shatters.

An ashtray full of cigarette butts, a handful of beer bottles, and a shower of stale pizza crust cascade across the floor as Uncle Terry flips the coffee table on its end, slides it across the dirty, worn carpet toward the window.

"Help me with this!" Terry yells. "Goddammit! Help me!"

Tossing the many-named sword aside, the Warlock takes one side of the table, tugging and pulling it toward the grimy window, where three hideous, bony, fleshy creatures crawl, leaving a smear of slime and gore behind them. The oozing trail reminds the Warlock of a sinus infection, phlegmy and bloody. The creatures' legs twitch back, tendons pulling taut, as they stab right into the glass, breaking through, a sharp barb of bone in the center of spiderweb fractures. Together the Warlock and his uncle slam the table against the window, blocking—albeit temporarily—the entry point.

The front door trembles in its frame, the thin faux wood grain bending in places, rupturing open as sharp legs poke through, ripping a path through the metal.

"Come on!" Uncle Terry rushes to the side of the checker-pattern couch. "Come *on*!"

The Warlock helps him move the couch as best he can with his shoulder screaming in pain from the gunshot wound.

The fabric reeks of cigarettes and sweat and spray freshener. A spring, poking out the back, stabs into the Warlock's hand, scraping across skin, almost drawing blood. As if this is attacking him too. They drag the couch across the room, tip it on its side, and shove it against the door.

Together they layer the makeshift barricade with Uncle Terry's recliner, with end tables, with dining room chairs, with the television. The mass of furniture trembles and creaks.

"It ain't gonna hold," Uncle Terry says. "They'll dig right through!"

But the Warlock has a much worse notion. There are more doors, more windows, more access paths, throughout the mobile home. These things aren't just going to stay in one place.

We'll never stop them from getting in.

The Warlock catches his uncle's eye for a fleeting moment. They're all each other has in this world—God help them both—and maybe they can't stand the sight of each other anymore, but they're clinging to that fragile familial bond for dear life, a life neither one of them valued all that much until this very moment.

The trailer groans and creaks under the siege of the misshapen creatures.

Shit. We're not getting out of here, are we.

"What are they?" Uncle Terry asks.

Like it matters.

"*What the fuck are they?!*" Uncle Terry screams.

The Warlock hears them, cracking the glass, crawling over the walls, digging through the home's metal sides, but he'd glimpsed them only briefly.

Thank God. Thank Arioch. Thank Crom. Thank the Dragon.

Just the quick look at their chittering, twitching bodies was enough to turn the Warlock's guts to jelly. They were made of bone, but red and gristly meat was stretched over their carapaces, the sinew twitching and pulling, stringy, moving the bony structure like—

"Meat puppets," the Warlock remarks.

Beneath his feet, the floorboards crack and splinter, heaving up, and the thin, filthy carpet tears. One of the "meat puppets" pushes its way through the ripping floor covering. Its rigid frame is covered in what looks like a baby's face, stretched like taffy, puffy in all the wrong places. As its muscles twitch, the baby's mouth opens and a gargling infantile wail peals from its trembling lips. The creature tears through the carpet and shreds it back. The jagged legs of even more of them push up through the hole in the floor, surging and shoving against each other as they seek entry.

Somewhere in the trailer, another window shatters. Pieces of debris rain down upon the Warlock.

Looking up, he sees more of the meat puppets ripping their way through the ceiling. Legs like skewers punch through the walls.

The sword! Where's my sword?!

In a frenzy, the monstrosities descend upon uncle and nephew. Their claws tear through clothing and flesh with equal disregard. Blood spurts in splattering arcs across the walls. A scream splits through the chittering, screeching, babbling sound of the atrocities.

At first, the Warlock thinks it's him. He's bleeding. But the one doing the actual screaming is Uncle Terry.

The creatures are busy dragging him, piece by piece, into the gaping holes in the floor.

Panic claws at the Warlock's mind as he reaches for what's left of Uncle Terry, grabbing one of the man's twitching hands. Two of the fingers on that hand are missing—they've been shaved off at the roots. The blood makes his hand slippery.

Uncle Terry's eyes fill with terror as he realizes all is lost.

He lets go of the Warlock's hand. And a moment later, he's gone.

The Warlock hears them now—all around—scratching at the feeble barricades, gnawing and rending and tearing their way through the floors, ceiling, and walls. Another window shatters. The floor creaks and snaps. The walls groan. The barricade tumbles apart, furniture clattering over the floor.

And most terrifying of all, the meat puppets cry out in human voices as they work their way inside.

"This isn't how I was supposed to die!"

"Somebody! Somebody help me!"

"Why is this happening?"

He almost recognizes some of the voices. Almost. And he's thankful that he can't.

The creatures are crying out in the voices of the people they've killed. Somehow, he knows it.

If that's the case, he might hear Uncle Terry bellowing at him, even after death, from underneath the floor.

The Warlock sobs. Tears burn in his eyes.

He never expected to feel sorrow at the loss of his pain-in-the-ass uncle, but it steamrolls over him just the same.

Sniffling, wiping his nose with his sleeve, he buries the surprising emotion beneath his instinct to survive and to fight.

Where—

At last he spots the sword, its hilt jutting out from under overturned furniture and tattered newspaper pages.

As meat puppets leap and slash at him, the Warlock dives for the weapon.

The blade, anointed with fanciful names, lashes out, cleaving a leaping creature from the air with a sickening squelch, shattering its body, spattering flesh and blood. The Warlock's injured shoulder throbs as he wields the blade, hacking and slashing his way through a sea of misshapen abominations. With every thrust, the sword rips through the mass, chopping bone apart, ripping muscle. But for each meat puppet he dispatches, another seems to emerge.

Are they putting themselves back together? Are they regenerating?

Like trolls or vampires or certain denizens of the lower planes.

His mind spins. *How do you combat monsters who regenerate? Fire or acid! That does me a fuck-ton of good right now!*

Sweat burns in his eyes as he keeps right on stabbing and slicing at the creatures. He wades down the hall, a path he's walked countless times. Only now he's not looking for the sanctuary of his bedroom, but for an escape route through the back door. The meat puppets chase after him, rise up to block his path, but they can't swarm him as easily in the narrow confines of the corridor.

Controlling the battlefield means understanding a monster's initiative, speed, and mobility.

But this isn't a game!

He keeps telling himself that.

Not a game! Not a game! Not a fucking game!

It's when he forgets to tell himself that, when he starts believing he's rolling dice across a battle mat covered in make-believe monsters, that whatever shreds of reality he's dangling from will finally unravel. *Maybe that won't be so bad!*

The back door hangs on its hinges, and meat puppets scrabble across the threshold.

The Warlock slashes at the creatures as he dives past.

Not a game!

His sword hacks a meat puppet in half. ***Critical hit!***

He lands hard on the ground, hard enough to rattle his teeth, but he keeps his grip on the sword. He rolls to his feet, and points his sword at the remains of the creature he just hacked apart.

The monster twitches on the ground. The wide, frightened eyes of what was once a person roll around in the eye sockets of a fleshy covering pulled over the thing's carapace.

This isn't a game!

The Warlock staggers away from his ruined home.

Everything he's ever loved—his posters, his dice, his miniatures, his books, even his uncle—is gone.

All he has left is his sword.

The trailer park is under siege.

The monstrosities swarm over the surrounding mobile homes. A few of the Warlock's neighbors scream as they pinwheel through the street, atrocities clinging to them, ripping at their flesh. One of the trailers is ablaze, burning creatures darting away from the structure.

Not a game.

The Warlock dashes across the yard, dodging snapping, hissing, biting clusters of meat puppets. The muddy ground shifts underfoot. He reaches the edge of the trailer park—the edge of the Warren—and doesn't dare look back. He runs for his life, knowing in his heart that nowhere on Wilson Island is safe, knowing that if he's going to survive, he must fight, willingly throwing himself into a realm full of monsters.

CHAPTER SEVENTY-NINE

JUNIOR FEELS HIS PULSE IN every muscle of his face. His lips are split open in several places. His mouth is full of jagged stubs that were once his teeth. One of his eyes is swollen shut. The other has blooded over, making his vision blurry.

It's not unlike the mask, he thinks. And the idea comforts him. *I'm so pathetic.*

His blood spatters the cold stone floor, right where—

Mother.

—stood earlier in the evening.

Right where she said good-bye and vanished. Tears spill from his swollen, blackened eyes, stinging as they roll over cuts and scrapes. He sits on the edge of the narrow jail cell bed, hunching over, elbows resting on his knees and hands clasped together. He can almost hear his father's voice, strained and weary from the ceaseless demands that the Mother—not *his* mother, not his father's wife, but *the* Mother—placed upon his shoulders.

She drained the life from him, just like from me.

From down the hall, he hears the metal cellblock door screech open once more. Footsteps approach. He doesn't rise from his seat or look away from his blood on the floor. He doesn't have the strength. Still, he feels Sheriff Buck's presence, notices the large man's shadow stretch across the floor. He acknowledges his presence with a grunt.

"You want to tell me what my deputies found at your house?" the sheriff asks.

Junior grunts again, this time shrugging his shoulders. *How should I know?*

"They went to your house to check on your mother, just like you asked."

Now he looks at the sheriff. "Mama?"

"We lost contact with them. I sent your friend Deputy Reed to follow up. Figured someone should stay here to watch over you, and it couldn't rightly be him."

"I didn't kill his friend."

"I don't really care about that right now. Your house—what did my deputies *find* there?"

"I tried to keep her satisfied," Junior replies. "I tried to heal her wounds, her sickness."

"What the hell are you talking about?"

"That's why I did what I did. I thought I was protecting the town."

"From what?"

"She said it was for the greater good."

"Who? Who said that? Your mother?"

"Not my first mother."

"Kid, you better start making some sense, and real quick."

"She's old. Older, maybe, than Wilson Island itself." Junior licks his ragged lips. "Ancient. That's what she is. And she needed my help. Can you imagine? Something so old and powerful, needing someone like me."

"Are you trying to say someone told you to kill Barry and Allison?"

"Not just them."

That takes the wind out of the sheriff's sails. "Who else?" he asks.

"There are sacrifices to be made."

"Oh God. Don't tell me this is some sort of ritualistic bullshit."

"She sacrificed her flesh when she tried to break free. My daddy made a sacrifice when he dragged her out of the water and set to tending and feeding her. I made a sacrifice when my daddy couldn't fulfill his sacred oath. And now—"

"Goddammit, Junior, what the *fuck* are you hiding at your house?!"

"She said," Junior says through bloody lips and broken teeth, "re-entry was a bitch."

CHAPTER EIGHTY

AT THE TUGBOAT SALOON, THE door flies open and Clifton Hodge spills in from the street. His face is bleeding, the skin peeled away, and he's missing an ear. Blood covers his left side, soaks into his clothing.

"Jesus Christ!" he screams. "They're using us for meat!"

Several of the customers drag Clifton to a seat before he collapses.

"I saw it!" he mutters through bloody bubbles on his lips. "They're cutting people up, taking their skin, their eyes, their lips, their tongues! They're taking whatever they want! And they're using our motherfucking parts to stitch their own bodies together!"

Delores stops tearing labels and drags herself away from the bar. Crossing the room, she opens the door. She steps just outside, taking one last look at the town she calls home before stepping back into the tavern and slamming the door closed.

She wishes she hadn't.

...

At Captain Bob's Tavern, patrons push barstools and chairs against the windows. They overturn the pool table and shove it against the door. They arm themselves with pool sticks and bottles and the hogleg Robert Hanratty keeps behind the bar.

And in their hearts, they know that all of this will do them no good.

...

Frantic questions fill the Tugboat.

"What the fuck are they?"

"How am I supposed to know?"

"Never seen anything like them!"

"Just stay inside! Stay quiet! Maybe they'll go away!"

But the creatures don't go away. They chitter and howl and screech, their strange sounds a myriad collection of cats yowling and dogs barking and birds chirping.

And people. Talking. Laughing. Shrieking.

With every passing moment, more human voices join in.

...

One of the creatures leaps through the main window of Captain Bob's Tavern, shattering neon filament, scattering shards of glass this way and that. It lands in the center of the room, scurrying around, regarding each and every patron. It looks like a pale crab standing on spindly, too-tall legs with too many joints. Bloody skin and tendons are haphazardly woven onto the bony appendages. The twitching convulsions and contractions of the flesh trigger a series of palpitations that cause the legs to move.

A person's face is stretched over the creature's shell.

Ray gasps. "That's Mildred Fairway! She works at the grocery store!"

Elongated lips part, and the creature speaks like a parrot. *"Paper or plastic? Paper or plastic? Paper or plastic?"*

"What the fuck?!" Ray says.

He takes aim with Captain Bob's revolver and blows the beast to kingdom come.

Four more of them leap through the window.

...

"We're not getting out of here, are we?"

With those words, Clifton utters his last rattling breath.

The customers of the Tugboat stand around the dead man, gaping at him, staring at each other, none of them saying a word.

The creatures outside speak for them.

Delores moves, stiff-legged, to the bar, hoists herself onto a stool. The bartender—Grant—stands before her.

Delores wishes she'd gone to Captain Bob's, not the Tugboat. She would much rather be face-to-face with Ray's Marlboro Man good looks than Grant's ugly mug.

"If this is the end," she remarks, "you might as well get me another beer."

Grant pulls a bottle from the cooler. He hesitates before popping the cap. "You sure you don't want something top-shelf?"

"Nah. The cheap stuff is fine. Might as well die like I've lived."

CHAPTER EIGHTY-ONE

MRS. CREWES'S HAND TREMBLES AS it hovers above the doorknob, the brass cold and unyielding beneath her tentative touch. Her heart thuds against her chest. Has she waited long enough? She still smells the chemical tang of the poison the exterminators left behind. She presses her ear against the bathroom door, holds her breath, and hears nothing.

"Rats," she whispers to herself in disgust.

She keeps a clean house. How could something like this happen to her?

She hasn't dared enter the treated room since the visit from Surefire Pest Solutions a few days ago. She wanted to give everything time to work, so she's been using the guest bedroom when she needed. The exterminators might have laid waste to the rats and—

So disgusting!

—roaches that spilled out of the hole, but she knew there were many, many more down below.

Now, though, she can wait no longer.

Her clean, pale fingers tighten around the knob and she pushes the door open.

Creatures scurry through the small room and surge out of the hole in the wall behind the toilet.

Oh, how she wishes they were just rats.

...

It dawns on Darla Conroy as she cowers behind a shelf full of potato chips, crackers, and pork rinds that Rudy's Mart has a lot of windows.

Windows upon which grotesque, twisted, dripping shapes are crawling.

Windows that tremble and crack under the jagged points of twisted, bony appendages.

"They're going to get in!" she says repeatedly, unable to stop herself. "They're going to get in! What do we do? There's gotta be some other way out of here!"

She and her five-year-old son had stopped in on their way home after visiting her mother in Goldsboro. Always a stressful trip, what with her mother constantly complaining about Darla's choice to get divorced from Liam, whom her mother adored, and raise Aidan on her own. *And on the coast, of all places?*

So, before heading home, she'd stopped at Rudy's for some Ben & Jerry's. They absolutely *deserved* it.

They'd just chosen cups of Americone Dream and Cherry Garcia when the sudden onslaught began.

"They're all over the place," Rudy says. "They're everywhere."

Rudy, pudgy and gray, grabs a shotgun from under the front counter, along with a box of shells. The shotgun can't have been fired in decades. It's covered in dust. He also yanks out a baseball bat, once painted deep blue but flaking along its length. He tosses that to Darla, who catches it awkwardly.

"God help us," Darla whispers, clutching her son's arm with slim fingers.

The creatures outside, their pale, twisted limbs a blur of scuttling motion, shatter glass and scurry inside. Boxes of canned foods and rolls of paper towels tumble from shelves. The awful things lurch through the store, their many-jointed legs clicking and snapping.

Rudy swings the shotgun up, his finger tensed on the trigger. But before he can fire, one of the creatures leaps at him. A claw like a switchblade slashes across Rudy's chest. He sprawls to the floor among packs of chewing gum and half-crushed candy bars. He batters the attacking creature away with the butt of the shotgun, pushing himself up.

He unloads the weapon, which works just fine as it turns out, one shot after another, at a pair of the things darting across the floor. They explode into a rain of blood and bone.

Darla screams for help, surrounded by the creatures, and she swings the bat in frenzied arcs, trying to fight her way to her son.

One of them crawls over Duncan's body. He's sitting on the floor, his back against a shelf, his legs kicked out before him, his fingers clutching feebly at his cup of Cherry Garcia.

The creature's limbs are long and slender, with hooked claws, all seemingly made of bone. The veiny tendons that crisscross over its hard shell contract and pull, and its hooks work rapidly, a skeletal mechanism not unlike the thresher separating grain from the stalk and also not unlike a loom guiding fibers. A sickening, juicy slicing sound accompanies each swipe of its claws as it tears through fabric and flesh. Dripping and squelching, the monster stitches the harvested meat onto itself, adding threads of bloody sinew to its already-exposed musculature.

"Get off him!" Darla screams, tears streaming down her face.

She swings the bat, knocking the horror away from her son. It's too late, though. Duncan's face, neck, and upper chest are nothing more than a red mess.

With a warbling shriek, the creature kicks out like an overturned horseshoe crab, rights itself, and scurries on another attack path.

Rudy reloads the shotgun, two shells, and in a split-second decision turns the barrels on Darla, ending her torment.

The creatures immediately go to work, peeling her skin and tissue away.

Rudy looks around his store, his home away from home, the shelves and refrigerated units, the candy bars and chips, the packaged doughnuts and fruit pies, the FOR CUSTOMERS ONLY sign on the restroom door. He's made a life here.

And now, with the windows shattered, blood spreading across the floor, and awful monsters crawling his way, that life is over.

He puts the barrel under his chin and fires the shotgun one last time.

...

Their masks discarded, the residents of the Golden Dunes stand in a semicircle around the moonlit field of death. Madhouse Quinn, with his preaching, with his sermons, had promised they would witness something special. Something sacred.

This, he'd said, was not their world—at least not yet—but they would bear witness to the birth of what came next.

When the Mother, he'd proclaimed, *is reunited with the Father!*

And they think it might be coming to pass. Resurrection and rebirth are finally upon them.

The dead animals draw breath once more, stirring in the field, bursting up from the shallow graves.

They twitch. They writhe.

A murmur passes through the crowd.

"Is this what was promised?"

"We should have kept our masks!"

"Something's happening!"

"Something's—"

Wrong.

From under the rotting animal carcasses, an army of terrifying creatures emerge. They resemble spiders or maybe crabs, their bodies composed of ill-formed bone. Each is at least the size of a cat, though some are larger. They scurry forth with grasping pincers and slashing blades and gnashing fangs.

Sorrowful wails and anguished screams fill the night.

When Madhouse Quinn returns—*if* he returns—his faithful followers will be nothing but a memory.

Maybe that's what he always knew would happen. Maybe that's part of the story he never bothered to tell.

Lost in a sea of panic, Abel turns around and around, reaching out for those who push and shove past him.

He knows he can't help them.

Arcs of blood and spatters of raggedly torn skin fly around them. Like confetti in a gore-fest party the little monsters are throwing for themselves.

So—no—no help. No salvation. No new world.

Can he provide some comfort, though, in their last moments?

For fuck's sake!

Madhouse is supposed to be the shepherd!

I brought many of these people here! I helped build this group! I brought them here to die like—

A bulbous horror, looking a bit like a bone-white football helmet with multiple long legs and spinning, concentric rows of fangs, leaps onto Abel's face, stirring his eyes, nose, and mouth into a meaty stew.

He flops to the ground.

His corpse is stomped by his community—his friends—a dozen or more times before Golden Dunes grows quiet once more.

CHAPTER EIGHTY-TWO

"**W**HAT *IS* THAT?"

Cocking her head curiously, Tessa rises from her seat, weaves around the partition, and moves toward the window of the police station. She stands there, looking at the world outside. She's confused, trying to make sense of what she's seeing.

"Sheriff?" Her voice quavers. "You . . . might want to take a look at this."

Pinching the bridge of his nose between his thumb and forefinger, Buck emerges from his office. "What ya got, Tess?"

Tessa looks back at him, her mouth opening and closing, as if she's lost the ability to form words. She points toward the window, and the rain-slicked street beyond. At last she manages to say, "There's something . . . moving . . . out there."

Crossing the room, Buck stands beside Tessa, both of them gazing out the window. At first he sees nothing but the familiar silhouettes of parked cars, the typical glow of the traffic light, switching from green to yellow to red. Then something darts across the pavement, its movements jerky and irregular.

"What the hell am I looking at?" he mutters, leaning closer to the glass. "Some sort of raccoon?"

Whatever it is, it most certainly is not a raccoon.

The creature in the street is a weird amalgamation of bone and sinew. About the size of a dog, it carries itself on three thick, hooked legs. Its gaping maw is filled with needle-like teeth that just seem to grow out of the bone. Though it has no eyes, it turns toward the station, almost as if it is looking back at Tessa.

It charges, moving faster than its warped and irregular legs should allow.

Without looking away from the window, Tessa reaches over, her hand clutching at Buck's forearm.

"Oh no," she breathes.

The window explodes, showering them both in shards of glass. Several jagged pieces of the window slice across Buck's face, cutting his cheek, cutting his nose, nearly taking out an eye. Tessa screams, throwing her arms up in front of her face, and stumbles backward, almost tripping over her own feet.

Perched on Eric Reed's desk is the . . . thing that leapt through the window.

The creature shrieks as it spins on top of the desk, knocking papers and pens over, turning to face Buck and Tessa even though it must be completely sightless.

Buck's Glock 22 springs into his hand. He doesn't understand the horror skittering around on the desk before him, but he knows damn well how to take aim, brace for recoil, and pull the trigger.

The gun jumps in Buck's hand, muzzle flare flooding the office, deafening thunder cracking, the shell spinning through the air. The bullet tears through the creature's bony structure, shattering its carapace, ripping through strangely stitched muscle, sending it toppling from the desktop and onto the floor.

Through the window, several more of the creatures—each one unique, each one just as terrible—crawl into the station. There is little consistency between them. Some have eyes. Some don't. Some have dozens of legs. Some pull themselves along on just two mantis-like arms. They are all made of bone, though, and all have claws or bladed hook arms.

All have mouths, that's for damn sure.

"Tessa!" Buck calls.

He means to tell her to run, but he doesn't even have time to bark that short command as the creatures throw themselves at him. He fires his pistol again and again. The muzzle flare paints everything into a weird slow motion as two of the leaping monsters are blown to pieces. A third, however, slams into Buck, hitting him square in the chest, throwing him sprawling over office chairs.

Even if Buck had ordered Tessa to flee, she might not have been able to do so. Her muscles stiffen and atrophy. Fear and disbelief and confusion petrify her as more of the creatures scurry into the room.

"What are they?!" she asks. "What are they?! What are they?!" As if she expects some unseen force to answer. As if she thinks that answer might save her.

Tessa's paralysis shatters when one of the creatures pounces, its claws raking across her arm, cutting her nearly to the bone. She screams, the pain jolting her into action. Stumbling back, she slams into her desk, sending papers flying as she tries to put distance between herself and the attacking beasts.

Bony legs scrabble across the floor as the abominations chase after her.

She sprawls over a chair, tumbling to the floor in a tangle of limbs and office furniture. She lands on her chin, her teeth chomping hard into the meat of her tongue, the taste of blood filling her mouth. The impact knocks the wind from her lungs, leaving her gasping as one of the creatures lands on her back.

Buck presses the muzzle of his gun against the attacking creature that pins him to the floor. He pulls the trigger twice, obliterating the monster, turning bone into flying dust and tissue into red mist. He rolls, clambers to his feet, and takes aim. He risks shooting Tessa, but the thing crawling on her back raises two hooks, preparing to drive them into the back of the woman's skull.

Buck fires. The creature flies across the room, slamming into the wall with a wet thud, sliding down, leaving a mess of bone and ooze across the wall.

Tessa squirms on the floor. Her blouse is soaked in blood, tattered in several places by the creature's sharp legs. Nasty gashes crisscross her skin. She pushes herself off the floor on trembling arms.

But as Buck examines the remains of the creature he shot, his blood runs cold. Spasming in pain, the thing stirs, its numerous bony legs twitching and writhing. As if it's knitting a sweater, it sews strips of Tessa's bloody skin that it took from her, using her flesh to patch up the bullet wounds.

"Jesus—"

Two more of the grotesque horrors scuttle across the floor, their appendages clicking as they charge toward Buck. Shots ring out in quick succession, each one finding its mark. The first creature explodes in a shower of bloody fragments. The second one spins wildly across the floor, losing a couple of legs.

Even more of the beasts leap and crawl through the window now, chittering and screeching.

The acrid smell of gunpowder fills the air as Buck empties his weapon, his movements fluid and precise. Shell casings clatter to the floor, mixing with the fragments of the creatures' shattered forms.

Click.

The empty sound echoes loudly through the room. But Buck pulls the trigger a couple more times as several monsters close in around him.

Click. Click.

He reaches with fumbling fingers to his belt, retrieving another magazine.

A blur of bone and sinew launches itself toward him. The creature's mouth—if that's what it is—is on its underbelly, a circle of tiny, twitching legs surrounding a tooth-filled orifice. Buck's eyes widen as he sees not one but three of the nightmarish creatures hurtling through the air, their limbs outstretched and grasping. His muscles tense as he prepares to dive out of the way, but he knows he's not fast enough.

The thunderous report of a shotgun booms in the office. Followed by two more concussive blasts. The three monsters explode in a shower of bone shards and viscera.

Buck blinks, his ears ringing from the sudden explosions. Through the haze of gun smoke, he sees Tessa standing there, her stance wide and solid, a shotgun from the gun cabinet in her hands. She pumps the weapon, the action clumsy but efficient. Her finger tightens on the trigger as another creature scuttles into view. The shotgun roars, its blast tearing through the unnatural shape.

A chorus of shrieks draws their attention to the window once more. A horde of the horrors pours in over broken glass and wood. They move with terrifying speed, their rigid limbs clicking against the glass shards and splintered wood.

"Oh God," Tessa whispers. "There are so many."

The things hop and leap from broken desks and overturned filing cabinets, their stolen flesh rippling as they propel themselves toward Tessa and Buck.

Buck fires at anything moving.

Tessa reloads, dropping spent shells to the floor. Despite her terror, her fingers move of their own accord, pumping the shotgun and taking aim once more. The shotgun's blast echoes through the devastated station, catching one of the leaping creatures midair, spattering it across the room.

Buck pivots, tracing the darting movement of yet another.

"Buck!" Tessa cries. "Look out!"

One of them, faster than the others, lunges at Buck's outstretched arm. With a sickening crunch, the beast's bony appendage slices clean through Buck's wrist, severing his right hand—the hand in which he grips his pistol—in one swift motion.

The gun spins across the blood-spattered floor.

Buck howls in agony, dropping weakly to his knees.

The beast, triumphant with its gory prize, scurries away, Buck's hand clutched in its horrific grasp.

The fingers still twitch, firing a phantom gun.

Blood gushes from the ragged stump where his hand had been, as Buck tries to scoot back away from the advancing monsters. The creatures, sensing weakness, swarm over him like a tide of writhing bones and sinew.

With her resolve breaking, Tessa watches, helpless, her finger quivering on the shotgun's trigger. The creatures tear into Buck, each piece vanishing into the writhing mass of bodies.

His screams are raw and gargling. But at least they end quickly.

The shotgun slips from Tessa's grasp, clattering to the floor. Warm liquid trickles down her legs as her bladder gives way, fear overriding all bodily control. Her legs are next, and she sinks to the floor, paralyzed once more.

"Please," she whispers, though she knows there will be no mercy. "Please, no . . ."

The creatures take her apart in seconds, her flesh strengthening the swarm.

CHAPTER EIGHTY-THREE

THE BATTLESHIP CAREENS DOWN the street . . .

. . . blasting past once-familiar streets that now look strange . . .

. . . swerving around the shredded dead that have been denuded of flesh . . .

. . . crunching over hideous, bony, flesh-and blood-covered creatures that scurry and slither and inchworm from corpse to corpse.

Sarah feels the car jostle as the wheels smash another of the little monsters into the pavement. She looks in the rearview, past the colorful, overlapping stickers covering the back window. Behind her, a bright spot in the darkness, is her home. Flames rage through the structure, pushing back the night. Billowing black smoke rises from the collapsing roof.

Somewhere in the conflagration, her mom and dad burn.

It was her father who set the fire, trying to use a lighter and her mom's hair spray to ward off . . .

. . . whatever the fuck these creatures are . . .

Her father's screams as the flames overtook him, folding back toward the spray can, rushing up his arms, racing up his face, setting his hair afire, will haunt Sarah for the rest of her days.

He'd been trying to save her mother as three of those bone-and-meat monsters ripped and tore at her with sharp, barbed legs. Her mom couldn't scream, because her throat had been slashed open. As she tried to speak, blood pumped in gushing bursts from her neck.

Sarah barely got out of there herself.

She winces, clutching at her left leg. One of the creatures had jumped her as she scrambled to the safety of the Battleship. It ripped through her jeans with what seemed like a half dozen knifelike claws. She'd kicked it away, but not before it left a long, wavering cut down her thigh, not too deep, but enough to hurt like hell and soak her pants leg in bright-red blood.

The Battleship rushes under low overhanging branches of the trees that line either side of the road. Sarah presses her foot down on the gas as hard as she can as there's a *thump* against the roof.

Sarah looks up, sees dimples punching into the metal, as something heavy and sharp-legged scrabbles overhead.

Another *thump* shakes the car.

And another.

They're in the trees. Holy shit, they're falling out of the trees and onto the car and they're going to get inside and then they're going to tear me apart next.

A jagged leg suddenly stabs through the roof, ripping the tattered ceiling upholstery, cracking the dome light from its mounting, as one of the creatures violently pushes its way into the car.

Sarah instinctively flinches away. Tires screech and the Battleship's roaring engine hiccups. The car loses speed, just for a split second, then lurches forward again.

"No, no, no, no, no!"

Now the creature on the roof has two legs jammed into the hole it made, wrenching the metal apart, ripping the cloth that covers the ceiling.

It looks in at Sarah with spinning eyes, the bloodshot eyes of a person.

The Battleship's engine sputters again, its momentum vanishing. The chance of escape slips through Sarah's fingers as fluidly as the blood gushing from her leg. Then the motor revs and the car surges ahead.

"No!"

As long as she's had the Battleship, she's never had an inkling of trouble. Now, though, when she needs it most, the vehicle shudders and rocks, the engine coughing, almost dying, coming back to life, then dying again.

The next time the Battleship loses power, it doesn't recover—the station wagon rolls to a stop in the middle of the street.

The rooftop creature batters against the gash it's made in the ceiling, pushing its way through into the cab, where it can hack and cut at Sarah and finish the job its brood-mate started when it sliced into her leg.

Two more creatures scrabble over the windshield and down the driver's-side window, trying to find their way inside. She can barely make out the shape of the beast to her left, concealed by the stickers wallpapering the glass. The monsters stab at the windows with their pointed legs. A crack forms across the windshield. The side window shatters.

But the stickers hold. The decals and labels cement the fragmented glass shards into place, preventing them from exploding across Sarah's face and the horrors from leaping in to rip and tear.

Gravity, friction, and faith.

But it won't hold for long.

The creature upon the sagging, crushed, decal-laden window shrieks and begins to shred its way through the vinyl covering.

Sarah throws herself away from the window, landing on her back across the front seat. Overhead, the first creature continues ripping open the ceiling while the others work at the windows.

She reaches back, her fingers pawing at the passenger-side latch.

As the door opens, Sarah drags herself across the seat, leaving a trail of blood across the cushions. She hauls herself out of the car, landing hard on the pavement. She rolls to her feet, springs up.

Abandon ship!

The three creatures climbing upon the Battleship scurry her way.

Sarah's arms and legs pump. With every step, a jolt of agony spreads through her thigh, threatening to bring her down. Maybe the cut is deeper than she thought and she's losing too much blood. But she doesn't check. She runs, not even sure where she's headed, three monstrous horrors zigzagging in pursuit.

CHAPTER EIGHTY-FOUR

MOM IS PLAYING THE PIANO. Not well, but well enough that Willa, upstairs in her room, can make out the tune. It's an old song, one of her mom's own compositions that holds the weight of the past. Willa has heard the stories countless times: the competitions won, the applause . . . then silence. Her mother never did explain why she stopped playing.

But Willa thinks she knows. Whispers of pregnancy fill in the blanks.

Willa's own guitars are propped up in the corner of her room, the wood gleaming dully. Willa wants to tell herself that she hasn't given up, not like her mom, but it's getting harder to cling to the dream.

Who am I kidding? I gave up a long time ago. And it has nothing to do with getting knocked up.

If that's the case, though, couldn't she regain her musical mojo?

She looks at her unused guitars and sighs.

The music from downstairs stops. Not with the lingering resonance of fingers lifted from keys at the end of a piece, but with a single, jarring, discordant note. Willa's heart skips a beat. That wasn't right. Her mother might be out of practice, but she plays with precision, even in her rustiness. The dissonant note sets Willa's nerves on edge, prickling her skin.

Willa slips off the bed, steps out of her room and into the hallway, her ears straining for any sound. She descends the stairs, each step hesitant and unsure.

"Mom?"

In response, explosive, destructive sounds rise from below. Glass breaking—sharp and clear—followed by the heavy thud of furniture being overturned.

"Mom!"

She takes a step, and another crash reverberates up the stairwell. Her hand grips the banister, knuckles whitening.

This might be another nightmare. It certainly *feels* like one of the horrifying visions that have recently plagued her sleep.

But you never realize you're having a dream when you're in it, do you?

No. *If you realize you're dreaming, you wake up.*

Willa forces herself to descend.

Step. *Crash.* Step. *Crash.*

Just as Willa's foot hovers above the bottom step, her father bursts from the living room. He falls backward with wide, unsteady steps, his face a mask of shock and blood. A sheen of sweat covers his skin . . .

. . . what's *left* of his skin . . .

. . . mixing with the crimson that masks his features, and his chest heaves with labored breaths.

"Da—" The word sticks in Willa's throat.

He sees her then, his eyes overly white orbs in the carnage of his face. His hand shoots up, signaling her to stop—to retreat.

"Go back! Y-your room! Lock your door!"

Red bubbles burst from the meat that was once his lower lip, as blood oozes down his chin.

Instinctively Willa obeys, starting to back up.

But the resolve in her father's eyes wavers, crumbles, as if he's glimpsed something behind her that claws and chews and ravages his decision. He corrects himself, his voice sharp with command. "No—get out! Just . . . just run!"

Then he charges back into the living room and out of sight.

Run? Leave him? Leave Mom?

In the fleeting moment of indecision, Willa remains frozen. Her father's sudden scream snaps her from her immobile state. She sees contorting shapes dance across the wall, hints of what's happening in the next room, shadow puppets playing out a violent scene. She has a choice to make. The front door, where she can flee out into the night, or the living room, where something awful has befallen her father and, in all likelihood, her mother. She can't just abandon them, no matter what Dad said, no matter what he wanted.

She throws herself headlong into the living room.

Every shard of reason and common sense tells her to shield her eyes, to turn her fucking head, to look away. She can't, though, even as tears blur her vision, rolling down her cheeks, trying to wash the sight from her memory. What she sees wrenches a startled gasp from her throat. Each awful detail etches itself into her mind, carves new wrinkles on her gray matter. She knows, with intense clarity, that if she survives this night, she'll forever remember every aspect of what she now witnesses.

This is just a nightmare, Willa tells herself.

The bay window is shattered, glass scattered across the carpet, the curtains billowing inward in the breeze. The carpet is wet with rainwater and blood. Strange tracks, winding through the room. Her mother is motionless on the floor, her music silenced, her legs twisted unnaturally over the toppled piano stool. A congregation of abhorrent creatures swarms over her, their forms a nauseating blur as they eagerly strip flesh from bone.

This is just a nightmare!

But she doesn't awaken.

Her mortally wounded father struggles against a growing horde of similar creatures. His movements are wild and frenetic, those of a man fueled by despair and love, determination and hate. Blood gushes in a sheet from his face and from the dozens of cuts and gashes and contusions all over his body.

This is just a nightmare!

Willa screams as the vile monsters gnash and tear at what remains of her mother.

The beasts surround her father, slicing at him, scraping at him, wearing him down, ripping him apart slice by slice.

Willa is still screaming, her throat raw, as she lunges toward her father. His shirt is in tatters, revealing deep lacerations that weep crimson tears. She grabs at him, tries to pull him away from the creatures. Their eyes lock for a fleeting moment—a silent plea for forgiveness, for understanding—and then are sundered as another creature pounces, its talons digging deep into her father's body for meaty morsels. Willa snatches up a shattered lamp base—she swings the improvised weapon, connecting with a sickening crunch against the thing's carapace. It reels back with an ear-piercing screech, momentarily releasing her father.

"Run, Willa! For God's sake, run!" Her father's voice anchors her in the middle of the madness.

"For fuck's sake," she cries, "let me help!"

And it dawns on her, she has never sworn in front of her father before.

Is that disappointment in his eyes?

Her father speaks again, even as more of them leap onto his back, tearing at him, pulling at him, tugging at him, laboriously trying to drag him away—

Where are they taking him?

—and his words come out as a choking gargle. Willa sees his mouth work, and even though she cannot make out the words, she knows what he's trying to say.

Run!

Get out of here!

And . . .

Good-bye.

One of the monsters scales her father's chest with spiderlike agility, its claws sinking into his skin as if it were soft earth. The creature's maw latches onto his exposed throat. A gush of blood erupts, a scarlet spray soaking over the monster's shell. Her father claws fitfully at the air. His eyes glaze over as his body convulses and he collapses to the floor.

The room spins, the walls stretching and contorting.

Willa's gaze fixes on the front door. With a shuddering, sobbing breath, she runs for the threshold, moving on pure survival instinct, knowing somehow that when she sets foot outside her home, she'll never see it again. She reaches the door, falls against it, weeps as she pulls it open.

A half dozen monsters are right there on the front steps, immediately surging toward her.

Willa screams, slamming the door closed. The creatures bash against it, the heavy wood cracking.

Spinning on her heels, she sees even more of the abominations scurrying down the hall from the kitchen, from the back of the house. There are even a few hopping and tumbling down from upstairs.

Willa runs back to the living room.

The creatures—there must be a dozen or more crawling through the room—now turn their attention toward Willa, advancing, chittering and hissing.

Some of them are . . .

—*wearing?*—

. . . pieces of her mother's face.

Sinew working her mother's distorted mouth like a puppet. Speaking with her mother's voice.

"You're out late! You're out late! You're out late!"

Willa clutches the lamp base, trying to ward off the horrors. They close in, undeterred.

"You should have called! Called! Called!"

The creatures—uncaring in the face of Willa's loss and sorrow—snap and slash at her.

Willa bolts for the window, fully aware that the jagged shards of broken glass will likely cut her deeply as she hurls herself outside.

What other option does she have?

A swarm of terrifying creatures has invaded the house. The front door feels miles away and out of reach. Hiding in her room only delays the inevitable. And trying to wake herself from a dream—

This is just a nightmare!

—isn't working.

If only she can manage to leap through the fragmented window—

Willa halts.

Countless chittering, squealing, snapping, hopping creatures swarm through the yard. They eagerly wait for her, poised and ready, like seagulls waiting for breadcrumbs to be thrown.

She hesitantly steps back, trying to blink what she's seeing out of her eyes.

Just a nightmare.

Please?

A nightmare.

A horn blares. An engine roars. The glow of headlights fills the shattered window and washes across Willa's face.

The creatures, startled—if it could be said about such monstrosities—by the sudden racket, scatter away from Willa.

At the last second, she throws herself out of the way.

A sleek black truck smashes through the window, through the walls of the house, splintering wood and shattering brick. The grille of the truck is slathered in the bits of bone and blood—the remains of creatures just like the ones that have slaughtered Willa's mom and dad. The front windshield is shattered and gore-caked.

Scraps, covered in sweat and blood, throws open the driver's door and almost spills out into the debris.

"Willa!"

He clutches a blood-coated tire iron. A thought spins through Willa's shattered senses: *In case of emergency, break glass.*

"How—"

"These little fuckers are everywhere!" Swinging the tire iron, Scraps sweeps his way through the room. "All over the yard! I ran over as many as I could! Mashed them good!"

His face is flushed, covered in sweat, twisted with fear.

He doesn't look like himself.

"Go, Willa!" Scraps gurgles.

Scraps stands over the ruined body of Wade Hanson. Small-town gangster. Willa's father. And maybe the only real friend Scraps ever had.

The bone-and-flesh horrors close in around Scraps, returning each slash of his tire iron with several of their own.

"Get your ass out of here!" Scraps yells.

He is barely standing, bloodied, his skin hanging in ribbons.

Several of the monstrosities are dead and oozing out on the floor, but even more scurry to take their place, jabbing and picking and cutting at Scraps.

Willa runs for the shattered window, slips past the ruined truck.

Bear, her father's other right-hand man, sits in the truck's passenger seat, wearing a frozen look of shock on his bearded face. His shirt is ripped open, his ribcage exposed for all to see. One of the creatures, dead, its shell crushed, lies on the seat next to him, still clutching his heart in its mandibles. The inside of the truck is painted with blood.

The ragged edge of the window scrapes against Willa's arm, and she hisses in pain. She's wearing only pajama bottoms and a tank top. Her feet are bare, and she must pick a path carefully to avoid the jagged shards of glass covering the ground.

She turns to her side and maneuvers through the narrow passage between the hulking mass of the truck and the broken window frame. Pressed between the metallic surface of the vehicle on one side and the sharp, splintered debris on the other, she moves as carefully as she dares, on her tiptoes, stepping between glittering glass. A few pieces of glass cut into her toes. She winces but keeps moving.

Once she is free, she runs.

Without a set of car keys.

Without her phone.

Without her mom.

Without her dad.

Every step is agony.

Not because of cuts on her feet.

Because of what she's leaving behind.

But she doesn't look back.

FRIDAY

HUMANITY ISN'T GOING OUT LIKE THAT, IS IT?

CHAPTER EIGHTY-FIVE

FROM THE PIER, KENNY TOSSES another duffel bag onto the wet deck of the *Jilly-Bee II*.

For the moment, the marina is quiet.

That was not recently the case. Couldn't have been. Not judging by the disarray around them.

The bait and tackle shop's door hangs ajar, the hinges barely clinging to the frame. The windows are a starburst of glass shards. The gravel parking lot is strewn with lifeless bodies, both of people and of the bone-horrors, many of which appear to have been crushed beneath the weight of squelching tires. Multiple motel room doors stand wide open, and all their windows are shattered or smeared with blood. Some doors stand firm, though, along with windows unscathed. Maybe, in those sealed rooms, survivors might cower.

The harbor itself is eerily still, devoid of any vessels venturing out or returning. Barely a ripple disturbs the surface of the water.

Nearby, the RV park is still. Who knows if any of the campers are still alive?

For now, no living bone-horror can be seen. They have moved on to more abundant hunting grounds. And Kenny's dad harbors no desire to wait around to meet up with them again.

In the distance, from town, screams can be heard.

People are dying out there. Willa might be—

"Take these cans, son." Kenny's father hurries down the pier, a red plastic gas can in each hand. He hands them off and starts to turn away. "I've got some more in the truck. I'll be right back."

Unease claws at Kenny's guts. "Dad—"

His father looks back at him, raising his eyebrows, an expression of curiosity—but also an expression that says *Hurry it up*—on his face.

"What about Willa?" Kenny asks.

"You know what's happening in town. You saw it firsthand. For pity's sake, son, we barely made it here ourselves."

The truck, parked in the marina's gravel lot, sports dozens of new dents. A nasty scratch, made by a six-fingered claw, meanders down the driver's side. The front window is cracked, the driver's-side window shattered. The tires are caked with bone and blood and mangled meat.

"You want to go find her," his father continues, "you be my guest. Take the truck if you want. I sure as hell don't need it. But I ain't waiting for you."

Kenny doesn't budge. There are monsters all over Wilson Island. Attacking and butchering people. *Monsters*.

And right now, as he prepares to leave his girlfriend to her fate, Kenny feels like one of them.

Not my girlfriend. My ex-*girlfriend. Let Dean save her. And the fucking baby.*

He knows that's his own fear talking, that he's trying to rationalize his selfish actions. He's fabricating excuses for leaving her behind.

He knows all of this and accepts it. Runs with it.

There's nothing he could do anyway. For all he knows, Willa is already gone, already dead. And the baby—

The baby's dead too.

A startled burst of mad laughter erupts from his lips.

His father hurries back to his truck.

They've loaded the *Jilly-Bee II* with supplies—food, water, beer, clothing, fishing gear, first aid kits, battery packs, a flare gun.

I'm finally getting out of here. Just not how I expected.

His father returns with two more heavy, dull cans of fuel. He hands them off to Kenny, who feels the heftiness of their contents, then steps onto the weathered deck of the boat.

"It's more than we need," Kenny's father says. "At least, I hope it is. I'd rather have too much and not need it than need it and not have near enough."

Something about his dad's words doesn't sit right.

"You think we might be out there for a while."

"Might be."

"You think this goes beyond Wilson Island?"

"How should I know?" His father scans the horizon. "We'll need to scout things out, figure out if it's safe to dock somewhere else. If it's not, if it looks dodgy, we'll stay on open water as long as we need to."

"What if those things can swim?"

"Didn't see any flippers on them."

The boat bobs in the water. The unlatched door to the bridge swings open an inch or two, then snaps against the frame, swings open again, then snaps closed once more. Kenny's dad makes his way up the short ladder to the bridge. He starts the engines. The *Jilly-Bee II* rumbles to life, water churning and frothing underneath.

"Cast us off."

Kenny unties the ropes from the cleats. With a shove off the dock, the boat pulls away from the pier, chugging past the rocky shoals, heading for open water.

Kenny watches as the marina—and the town beyond—gradually recede into the distance, becoming smaller and darker with each passing moment. Wilson Island becomes nothing more than an outline, a silhouette dotted with tiny specks of light, barely visible on the horizon.

"Better stow those supplies," his dad says.

"Yes, sir."

As Kenny moves to open the loose hatch door leading to the boat's hold, the last traces of the island's outline dissolve into the engulfing darkness, leaving an inky sea stretching in every direction.

The hatch swings open on its own.

Seven or eight skeletal creatures surge forth, jaws snapping and claws slashing. Kenny stumbles, landing hard on his ass. He kicks across the slick deck, trying to get away from the beasts. One of them lunges, its bony neck extending, sharp teeth biting through Kenny's deck shoe, taking half his foot in a flash of searing, bone-crunching, flesh-shredding pain.

Kenny howls as the creature spits out the bits of shoe and foot.

One of its companions gathers them up, almost tenderly.

"Kenny!"

His father moves toward the bridge ladder, only to find himself face-to-face with a trio of creatures climbing up to greet him.

Cans of fuel and boxes of supplies are knocked over, rattling into one another, spilling their contents. Blood pools across the deck. Gurgling fuel spills in spurts from one of the overturned cans.

As the creatures advance on Kenny, he gropes blindly, fingers digging through bags of snack food and tangles of fishing line, over rolling and clinking beer bottles, for anything that might serve as a weapon. His hand closes around the handle of the flare gun.

Somewhere—it seems even farther away than the town they've left behind—he hears his father scream, an alien sound he never thought the man could utter.

Kenny aims the gun and pulls the trigger.

A searing white heat instantly envelops him.

From the shore, any observer still alive might witness the *Jilly-Bee II* explode into a spectacular flower of flame, its smoldering debris soaring high above the open water before descending in a downpour of smoke trails.

CHAPTER EIGHTY-SIX

HE DOESN'T LIKE TO THINK of it as blood.
That's what it is, yes, dripping down the length of the many-named sword. The blood of animals, of men and women. The blood of those things.

The blood of *meat puppets*.

His own blood, too, running down his arm, oozing through the grooves of the sword's hilt, traveling along the blade to mix with the ichor of his enemies.

He is cut and torn and sliced in a dozen places. His right arm, his left leg, his back, his face. The bullet wound on his shoulder throbs and bleeds as well, soaking into his clothing. If he stops moving for more than a few seconds, his muscles tighten and his arm grows heavy. Luckily—or perhaps unluckily—he hasn't had much of an opportunity to stand still, not with all the hacking and stabbing and slashing. The asphalt on the street beneath him looks almost comfortable, he thinks, and it might be pleasant to lie down and take a long nap.

The Warlock no longer hides as he moves through the Plaza of Lies. He limps down Beaumont Street for all to see. Guttering streetlights herald his passage.

His sword is in hand, the blade pointed down, held at the ready.

The town smells like a slaughterhouse with AC problems on the hottest day of the summer.

The windows of Island Outfitters are blown out, and the clothes on the racks within sway like ghosts. At Island Ice Cream, the ice cream has melted and mixed with blood.

The meat puppets leave cast-off remains littering the streets, in some cases taking everything and in others only specific bits of flesh, some corpses picked clean, raw down to the bone, some missing sections, either raggedly torn off or almost surgically removed.

The creatures, he realizes, are using the skin and muscle and tissue of their victims, using it to weave tendons and muscles on top of their strange, misshapen bone bodies, using palpitations to pull the strings of flesh and blood to spur legs and claws and mandibles into action.

They're animating the dead the way necromancers in worlds of fantasy and horror animate the dead.

Only, rarely do necromancers animate themselves. *Unless we're talking about a lich.*

A supremely powerful archmage might use magic to cheat death as an undead creature. *If this is a lich, though, this is a whole new ballgame.*

Either way, the meat puppets are acting with purpose. They're harvesting flesh. The way the Ripper . . . the way Junior did.

Junior knows what's going on. Maybe he knows how to stop it. If he's still alive.

In the distance, the Warlock hears screams. He cannot be sure, though, that he's hearing what he thinks he hears. They sound human, yes. But the meat puppets are like mockingbirds. Like sirens of the sea.

Will-o'-the-wisps. They lure their prey.

Their ghostly mimicry might lead the Warlock straight into a trap.

Three of the hideous creatures skitter out of the shattered windows of the Almighty Deli. They crawl toward the Warlock, their claws clacking, knifelike appendages eagerly flexing. One of them moves on a dozen twitching legs, or maybe they're rib bones. Another slithers back and forth, carried on a writhing spinal column that leaves a snail trail of gore behind it. And the third drags itself along, a skull-shaped body pulled by a waving, intestine-like tongue.

One of them meows. Another squeaks like a squirrel. There's one making an all-too-human sobbing sound.

The meat puppets surround him, clawing at him with sharp legs, biting at him with gnashing teeth, lashing at him with spinal column tentacles. Blood spatters from the end of the many-named sword as the Warlock swings it against the monstrosities.

More blood—

No. Not blood. Ichor. Slime. Goo. Not blood.

—sprays as he hacks and stabs and cleaves.

With these three meat puppets left dead and in pieces, the Warlock wearily turns in a circle, looking for more enemies, for anyone who might need help, looking for someone who might help *him*, looking for an ally to prove that he's not alone.

What he finds is Madhouse Quinn.

The raggedy man steps out of the deli. He's got a cold, half-eaten hoagie in his hand and casually takes a bite of it. Wilted lettuce and mayonnaise-covered turkey drip down his chin.

"Look at you," he says, "the big, bad monster killer."

"What are these things?!" the Warlock shouts.

"You know what they are."

"Meat puppets."

"They've had other names." Madhouse Quinn cackles and coughs. "Older names. Much older. But I like that. Suits them. Suits us."

"They're all over the island," the Warlock says. "They're killing everyone in sight. We need to help where we can. *If* we can."

"Not my job," Madhouse Quinn says.

"What the hell is *that* supposed to mean?"

"Means it's not yours either."

"You're still going on about being chosen, about destiny."

"Yeah. And you still don't get it."

Maybe not, but I've been playing games about destiny for a good chunk of my life.

The stalwart warrior doing battle with a terrible wyrm. The young apprentice wizard on a quest for true power. The cunning rogue braving trap-infested warrens in search of fortune and glory. The Warlock knows a little something about these stories, knows these archetypes, the hero's journey.

We have jobs to do, you, me, each and every one of us. No application necessary. No interview required. That's what Madhouse—the doomsayer—had said. *You, me, them others who were out on the beach that night. We were chosen. Recruited. Conscripted. Enlisted.*

Behind Rudy's Mart, where all great prophecies are delivered.

"Explain it to me," the Warlock says. "What do these things want?"

"When angels wage war, it's not because of what they want."

"We're not talking about angels here." *At least, I hope not.*

"She started small," Madhouse says, "but now she wants it *all*."

Another meat puppet, this one unbelievably gliding on wings of veiny, tattered skin, swoops out of the sky. The many-named sword spins in the Warlock's hand, slicing the creature apart.

"They can fucking fly?!" the Warlock exclaims.

"It would appear they can now," Madhouse Quinn says.

The mangled meat puppet convulses on the street, its body unevenly split in half. Though it isn't precisely gasping for air, it most certainly struggles to hold on to its flimsy mockery of life. On one fleshy wing is the tattoo of a coiled dragon with butterfly-like wings of its own. With every jerking movement, the dragon seems to undulate weirdly.

The Warlock recognizes the tattoo. It had been on the shoulder blade of Kayla, the waitress at the Red Eye.

"You told me a few days ago we have jobs to do. Is that related to all this?"

"Haven't you been having the dreams?" Madhouse asks.

"I—"

He starts to say that he hasn't, but he realizes that's not true. He's seen the strange man lurking outside his window. He's drawn weird shapes in his notebooks, written as—

"The Caller."

"That's right," Madhouse says. "The Caller from the Void."

"I drew it."

"You were there. Same as me. Same as Lucas Simms. Same as Willa Hanson and that boyfriend of hers, rutting like animals in the back of a truck. You might have been stoned out of your mind, you might not remember, but you were *there*."

"So what?"

"No one witnesses an angel fall without being fundamentally changed."

The Warlock can't argue.

He may not remember how the meat puppets came to Earth, but he definitely *feels* different.

Angels, though? I don't think so.

"Listen," he says, "I might have an idea. It's a long shot, I know, but it might be our only chance to save the town, to save anyone who's still breathing. Junior Simms—"

"He was not among the chosen," Madhouse says.

"I saw him, though. He attacked Willa Hanson. I stopped him."

"You've picked a side, then."

"I saved someone who needed saving."

"The Mother cannot be twice-embodied," the doomsayer says, speaking as if he is reading bizarre scripture. "The Caller sees her as weak, and so he wants her to be born anew, born of the flesh of the Hanson girl."

"I don't know what that means."

"To spare the girl is to curse the Mother. What lives cannot be reborn."

"Whatever's happening, maybe I can stop it."

"You think so?"

"Junior Simms knows about these things. He was fucking wearing one of them on his face like a fucking mask! I think he was killing people on their behalf and, now that he's locked up, they're running rampant. Maybe he knows a way to stop them."

Madhouse Quinn laughs. "You serious?"

"Let me guess," the Warlock says. "Not our job?"

"No. I mean, you think there's a way to stop all this?"

"What else am I supposed to do?"

For fuck's sake, I've got a sword, after all.

The thought springs into his head. He almost says it aloud. It's not sarcasm or a joke. He means it.

Maybe I'm losing my mind.

Maybe I am *losing my mind.*

"Well, go on, then." Madhouse Quinn waves him off. "If that's the path you need to take, I won't stop you. That's part of your story, and I'll tell it when you're gone."

"But you won't help either."

"I'm here to tell the story," Madhouse Quinn replies, "to spread the gospel."

"And me? What am I supposed to do?"

"By the time you figure that out, it'll be far too late."

CHAPTER EIGHTY-SEVEN

Everyone she cares about is dead.

Willa feels it deep in her bones. Her mom and dad for sure. But Kenny too. Dean. Sarah.

Oh God, Sarah.

How could *any* of them survive? How will *she*?

Willa feels death creeping in around her. At one time, maybe, she wouldn't have recognized it, but she most certainly does now. It feels like exhaustion. Like weariness flowing through her veins instead of blood. A weakness that can't be shaken.

Death creeping in from all around. Life creeping in from within.

It feels like giving up.

As she shuffles down the street, she pinches her arm over and over.

This is a nightmare.

Willa hobbles along the street. Palm trees line the road like sentinels, their fronds rustling and whispering in the breeze. Otherwise, everything is still, and the shuffling of her bleeding bare feet is almost too loud.

Smith Brothers Cigar and Pipe, where her dad would sometimes spend a couple of hours smoking stogies and socializing with locals, now stands in ruins. The front window has been blown outward, jagged shards littering the street. A dark, bloody drag trail parts the sea of glass where someone—maybe one of the Smith brothers—was dragged away.

A skateboard lies abandoned, snapped in two, along the sidewalk.

Nearby, the lifeless body of a woman, perhaps thirty years old, clings desperately to the replica of the Cape Jordan Lighthouse. Her arms encircle it as though it were a life preserver. She didn't dare let go as she was attacked, even when her legs were severed from the rest of her.

Willa's hometown, besieged by monsters. Family and friends and neighbors, people she's known all her life, sprawled in their houses, in their yards, on the street, stripped of their skin and flesh. Awful bone creatures skittering about, holding organs and severed limbs, not unlike the fiddler crab back at the beach from what seems like years ago now, holding Willa's last cigarette like some sort of award.

This is a nightmare.

Her *last* cigarette.

She thinks about her unborn baby, who may never know its father, who may not live to be born. A baby Willa isn't even sure she wants to bring into this fucked-up world.

My baby.

Her arm is bruised, she's pinching so hard.

This is a nightmare.

This is a nightmare.

This is a nightmare.

If it isn't, then she wants to curl up in the dark somewhere, close her eyes, and retreat into a nightmare forever.

Her fingernails puncture her flesh, scratching bloody crescent moons into her arm. The world around her, though, remains the same.

Surely this must be another of her surreal dreams. But no.

"Please," she mutters to anyone who might listen.

She prays for an endless nightmare. Because it has to be better than this reality.

And if this *is* reality, she longs for a sign, for some kind of omen, for a guiding light, like the long-extinguished signal of the Cape Jordan Lighthouse showing her the way through the dark. Her hand over her belly, she hopes for a reassuring kick from the baby, but it's too soon for anything like—

"Psssst."

Willa jumps at the sound.

"Over here." A whisper from the shadows. Sarah's voice.

Behind a trio of alleyway trash cans, a shape detaches itself from the surrounding darkness.

"Willa."

"Sarah . . . ?" Willa whispers back. She takes a step, then stops herself. Back at the house, one of the creatures had actually spoken, mocking Willa by using her dead mother's voice. Could this be the same lure, taunting her now, mimicking her best friend?

"Is that you?" Willa says.

But it can't be. Willa already knows. Sarah must be dead and gone, just like everyone else.

"It's me," Sarah's voice says. "What the fuck are you doing out in the open? Get off the street, dummy. Take cover."

"What's the point of hiding?" Willa asks. "This—whatever's happening—is already over."

"You're not dead yet."

But I am, just like everyone else.

"How can I be sure," she asks, "that's really you?"

"You're kidding. Tell me you're kidding."

Willa shakes her head slowly.

Because those nasty little creatures can speak with the voices of the dead, the voices of people they've killed, and maybe they can take vocal cords as easily as they take faces and lips and tongues, and maybe they somehow take memories too, and if this isn't all in Willa's head, then her father and mother and probably Sarah too really are dead, and if the only way to communicate with them is through the creatures that killed them, then maybe that part of the surrounding slaughter isn't a nightmare at all, but a—

"A good dream," Willa whispers.

"Christ on a Popsicle stick. Snap out of it, Willa."

The shape steps out into the dim light. A feeling of painful relief washes over Willa, and she almost falls, her legs giving out under her.

Sarah is ashen, limping, wincing a little with every move, her clothing spattered in blood, her face smudged with soot. One sleeve of her jacket has been torn off and tied tightly around her left leg as a makeshift bandage.

It's really her!

Willa collapses against Sarah, hugging her best friend tightly, weeping.

"You," Sarah says, "look like shit."

And, despite everything, regardless of everyone she's lost, or what may yet happen, Willa's tears turn into racking laughter. She's never been so happy to be so wrong.

CHAPTER EIGHTY-EIGHT

"**I**'D LIKE TO MAKE A special request," Slim says.

Along with Bo, Duncan, Jerry, Matty, and Li'l Winslow, he stands outside the Surefire Pest Solutions office. Three company trucks, each adorned with comically dead, smiling fiberglass insects on top, are parked in a wall-like formation. A barricade against the monsters in the night. Duncan and Jerry look out from behind one of the trucks, watching the surrounding neighborhood. They each have a hunting rifle at the ready. Matty sits on his ass, his back against a tire, arms draped over his knees, head down. Li'l Winslow paces, his phone pressed against his ear. At the tailgate of one of the vehicles, Bo fidgets with a metal canister and hose, using a wrench to tighten bolts.

Bo looks up from his work.

"What did you say?" he asks.

"A request," Slim says, "for the Death Request Line."

Bo returns to his task, the muscles in his arms tensing as he twists the wrench. Next to the canister are a dozen mason jars, all filled with gasoline, tangles of cloth stuffed into their mouths.

"I want to kill them all," Slim says. "Every last one of them."

Duncan and Jerry look toward Slim.

Li'l Winslow lowers the phone from his ear.

Matty doesn't look up, but he chokes out a laugh.

"Sounds like a plan to me," Bo says.

"No." Li'l Winslow waves his arms in sweeping defiance. Flag on the fucking play. "You're all crazy as hell if you think I'm letting you do this."

"We weren't asking," Bo says, as he continues his "arts and crafts" project.

"You're talking about using my property," Li'l Winslow says. "My chemicals. My trucks. I won't let you."

"My guess is we're all done taking orders from you," Bo says.

"Those things are swarming all over town," Slim says. "They're killing everyone they see. Sooner or later they're gonna come this way. What do you think you're going to do then? Hide in your fucking office?"

"We kill them," Bo says, "before they kill us."

"We should just keep our heads down," Li'l Winslow says, "until this blows over."

"What makes you think this is going to blow over?" Slim says. "Who are you calling anyway? The cavalry? By the time anyone gets here, there won't be any of us left."

Li'l Winslow looks helplessly at the phone clutched in his hand.

"It's an infection." Satisfied with his work, Bo steps back from the truck. The smell of gasoline curls around him. "It's kill or be killed."

"I won't allow it," Li'l Winslow says.

"You think you can stop us?" Bo asks.

He steps toward Li'l Winslow. Duncan and Jerry turn away from their watch. Even Matty looks up coldly.

"I won't be a part of this."

Bo regards the other men, then shrugs.

"We don't need three trucks," he says. "You want to clear out, now's your chance."

Li'l Winslow eyes them. A curse forms on his lips, but he doesn't dare voice it. All he says is, "You're all fired. I hope you know that." With a grunt of disgust, he moves for one of the trucks. He pulls himself into the cab, cranks the engine, looks at his team one last time . . .

. . . then hauls ass.

The tires spit gravel at the exterminators.

Slim imagines that's the last they'll see of their boss—their former boss—one way or another.

"Killing is my business," he remarks, "and business is good."

CHAPTER EIGHTY-NINE

WHEN THE WARLOCK FINDS THE two girls, they look dead on their feet.

A trail of bloody footprints meanders along the sidewalk. This was the trail he followed, which brought him to them. Willa's feet, he can see, are bare, bleeding from a few scrapes and cuts, and he imagines every step she takes is painful. Her friend—the Warlock knows Sarah even though she's barely said a handful of words to him in her entire life—is limping too. Despite the temporary field dressing wrapped around her leg, her jeans are so dark with blood that they look almost black.

They look like badass warriors of the apocalypse, he thinks. Then a more realistic thought pops into his head. *They're not going to make it.*

When they notice him, when they hear him following them, they jump, nearly screaming. They must have expected to see these goddamn meat puppets stalking them. What they see, though, is a guy in a hoodie and jeans and black Converse with a gore-and-goo-dripping sword decorated with many names. It has served him well in these dark moments.

"Willa?" he calls out.

"Warlock?" Willa says. "You're still alive!"

"Nice sword," Sarah says.

Her voice trembles, barely a whisper, and she forces herself to swallow down her obvious pain.

The Warlock looks at the bloody weapon, almost as if seeing it for the first time. "Thanks."

"Do you know what's happening?" Willa asks. "I mean, do you know *why* it's happening?"

"Really, I feel like I've only picked up bits and pieces," the Warlock says. "And I'm not sure I believe any of it."

"Bits and pieces," Sarah says. She's barely able to stand, and she can't take her eyes off the viscera dripping from the end of the sword. "I don't know that I like that description."

"That's more than we know," Willa says.

"Something fell from the stars," the Warlock says.

"What? Are we talking about aliens here?" Sarah asks.

"I don't know," the Warlock continues. "Whatever it is, it fell like a comet or shooting star, and it splashed down not far from here. I was there, I guess, even though I don't really remember it. So were Madhouse Quinn and Lucas Simms. So were you, Willa."

"Me?" Willa asks.

"You and your boyfriend both," the Warlock says.

"When was this?" Willa asks.

"A couple of months ago," the Warlock says.

"Kenny and I—" Willa stops herself.

"You were out there," Sarah asks, "on the night you got knocked up?"

"Wait." The Warlock stammers, shakes his head slightly. "You're pregnant?"

"Keep up," Sarah tells him, then turns her attention to Willa again. "How about it? What about that night?"

"I don't know," Willa says. "Maybe. Probably. We were out there a lot."

"Were you out there on the night of a falling star?" Sarah asks.

"What's it matter?" Willa's voice rises. "I know you. You don't believe any of this."

"Maybe not," Sarah says, "but I feel like I need to set the boundaries of our collective crazy."

The party's starting to go off in wild directions. The Warlock thinks like a Dungeon Master. *I need to bring them back to the story.*

"Listen," he says. "I know this is messed up, all right? I'm trying to figure it out myself, and this is everything I have to go on at the moment. These things, the meat puppets—"

"The what?" Willa asks.

"The meat puppets."

"Like the band," Willa says.

The Warlock smirks, impressed. "Guess so."

"That's disgusting," Sarah says. "Appropriate, but disgusting."

"I think they're connected to whatever fell that night. Madhouse said something about a 'Mother.' I think he was talking about a hive queen or something? You know. Like an aboleth, maybe."

"A what?" asks Sarah.

"Sorry," the Warlock says. "It's from Dungeons and Dragons."

"That's not helping."

"Hear him out," Willa says.

"N-no." The Warlock looks from Willa to Sarah and back to Willa again. "She's right. This isn't a game." *I have to remember that.* "I think maybe these meat puppets have a nest somewhere. I think they're gathering meat, harvesting food, to feed something in that nest."

"A queen," Willa says.

"A meat queen," Sarah clarifies.

"Whatever this thing is," the Warlock says, "it's more than just an animal. Maybe it *is* an alien. An angel. A god, if you believe in that sort of thing. Maybe it's something else altogether, which we weren't meant to understand at all."

"Mission fucking accomplished," says Sarah.

"When it fell that night, the night of the shooting star, it latched on to anyone who was there, got its hooks in us, connected us in an unexpected way, gave each of us our own destiny."

"Destiny," Willa says.

"Like a job," the Warlock says.

Sarah rolls her eyes. "She knows what a destiny is, dummy."

"Okay, okay." Willa holds her hands up, trying to frame their situation. "Who did you say was on the beach that night? Lucas Simms. Junior's dad."

"He must have been chosen to protect the queen, to provide for her."

"He was killing people to feed her or something," Willa says.

"And for some reason," Sarah adds, "his kid took over for him."

"Then," Willa continues, "there was Madhouse Quinn."

"He believes," the Warlock says, "that he's some kind of prophet or disciple. Like, he's supposed to chronicle the life story of the meat-queen or whatever."

"What about Kenny and me?"

The Warlock notices that Willa touches her stomach when she asks the question.

"I don't know," he says. "Sorry."

I'm cracking up, the Warlock thinks. *That's what she believes. I can see it on her face. She believes I'm trying to rationalize what's happening, painting all the horror and violence and death in colors I understand, reframing it as some sort of sword-and-sorcery adventure. Maybe I am, but what else am I supposed to do?*

"I'm not crazy," the Warlock says.

"Nobody said that," Willa says.

"Might've thought it, though," Sarah chimes in.

"Stop it," Willa tells Sarah, then looks at the Warlock. "What about you? What were you chosen for?"

"I think . . ." The Warlock looks down the length of his sword. "I think I'm supposed to kill it."

"The meat-queen gave you this job?" Sarah asks. "So—what?—she's suicidal?"

"You know what they say," the Warlock answers. "Mysterious ways."

"Do you think you can kill her?" Willa wants to know.

"I can fucking try," the Warlock says.

"You know where it is?" Sarah asks.

"Not yet," he says, "but I think I know someone who might. Junior Simms was . . . serving this thing . . . like some sort of fucking Renfield or something. That's why he was killing people. He was *feeding* it. When he got caught, that's when the meat puppets spilled out into the world."

"Why then?" Sarah asks.

"Maybe they were hungry," Willa says, "and without Junior to feed them—"

"They're animals," Sarah says. "Bugs. How would they even know Junior was caught? How would they know he couldn't feed them?"

"It wasn't the meat puppets," the Warlock says. "It was the queen. And I don't think they were after food."

He fixes Willa with a stare.

"Me?" she asks.

"You're pregnant," the Warlock says.

Sarah bristles. "Hey, weirdo—"

Willa stops her, a hand on her arm. "Yeah," she says. "And?"

"You got pregnant," the Warlock says, "on the night the queen fell."

"I don't like where this is going," Willa says.

"What is living," the Warlock says, "cannot be reborn."

"Are you saying that the queen did something to my baby?"

"I'm saying you're carrying something that might not be human."

"Oh, fuck off," Sarah says.

"I think your baby might be connected to the queen," the Warlock tells Willa. "I think the queen might want you dead because of it. But we might be able to stop her before she gets her wish."

"How?" Willa asks.

"Junior Simms. He was all wrapped up in doing the queen's bidding, so he might know where to find her. If we find her"—the Warlock tests the weight of his sword—"maybe we can kill her."

Suddenly Sarah grabs the Warlock's arm, squeezes. She's looking past him, her eyes wide.

"You might be looking for their queen," she says, "but the . . . meat puppets . . . have found us."

At least a dozen, maybe more, of the creatures skitter toward them with outstretched claws, stolen muscle working to animate their skeletal frames. It's almost impossible to count them. They dart about in weaving, crisscrossing paths, hopping and clambering over one another.

"Get behind me," the Warlock tells them.

A sea of horrors converges upon the three of them. They huddle together, spinning in a slow circle to keep an eye on all the monsters, Willa and Sarah clutching at one another, the Warlock waving his sword to ward the creatures away. Hissing, the meat puppets stab out with claws and barbed appendages and serrated limbs. The many-named sword parries the attacks, batters the beasts back.

But they keep returning for more.

They move toward Willa, reaching for her, most of them completely ignoring the Warlock and Sarah.

"They're fixated on you!" Sarah says.

"Why me?" Willa asks.

Once again, instinctively, impulsively, Willa touches her stomach, placing her hand over it protectively. *Oh. She's pregnant.*

And with that, the Warlock understands his destiny. Fuck killing the meat-queen. He's here to protect Willa above all else.

He doesn't fully grasp the intricate whys and wherefores that weave the tapestry of fate. That's not, he supposes, how providence operates. But he trusts his instincts.

He's witnessed it unfold countless times. The innocent mother-to-be, carrying the would-be savior within her womb. Her belly cradling the promise of hope.

The Warlock's been tossing around words like "chosen" and "destiny" with abandon. Now the weight of their meaning slaps him with startling clarity.

Willa's unborn child might be the key to vanquishing the meat puppets. The baby might grow up to be a savior in dark days to come. And he is her guardian.

For the first time ever, the Warlock understands his purpose on this earth. He saved her from the clutches of Junior Simms. Now he stands resolute, battling an ever-growing horde of crawling monstrosities determined to end her life.

Excalibur. Blackfyre. Sting.

The names he has given the sword over the years race through his head as he draws on the weapon's strength.

He hacks one of the creatures apart.

Scalpel. Andúril. Blackrazor.

With a stab, he skewers another.

Frostmourne. Stormbringer. Grayswandir.

He kicks a third creature away, sending it tumbling across the street.

He is a warrior. A knight. A paladin.

"Stay behind me!" he cries.

"How are we supposed to do that?!" Sarah yelps. "They're coming in from every direction!"

One of the meat puppets swiftly ducks past the Warlock's sword, making its move at him. The monster's gaping mouth is set vertically within its skeletal frame instead of horizontally, serrated teeth seeming to grow from the jaw, each point like a shark's tooth. The creature's maw is pulled open by tendons resembling taut rubber bands, before snapping shut like a bear trap. The meat puppet jerks backward, propelled by the spasmodic twitching and contracting of its sinewy tendons, wrenching fragments of the femur and tibia from the Warlock's right leg.

He screams, falling to his knees, the agony of the bite so intense that he barely registers the jolt running up his leg as the mass of ruined meat and bone smashes into the street.

Willa clutches his shoulder, attempting to hoist him to his feet. His right leg, however, dangles uselessly, resembling more a fleshy sock than a functional limb. With a groan of pain, he collapses once more, bracing himself on one arm while the other swings his sword. Blood spreads across the street. Willa's foot slips in the slick puddle, but Sarah swiftly yanks her back, rescuing her from another biting, slashing meat puppet.

The Warlock bellows, his throat raw, spittle flying from his lips, tears streaming down his cheeks.

He thrusts the point of his sword into the meat puppet, twisting the blade, ripping the creature apart.

More of them close in.

Doomgiver. Mourneblade. Chaoseater.

Now the awful creatures forget about Willa, just for a moment, and turn their full attention toward the Warlock as they shred and rip, bite and tear, snap and slice.

On his knees, the Warlock slashes the legs out from under one of the monstrosities.

Thorn. Graywand. Brightroar.

His head spins as he smashes another with three quick, brutal strikes.

Longclaw. Sorrow. Witch's Fire.

His vision blurring, he stabs the last one in its snapping mouth.

Bleeding from dozens of deep, gushing wounds, the Warlock lets the many-named sword fall from his grip and clatter to the street.

A memory flickers through his mind. Uncle Terry's eyes filling with panic as those things dragged him away, as he realized all was lost.

He flops over, falling on his side. He blinks rapidly, the world around him vanishing, then reappearing, vanishing, then reappearing.

He sees more creatures crawling out of the shadows, and he knows he was wrong. His destiny was not to fight, to protect Willa. His destiny was to fail—to show anyone who might be watching how hopeless it is to fight against these horrors.

Destiny fulfilled.

He gazes toward Willa and Sarah, his vision blurring as the world around him fades into a murky grayness.

Willa rushes to his side, falling to her knees beside him, her eyes wide with shock.

"Oh God," she murmurs. "Oh God. Oh God."

She doesn't even know my name, not my true name. But he lacks the strength to voice it.

Just as he can't warn her that the fight is futile, that she's already lost, that she should surrender to the horrors that await.

He hopes his actions—his failure—have illustrated that lesson.

With a feeble effort, he reaches for his cherished sword, his fingers flexing open and closed.

He's not dead yet.

Close enough.

"Thank you," she whispers. "Thank you, Denny."

And the utterance of his name—his real name—releases him from a world of hurt and pain, and he feels himself go weightless, dropping into an infinite void, nothingness.

She knew.

Willa takes hold of the sword for herself. The Warlock hears the metal scrape harshly against the pavement.

"We need to be able to protect ourselves," she says.

As darkness envelops the Warlock completely, he senses a gentle tug at his legs.

"And what are you doing now?" Sarah asks.

"I need shoes too."

CHAPTER NINETY

THE FAMILIAR ARCHING SILHOUETTE OF the Walters Memorial Bridge looms ahead, connecting Wilson Island to the mainland.

In his Surefire Pest Solutions truck, Li'l Winslow slams his foot on the gas. The engine roars.

He knows the state police must be en route, alerted by the dozens, possibly hundreds, of calls from the area, including his own. The reports were bizarre, sure. Freakish monsters slaughtering the town! But their sheer volume would demand attention.

Still, Li'l Winslow has no plans to stick around for the cavalry.

His escape, though, is blocked by a chaotic jumble of vehicles—cars and trucks haphazardly clustered together, like an abandoned traffic jam.

Cursing, Li'l Winslow hits the brakes.

Some vehicle doors hang ajar, swinging gently in the breeze. Engines still purr, creating an eerie symphony of idle hums. Headlights pierce the night, casting long, ghostly shadows across the bridge. But there is no trace of drivers or passengers, as if they've vanished into thin air.

Amid the wreckage, a state police vehicle stands out, its nose pointed ominously toward Wilson Island. The driver's-side door is wide open. The blue light spins lazily, painting the roadway in light.

Winslow climbs out of his truck, the door creaking as it swings shut behind him.

The fiberglass insect on top of the truck bounces on its springs.

Li'l Winslow creeps past the abandoned vehicles crowding the road. Approaching the nearest car, a Kia Sportage, Winslow peers through the grimy window.

Inside, the upholstery is drenched in a dark, crimson stain. A pair of hands, cleanly severed at the wrists, grips the steering wheel, lifeless fingers locked in place.

Ten and two.

Li'l Winslow barks out a mad laugh.

His stomach churns violently, bile rising in his throat. He clamps a trembling hand over his mouth, to stanch both the possible puke and more possible mad laughter. He stumbles away from the Sportage. His feet brush up against something in the road.

Whirling, he sees the body of the state trooper slumped against a nearby vehicle.

Just the body, though. The trooper is missing his head.

It, too, has been almost surgically removed. A trail of crimson streaks across the pavement into the tall grass. The trooper's head, blood-soaked, eyes wide, peers back over the gently swaying blades.

Li'l Winslow spins in place, looking at all the empty cars around him. They're blocking the road, yes, but several of them are still running. He can move them aside. Better yet, he can just take one and get the hell out of there. He has a feeling that the people who were driving the cars won't miss—

Behind him, in the middle of the road, is the fiberglass bug from the top of his truck.

How? Had it fallen off?

It *isn't* the ornamental insect at all. The Surefire Pest Solutions mascot is still perched atop the truck, right where it's always been.

The creature on the street is the same size. Its pale, chitinous body looks like the shell of an insect. Where the Surefire ornamental bug smiles, though, this creature hisses with a maw full of concentric rows of teeth.

Some of them are pointed and sharp, others are blunt, human.

The creature scurries with shocking quickness toward Li'l Winslow.

Desperately he glances around for some avenue of escape and sees the state trooper's head bobbing toward him through the grass. It sits atop another insectile horror, blood leaking from the stump in little rivulets all along the monster's shell, threadlike veins woven into the meat that animates the creature.

"It's got me!" the creature screeches. The veins spasm and pull, making the severed head's mouth open and close. "It's got me!"

And in that moment, Li'l Winslow knows they've got him too. The dead X eyes of the fiberglass bug witness his final moments.

...

The little black-and-white dog runs breathlessly through the neighborhood, tongue lolling out the side of his mouth, tags upon his collar jangling. The night air tastes of salt and seaweed, of rain and mud, of sweat and blood.

Of panic. And death.

All around, the shadows birth strange shapes that reach, chittering, for the dog.

Buster rips through a wet yard and jumps a broken fence, sprawling on the other side, his short legs kicking up tufts of slick grass.

Behind him, the shuffling creatures slip out from behind brush, out from dark alleyways, out from sewer drains.

Buster scurries around the corner of a house that smells of mildew and rot, paws sliding, and dashes past a stack of old crab pots and a fishing boat on cinderblocks. Losing his pursuers, he hunkers down, catching his breath. He hides behind a rusting cast iron tub not too different from the tub in which he used to get his much-hated baths. Nearby, a bug light pops and zaps worrisome insects into smoldering ash.

One by one, the things slide across the yard, searching for him. The glow of the bug light shimmers over their slick forms, revealing too many eyes or none at all, too many joints, too many claws, too many snapping and hungry jaws. Some have faces that are almost human. Some have no faces at all. Some have mouths that suction open and closed. Some are silent. Some hiss or squeal. Some speak in weird human voices.

Feeling their closeness . . .

. . . feeling mounting fear . . .

. . . Buster makes a break for it.

He tears toward the street in one great leap, running across the pavement, launching himself through a string of yards, seeking holes and ducking under the fences this time, where unfamiliar smells mix with rain. His little legs pump as hard as they can.

As Buster bounds past a swing set, one of the creatures springs out of hiding. Buster dodges left, but the creature closes on him, a claw stabbing out, grabbing the fabric of his collar. Yipping, he yanks away, but the collar holds, drawing him closer to the creature's rapidly snapping jaws. Growling, he twists and writhes, trying to free himself.

At last the claw tears through the collar. Buster's tags spin through the air, falling to the ground.

Buster is halfway across the yard by the time the collar comes to a rest.

But another one leaps at the dog, smashing into him, its weight sending him sprawling through the mud. His world spins, a wheeling rush of dark sky and bright porch lights filling his vision. He rolls across the ground, kicking and scrambling to regain his footing.

Yet another springs at him, reaching. But he hops back, ducks beneath the grasping claw, and comes up with a bite of his own.

His teeth clamp down on the thing's outstretched arm. He shakes his head, back and forth, until something gives way and the claw snaps off.

The creature staggers back. This was not expected.

Buster bolts, too fast for the injured creature to recover, a black-and-white blur through the shadows. He leaps proudly, running like he might not ever stop, carrying his prize—his enemy's arm—in his jaws. He vanishes, triumphant, into the waiting night.

...

Madhouse Quinn listens to the distant screams and howls from town. He settles back against the bars of a multicolored jungle gym/swing set/monkey bar play station, reaches into his jacket for a smoke, and lights up. Around him, the playground, with its seesaws and sandboxes and merry-go-rounds and shredded foam rubber turf, is quiet.

He imagines no children will ever play here again. It makes him a little sad, but there's not a damn thing he can do about it. He will tell their stories.

The meat puppets are rapidly spreading across Wilson Island.

With every kill, their numbers grow.

Soon they will scatter into all of Fredericks County. From there, they will take the state, and the country, maybe even the whole of the continent.

If that didn't give the Mother a big enough army . . . if she still couldn't defend herself . . . then the world would be next.

The Mother had struggled to liberate herself from the influence of the Caller from the Void. From the pull of this world.

She had thrown herself to the stars, even though gravity clung to her like heavy chains. She had almost broken free.

Plummeting back to the earth, frying in the atmosphere, she'd found herself weakened, her defenses shattered, leaving her exposed and vulnerable.

Inevitably, the Caller will seek her out once more.

With escape beyond her grasp, she will fight. For the war to come, she needed soldiers. *This is the story I have been chosen to tell.*

Madhouse Quinn will be here to guide the human survivors. He will preach the gospel.

In time, the survivors will come to understand. They will accept the sacrifices that were made. They will come to love the Mother for the battle she has won.

He is not afraid when a dozen meat puppets scurry out of the shrubbery, moving toward him with their snapping claws and clicking blades. They are awful, hideous atrocities cobbled together from the bone of the Mother and the sinew of the residents of Wilson Island. But they mean him no harm.

He is, after all, their messenger.

Watching the misshapen creatures inch closer, Madhouse takes a drag on his cigarette, lets smoke explode from his nostrils.

Smiling and clucking his tongue, he crouches down, reaching out with one hand.

The creatures crawl toward him, their claws flexing open and closed, their jaws clamping open and shut, their serrated and bladed antennae waving back and forth.

"You know me," Madhouse says.

The wet and seeping flesh that's stretched over their bodies flexes, pulses, pulls taut, then relaxes.

Pulls taut, relaxes.

Madhouse Quinn snaps his fingers. "Come on. Let me get a closer look at you."

One of them reaches out timidly.

"There we go," he says.

A lightning-fast snip of its claw, and the meat puppet severs three of Madhouse Quinn's fingers.

With a gasp of surprise—because pain hasn't set in just yet—Madhouse recoils. Blood jumps across the playground's mulched rubber. His fingers bounce and tumble away.

"Wh-what are you doing?!" he shouts as the creatures converge. "I'm meant to spread the gospel! You fucking *idiots*! You're not supposed to hurt me! I was chosen to tell your *story*!"

The atrocities chitter back at him with the voices of those they've killed, consumed, and reimagined.

"It's biting me! It's biting me!"

"Did you remember to take out the trash?"

"I made reservations for next Friday!"

"Oh my fuck! What is that?"

So many stories, the totality of Wilson Island, in fragments.

The meat puppets keep right on gibbering as they rip and tear and slice and gouge.

As he screams—because now both the pain and the shrieking have set in—Madhouse Quinn understands that the monsters . . . the Mother . . . no longer need him.

They will tell their own story from here on out.

CHAPTER NINETY-ONE

THE LAST TIME SUREFIRE PEST Solutions visited Mrs. Crewes's house, they'd knocked politely on the door. They had been invited inside. They had worn plastic booties on their feet. This time, the door is locked up tight. This time, no one answers. This time—

Fuck the plastic booties.

Matty cracks the front door open with a crowbar, then steps aside.

Bo, a tank strapped to his back and a sprayer in hand, moves into the house.

He looks, Slim thinks, *like a World War II soldier armed with a goddamned flamethrower.*

Slim, Jerry, Duncan, and Matty follow. Slim and Jerry hold sprayers and handheld jugs filled with chemical poison—Bo's special recipe. They look more like gardeners, maybe. Duncan carries a couple of tenderloin roasts and a turkey, all raw, so he looks a bit like a butcher.

Last time, they'd left poison behind. To kill the rats. They were giving it a few days to do its work.

They each have a few gasoline-filled mason jars in bags at their sides.

None of them bother with plastic coverings for their boots as they tread through the house.

Bo checks and clears each room, soaking the floors, walls, and ceiling with a sizzling, foaming combination of deadly poison.

Slim nods toward the back of the hall. "That's the bathroom," he says. "That's where we saw the hole in the wall."

In the living room, they find a skeleton, its bones stark and polished, glistening with a sheen of crimson. The remains, seated on the plastic-covered couch almost as if calmly waiting for a favorite afternoon soap opera to come on the tube, are encircled by the tattered shreds of what once was a floral print dress.

"Mrs. Crewes," Slim notes.

"What's left of her," Duncan says.

The team approaches the bathroom door. Bo pushes it open with the sprayer nozzle, and rotting meat stink hits them with monstrous force.

"The bugs," he says. "They're gone."

"Not really bugs, are they?" Jerry says.

"Don't get technical on me now," Bo replies.

The bathroom is smeared with blood and filth. *I keep a very tidy home*, Mrs. Crewes had said.

The hole behind the toilet is far bigger than it was before. Whatever had boiled up from below wasn't a cockroach, centipede, or rodent. Bo crouches, sprayer at the ready, peering into the darkness.

"Rats and roaches," Bo says, "tried to escape the bugs."

And now, Slim thinks, *for us, there's nowhere left to run*.

"Bring the meat," Bo says.

"You think this is gonna lure them out?" Duncan asks as he hands the roast over.

"I don't know," Bo says. "Maybe. They like meat, near as I can tell. Here's hoping they won't turn down a free meal."

Bo takes the roast, which he personally pumped full of the same poisonous concoction sloshing in the tank strapped to his back, and he shoves it into the opening behind the toilet. He scoots back across the floor, puts his boot on the hunk of meat, and kicks it down into darkness. The roast topples into the tunnel beyond, thumping against the cavernous walls.

"Just need a couple of them to take the bait," Bo says. "They'll spread it to the nest, wipe them out at the source."

"What if they don't behave like regular bugs?" Matty asks. "What if it doesn't work?"

"It'll work," Bo says.

"Maybe they don't have a nest," Matty says.

"They look like fucking bugs," Bo says. "They've got a nest like fucking bugs."

"No bug I've ever—"

"Listen!" Slim leans closer to the wall. Something screeches down below.

"All right." Bo rises. "Let's move."

"And then what?" Jerry asks.

"We find and poison as many of those little fuckers as we can," Bo says. "More poison we spread, the faster the hive dies."

"They're not bugs," Jerry says again. "Not exactly. So, how do we know this is gonna work?"

"We don't," Slim says, "but we gotta try. Something. Anything. We gotta hope it makes a difference."

Bo regards him, smiles.

"One last job before we find ourselves in the unemployment line."

Slim knows that's wishful thinking.

When they emerge from the house, they find themselves surrounded. Dozens of the creatures move toward the house, scurrying across the street, crawling through trees, scrabbling over the roof.

Bo clutches the sprayer tightly.

Slim reaches for one of the gasoline-filled mason jars.

In his head, he recites a litany of bands and songs. He builds a playlist for his lighthouse radio station. Ratt and Poison and Mötley Crüe and Bon Jovi and the Scorpions. The list goes on and on. All playing a dirge for a dream that will never come to pass. He hears the songs playing in his skull, from this moment until the end, even when everything goes red and agony-filled.

"For Barry," Slim says, dedicating his final request.

CHAPTER NINETY-TWO

WILLA'S FINGERS CURL AROUND THE hilt of the many-named sword. She tests the weight of the steel. The weapon is bulkier than she expects, heftier, a little awkward in her grasp.

The Warlock made it look easy. *When he saved me. From Junior. From the meat puppets.* Until it wasn't so easy after all.

Together, she and Sarah walk along Beaumont Street, now a wasteland of shattered storefronts, gore-splattered sidewalks and pavement, and abandoned vehicles with slashed tires and shredded engines and shattered windshields.

They pass the music store where Willa once spent countless hours. The windows are broken out. A light flickers and pulses somewhere within.

Nearby, a child's teddy bear, not too different from Willa's own Mr. Bigsby Bear, lies in the gutter, soaked in blood.

Corpses lie here and there in the street.

Willa remembers how this all started for her, with human organs scattered across Killdeer Avenue.

Now I'm going to end it. That's what she tells herself, how she tries to convince herself to keep moving.

The sword seems to grow heavier by the second. Her fingers tighten and loosen, tighten and loosen, upon the weapon's hilt.

It's not that *heavy.*

She tests the weight.

And I'm gonna drive it right into the heart of—

Of who? Of what?

In the aftermath, a stillness lies over the street like a heavy blanket. *Or a shroud.*

"Everything's so quiet," Willa says.

"It's like those creatures," Sarah says, "the . . . meat puppets . . . have gone into hiding."

"They're still out there," Willa says. "I think maybe they're taking everything they've harvested back to their nest. And they've harvested a *lot*."

"That's a cheery thought," Sarah says. "And what are we doing with our brief reprieve? Where are *we* going?"

Willa warily watches the street. "The Warlock said something about Junior. He thought he might know something about those things. Where they came from. Maybe even how to stop them."

"Come on, Willa. It's too late for all that."

For some of us, Willa thinks. *For my mom. For my dad. For your parents. For the Warlock.*

She stops herself before she falls down the rabbit hole of naming everyone she knows.

"It's not too late for you," Willa says.

"What?"

"I don't want you to come with me."

"What?" Sarah says again with a humorless laugh. "Knock it off."

"We'll find a car that still runs, one with keys, with gas in the tank." Willa is already scanning the streets for a suitable ride. "I want you to drive it as fast as you can, as far as you can, until you're running on fumes. Just get as far away from here as possible."

"Just me?"

"I'm staying. I'm going to the sheriff's station. Ask Junior to help me stop this whole thing."

"Come with me," Sarah says.

"I can't."

"That's bullshit."

"Maybe so, but I'm not leaving, not yet."

"All right." Sarah takes a deep breath, steeling herself. "So, listen."

"I need you to leave." Willa looks at her best friend, pleading with her. "I need you to survive."

"I need you to do that too!"

"Maybe I will."

"So, listen." Sarah's mouth moves into a toothless smile as she repeats herself. "You're my best friend, Willa. I love you."

"I—" Willa starts.

"But," Sarah interrupts, "if you insult me again by telling me to leave, by telling me to abandon you, well . . . sword or not, I'm going to kick your ass."

And that ends the argument. Willa knows better than to push the issue now that Sarah's made up her mind. Because Sarah *would* make good on her threat. She's not going anywhere.

Willa would never say it out loud, but thinks, *Thank God*.

"We're heading to the sheriff's department, then," Sarah says.

"I think Junior is our best bet."

"What makes you think he'll help us?"

Willa holds the Warlock's sword out before her. "Fuck it—I'll make him."

CHAPTER NINETY-THREE

SHE'S MADE A MISTAKE.
There's no way, Willa thinks, *anyone survived whatever happened here.*

The sheriff's department is in ruins. Windows are shattered. Doors hang off the hinges. Inside, the floor is covered in glass shards and scattered paperwork that'll never be filed and splattered blood droplets, and furniture is overturned and strewn about and splintered.

Willa's heart sinks.

"Maybe they survived." Sarah senses her friend's worry. "They're trained for crisis situations. They've got guns."

Willa shoots a disbelieving look her way. Blood oozes down the walls.

"Maybe . . ." Sarah says, her voice withering.

Sword in hand, Willa steps across the fragmented picture window. She reaches behind her, takes Sarah's hand, and helps her across.

Sprawled in the debris lie the bodies of Tessa Kendry and Sheriff Buck. The cuts decorating their prone forms are a mix of surgical precision and vicious carelessness. A hand is missing here, an eye there. Lips. Teeth. Skin is flayed and bone and muscle have been removed from within. They've been—

Harvested.

Weapons lie near the corpses—pistols, shotguns—and the smell of gun smoke hangs almost as heavy in the air as the smell of urine and blood.

They didn't go down without a fight.

There are no dead creatures to be found, though. They seem to leave the remains of humans where they lie, taking only what they need or want, casting the rest aside, but they don't dare leave one of their own behind.

That's how ants do it, right? They drag their dead back to their hives or warrens or anthills or whatever. Back to their queen.

Willa barely realizes that she's holding one hand protectively over her stomach.

She grabs up a phone, flinches away from the incessant buzzing that emerges. Circuits are overloaded. Or the phone lines are down. Either way, the phone's useless.

The door to the holding cells is closed and locked. There's no sign that the meat puppets gained access to that area.

"Junior might still be alive," she says.

"Yay?" Sarah replies.

Across the room, Willa spots a bright-red first aid kit mounted on the wall.

"There we go," she says. She grabs a nearby wooden chair and slides it next to Sarah. "Sit."

"What?"

Not missing a beat, Willa makes her way across the room, almost tiptoeing in the shoes she took from the Warlock's body. It feels somehow disrespectful, sacrilegious even, to disturb the scene. Like walking across graves.

If that's the case, though, I should be treading lightly across the entire town.

Retrieving the kit, she flips the metal clasp and opens it up, checking the contents: white bandages, small bottles of antiseptic, and various sizes of gauze pads, each nestled in its designated compartment.

Sarah still stands beside the chair. "What are we doing?" she asks.

"I said—sit."

"Yes, ma'am," Sarah says as she plops into the chair.

"We need to clean your leg, bandage it properly."

Willa crouches down in front of Sarah. She's not exactly sure what she's doing, but she cleans the cut on Sarah's leg with antiseptic and wraps the wound snugly with the bandages. When she's done, she gently pats the dressing.

"Feel all right?"

"Feels great, Doc," Sarah says, "almost like a meat puppet didn't try to eat me. There any painkillers in that box?"

Willa tosses her a couple of Advil from the kit, then hurries across the carnage-filled room once more.

She crouches next to what remains of Sheriff Buck, taking the ring of keys from his belt. She has pangs of regret about her last interaction with the man. She had nearly squared up on him, making vague threats about her father and his influence in the town. All so she could stand at Kenny's side in his moment of need.

And how did that turn out?

She rises, crosses the room carefully, tentatively, not stepping on any more glass or blood, and stands at the cellblock door. She sets the Warlock's sword against the wall. She tries one key after the other, fishing through them for the right one.

Something clatters in the room, and Willa tenses, looking over her shoulder, reaching blindly for the sword.

Sarah holds up a pistol that she's grabbed from the floor. "Might be more effective than that Ren Faire pigsticker," she notes.

"You know how to use one of those?"

Shrugging, Sarah regards the pistol. "I'll figure it out."

At last the lock clicks and the door groans open.

Willa steps into the hallway beyond, unsure what she'll find. She holds the blade at the ready as she passes the barred cells. Sarah follows close behind. She fidgets with the gun.

They find Junior Simms in the last cell, his face a display of cuts and scrapes and dark bruises and swollen flesh.

"You," Sarah says, "look like shit."

Maybe Sarah hasn't figured the gun out yet, but she aims it like a pro, right at Junior's ruined face.

He barely looks like a person, Willa thinks.

"What happened to you?" she asks.

He looks at her, recognizing her, wincing away from her. "*You* did," he says.

"Wow. You didn't tell me you gave this guy a beatdown." Sarah raises an eyebrow. "Nice work."

"I didn't do this, and neither did the Warlock."

"I tried to do the Mother's bidding," Junior says, sniveling, "and I failed."

"Mother?" Willa says. "We've been thinking of her as a queen."

"She's very old," Junior says, "and she's had many names."

"What is she?" Willa asks.

"Maybe she's a god," Junior says.

Sarah scoffs. "You really believe that shit? She's all-powerful but needed—no offense—*your* help?"

"She was weak. Afraid. She needed to be . . . tended to."

"I don't know about you," Sarah says, "but I'm officially grossed out."

"My father was chosen to protect her," Junior says, "and then it fell to me."

Willa looks to Sarah, who shrugs.

"She tried to get away," Junior says, "to leave this place."

Her and me both, Willa thinks.

"She escaped," Junior continues. "She leapt clear, thousands of years gone by, but she was dragged back."

"What are you even talking about?" Sarah says.

"She was snared by the world," Junior says, "caught for so long in a decaying orbit."

"You said you were doing her bidding," Willa says. "What did she want you to do?"

"She needed meat," Junior says.

Sarah makes a gagging noise.

"She needed to be restored."

"What else?" Willa asks.

Junior raises his swollen eyes. "She wanted me to kill you."

"You know," Sarah says, "those meat puppets were all about *you* out there. And this guy was sent to kill you as well. Why does this bitch hate you so much?"

"She said"—Junior rises painfully and approaches the girls—"you were in her dreams."

That's how I feel about her, Willa thinks.

Sarah motions with the gun. "Why don't you back up a little?"

Junior does as he's told. "She told me you were dangerous."
"Yeah," Willa says. "She's about to find out."
"Huh." Sarah smirks. "You almost sounded like a badass just then."
"Thanks."
"Do you believe it?"
"Maybe?"

CHAPTER NINETY-FOUR

JUNIOR SIMMS, THE WILSON ISLAND Ripper, leads Willa and Sarah back to where it all started.

Back to the beach.

The sky is brightening. A pale grayish-blue seeps into the inky darkness, as the sun sluggishly begins to rise. Seagulls wheel and squawk in the early-morning sky. In the distance, shadowy, rocky, cave-dotted cliffs appear. They're not too different—and not too far—from the area where Dean created his underground gallery.

She thinks about Dean, wondering if he's all right, wondering if he managed to escape the mayhem surrounding them.

She hopes so.

Junior treads across damp sand. Willa stays only a few steps behind him, pointing the many-named sword at the back of his head. Armed with the pistol, Sarah follows. She has a satchel thrown over her shoulder. When she found it, the bag had been full of yarn and knitting supplies, most likely Tessa's. Now it is filled with more immediately useful items scrounged from the sheriff's station—ammunition, road flares, a flashlight.

Junior speaks over his shoulder. "This is where my father brought her."

It surprises Willa that he agreed to help them at all. When she saw him last, he'd tried to murder her. That means—and she can almost hear Sarah's jaded voice ringing in her mind—that this is more than likely some sort of trap.

If it is, I'll take him with me.

"This is where she fell," Junior says, "where my father found her."

"We're near the Point," Sarah says.

She nods toward the dunes, where horny kids park and hook up, where Willa and Kenny had screwed in the back of his truck.

All very romantic.

Shooting stars, blah, blah, blah.

This is where she got pregnant.

This is where she fell.

They're not far from Dean's gallery, Willa realizes, and she feels her heart sink, wonders if Dean is all right.

Or if he's—

She doesn't want to think about it.

Through eyes swollen nearly shut, Junior watches the caves. "He thought she would be safe here," he says.

"And *who* are we talking about?" Sarah asks.

"He wanted her to rest," Junior says, "to heal."

Willa takes her eyes off Junior for just a second, looks at Sarah, and shrugs.

They approach the caves. The entrance is a low-hanging and jagged-toothed mouth.

"She's in here," Junior says.

"*Who* is in here?" Sarah asks.

"The queen."

It's not Junior who answers, though.

It's Willa.

"A queen?" Sarah asks. "You're talking about the lord high mama of all those little meat puppets who have been scurrying around the island. And you want to—what?—talk with her? Negotiate with her?"

"Maybe," Willa says.

"With him"—Sarah nods toward Junior—"as your guide."

"I tried to get you to leave," Willa says.

"And I'm starting to understand the error of my ways."

"You don't have to come."

"Interestingly enough, I don't even *want* to come with you."

"So—"

"So, nothing. I'm not turning my back on you now. But I reserve the right to complain about this suicide mission as much as I want until the sweet release of blissful oblivion."

"All right." Willa points the sword at Junior, the muscles in her forearms straining, then motions toward the cave. "Let's go."

Sarah digs in the satchel at her side, retrieving a flashlight. She clicks it on, then off, then on again, testing the light.

"I knew we were going to need this," she says.

Junior ducks low, squeezing through the cave entrance between the slimy rocks. He grunts with the effort. He looks back, his bruised and swollen face monstrous in the shadows falling over him.

He doesn't need a mask, Willa thinks.

And then he vanishes from sight.

Willa follows, looking back at Sarah as she crouches under the cave's jagged stone teeth.

Be careful, Sarah mouths silently.

Willa half expects Junior to brain her with a rock as she emerges on the other side or a legion of so-called meat puppets to spring at her.

Perhaps the cave mouth itself will slam shut on her, chew her to a pulp, and spit her back out.

Instead, she finds Junior waiting patiently for her.

Sarah joins her, shining the beam of the flashlight into every nook and cranny, watching for attacking monsters.

Only a little of the morning light seeps into the cave.

It's much darker than Dean's gallery, the tunnels far narrower.

"My father didn't need much light," Junior says, "not once he started wearing his No-Face."

"The mask," Willa says.

"It provided a connection to Mother." Junior's fingers rise, tracing the angry red scars that outline his face. "That's how he heard her. That's how I heard her. That's how she lied to us."

There it is, Willa muses. *That's why he's helping us*.

For whatever reason, Junior feels betrayed, abandoned, cast aside, by the meat puppet queen.

"Eventually he didn't need to come here." Junior treads deeper into the cave. "He ripped a hole in the floor of our house. I helped him do it. After that, that's where he fed her. Where I fed her. That's where she sent her brood—"

"The meat puppets," Sarah says.

"—to fetch the sacrifices we made."

He talks about it like it was some sort of game he used to play with his dad, like football, like tossing a Frisbee or flying a kite, like catch.

As they navigate the dim labyrinth, numerous side passages branch off from the main tunnel, veins diverging from a primary artery. Sarah reaches into the knitting satchel, retrieving road flares. She ignites the flares at intervals, each one casting a fiery glow, and throws them along the rocky walls.

"To find our way back out," she says.

Willa recalls Dean saying that the cave system sprawled for miles, twisting and turning beneath the surface of Wilson Island.

Maybe that's how the meat puppets spread all over the island so quickly.

Again, she wonders if Dean is okay.

Again, she pushes the thought down.

"I've never been here," Junior says. "After everything I did, this is the only time I've ever set foot in these caves. Only my father came here."

"What happened to him?" Willa asks.

"He came back," Junior says. "To this place. Without his mask."

Without his mask. Like Junior. Right now.

"And Mother," Junior continues, "accepted his sacrifice."

"You're hoping to see him again," Willa says.

"No." Junior stares through the gloom. "He's gone."

With only the glow of Sarah's flashlight to illuminate their way, they follow meandering tunnels deeper into the earth.

"No one comes here without a mask," Junior says, "unless they *want* to die."

CHAPTER NINETY-FIVE

DEEP IN THE DARK, DEEP in the caves, the Mother greets them.
She's sick.
Willa knows it as soon as the beam of Sarah's flashlight washes over her.

The Mother crouches, her arms and legs long and spindly and bent in upon themselves, drawn up like a dying spider, in an expansive chamber. The dripping domed ceiling is supported by columns of wet and slimy rock. Numerous tunnels stretch out from the cave, their entrances yawning like dark mouths. Some are vast, spacious enough to accommodate a person with ease, while others are so enormous that even the Mother herself could glide through without hindrance. A few passages are narrow and confined, just wide enough for the slender meat puppets to slip through, the walls brushing against their sides as they navigated the labyrinthine network. The air is cool and damp, heavy with an earthy, mineral scent.

And the stink of rotting meat.

They stand together—Willa with her sword, Sarah with her flashlight and pistol held close together, and Junior with his utter surrender, complete awe, and fealty—no more than a couple of yards from the behemoth.

The Mother resembles, in equal parts, one of the foul creatures causing devastation throughout the town, a human woman, and a tangle of rotting driftwood. She's massive, curled up in the chamber. She has no flesh of her own. Instead, she's draped in flaccid sheets of animal hide and human skin, pieced from patches of stolen, festering meat stitched together to form tendons and muscles to move her ponderous limbs.

The large, round eye sockets of her misshapen skull are stuffed with human and animal eyes, clustered like grapes.

She's dying.

Her creaking bones are in a constant state of growth and mutation. Here and there among her arms, legs, ribs, and spine, jagged spurs blossom like flowers. The growths from the Mother's bones remind Willa of her Magic Crystal gardens, only they're growing so, so fast. The fruiting nodules look like pale, lifeless insects or crabs shaped from coral polyps cast up from the sea.

Meat puppets, Willa realizes.

Without the aforementioned meat.

These are her spawn. Her children. Sprouting from her body, born dead, but animated by harvested tissue.

Even more of the atrocities, all dead or dying, litter the ground around the Mother. Some twitch and spasm. Others breathe—or whatever such a thing does instead of breathing—a white, foamy substance from distorted mouths and nostrils and blowholes. Some are decaying, their stolen flesh peeling back and falling off and turning black and cancerous, their shells crumbling like dry rot.

"Oh no!" Junior kicks a path through dead creatures, reaching lovingly for the queen, for Mother. "What is this? What's happened to you?"

He might feel betrayed by her, but he still loves her too, in his own twisted way.

Jesus.

Then, a heartbeat after Junior asks his question, he answers. "*My children,*" he says, his voice deep and cold, "*have been poisoned.*"

"Let me help you." Junior's voice shifts back to normal. He runs his hands over her pale, bony body. "What can I do?"

His tone changes again. "*There is nothing to be done. My children . . . brought the toxins back to me.*"

She's speaking through him, Willa realizes, *using his tongue because she doesn't have one of her own.*

A tongue must not have been harvested for her. Or maybe she rejected the tissue.

"Let me bring you offerings," Junior says, answering in his normal voice, "so you might heal yourself."

Willa swings her sword in his direction. "Like hell you will."

Junior doesn't acknowledge the threatening gesture. He only looks up at the Mother. The massive creature herself, though, turns her dark gaze toward Willa. Junior's voice, deep and resonant, answers.

"*Mother,*" he says.

"Yes. I know who you are," Willa replies.

"*Not me,*" Junior says.

Once more, Willa puts her arm protectively over her stomach.

"*I have lived on this world for so long,*" Junior says in the voice that is not his own, "*and for all those vast ages, I have waited to serve as bride for the Caller from the Void.*"

An echo—the distant rumble of waves—reverberates through the cave.

"*He waits, out in the depths, for the day he will claim my body for himself.*"

Thick, viscous tears drip from the horror's cluster-eyes.

"*This is not what I wanted for myself,*" Junior says.

Fuck, Willa thinks. *Don't let me relate to this monster.*

"*I tried to flee,*" Junior says, "*to leap from this world to the next, but I was dragged back down.*"

"I was there the night you fell," Willa says, "me and Kenny."

"*As my flesh burned from my body, I glowed like a star in the night.*"

Like witch's fire.

"*The Caller must have seen,*" the Mother says, speaking through Junior, "*must have awakened. He stirs—oh-so-slowly—and he is coming for me, coming to pull me into the darkness to serve his whim.*"

"You attacked us," Willa says, "attacked everyone on the island."

"*I needed to rebuild,*" Junior says.

Another bulbous piece of bone protrudes from the side of the Mother's skull, swelling and inflating, breaking free and tumbling to the cold, damp cave floor below.

"You killed so many people," Willa says.

"*I needed flesh and blood for myself . . . and for my children,*" Junior says. "*With my children, with my brood, my swarm, my army, I can stand against the Caller, against my fate.*"

"This"—Sarah speaks in breathless disbelief—"sounds like complete bullshit."

And Willa knows her friend is right.

The Mother's just saying things she thinks we'll understand. She's lying. And she's not even using her own tongue to do it.

"You were there," Junior says, "and you were touched by the light, touched by the Caller's will. And, so, even as I have tried to rebuild, even as I have prepared for the war to come, I will be reborn in you."

"In me?"

No. In my baby.

I'm the mother.

"You cannot want this," Junior says. "Not for yourself. Not for your child. Not for me."

The mother of the Mother.

The Caller wanted the Mother to be reborn. In Willa. In Willa's child.

All because I was on the beach that night. Along with Kenny.

Along with—

So many names had been painted along the blade. Names from books and movies and games.

None of them, though, had ever stuck. Not for Denny Finn Danvers.

But Willa knows the sword's true name. It materializes in her head.

The Warlock.

If she survives the night, she'll paint it on the steel alongside all the others.

Willa's fingers clench around the sword's hilt, her knuckles whitening. She's endured enough. She's not going to let this island . . . or her baby . . . or some sort of living alien bone garden shackle her to a fate she never chose. The losses she's suffered—her parents, her friends, maybe now even her own sanity—harden her resolve. She raises the blade, her muscles tensing as she prepares to drive it into the Mother's heart.

"No!" Junior screams, his own voice once more.

"Watch out!" Sarah cries.

She aims the beam of the flashlight. The pistol's barrel.

Junior throws himself at Willa, grabbing at her.

A gunshot rings out, the sound bouncing off the cave walls, and a flare of light plumes—

—like witch's fire—

—in the darkness, painting the chamber in slow-motion brightness.

The recoil of the weapon hurls Sarah back against the wall.

Junior spasms in pain, teetering on weak legs, reaching for his back, and the bullet Sarah planted between his shoulder blades.

Willa lashes out with the sword. The blade rips across Junior's face and he screams, pulling his blood-covered hands away from the gunshot wound in his back.

He grabs at his face, blood spilling out from under his palms.

He has no eyes.

Willa swings the Warlock back the other way, this time drawing it across Junior's throat.

Eyeless, Junior Simms clutches at his face, moves his other hand to his gushing throat, then to his back, then to his throat, then to his ruined face again. He takes a step toward Willa. At last, all the strength flees from his muscles and he collapses to the cave floor.

Willa draws the Warlock back once more, and she's shrieking now, a deep bellow filled with sorrow and hatred and fear, as she stabs the blade deep into the Mother's inhuman body.

The Mother opens her mouth impossibly wide.

Junior, squirming fitfully on the floor, screams with his final breath. He screams for her.

The sword still embedded in her body, the Mother rears back, almost wrenching the weapon from Willa's grasp. She raises a ponderous arm and brings it down with a crash onto the Warlock. The blade shatters under the impact, splintering into a jagged point halfway along its length. The broken point of the blade juts from the Mother's body. Where blood should come forth, a white foam-like dust puffs and oozes and dribbles out.

In the bouncing glow of the flashlight, the Mother appears like a huge, twisted, spectral tree. Her overlong, near-fleshless bones creaking, she reaches out with her great arms. Her massive hand, adorned with razor-sharp claws, arcs toward Willa.

Dodging the attack, Willa trips over a dead meat puppet and falls on her ass. The Mother's monstrous body rises above Willa, her head swinging back and forth, her mouth open in a silent scream.

Three more gunshots ring out. Foam and bone fly from the Mother's body.

The chunks of bone clatter to the floor, twisting, growing, sprouting lifeless claws and legs.

"Run!" Sarah screams.

Willa rolls to her hands and knees. At her side, Sarah grabs Willa by the crook over her elbow. Together, they flee.

The Mother follows.

CHAPTER NINETY-SIX

STILL CLINGING TO THE BROKEN sword, Willa runs for all she's worth. The Warlock's weapon in hand, his shoes on her throbbing feet.

Sarah is at her side, the beam of her flashlight careening wildly along the walls with every frantic step. There's no time to retrace their path, no chance to follow the flares—the breadcrumbs—they left behind. They're lost, their odds of survival dwindling. Sarah swings the light behind her, and the yawning cave ahead plunges into vast shadow.

"Sarah!" Willa cries. "What are you—"

She pivots, catching only the briefest glimpse of the pursuing horror, and her eyes swell with fright.

In the bouncing light, the Mother fills the tunnel. Her heavy, stomping, many-legged footfalls echo like thunder, shaking the ground. She lashes out with overlong arms, smashing through stalagmites and stalactites and natural columns. White foam—or maybe puffing, bone-like dust—cascades from her lipless mouth as she roars.

"THIS IS NOT WHAT I DESERVE!"

Almost sprawling forward, Sarah wheels around, lighting the treacherous path ahead.

But Willa will never not see the Mother. She knows it. The image of the monster will haunt her for the rest of her life. If she lives.

"I WON'T LET YOU GIVE ME TO HIM!"

The Mother's booming voice echoes through the hall.

But Junior's dead! If he was her voice, how is she still screaming?

"I WON'T LET YOU GIVE ME TO HIM!" she howls once more.

Sarah trips on the uneven ground, stumbles, and almost falls. Just one faltering step and the Mother is upon her, striking out with her gigantic arm, catching Sarah mid-stride, silencing her mid-scream, throwing her like a rag doll across the tunnel to smack into the stone wall.

The flashlight spins through the air, cracks against the ceiling, and goes dark.

"Sarah?"

Even in the dark, Willa is acutely aware of the Mother's presence. The ground quakes as the creature stomps around, looking for her prey.

Willa drops to her hands and knees, the cold stone pressing against the palm of her free hand, the knuckles of the hand clutching her shattered sword.

The Mother's massive arms swing wildly in the dark. Willa can't see the attack—and she's grateful—but she feels the rush of wind. If she hadn't thrown herself to the floor, the Mother might have taken her head off.

Willa feels her way across the wet and gritty floor.

"Sarah!" she calls out.

She receives only silence in response.

Her fingers find something warm and wet smeared across the stone—something viscous and coppery and unmistakably sticky.

Blood.

She urges her fingers forward, away from the blood, until they touch the cold metal shaft of the flashlight. She grabs it, her thumb flicking the switch. When nothing happens, she gives it a sharp tap against the Warlock's handguard. A glow flares in the darkness—

—right into the hideous face of the Mother.

"YOU ARE NOT MY MOTHER!" With all her might, Willa swings the sword, the jagged edge striking the creature's face with a sickening crunch.

The Mother wheels away, but only for a second.

Willa rolls across the floor, narrowly evading one of the entity's bladelike legs.

She springs to her feet and sprints away, flashlight beam bobbing.

Oh God! Oh God! Sarah!

Willa can't afford to look back, can't afford to check on her friend. She knows the monster is right behind her, knows it is closing in, knows that—even though it's dying itself—it will stop at nothing to kill her so that it will not be reborn in human flesh. She won't let the creature catch her, won't let it rip her apart, won't let it kill her baby.

Willa scrabbles up a slippery slope of wet stone, falling again to her stomach, clawing at the stone, breaking her nails, as she slips an inch, climbs an inch, slips an inch, and climbs three. She reaches the crest, using her sword as an anchor, and pulls herself over the edge. She sprawls head over heels down the other side.

The Mother leaps into the air and crashes down. Bits of stone scatter through the air.

Willa tumbles clear, narrowly avoiding the monster, landing—

Face-to-face with Dean.

Ghostly pale, his eyes are wide open, staring, startled for eternity. Patches of his skin and muscle are missing as if scissored away. His stomach is splayed apart and hollow, his innards torn out and snaking across the cold floor.

"Ah—"

A sob begins to form on Willa's lips. The weight of loss presses down on her, suffocating her, crushing her to the stone floor. Death creeping in all around.

Dean is gone, and Willa despises herself for rejecting him, when all she had to do was agree to see him again.

Her mother is gone, and guilt gnaws at Willa's breaking heart for being the cause of abandoned dreams.

Her father is gone, and regret fills Willa's mouth like bile because she never told him how proud she was of him, no matter what he did for a living.

The Warlock's life has ended, and instead of mourning, Willa seized his weapon and his shoes.

Sarah is most likely dead or on the brink of death.

And I abandoned her.

Kenny is probably dead too, and he'll never know the joy of meeting—

His baby.

Life is creeping in from within.

Willa cannot afford the luxury of grief. Not right now. Not if she wants to live. Not if she wants her baby to survive. She scrambles to her feet, leaving Dean's lifeless form behind. Ahead, she glimpses the mouth of the cave, daylight streaming in, promising freedom.

She knows this place. Knows this cave.

She's found her way back to Dean's gallery.

The flashlight falls from her fingers, clatters on the rock, goes dark one last time.

Behind her, the Mother looms closer, reaching out, threatening to pull Willa back into darkness.

She screams with an unknown voice: *"I WON'T LET THE CALLER HAVE ME!"*

Willa races past Dean's gallery. Past wild horses. Flowers and waterfalls. Bird-headed people eating burgers and drinking shakes.

Past herself.

The portrait Dean—*oh God, Dean!*—had painted on the cave walls watches silently as Willa flees.

Caught me in a moment.

The Mother thunders after her.

Willa dives from the mouth of the cave into the cool air, into the spray of salt cast up from tumbling waves. Her feet slip on the slick, uneven stones, and she stumbles, arms flailing, falling to the pebble-covered beach. Breathless, she crawls across the wet sand and stone, her fingernails breaking, and she picks herself up, clambering into a terrified sprint.

A cloud of seagulls, startled by the commotion, plumes from the rocks, screeching wildly.

A towering figure of sinew and bone, the Mother drags herself out of the cave on immense, skeletal arms and legs. With every shuddering step she takes, more lifeless creatures—not meat puppets but bone puppets—sprout and puff up and blossom. The stillborn atrocities clatter to the wet rocks and sand. She raises lethal, hooked legs high, preparing to drive them down.

"HOW COULD YOU DO THIS TO—?"

Where?

"HOW COULD YOU DO THIS TO YOURSELF?"

Where is that sound coming from?

"TO YOUR OWN CHILD?"

Who is speaking on the Mother's behalf now?

Drenched in sea spray, her chest rising and falling with panting breaths, weakness seeping into her muscles and bones, Willa turns. The morning sun fails to offer any warmth. The ocean sighs and growls, waves breaking upon the rocks and washing across the sand. She lets the sword fall to her side for a moment, the weight of it pulling her arm down. She plants her feet, clad in the Warlock's shoes, upon the wet shoreline rocks.

And faces the Mother.

Everything about the creature before her defies the very concept of life. Her eye sockets are hollow, gaping. Her lipless mouth clacks open and shut. Rotting flesh and skin cover crumbling and creaking bone, the stretching and tugging and twitching of appropriated meat giving her the gift of movement as she stalks—slowly now, deliberately—in for the kill.

Perhaps Willa could run. Her own bones aren't as weary as they felt. Her own muscles aren't about to snap.

But she feels as if her body will give up the flight before the Mother gives up the chase.

With escape beyond her grasp, she will fight.

Willa grips the sword's handle with both hands.

The Mother closes in. Screams. But she has no voice of her own.

The scream comes from within.

From Willa's unborn child.

The world around them seems to hold its breath. The Mother doesn't have any of her own.

Dozens of flapping shadows cascade across the Mother's titanic, pallid, gnarled shape.

Sharp-beaked seagulls swoop and dive at the Mother, their wings beating the air as they descend upon her in frenzied hunger. They rip and tear at her flesh with abandon, their squawking and squealing like maddening laughter. The dark, living cloud contracts and expands, contracts and expands, relentless as the birds nosedive and flutter, flap and careen through the air. Their beady eyes glint ravenously as the gulls peck and snatch and rip at the skin and meat that cover the Mother's body. As assuredly as they might abscond with stale bread thrown out over the sea, the birds steal the flesh that stitches her bony frame together.

Stealing stolen meat.

The Mother shrieks without a sound, her silent agony resonating forever in Willa's brain.

The seagulls continue their merciless attack, ripping and tearing at the Mother as she flails fitfully, her arms swinging in vain to fend off the avian assault. She stomps and staggers away from the jagged rocks, her legs unsteady on the uneven ground, swatting frantically at the circling gulls. A winding trail follows her across the scattered pebbles and damp sand. She appears to be trying to reach the surf, hoping the water will wash away the murderous birds. Her movements become increasingly weak and futile, her strength ebbing away with every shred of muscle the voracious gulls rob from her frame.

Her body atrophies in real time.

A seagull's sharp, hooked beak delves into the hollow of the Mother's eye socket. With each peck and tug, it shreds the soft, decaying remnants of myriad eyes within.

Alerted to the morsels hidden within the Mother's skull, another bird joins the attack.

And another. And another.

The seagulls strip the Mother back down to the bone.

The bones waver slowly, as if there is still intelligence within them, as if they are trying to remember how to move. No new bony creatures metastasize from the Mother's body. With a groaning creak, the Mother collapses onto the beach, her skeletal structure imploding, lifeless, into broken fragments.

Willa stands over the pale, unmoving driftwood shape.

"Remember the fucking Tasty King, bitch."

The surf rolls in, foaming around the Mother's bones, already tugging at her, starting to drag her into the ocean's depths.

Willa watches the churning waves, listening to the seagulls as they screech and squeal, satisfied only for the moment, already anticipating their next meal.

There's something out there.

She can almost discern its form, a swelling in the water, a hint of something massive poised to breach the surface and reveal itself.

Whalelike. Mammoth.

To her surprise, she realizes that her hand remains clenched around the hilt of the broken sword—the Warlock. She grips it so tightly that blood wells between her palm and the metal, binding them together for all time.

Come and get her.

The mysterious shape within the water—whatever it may be—begins to recede, its presence fading back into the depths.

It will wait.

A voice calls to Willa.

At first she thinks it might be the thing out in the depths.

What is it?

The Caller from the Void.

Then she thinks it might be the Mother, crying out from Willa's memories.

Willa places a hand over her stomach. Or from within Willa's own body.

But then—then—she thinks the sound is coming from the cave itself.

A shadowed shape emerges, limping, from the mouth of the cave, stumbling, slipping on the wet rock.

Sarah?

Through the veil of sea spray, she hobbles toward Willa. For a long, nearly frozen moment, silence stretches between them as they lock eyes, each of them unable to believe the other has survived.

"You look like shit," they say simultaneously.

"How?" Willa questions, her voice barely above a whisper, not really directing the question to Sarah but rather casting it into the vastness of the ocean, to the gulls wheeling above, even to the life growing within her belly.

She doesn't need an answer. It doesn't matter.

All that matters is that her friend is standing before her, alive and breathing, when so many others have died.

They collapse, crying and laughing, into each other's arms.

"How?" Willa repeats, her voice tinged with desperation. "How am I going to get through this?"

"Same way as always." Sarah smiles through her tears. "Gravity, friction, and faith."

ONE YEAR LATER

WILLA STEERS THE BABY CARRIAGE down the crowded sidewalk. Her eyes dart from face to face in the sea of strangers who hustle and push and shove, not unlike seagulls vying for a morsel of food. No one smiles. No one nods. No one waves. No one recognizes her. No one knows—or wants to know—her name. She's lost in the crowd.

That's the way she likes it.

She hasn't set foot on Wilson Island in a year and has no intention of ever doing so again.

There's *no one* there now.

It's completely abandoned. The people who survived all packed up and left, fearful of a repeat occurrence.

Willa doesn't blame them.

Public record states that Wilson Island was evacuated and quarantined due to chemical contamination, dioxin or some other such nonsense. It made the evening news in a few places. But Willa knows the truth.

The island, or so she's heard, is a ghost town.

And the problem with a ghost town is all the ghosts.

Living on the road, never staying in one place too long, always moving.

It isn't easy.

She had taken what she could from the town, including a sizable amount of money her father had squirreled away. It didn't last long, of course, but there were still people out in the world who remembered Wade Hanson, small-town gangster that he was, and still honored the favors they owed.

Thanks, Dad.

He's still looking out for her.

And for his granddaughter.

In the carriage, the baby kicks and gurgles softly.

Willa pauses, reaches down to adjust the blankets.

She takes her eyes off the street, off the surrounding crowd, for no more than a second. That's enough. A man in a well-tailored suit bumps into her, jostling the carriage and nearly knocking Willa off-balance.

"Watch it!" he snaps. "You can't just stop in the middle of a walkway!"

Willa mumbles an apology as he rushes past.

She watches him weave through the crowd.

Her heart races. Her face flushes. Sweat rolls down her neck.

She takes a deep breath.

Once he vanishes into the throng of people, she continues on her way.

You're being paranoid, she tells herself. *You're safe here. The baby's safe here.*

She had chosen—

No, she hates that word.

She'd *found* her way to Atlanta because the city's landlocked location offered her a sense of security.

Truth be told, though, she knew the horrors she'd encountered on Wilson Island could reach her anywhere. If they wanted.

And, oh, they longed to find her.

Willa's paranoia, her conviction that the baby girl would forever be in danger, had often been a point of contention between her and Sarah. Especially in the days immediately following the massacre on Wilson Island.

When Willa believed wholeheartedly that she could still hear the Mother speaking to her from within her own body.

When Sarah argued that maybe—if the baby was going to be the source of so much pain—Willa should just get rid of it.

When Willa, for reasons she couldn't really explain, was unwilling to do so.

When neither of them could forgive themselves for surviving at all. God, the friendship-ending fights they'd had.

Waiting along with a dozen other people at a crosswalk, Willa hears a familiar tune. Her gaze is drawn to a street musician playing guitar on the corner. It's an old Guns N' Roses song about love and murder. Jolly, despite the subject matter. Once upon a time, it was one of her faves. The melody tugs at something deep inside her, a bittersweet reminder of the life she's left behind.

Not by choice, though.

That life was taken from her.

The baby mewls and squirms in its carriage.

The musician, strumming his strings, bobs as he plays and sings. He turns in Willa's direction. The smile on his face is too wide. His eyes are too dark. Too hollow.

The crosswalk light changes, and Willa pushes forward, trying to get ahead of everyone else, trying to race them to—

Nowhere in particular.

Amid all the movement, all the hustle and bustle, a flash of . . . stillness . . . catches her eye. A figure stares back at her from a nearby alleyway. For a moment, its silhouette seems impossibly thin and angular. Willa blinks, and the figure is gone.

The baby stirs, her tiny fists reaching up toward her mother.

Willa's expression softens.

"What a precious little baby." An older woman leans over the carriage, smiling, clucking her tongue, and waggling her fingers.

Willa blinks. She hadn't seen the woman approaching. If she had, she would have quickly walked the other way.

"What's her name?" the old woman asks.

Willa hesitates for a second before answering.

"Denny."

"Oh, what an interesting name!"

The baby, though, has gone by many names.

Sue. Sarah. Deana. Scraps.

Next week—hell, even tomorrow—if someone asks, they'll likely get a different answer.

None of the names seem to stick.

"What a precious little baby," the woman says again.

Almost as if programmed to utter those words. Her eyes are empty. Hollow.

Willa jerks the carriage away, turns, and hurries off.

She doesn't need to look back to know that the old woman is following her. She calls them "the Empty Ones." She's encountered them a few times. They're always out there in the world, always searching for her.

The Mother had her meat puppets.

So too, apparently, does the Caller from the Void.

His are just a little more difficult to spot.

They want the baby—the vessel of the Mother reborn—for their master.

Of that, Willa is certain.

She weaves through the crowd, certain that the old woman—the Empty One—is moving along in pursuit. She tries to control her breathing, her heartbeat. She forces her eyes forward.

She's actually scared she might look back and the woman won't be there.

Because that might mean that Willa's cracking up.

"Denny" giggles in the rattling carriage.

Willa looks back. For a second, she doesn't see the old woman. Then, emerging from behind some of the blank faces in the crowd, she appears, moving faster than should be normal, still smiling.

Willa strides down the street. It's familiar. She's plotted out the path.

But she wants to move faster. Put distance between her and the latest Empty One.

Breathless, she jags the carriage to the side and hurries down an alley. Just a few steps, and she's left the busy street behind. No one notices her as she rushes along the shadowy, dumpster-lined path.

No one but the old woman.

She sure as hell follows.

"What a precious little baby," Willa's pursuer calls out.

Most nights, sleep is elusive and fleeting. When Willa does sleep, she dreams.

Not of the Mother. But of birds. Surprisingly, not seagulls—she dreams of killdeer.

When Kenny almost ran the Ripper over in the dead of night, it had been on Killdeer Avenue. Maybe the nightmare had started the night the Mother fell to the beach. But, in so many ways, it felt like it had started right there on that street, named after the common shorebird. With its distinctive *kill-deer!* call.

Brown and white feathers, black banded markings around the breast, vibrant tail, and long, thin legs. And with its "broken wing" behavior.

When a predator drew too close to the nest, the bird would hop about, drag its wing in the sand, acting as if it was injured and helpless, drawing the hunter away.

It's a dangerous tactic.

A lot of mothers got themselves eaten while saving their nest.

"We'll be okay," she whispers, as much to herself as to the baby. "We have to be."

The old, smiling woman draws closer, reaching out for Willa with eager fingers.

The agents of the Caller come for her when she is alone.

A whistle cuts through the alley. The old woman stops, turning.

Standing at the mouth of the alley, with a crowd of unobservant and uncaring people walking past, stands Sarah. She holds a broken sword, the blade decorated with dozens of painted names.

The old woman hisses.

Willa and Sarah had spent hours and hours talking about destiny. About being chosen. About moving inexorably toward a fate someone else—some*thing* else—had chosen for them.

Willa had thought that if she killed the Mother, she might sever the threads of providence.

She's come to understand, though, that they were never serving the Mother's purpose. It was the *Father*—the Caller from the Void—who'd cursed them in such a way.

The child in the carriage is the Mother reborn. The Caller had willed it so. And he would have her.

Willa looks past the Empty One toward Sarah, who smirks and adjusts her grip on the sword's hilt.

Over our dead bodies, she thinks.

ACKNOWLEDGMENTS

If writing a book is a battle—and this one felt that way at times—it's important to recognize the team who was right there in the trenches with me. First and foremost, I must give another shoutout to Cindy and Roman. Yes, yes, I dedicated the book to them! But they deserve a little more recognition, since they witnessed firsthand just how real the struggle could be! I'd like to thank my editor, Ed Schlesinger, and my agent, Charlie Olsen, for getting this across the finish line. I'd also like to thank Josh, Greg, Tim, and Scott—the Dangerous, Disheveled Dilettantes—for having my back and giving early versions of this book a read. My friends JimmyZ, Aaron, and Beth also read some early chapters, and I'm grateful to them for their feedback, as well as Joal Hetherington, who copyedited the final manuscript. And, finally, I want to thank all the members of Cullen Bunn's Monster Club for keeping me company through the process, and everyone who has supported my work over the years. It truly means the world.

ABOUT THE AUTHOR

One morning, when he was four years old, **CULLEN BUNN** woke up and realized that to *be* the man, he had to *beat* the man. From that day forward, he set out to conquer the worlds of comics, prose, gaming, competitive Komodo dragon wrangling, and the delivery of joy to well-behaved children worldwide every December 25.

Cullen has written comics for nearly all major publishers, including Marvel, DC, Image, Dark Horse, Vault, Valiant, Boom!, Oni Press, Titan, IDW, Dynamite, Outland Entertainment, New England Comics, and many others. He is the *New York Times* bestselling writer of creator-owned comic books, including *The Sixth Gun*, *Harrow County*, *Bone Parish*, *The Damned*, *The Empty Man*, *Regression*, *The Ghoul Next Door*, *Basilisk*, and *Deluge*. He has also written *Deadpool Kills the Marvel Universe*, *Uncanny X-Men*, *X-Men Blue*, *Magneto*, and *Asgardians of the Galaxy* for Marvel; *Sinestro* and *Lobo* for DC; and *Shadowman* and *Punk Mambo* for Valiant.

Cullen curates and edits a horror imprint, Outer Shadows, for Outland Entertainment. For the imprint, he has edited books such as *Swords in the Shadows*, *I'll Kill You Last*, and others. His middle-reader horror novel *Crooked Hills* was also published under the imprint.

He has fought for his life against mountain lions and performed onstage as the "World's Youngest Hypnotist," but these days he lives in Missouri with his wife and son.

When he's not dreaming about what's next, he's having nightmares about what very well might be.

He hosts the horror-centric video podcast *The Cullenoscopy* at www.youtube.com/@TheCullenoscopy.

Visit his website at CullenBunn.com.

And, yes, he is taking credit for the kindly work of Santa Claus.